THE

R'S

MILLS BOON

Published in Great Britain 2014
by Mills & Boon, an imprint of Harlequin (UK) Limited,
Eton House, 18-24 Paradise Road, Richmond, Surrey, TW9 1SR

© 2014 Sharon Kendrick

ISBN: 978-0-263-24993-4

Harlequin (UK) Limited's policy is to use papers that are natural,
renewable and recyclable products and made from wood grown in
sustainable forests. The logging and manufacturing processes conform
to the legal environmental regulations of the country of origin.

Printed and bound in Spain
by Blackprint CPI, Barcelona

'Surely there must be somebody else who could do it?' Carly said.

'But I don't want anyone else doing it—I want you,' Luis said. 'After all, I am the one paying your salary, aren't I?'

Carly's hands balled into two fists, because now he had her in a corner and they both knew it. He paid her a generous amount of money, most of which she squirrelled away towards her goal of getting to medical school.

The smile had now left his lips.

'I am growing bored with this discussion,' he snapped. 'Are you prepared to help me out or not?'

She recognised the implicit threat behind his words. *Help me out or else.*

Or else what? Go out and find a new job?

Go out and find a new job? One which wouldn't leave her with so much free time to study for her medical school exams?

'I'd be prepared to do it if you were prepared to give me some sort of bonus,' she said suddenly.

'Danger money, you mean?' he mocked.

With a grimace he swung his long legs over the side of the massage bed, but not before Carly had seen a peek of hair-roughened thigh as the robe flapped open.

'Yes, that's right. Danger money,' she croaked, quickly averting her gaze once more. 'I couldn't have put it better myself.'

AT HIS SERVICE

From glass slippers to silk sheets

From washing his sheets to slipping between them,
from ironing his shirts to ripping them off…
When the job description said 'full benefits package',
this wasn't quite what she had in mind!

But when you work for a man who's used to
getting everything he wants, how do you stop yourself
becoming his latest acquisition?

Other titles in this series:

THE CONSEQUENCES OF THAT NIGHT
by Jennie Lucas

MAID FOR MONTERO
by Kim Lawrence

AN ENTICING DEBT TO PAY
by Annie West

*Look out for more **At His Service** stories coming soon!*

Sharon Kendrick started story-telling at the age of eleven, and has never really stopped. She likes to write fast-paced, feel-good romances with heroes who are so sexy they'll make your toes curl!

Born in west London, she now lives in the beautiful city of Winchester—where she can see the cathedral from her window (but only if she stands on tiptoe). She has two children, Celia and Patrick, and her passions include music, books, cooking and eating—and drifting off into wonderful daydreams while she works out new plots!

Recent titles by the same author:

SEDUCED BY THE SULTAN *(Desert Men of Qurhah)*
SHAMED IN THE SANDS *(Desert Men of Qurhah)*
DEFIANT IN THE DESERT *(Desert Men of Qurhah)*
THE GREEK'S MARRIAGE BARGAIN

With special thanks to George Tilbury and Erika Ring,
for teaching me how bodies heal.

Also, for invaluable insights
into the world of motor racing, thank you to
Keith Roberts and team-owner Roland Dane. Roland,
in particular, helped breathe life into Luis Martinez!

And to Peter Crone for his invaluable help with
wind-farms (although they appear in Murat's book—
SEDUCED BY THE SULTAN!)

CHAPTER ONE

CARLY'S FINGERS STILLED as the angry voice echoed through the house like a low rumble of thunder.

'Carly!'

She stared at the cornstarch which had lodged itself under her fingernails.

Now what?

She supposed she could try ignoring him but what would be the point? When her fractious, brilliant, mercurial boss wanted something he wanted it ten minutes ago; preferably sooner. He was driven, committed and single-minded—even when operating at fifty per cent of his usual capacity. It was just that fifty per cent of Luis Martinez's capacity would be full throttle for most men.

She pulled a face. Hadn't he already disrupted the peace enough times over the last few weeks with his incessant orders and his bad temper? She supposed that he'd had a pretty good reason to be more demanding than usual, but even so... She had lost count of the times she'd been forced to bite her tongue, when he'd snapped out yet another arrogant command. Maybe that quicksilver mind of his would focus on something else if she pretended she hadn't heard him. Maybe if she wished hard enough, he might just go away and leave her alone.

Preferably for ever.

'Carly!'

Maybe not. The shout had grown even more impatient now, so she took off her apron and shook her ponytail free. Quickly washing her hands, she set off towards the gym complex at the back of the house, where Luis Enrique Gabriel Martinez was currently undergoing another rehabilitation session with his physiotherapist.

Or rather, rehabilitation was what he was *supposed* to be doing, following the car crash which everyone said he'd been lucky to survive. Lately, Carly had wondered if the daily sessions had slipped over the boundary from the professional to the personal. Which might explain why the previously cool physiotherapist had started adding significant amounts of make-up before her visits, and spraying herself with a cloud of gingery-lemon scent just before she rang the doorbell. But that was par for the course, wasn't it? Luis had something special when it came to women. Something to do with those rugged South American looks and an unquenchable appetite for life which frequently courted danger.

Luis came, saw and conquered—though not necessarily in that order. He had an unerring ability to turn women into puddles of meek surrender, even if he happened to be lying stricken on a hospital bed at the time. Hadn't half the nurses who had treated him turned up here after he'd discharged himself? They had trooped through the door, bearing nervous smiles and sad little bunches of grapes—along with some pretty flimsy excuses about why they were visiting. But Carly had known exactly why they were visiting. A bed-bound and very sexy billionaire was an irresistible target, though to her surprise he'd given them all short shrift—even the platinum blonde with the legs which seemed to go all the way up to her armpits.

Carly was just grateful to be one of the few women immune to the Argentinian's careless charm, even if the truth of it was that he'd never actually *tried* to charm her. Maybe that was one of the advantages of being known as a dedicated 'plain Jane'—that your sex god of a boss would inevitably look through you as if you were part of the wallpaper. Which left her free to do her job and work towards a brighter future. And to remind herself of Luis's many negative qualities: his selfishness, restlessness and disregard for his own safety—as well as his annoying habit of leaving tiny espresso cups all around the house, which she was always finding in the most unexpected places.

She reached the gym complex and hesitated for a moment, wondering if it might be better to wait until he had finished his massage.

'Carly!'

Had he heard her approaching, even though in these old sneakers her footsteps were practically silent? She knew it was said of Luis Martinez that his senses were as finely tuned as his cars and one of the reasons why he had dominated the racing scene for so long.

Still she hesitated.

'Carly, will you stop skulking around outside the door and get yourself in here!'

His raised tone was arrogant and peremptory and she guessed that some people would have found it offensive to be spoken to in such a way, but Carly was used to Luis Martinez by now. She knew what his entourage said about him. That his bark was worse than his bite. Though she wasn't sure if that bit was strictly true. His last but one girlfriend had seemed rather *fond* of his bite. Why else would she have kept appearing at breakfast during her brief tenure as his lover sporting bruises on her neck with a kind of joyful pride, as if she'd spent the night with some obliging vampire?

Knowing that she couldn't put it off any longer, Carly opened the gym door and walked into the room where her famous employer was lying on his back on the narrow massage table. His dark head was pillowed on his clasped hands and his golden-olive body was outlined against the white sheet. His gaze alighted on her and his black eyes narrowed with something which looked like relief.

Which was weird. She thought that they tolerated each other pretty well, but there wasn't what you'd call any real *affection* between them.

Or maybe it was not so weird after all. Quickly, she became aware of the tension in the room and of two things which couldn't go unnoticed. That Mary Houghton, the physiotherapist, was standing on the far side of the room breathing rather heavily as she stared fixedly down at her shoes. And that Luis was completely naked, save for the trio of small white towels which were strategically placed at his groin.

A wave of colour swept into Carly's face and suddenly she felt angry. Wouldn't it have been polite for him to have covered up before she arrived? Surely he must have known that it simply wasn't done to greet a member of your staff in such a way. That she might find it...*embarrassing* to see that rippling chest and broad shoulders on display. Or that it was *arrogant* to flaunt those long, bare legs, which were currently sprawled out in front of him?

She kept away from men and all their complications—and with good reason. Experience had made her wary; but for once, all her latent fears and hang-ups about the opposite sex were put on hold as she stared at her boss with reluctant fascination.

Looking at him now, it was easy to see why women adored him. Why the newspapers had nicknamed him The Love Machine, when he'd been at the peak of his powers, and motor-racing champion of the world. Before her time, of course, but Carly had heard of him, even then. Everyone had.

His face had been everywhere—on or off the track. When he hadn't been standing on podiums, garlanded in the winner's laurels and spraying champagne over the adoring crowds, he had been an advertiser's dream. Magnified images of Luis Martinez wearing expensive watches, with that famously devil-may-care smile on his face, were regularly emblazoned over giant billboards. Off-duty, his fascination had been equally compelling. Hunky South American billionaires always provided good copy—especially as he was rarely seen without the requisite blonde clinging possessively to his arm. And if some perceptive journalist had once remarked that his jet-dark eyes looked almost *empty*—perhaps that only added to his appeal.

Because Luis Martinez wasn't just good-looking—even Carly recognised that. There was something *wild* about him. Something untamed. He was the trophy which was always just out of reach. The desired object which no woman could hold onto for long. That mane of slightly too-long black hair gave him a reckless, buccaneering look and those black eyes were now studying her in a way which was making her feel distinctly uncomfortable.

Turning away from his scrutiny, she looked at Mary Houghton, who had been coming to his English mansion for weeks now. With her neat figure and shiny hair, the physiotherapist looked as pretty as she always did in her crisp white uniform, but Carly thought she could see a shadow of hurt clouding the other woman's features.

'So there you are, Carly,' said Luis, his voice heavy with sarcasm. 'At last. Did you fly in from the opposite side of the world to get here? You know I don't like to be kept waiting.'

'I was busy making *alfajores*,' said Carly. 'For you to have with your coffee later.'

'Ah, yes.' He gave her a grudging nod. 'Your timekeeping may be abysmal, but nobody can deny that you're an excellent cook. And your *alfajores* are as good as those which I used to eat when I was growing up.'

'Was there something special you wanted?' questioned Carly pointedly. 'Because this particular kind of baking doesn't lend itself kindly to interruptions.'

'As the world's worst timekeeper, I don't think you're in a position to lecture me on time management,' he snapped, turning his head to look at Mary Houghton, who for some reason had gone very red. 'I sometimes think Carly forgets that a certain degree of submissiveness is a desirable quality in a housekeeper. But she is undoubtedly capable and so I am prepared to tolerate her occasional insubordination.

Do you think she can do it, Mary—can someone like her get me back to my fighting best, now that you are intent on leaving me?'

By now, Carly had stopped thinking about the Argentinian cakes which were Luis's favourites, or his arrogant sense of entitlement. She was too interested in the fraught atmosphere to even object to being talked about as if she were an inanimate object. She wanted to know why the previously cool physiotherapist was now chewing on her lip as if something awful had happened.

Had it?

'Is something wrong?' she asked.

Mary Houghton gave Carly a lukewarm smile accompanied by an awkward shrug of her shoulders. 'Not exactly…wrong. But my professional association with Señor Martinez has…come to an end. He no longer requires the services of a physiotherapist,' she said, and for a moment her voice sounded a little unsteady. 'But he will continue to need massage and exercise for the next few weeks on a regular basis to ensure a complete recovery, and someone needs to oversee that.'

'Right,' said Carly uncertainly, because she couldn't see where all this was leading.

Luis fixed her with a piercing look, his black eyes boring into her like twin lasers. 'You wouldn't have a problem taking over from Mary for a while, would you, Carly? You're pretty good with your hands, aren't you?'

'Me?' The word came out as a horrified croak.

'Why not?'

Carly's eyes widened, because suddenly all her fears didn't seem so latent any more. The thought of going anywhere near a half-naked man was making her skin crawl—even if that man *was* Luis Martinez. She swallowed. 'You mean, I'd be expected to *massage* you?'

Now there was a definite glint in his eyes and she couldn't work out if it was displeasure or amusement. 'Why, is that such an *abhorrent* thought to you, Carly?'

'No, no, of course not.' But it was. Of course it was. Wouldn't he laugh out loud if he realised how little she knew about men? Wouldn't she be the last person he'd choose as his temporary masseuse, if he knew what a naïve innocent she was? So should she tell him the truth—if not all of it, then at least some?

Of course she should tell him!

She shrugged her shoulders, aware of the heightened rush of colour to her cheeks as she mumbled out the words. 'It's just that I've…well, I've never actually given anyone a massage before.'

'Oh, that won't be a problem.' Mary Houghton's cool accent cut through Carly's stumbled explanation. 'I can show you the basic technique—it isn't difficult. If you're good with your hands, you won't have a problem with it. The exercises—ditto. They're easy enough to pick up and Señor Martinez already knows how to do them properly. The most important thing you can do is to ensure he keeps to a regular schedule.'

'Think you can do it, Carly?'

The silky South American voice filtered through the air and as Carly turned, the intensity of his gaze suddenly made her feel *dizzy*. And uncomfortable. It was as if he'd never really looked at her properly before. Or at least, not like that. She got the feeling that he had always regarded her as one of the fixtures and fittings—like one of the squashy velvet sofas which he sometimes lay on in the evenings if he'd brought a woman back here. But now his eyes were almost… *calculating* and she felt a stab of alarm as he assessed her. Was he thinking what countless men had doubtless thought before? That she was plain and awkward and didn't make the best of herself. Would it surprise him to know that she liked it that way? That she *liked* to fade into the background? Because life was safer that way. Safer and more predictable.

Pushing away the nudge of dark memories with an efficiency born of years of practice, she considered his question. Of course she could learn how to massage him because—as he'd just said—she was very good with her hands. She ran his English home like clockwork, didn't she? She cooked and cleaned and made sure the Egyptian cotton sheets were softly ironed whenever he was in residence. She arranged for caterers to arrive if he was hosting a big party, or for prize-winning chefs to be ferried down from London if he was holding a more intimate gathering. She had florists on speed dial, ready to deck his house with fragrant blooms at the drop of a hat or to float candle-topped lilies in his outdoor pool, if the weather remained fine enough.

What she wished she had the courage to say was that she didn't *want* to do it. That the thought of going anywhere near his body was making her feel…*peculiar*. And even though her dream of being a doctor was what kept her in this fairly mundane job—she didn't want her first experience of the therapeutic to be with a man with the reputation of Luis Martinez.

Imagine having to touch his skin, especially if he

was barely covered by a few meagre towels, as he was at the moment. Imagine being closeted alone in the massage room with him, day after day. Having to put up with his short fuse and bad temper in such an intimate setting. Luis Martinez she could cope with, yes, but preferably with as much distance between them as possible.

'Surely there must be somebody else who could do it?' she said.

'But I don't want anyone else doing it—I want you,' he said. 'Or do you have other things which are occupying you, Carly? Things which are making too many demands on your time and which will prevent you from spending time doing what I am asking you to do? Is there something I should know about? After all, I *am* the one paying your salary, aren't I?'

Carly's hands balled into two fists, because now he had her in a corner and they both knew it. He paid her a staggeringly generous amount of money, most of which she squirrelled away towards her goal of getting to med school.

She had the cushiest of positions here, which left her plenty of time to study. As jobs went, she would go so far as to say she loved working here. She loved it most when Luis was out of the country, which was most of the time. He had gorgeous homes in far-flung corners of the world, sited wherever he had business interests, and his English residence was usually bottom on his list of visits. She wasn't even sure why he bothered keeping this vast, country house until one day she had summoned up the courage to ask his burly assistant, Diego. 'Tax,' had been the ex-wrestler's terse reply.

Carly's role was to keep the house in a constant state

of readiness in case Luis should decide to pay an unexpected visit. In fact, he wouldn't be here now were it not for the charity car race which she thought he'd been insane to enter and which had ended with him smashing his pelvis and spending weeks in hospital.

She looked at him—thinking about his general high-handedness and arrogance and whether she would be able to tolerate it on a far more intimate basis. How could she possibly massage him without giving into the temptation to sink her fingernails into that silken olive flesh of his and make him squirm? How on earth would she be able to *touch* such a notorious sex god, without making a complete and utter fool of herself?

'I just wonder whether you might be better getting another professional in,' she said stubbornly.

He flicked a glance at Mary Houghton, who was still standing in exactly the same position and Carly saw his mouth twist with undisguised irritation. 'Can you give us a moment, please, Mary?'

'Of course I can. I'll…I'll talk to you when you've finished in here, Carly.' There was a pause, before Mary held her hand out. 'Goodbye, Luis. It's been… well, it's been great.'

He nodded, but Carly thought how *cold* his face looked as he propped himself up on one elbow, before shaking the physiotherapist's hand. Whatever Mary had said or done had not pleased him.

'Goodbye, Mary,' he said.

There was silence as she left the room and Luis sat up—impatiently gesturing for Carly to hand him the robe hanging from a hook on the back of the door.

She did as he wanted—quickly averting her eyes

until he'd covered up with the black towelling robe, but when he spoke, he still sounded irritated.

'Why are you so reluctant to do what I ask?' he demanded. 'Why are you being so damned stubborn?'

For a moment Carly didn't answer. Would he scoff if he knew that his proposed intimacy scared her? Or would he just be shocked to learn that she had allowed one horrendous experience to colour her judgement—and she'd spent her life running away from the kind of personal contact which most women of her age considered perfectly natural? Someone like Luis would probably tell her to 'move on', in the way that people did—as if it were that easy.

And this was about more than what had happened to her, wasn't it? She could see nothing but trouble if she agreed, because rich and powerful men like Luis *were* trouble. Hadn't her own sister been chasing that kind of man ever since she'd first sprouted breasts, and didn't she keep on going back for more—despite getting knocked back, time after time?

Thoughts of Bella's inglorious escapades flitted through her mind as she met Luis's luminous gaze. 'I don't want to neglect my housekeeping duties,' she said.

'Then get somebody else to do the cooking and the cleaning instead of you. How difficult can it be?'

Carly flushed. She knew that housekeeping wasn't up there with being a lawyer or a doctor, but she still found it faintly humiliating to hear Luis dismiss her job quite so flippantly.

'Or get in a professional masseuse who could do it better than I ever could?' she suggested again.

'No,' he said, almost viciously. 'I'm sick of strangers. Sick of people with different agendas, coming into my house and telling me what I must and mustn't do.' His mouth hardened into a forbidding line. 'What's the matter, Carly? Are you objecting on the basis that providing massage for your recuperating boss isn't written into your contract?'

'I haven't got a contract,' she said bluntly.

'You haven't?'

'No. You told me when I interviewed for the job that if I didn't trust you to give me your word, then you weren't the kind of person you wanted working for you.'

An arrogant smile spread over his lips. 'Did I really say that?'

'Yes. You did.' And she had accepted his terms, hadn't she, even if the logical side of her brain had told her that she'd been a fool to do so? In fact, she'd practically bitten his hand off, because she had recognised that Luis Martinez was offering her the kind of opportunity which wasn't going to come her way again. A place to live and a salary big enough to make substantial savings for her future.

The smile had now left his lips.

'I am growing bored with this discussion,' he snapped. 'Are you prepared to help me out or not?'

She recognised the implicit threat behind his words. Help me out or else.

Or else what?

Go out and find a new job? One which wouldn't leave her with so much free time to study for her exams? She frowned as she thought about the champagne bill from his last party and a new resolve filled her.

'I'd be prepared to do it, if you were prepared to give me some sort of bonus,' she said suddenly.

'Danger money, you mean?' he mocked. With a grimace he swung his long legs over the side of the massage bed, but not before Carly had seen a peek of hair-roughened thigh as the robe flapped open.

'Yes, that's right. Danger money,' she croaked, quickly averting her gaze once more. 'I couldn't have put it better myself.'

He gave a short laugh. 'Funny. I never really had you down as a negotiator, Carly.'

'Oh? And why's that?'

Luis didn't answer immediately, just concentrated on stretching his hips, the way that Mary had shown him. He wouldn't bother telling his plain little housekeeper that she had merely confirmed his belief that everyone had a price, because that might upset her, and there was no point in upsetting a woman if it could possibly be avoided. Often, of course, it couldn't. Usually because they weren't listening to what you were saying, or they thought they could change your mind for you.

Or they started falling in love with you, even though you hadn't given them the slightest encouragement to do so. His mouth hardened. That had been Mary Houghton's mistake. He'd seen it growing day by day, until in the end she could barely look at him without blushing. She'd made it clear that she was keen for a...*liaison* and, yes, he'd been tempted. Of course he had. She was a good-looking woman and hadn't he read somewhere that physiotherapists made great lovers because they knew how the body worked? But it had been highly unprofessional of her, and some deep-rooted and rather old-fashioned prejudice against such things had appalled him.

He turned his attention back to Carly. At least in her he had nothing to fear because sexual attraction was unlikely to rear its head. He found himself wondering if she bothered keeping a mirror in her bedroom, or whether she just didn't see what the rest of the world saw.

Her thick brown hair was tugged back from her face in a ponytail and she wore no make-up. He'd never seen mascara on those pale lashes which framed eyes the colour of iced tea, nor lipstick on her sometimes disapproving lips. A little blusher would have added some much-needed colour to her pale skin, and he'd often wondered why she insisted on wearing a plain blue overall during working hours. To protect her clothes, she said—though, from the glimpses he'd caught of them, hers were not the kind of clothes which looked as if they needed much in the way of protection. Weren't man-made fabrics notoriously hard-wearing? They were also very unflattering when stretched tightly over unfashionably curvy bodies like hers.

Luis was used to women who turned femininity into an art form. Who invested vast amounts of time and money making themselves look beautiful, then spent the rest of their lives trying to preserve that state of being. But not this one. Oh, no. Definitely not this one.

His lips flattened into a wry smile. What was it that the English said? Never to judge a book by its cover. And the old adage did have some truth in it—because despite her plainness and total lack of adornment, nobody could deny that Carly Conner had spirit. He could think of no other woman who would have hesitated for more than a second at the thought of—literally—getting their hands on him. Which of course was precisely the reason why he wanted her for the job. He needed to get fit, and he needed to do it as quickly as possible—because this inactivity was driving him crazy.

All he wanted was to feel normal again. He loathed the world passing him by, so that all he could do was watch it. Because inactivity left you with time to think. It left you feeling as if something was missing. He wanted to get back on the ski slopes. He wanted to pilot a plane again. He wanted the challenge of dangerous sports to fill him with adrenaline and make him feel alive again.

His mouth twisted as he levered himself off the bed.

'Hand me my crutches, will you, Carly?'

She raised her eyebrows.

He gave a small growl. 'Please.'

Silently, Carly handed them over and watched as he grasped them, straightening up to his full and impressive height. It still seemed strange to see a man as powerful as Luis needing crutches, but at least he was well on the road to recovery now. Almost unscathed, he had come through an accident the doctors said he'd been lucky to survive.

He hadn't raced professionally for five years, but the lure of an enormous charity prize organised by one of the big car manufacturers had proved too much to resist. That, and an inbuilt arrogance that he was indestructible…and a nature which loved to embrace danger in its many forms.

She remembered the day it had happened, when she'd received the phone call to say he'd been rushed to hospital. Her heart had been racing as she had driven through the narrow country roads, reaching the accident and emergency department and fearing the worst, to be told that he'd been taken to Theatre and they weren't sure how bad it was.

His entourage had been going crazy. There had been people rushing around all over the place and getting in the way of the medical staff. Security people. PR people. Diego, his swarthy assistant, had been dealing with the press, and his lawyers were busily engaged with threats of litigation, claiming that the racetrack had been unsafe.

Carly wondered if any of them had actually remembered that they were all there because a man was sick and wounded. And that was when her old pattern of wanting to care had kicked in. She had crept upstairs to the intensive care unit, where the nurse had let her sit with him and everyone else had been barred, on the grounds that any more excitement might hinder his recovery. She remembered thinking how *alone* he looked, despite all his money and success. There had been no family to visit. His parents were dead and he had no brothers or sisters. Carly had been the only one there for him.

All that night she had stayed put, holding his motionless hand and running her fingertips over it. Telling the unresponsive figure who dominated the narrow hospital gurney that he was going to be okay. But the experience had been a strangely powerful one. It had been a shock to see him looking so *vulnerable* and for a short while Carly's feelings towards her irascible boss had undergone a slight transformation. For a while she had felt almost *tender* towards him...

Until he had started recovering and had become his usual arrogant self. She had been elbowed out of the way then, when the first of a long stream of women had arrived, all vying with each other in their tiny leather miniskirts—because everyone knew that the ex-world champion was turned on by leather. She remembered turning up at the ward one day to find a stunning blonde in thigh-high boots groping him under the bed-sheet. And Carly hadn't bothered visiting again. She hadn't seen him again until he'd discharged himself home against his doctors' advice.

But she suspected that the accident had changed him, as she knew that near-fatal accidents sometimes did. Even though the house was vast, it had seemed overcrowded with his people mooching around the place, not sure what to do with themselves while their boss was recovering. And Luis had been even more bad-tempered than usual. He hadn't liked people trailing in and out of his room to speak to him, saying that it made him feel like a dying king. Demanding peace, he had sent his entire entourage back to Buenos Aires— even Diego. Carly remembered their astonishment at being sent packing. And hers. Because once again, Luis Martinez really was on his own. Only this time, he was alone with *her*.

Emerging from her silent reverie, she realised that his eyes were trained on her and that he was waiting for the answer to a question which, in reality, was little more than an order.

'Yes, I'll do it.' She sighed. 'I'd better go and talk to Mary and get her to run over exactly what it is you need, though I don't know why you couldn't just have carried on paying for her to see you privately.'

She soon discovered why, when she found Mary Houghton in the garden room, staring rigidly out of the French windows at the rain-soaked gardens outside. The bright hues of the summer flowers looked like fragments of a shattered rainbow, but all Carly could see was that the physiotherapist's shoulders were shaking slightly.

Was the cool Englishwoman *crying*?

'Mary?' she questioned gently. 'Are you okay?'

It was a few moments before Mary turned round and Carly got her answer from the telltale glitter in the other woman's eyes.

'How does he do it, Carly?' Mary questioned in a shaky voice. 'How does he get usually sane women like me to fall for a man they don't even *like*? How come he's dumped me in the coldest way imaginable and I still end up thinking he's the greatest thing since sliced bread?'

Carly tried to crack a joke, anything to lighten the atmosphere and to take that terrible look of *pain* from Mary's face. 'Well, I've never been a great fan of sliced bread myself—which is why I always make my own.'

Mary swallowed. 'I'm sorry. I shouldn't have said anything. Especially not to you. You work for him all the time—you probably deserve my sympathy, instead of me asking for yours.'

'Don't worry about it. You're not the first woman he's reduced to tears and you won't be the last.' Carly shrugged. 'I don't know how he does it, to be honest. I don't think it's calculated, or even intentional. He just seems to have that indefinable something which makes women go crazy for him. Maybe it's inevitable

when you're that good-looking and rich and powerful and—'

'Do you know,' interrupted Mary, her voice suddenly
urgent, 'that I've never fancied a male patient before?
Never. Not once. The thought had never even crossed
my mind—though obviously not many men like Luis
Martinez end up on the hospital wards. I can't believe
that I allowed him to see it.' She bit her lip. 'It's so…
so…*unprofessional.* And so humiliating. And now he's
asked me to go, and you know what? I deserve to be
let go.'

Carly didn't know what to say. She found herself
thinking that things were rarely what they seemed.
She'd always thought of Mary Houghton as cool and
unflappable. She'd seen her as one of those composed
Englishwomen who knew exactly what they were doing
and where they were heading. And yet one lazy look
from the smouldering black eyes of Luis Martinez and
she was as jittery as a schoolgirl who'd just seen her
pop-star idol in the flesh.

Carly looked at her. *Maybe she should be glad of the
hard lesson she'd learned all those years ago.* Because
didn't they say that heartbreak was almost as painful
as bereavement? And who in their right mind would
want to be going through what the physiotherapist was
clearly going through right now?

She looked at Mary. 'I'm sorry,' she said.

Mary pursed her lips together. 'Oh, I'll get over it.
And maybe it's all for the best. Maybe I'll start dating that sweet young doctor who's been asking me out
for weeks, and forget about a man who's famous for
breaking women's hearts. Now,' she said briskly. 'Let

me show you what you need to do to get Luis back to full fitness.'

'If you're sure you're okay?'

'Carly, I'm *fine*!'

But Carly noticed Mary delving into her handbag for a tissue and that she blew her nose for a suspiciously long time afterwards.

CHAPTER TWO

CARLY COULD FEEL her heart racing like a train, because this was weird.

It was weirder than weird.

Her hands were unsteady as they positioned themselves above Luis's bare back and she drew in a deep breath, praying he wouldn't guess how nervous she was. Praying that she wouldn't behave like a ham-fisted failure as she began to do exactly what Mary had taught her. It wasn't difficult, she told herself fiercely. Massage was a skill, yes—but it was one that thousands of people did every single day.

But even though the thought of touching Luis's skin was making her mouth grow dry with fear, it seemed there was no way she could avoid it. He was paying her a bonus. They had agreed that this was a deal. And wasn't it crazy to have reached this age and still be scared of touching a man? She lowered her hands towards his gleaming skin and thought about the way she'd let the past impact so profoundly on the present. Was she going to let some worthless piece of scum ruin her life for ever?

Because if she was ever going to fulfil her dream of becoming a doctor, she was going to have to touch people like this every day.

Pressing the heels of her palms deep into his silken flesh, she began to move her hands, glad he couldn't see her face. Wouldn't he laugh himself silly to know that she was flushed with embarrassment?

It was distracting seeing him like this—wearing nothing but a pair of close-fitting black briefs. Catching sight of him and his billionaire buddies lounging around the pool during one of the few hot days last summer while she carried out a tray of drinks was not the same thing at all.

She thought how pale her hands looked against the olive hue of his skin and noticed that her fingers were trembling slightly as they moved over his warm flesh. But to her surprise her nerves soon left her once she got into some kind of rhythm. If she concentrated on the healing aspects of the task, it was easy to push away her uncomfortable thoughts. In a way, it was the opposite of working with pastry, which needed cool, quick movements. For this, her hands were warm and oily and her movements slow and deliberate. She pushed deep into his latissimus dorsi muscles and he gave a little groan.

'Is that okay?' she questioned nervously.

He gave a grunt and she wasn't quite sure if he was agreeing with her or not.

'I'm not hurting you, am I?'

Luis shook his head and shifted a little, the rough towel rubbing beneath his crotch, which was precisely where he did *not* want to focus his attention. *Santo cielos!* No, she was not hurting him—but he wondered if she was trying to torture him. Resting his cheek against his crossed arms, he closed his eyes, unable to decide whether this was heaven or hell. Or perhaps a mixture of both.

What the hell was happening here?

He could feel her hands moving further down his back, skating tantalisingly over the taut lines of his buttocks before alighting on the tops of his thighs. He swallowed as the minutes ticked by and suddenly he found himself lost in the sensations she was producing. If she was nervous, you would never have guessed it. Apart from that nervous flutter of her fingers at the beginning, she had taken to it as if she had been born to stroke at a man's skin like this. Who would ever have thought that his mousey little housekeeper had the touch of an angel?

Yet she had been the model of brisk proficiency from the moment she'd greeted him, with nothing but a brief smile as he had lain face down on the bed. She certainly wasn't flirting with him, which made him wonder what was making him feel so *aroused*. How could Carly—plain little Carly—manage to make him feel like this? Was it because she *wasn't* flirting with him and he wasn't used to that? For a moment he imagined her requesting briskly that he lift up his buttocks, so that she could slide her hands underneath him. He thought about her taking his rapidly growing hardness between her fingers and stroking him to a blessed and swift release.

His mouth dried.

'No, you're not hurting me,' he said eventually, when he was certain his voice wouldn't come out sounding like some kind of strangled groan.

She continued to work in silence. He could feel her fingers sinking deeper into his flesh and as the muscles began to loosen up beneath her touch he couldn't seem to stop himself fantasising about her some more. He wondered what her breasts might look like if she were to remove that hideous overall she was wearing. An image of pale mounds tipped with rosy points swam into his mind with disturbing clarity. He pictured his tongue tracing a slow, wet circle around one puckered nub and he shifted his aroused body again in a vain bid to make himself comfortable.

The movement must have registered, for her hands stilled.

'You're sure I'm not hurting you?'

Against the lavender-scented doughnut of a pillow on which his cheek was resting, Luis shook his head. 'No,' he said huskily. 'You have a very...*natural* touch. I can't believe you haven't done anything like this before.'

'Mary was very helpful. She showed me exactly what to do. She said that if I pressed firmly on key parts of the body...like *this*...that it would be effective. And then last night I studied lots of technique and tips on my computer.'

His instinctive groan of satisfaction made his words come out as a muffled drawl. 'You have nothing better to do on a Friday night than look up massage technique?'

There was a pause.

'I like to do a job properly. And you're paying me a very generous bonus to do this.'

Her emphasis on the financial made him feel comfortable about interrogating her, although it didn't occur to him until afterwards to wonder why he should be interested in her social life. 'So is there no irritable boyfriend wanting to know why your boss is demanding so much of your time?'

There was another pause, a slightly longer one this time. She seemed to choose her words carefully. 'I don't have a boyfriend, no,' she said. 'But if I did, I don't really think this job would be compatible with it. Not if it was a serious relationship.'

'Why not?'

'Because when you're here the hours are long and erratic and because I'm living in someone else's house and—'

'Not why a live-in job isn't compatible with a relationship,' he interrupted impatiently. 'You wouldn't need to be a genius to work that one out. No, I meant why don't you have a boyfriend?'

Carly rubbed some more oil into the palms of her hands. It was difficult to come up with a reasonable answer to his question. Difficult to come up with anything which sounded sensible when her hands were in contact with his skin like this. If she hadn't been feeling so disorientated by what was happening, she might have told him that her social life was none of his business. Or she might even have hinted that one dreadful experience had put her off men for ever. But she couldn't really think of anything except how gorgeous he felt. She was being bombarded with powerful sensations and none of them were welcome—or expected.

All the blinds had been drawn and the semi-darkened room felt claustrophobic because the dimensions seemed to have shrunk. Candles were wafting out a subtle sandalwood scent and there was faint whale-like music coming from the sound system, just as Mary had suggested. She knew these small additions were intended to create a relaxed atmosphere and maybe it was working for Luis, but it certainly wasn't working for her.

Because the unimaginable was happening. Instead of being frozen with fear, all she could feel was a slow-building pleasure whenever she touched him. She stared down at his olive-skinned body, because where else was she going to look? And even though he was wearing a pair of black briefs instead of those three terrifyingly small towels which had been covering him yesterday, they weren't nearly as much of an advantage as they should have been. Because yes, they provided a necessary barrier of modesty—but they also emphasised the very masculine outlines of his body. They made the rocky globes of his buttocks look as if they'd been coated in liquorice, and liquorice had always been her favourite kind of sweet.

'I'm not really interested in men,' she said at last, her words making a mockery of her thoughts.

'Ah. You prefer women?'

'No!' She was shocked by his openness, and unreasonably hurt by his assumption. She told herself that he was perfectly entitled to think what he liked about her, just as she was perfectly within her rights to tell him that her sexuality was none of his business. But something made her answer him. As if she wanted him to know. *Needed* him to know. 'I'm...straight.'

'Ah.' He turned his head to the side and she could see the faint smile which curved his lips. 'So why is there no man in your life?'

'It drives me mad when people say that. It's the first thing people ask a single woman.' She started massaging again, pressing the heels of her hands hard against the firm flesh, aware that she was running the risk of sounding defensive but suddenly she didn't care. 'You don't have a girlfriend, do you? But I certainly don't make it sound like some kind of character fault, or start interrogating you about it.'

'I don't have one particular partner, no, but I certainly have girlfriends from time to time. You, on the other hand, don't.'

Her hands stopped mid-stroke and she stared at them. She thought they looked like pale starfish in a sea of gold. 'How do you know that, when you're not here most of the time?'

'Because my estate manager keeps me up to speed with what's going on. I like to know what's happening with someone who has the entire run of my house while I'm not here, so obviously I enquire about you from time to time. Not that he tells me anything very interesting since, apparently, you live the life of a nun.'

Carly tensed, hearing the implicit criticism in his tone. 'There's nothing wrong with nuns,' she said.

'I didn't suggest there was. But you haven't taken any vows since you came to work for me, have you, Carly? Certainly not poverty or obedience,' he persisted mockingly.

'Actually, as an employer you do seem to require total obedience from your staff—though I can't deny that you pay very well.'

'Which only leaves chastity,' he said. 'Doesn't it?'

Carly's heart thundered again as she forced herself to restart the massage, trying to concentrate on the slow, circular movements instead of the bizarre turn of their conversation. 'What I do in my spare time is none of your business.'

'He said that you always seem to have your head in a book,' observed Luis, as if she hadn't spoken. 'And that you go to evening classes in the nearby town.'

'And is there something wrong with wanting to improve myself?' she demanded. 'Perhaps I should throw a wild party when you leave. Give the gardeners and the estate manager enough ammunition to earn me a reputation.'

'Why, do you like wild parties?' he challenged.

'No.'

'Me neither,' he said unexpectedly.

'So how does that work?' she asked, with a frown. 'When you throw them on a regular basis. The house is always full of people. Why, you could almost employ a full-time party planner.'

'I agree—they have become something of a habit. A hangover from my racing days when wild parties were *de rigueur,* but recently I have grown bored with them.' His bare shoulders rose in a shrug. 'I find that they are all exactly the same.'

Carly blinked. How peculiar. She'd thought he'd loved the crazy gatherings which all the locals talked about for weeks afterwards. When hordes of the rich and beautiful converged onto his country estate—some of them travelling from as far as Paris and New York. The women were usually the generic blondes he was so fond of, with their tiny dresses and seeking eyes. On more than one occasion, Carly had been standing making pots of coffee at four in the morning, while some poor creature sobbed her eyes out over the kitchen table, because Luis had taken some other woman to bed instead of her. On another memorable occasion, she had opened the door to the drawing room and found a

French supermodel lying completely starkers on a fur rug, waiting in vain for Luis and not realising he was already on a plane which was heading for Morocco.

'There.' Carly stopped massaging at last, suddenly aware of the slow trickle of sweat which was sliding in a path between her breasts. Was it the heat which was making them feel so much bigger than usual? Making their tips feel so uncomfortably hard and prickling against her uniform so that she found herself wanting to rub at them. And why was she suddenly looking at the golden gleam of his bare back and thinking it was so physically perfect that it would work as an illustration in the pages of an anatomy book? She swallowed. 'Feeling better?'

'I'm feeling…good,' he said indistinctly.

Hastily, Carly wiped her hands on a towel. She had to stop thinking like this. She had to start regarding him with the impartiality she'd always had before now. 'I think that's enough for now, don't you?' She kept her voice brisk. 'We can have another session before…er, before you retire for the night. You can get up if you like, Luis.'

But Luis didn't want to get up. Or rather, he didn't feel capable of getting up, not in the way that she meant and not without making it very clear that he was having very erotic feelings about her. He could feel the hard throb at his groin and the sharp aching in his balls and found himself in the unthinkable position of being aroused—*by Miss Mouse.* And he still wasn't sure how that had happened. Surely it couldn't just be because she was *touching* him, because if that was the case then he would have felt something more potent than irritation towards Mary—the physiotherapist he had just sacked.

The aching intensified, but his impatient squirm only made the hardness worse, instead of relieving it. He scowled into the stupid scented doughnut of a pillow. Weeks of doing nothing had driven him close to crazy with no work, no play and no sex. Worse still, his confinement had left him with time to think and he was a man who preferred to *do*. Stripped of his constant need for action, he was forced into the unwanted position of introspection.

His incarceration in hospital had made him stop and take a look at his life and realise what a circus it had become. He'd thought about his different homes dotted around the world and the swollen entourage who accompanied him everywhere, and it had been like looking at the world of someone he didn't know. When had he managed to acquire so many hangers-on? He remembered their barely disguised shock when he had sent them to his main base in Buenos Aires, with Diego at the helm. And the strange calm which had descended on the house once they'd gone, leaving him alone with his mousey housekeeper.

He shifted his thigh a fraction as he thought how efficiently Carly had slotted into her new role as temporary masseuse. It seemed she was as proficient at rehabilitation as she was at running his house for him. Minutes before his massage, she had overseen the daily ballet exercises intended to strengthen his damaged pelvis. She hadn't made any predictable jokes about men doing ballet, but had simply stood beside him, counting the small elevations of his legs, with a look of fierce determination on her face.

'How about a swim now, Luis?'

Her soft voice ruptured his disturbing thoughts and it was with a sense of relief that he realised that his erection had subsided.

He yawned. 'Is that a suggestion?'

'No, it's an order—since you seem to respond much better to those.' She pulled up the blind and peered outside. 'Oh, dear, it's raining again.'

'It's always raining in this damned country.'

'That's what makes the fields so green,' she said sweetly. 'Never mind. At least we can use the indoor pool.'

'But I don't like the indoor pool,' he growled. 'You know that. It's claustrophobic.'

'And this room isn't?'

'I'm not planning to swim in here,' he snapped. 'So why don't we just go outside and use the big pool? Live dangerously for once.'

Carly turned back from the window, her mouth flattening with a disapproval she couldn't quite hide as she looked at him. She knew that was the kind of crazy thing he did. She'd witnessed people diving into his rain-lashed swimming pool, fully clothed, and she'd come down early the next morning to find glasses full of rain and champagne. Once she had even found a pair of knickers hanging from one of the flagpoles and one of the gardeners had been forced to shin up and get them back down again. What must it be like to live a life as decadent as his? she wondered.

'Because I don't like to live dangerously,' she said repressively. 'And perhaps if you didn't, then you wouldn't have ended up occupying a hospital bed for so long and probably blocking it for someone who really needs it. As it happens, the grass is absolutely sodden and the tiles around the swimming pool will be wet and slippery.'

'Sca—*ry*,' he said sarcastically.

She didn't react to his taunt, even though he seemed to be spoiling for *some* kind of fight. What was the matter with him today? He was even more bad-tempered than usual—and that was saying something. She set her lips into a disapproving line. 'So unless you want to risk falling over and complicating your recovery, then I'd advise playing safe and using the indoor pool, which was designed with rainy days like these in mind.'

'Don't you ever get tired of being the sensible voice of reason?'

And don't you ever get tired of being the perennial bad-boy playboy? It was only with difficulty that she stopped herself from saying it out loud as she turned to face him. 'I thought that's what you were paying me for.'

'That, and your cooking.' He paused, his thick black lashes half veiling his eyes. 'So you don't like living dangerously?'

Emphatically, Carly shook her head. No, she certainly did not. On the contrary, she had always wanted to live safe. She had craved a security and stability which had always eluded her. But Luis didn't really want to know that, did he? He was asking the question in that throwaway way he sometimes did, like an owner throwing his dog a scrap of food from the table. He wasn't interested in her as a person; she was just a tiny cog in the giant wheel designed to keep his life running smoothly. 'Not really,' she said. 'You do enough danger for both of us.'

He gave an exaggerated sigh. 'Okay, Miss Sensible—you win. The indoor pool it is. Go and find your swimsuit and meet me in there.'

But his mocking was ringing around her head as Carly ran upstairs to change into her costume, because he had touched a nerve. Being sensible wasn't something most people aspired to but she'd always been that way. At school she had been the reliable first choice if you needed someone to help with your science homework, or to spend a whole playtime looking for a lost charm from somebody's bracelet. *Careful Carly*, they had called her and as a nickname she hadn't particularly liked it. It wasn't cool to be careful—it was just the way she'd been made.

She reached her room at the top of the house and shut the door behind her, leaning against it to get her breath back. The attic space was large, with sloping ceilings and a dramatic view over the gardens and the fields beyond. Up here she was among the treetops. Up here you could see the most amazing sunrises and sunsets, which filled the room with a rich red light. There was a little desk, on which she did her studying, and on the wall above the small fireplace hung the little watercolour her father had painted, the year before he'd become too ill to hold a brush any more.

Sliding open one of the drawers, she fished around and found her swimming costume, knowing that the last thing she wanted was for Luis to see her in it. She was too fleshy. Too pale. Too everything. And although she knew that comparison was pointless, she couldn't help thinking about the women who usually shared the

pool with him. Leggy supermodels, wearing tiny bits
of string which they called bikinis. She shivered as she
stripped out of her bra and pants, her skin cold and resistant as she tugged on the one-piece. She thought how
faded it looked and how, rather alarmingly, it seemed
to have shrunk.

The rain was bashing hard against the window and
some of the showier plants in the flower beds had been
flattened to the ground. The dark blue petals of the delphiniums lay scattered on the sodden earth, as if some
exotic bird had recently had its feathers plucked. Carly
found herself remembering that expression her mother
used to say: *Fine feathers make a fine bird.*

But now wasn't a good time to remind herself why
her doll-like sister had always been given the cream of
the crop, while she had been dressed in more practical
outfits. After all, why would ungainly Carly be given
the delicate clothes favoured by a thespian mother, desperate to create a mini-me image of herself?

When she'd been old enough to buy her own clothes,
she had become more adventurous, until that disastrous
night which had ended up with her at first wanting to
die and then to just fade into the background. And she
had become very good at doing that.

She thought about the questions Luis had asked her.
Intrusive questions about her sex life or, rather, the lack
of it. For a moment she forgot the indignation that her
employer should be arrogant enough to question her
about something like that. Suddenly she got a glimpse
of her life as others must see it. As someone who never
went out and never had boyfriends. Who lived in the
billionaire's house and polished and cleaned it even
when he wasn't there. As someone who lived in a staid

little world which kept her safe, but which now seemed to mock her.

And Luis didn't know about her ambitions, did he? He didn't realise that behind her dull image was someone who was going to do good some day. Someone who could hopefully use the brain she'd been given and not have to rely on her looks to better herself.

Pulling on a towelling robe, she hurried down to the pool to find Luis waiting for her and she couldn't help the instinctive shiver which ran down her spine. Silhouetted against the enormous curved window which overlooked the woods, he was wearing nothing but a moulded pair of swim-shorts and, from where she stood, Carly thought he looked almost completely fit again.

Despite the severity of his injuries, he had certainly regained his physical strength very quickly—probably because he had been at the peak of fitness before the accident. His dark body still looked immensely tough, despite the crutches he was leaning on. Wavy black tendrils of hair kissed the base of his neck and he seemed lost in thought as he stared out at the Indian Leaf trees whose summer blossoms were creamy-white against the greyness of the day.

He turned as she walked in, and something very peculiar happened to her as their eyes met across the turquoise pool. It was like the disorientation she'd felt when she'd massaged him earlier, only it was worse. Much worse. She stared at him across the echoing space and there was no sound other than the quiet lapping of water and the unnaturally loud pounding of her heart. She could feel her breath drying in her throat and suddenly her chest was tight and she was having trouble breathing. It was happening again and she didn't want it to happen. She didn't want to look at a man like Luis and *desire* him. She didn't want to feel this hot little ache at the pit of her belly or the sudden warmth which had started flushing over her skin. Why him, and why *now*?

Was it because she had touched him in an intimate way and broken a taboo which had haunted her for such a long time? She had run her fingers over his almost naked body and had been able to do so because everyone knew that the massage was a kind of *healing*.

But maybe she had been wrong. Maybe it had been more than that. What if that touch had woken something she'd thought was dead, but which had been lying dormant all this time? Something which was now assuming a life of its own and making her look at him with a terrible and tearing kind of *hunger*.

She blinked, wanting to clear her vision and make everything go back to how it had been before. She wanted to go back to thinking of Luis as a generous but extremely arrogant boss. She wanted to be troubled by nothing more onerous than trying to get her head round the book on quantum physics she was currently reading. Because she didn't *do* desire and all the dark stuff which came with it. Wasn't she a total failure in that department? *Hadn't she been told that in no uncertain terms?*

She saw him glance across as she slipped off her robe and that glance, more than anything, killed off some of the feelings which had been multiplying like bacteria inside her. Was that *disbelief* she could read in his eyes? Of course it was. He'd probably never seen a woman who wasn't a size zero. Looking at her curvy body, he might think that she usually finished up all the *alfajores* once he'd flown back to wherever was next on his exotic list of destinations. And he would be right.

Forcing a quick, professional smile, she walked towards him. 'Ready?' she questioned.

'I've been ready for quite some time,' he said acidly. 'But, as usual, you were late.'

'It took me a while to find my costume.'

'Sorry for the inconvenience,' he said sarcastically. 'Perhaps I should have given you more warning. Written it down in triplicate and signed it first.'

She decided not to react. To just pretend that nothing was the matter, but it wasn't easy when she was being confronted by a bare and powerful torso which was making her want to squirm with embarrassment. 'Anyway, we're here now,' she said brightly. 'Just make sure you go backwards down the ladder.'

'I think I know how to get into the damned swimming pool by now.'

Carefully, she took the crutches from him and propped them up against the wall. 'I was only trying to—'

'Well, stop trying,' he snapped. 'I'm fed up with people *trying*. I've been doing this damned regime for weeks and I think I've just about managed to get my head round it. Next thing you'll be teaching me how to cut up my meat using a knife and fork. Or maybe even start spoon-feeding me.'

For Carly, it was the final straw. Coming on top of the insecurity she was feeling at having to stand in front of him, shivering half to death in an unflattering swimsuit, and the fact that she had been shoe-horned into a role she didn't want, something inside her flipped. She turned and glared at him. 'Do you have to be *quite* so bad-tempered, when I'm only trying to help you?'

There was a pause as their eyes clashed in a fierce and silent battle. She felt herself tense to find herself caught in that intense black spotlight and she wondered what snapped insult he was about to come out with next. And then, unexpectedly, he sighed.

'I know you are,' he said. 'It's only frustration which is making me so unbearable. The aftermath of this damned accident has gone on for weeks and sometimes it feels as if it's never going to end.'

'Yes.' She chewed on her bottom lip. 'I suppose that's one way of looking at it.'

He raised his brows. 'Unless you're about to tell me that I am pretty unbearable generally?'

Quickly, she glanced down at his bare feet, thinking how pale and perfect his toenails looked against the dark olive of his skin. 'That isn't for me to say.'

'No instant denial, then, Carly?' he mocked. 'Leading me to conclude that I *am* unbearable?'

She lifted her head then and met the mocking challenge in his eyes. 'You aren't exactly known for your sweet and even temper,' she said, and to her surprise he actually laughed as he lowered his powerful body into the pool.

'No, I suppose I'm not. Come on, Carly—aren't you coming in?' he questioned, hitting the surface of the water with the flat of his hand so that an iridescent little plume of spray went showering upwards and fell in tiny droplets which gleamed against his dark skin. 'Mary always did.'

I'll bet she did, thought Carly as she slipped into the

water beside him. Yet wasn't *she* doing exactly what Mary had been guilty of doing? She was having some *very* inappropriate thoughts about her boss, only she was also being a bit of a hypocrite, because hadn't she disapproved of the physiotherapist's behaviour?

She waded further into the water and shivered as the cool water reached her tummy. Goosebumps iced over her skin and she felt the tips of her breasts hardening again, just as they'd done earlier.

In an attempt to conceal it, she leaned back against the tiled wall and splashed water over her arms. 'You're supposed to do ten lengths.'

'I know I am, but I'm planning to do twenty.'

'Do you think that's wise?'

He gave her a hard smile. 'Let's find out, shall we?'

She watched as he struck out, making no concessions towards his injuries as he cleaved through the water like a golden-dark arrow. He swam with the same energy and determination which he applied to everything in life, but after twelve lengths she could see that he had grown pale and his mouth was tight with tension.

'Stop now,' she said, as he came up for air, his black hair plastered to his head like a seal. 'For heaven's sake—slow down, Luis. You're not in some kind of race.'

But he was stubborn, of course he was, and for him life *was* a race. She wasn't surprised when he shook his head and continued but when he'd finished, he was exhausted. Hauling his body out of the water, he propped his elbows onto the edge of the pool and rested his head on them, saying nothing until he had regained his breath.

At last he looked up at her, his eyes gleaming blackly from between wet, matted lashes. 'How was that?'

'You know exactly how it was. You did twenty lengths—double that recommended by the physiotherapist. You want praise for disobeying her instructions?'

'*Sí.* I demand praise. Heaps of it piled high onto my head. So why don't you wipe that disapproving look off your face for once, and tell me how good I am?' His mouth curved into a provocative smile. 'You know you want to.'

Carly stiffened as something unfamiliar prickled over her skin. Was he *flirting* with her? She stared at him, her eyes blinking. Surely not. Unless flirting was almost like a reflex action for him, a bit like a goldfish gasping for air if somebody tipped its bowl onto the floor. *It's just sweet-talk and it doesn't mean anything,* she told herself fiercely. *So don't act as if it does.* 'You probably overextended yourself, but, yes, you were good,' she agreed grudgingly. 'Actually, you were very good.'

He raised his wet eyebrows. 'Why, Carly,' he murmured. 'Praise from you is praise indeed.'

Flustered now, she tried not to let it show, dipping down below the surface of the water, mainly to try to distract herself again. But when she stood up again she could see that Luis's eyes had narrowed and it took a moment for her to realise that he was staring at her with fascination. Or, more specifically, he was staring at her breasts.

The stretchy fabric of her modest one-piece had suddenly become tight and shiny and was clinging to her like a second skin. Embarrassingly, she could feel her nipples pushing against the wet fabric like two little bullets.

Had he noticed that?

Oh, God. What if he had?

'I think you ought to get out now,' she said quickly. 'Before you get too cold.'

'Or too hot,' he amended, but his words were so indistinct that she told herself she must have misheard them. She *must* have done. Unless she was seriously imagining that Luis Martinez—one of the world's greatest lovers—was making a suggestive remark to *her*.

'Let's go,' she said, and dived beneath the water to escape his watchful black eyes.

She swam further than she had intended but she needn't have bothered, because the cold water failed to have the effect it should have done. And when she rose to the surface, gasping for breath, she still had that same terrible aching in her breasts when she looked at him.

CHAPTER THREE

IN A STREAM of impatient Spanish, Luis cursed loudly and eloquently. Outside, the wind howled and rain battered remorselessly against the tall windows. Neverending rivulets slid down the glass as the sound of the summer storm served as background noise in the scarlet and gold drawing room.

When was this damned rain ever going to stop?

Redirecting his gaze to the table at the far side of the room, he watched as Carly bent over a tray and poured him a tiny cup of espresso.

He felt another unwelcome jerk of desire, jackknifed through his groin with an exquisite precision which made him want to squirm. He scowled instead.

He was bored.

Bored and frustrated.

And one must be as a direct result of the other, he reasoned. Because why else would he be feeling such powerful pangs of lust for someone like little Miss Mouse?

Unobserved, he let his eyes drift over her, trying to work it out. For once, the shapeless cut of her jeans managed to enhance her figure, though not through any deliberate intention on her part. When she bent over like that, the denim stretched tightly over her bottom and emphasised the generous curves of her derriere. She ought to wear close-fitting clothes more often, he thought hungrily. Just as he ought to be in his study analysing the stock market, or reading through the stack of emails which Diego had sent through to him earlier. His mouth tightened and the need to distract himself from her luscious body became paramount.

'Play cards with me, Carly,' he said suddenly.

She turned round to look at him, her expression at first startled, then decidedly wary.

'I don't play cards,' she said.

'Then I'll teach you.'

Still she hesitated.

'What's the matter?' he drawled. 'Afraid I'll corrupt you? One game of poker and you'll be gambling away all your hard-earned wages?'

Wishing that he would stop looking at her like that, Carly straightened up and carried his coffee across the room, putting it down on the table beside him.

Corrupt her? She wondered if he had any idea what a good job he'd already done in that department. Wouldn't he be appalled if he knew how much he was on her mind these days? If he realised that she lay in bed thinking about him at night, when the silence and the darkness of her room seemed to magnify her thoughts. Thoughts which felt like longing, but which were closely followed by terrifying memories. Yet even those memories weren't enough to prevent the tingling in her breasts, or the molten ache low in her belly as she lay beneath the feather-soft duvet.

She had felt...*frustrated*...but had found herself recoiling from needs which she had repressed for so long. She kept telling herself that all she needed was to maintain some kind of balance, until things got back to normal again.

But when would that be?

When her boss was well enough to go back to Buenos Aires, or New York, or France or wherever he was planning to take up residence next? When he put some natural distance between them, so that all these stupid feelings would fade away? When she could go back to the quiet, studious life she had forged for herself here and put him out of her mind.

And sitting playing card games wasn't going to help, was it? Not on top of all the increasingly intimate massage sessions and those long and distracting sessions in the pool. She needed to spend less time with him, not more.

'I don't think we have any cards,' she said.

'Yes, we do. In my bedroom,' he said. 'In the desk. Second drawer, on the left. Go and get them, will you, Carly?'

She raised her eyebrows.

He sighed. 'Please.'

'What if I told you that I don't particularly want to play cards.'

'Then I might be forced to pull rank.'

'So it's an order?'

He slanted her an arrogant smile. 'Most definitely it is.'

Carly turned and left the room without another word but her footsteps felt heavy as she mounted the stairs. She felt trapped—like a fly caught in the sticky temptation of a spider's web. The weather had effectively kept them prisoners in this big house so that sometimes it felt as if they were the only two people in the world.

And meanwhile, her dilemma was compounded by her growing feelings for him. Because even she recognised that something had changed.

In the past she had thought of him as a distant and demanding figure, but hadn't that been preferable to *this*? To finding that she was actually enjoying his company in a perverse sort of way. Just her and him and the worst summer rains the country had known for a decade. Cooped up and going stir-crazy, with the lanes around the estate thick with mud and puddles. Luis couldn't drive and he didn't want to take the train to London. And he told her that he didn't want people coming over, drinking his wine and eating his food, and taunting him with all the things he found himself unable to do.

The most disturbing thing of all was that Carly was discovering how much she *liked* having him all to herself.

Pushing open the door to his bedroom, she entered the oak-panelled suite which took up almost all the first floor of the stately home. She'd been up here earlier, making his bed as she always did, changing his expensive Egyptian sheets, which were inevitably tangled—even when he slept alone.

Walking over to his desk, she found her gaze drawn to the two photos standing at either end of the gleaming surface. One was of his mother with her sad eyes and raven hair and the other an iconic shot of Luis, taken the first time he'd become world champion. His hair was wet with the spray of champagne and he was holding a massive silver trophy aloft.

It was funny, she'd seen these photos countless times and most days she dusted around their heavy silver frames without really noticing them. But today she felt like an intruder snooping around. As if her role in this house had subtly changed and she wasn't sure how to deal with it.

'Carly!'

Luis's impatient voice rang through the house, and quickly she found the pack of cards and ran back downstairs to find him sitting where she'd left him.

He glared at her. 'What kept you?'

'I didn't realise I was being timed. I was just daydreaming.'

'And what were you daydreaming about?' he questioned silkily.

She could feel the hot lick of colour to her cheeks, terrified he might guess. 'Nothing,' she said quickly and walked over to the card table.

Wincing a little, Luis levered himself to his feet before joining her and, for some reason, he became aware of the lamplight making intriguing shadows on her rather square face. He noticed the way her breasts moved as she fidgeted with the cards. And he wondered what she'd say if she knew that he'd been sitting here wondering what she would look like naked. He pulled out a chair and sat down, wondering how long this madness was going to continue, and his mouth hardened. Because he had never slept with anyone on his payroll—and he didn't intend to start, not with Carly.

He held out his hand for the pack.

'So what are we going to play?' she questioned.

It was unfortunate that her innocent question only fuelled his frustration, and suddenly all he could think about was the brush of her skin against his as he took the cards from her and he wanted more of it. He wanted to play a game which had nothing to do with hearts or clubs or diamonds. He wanted to play a very grown-up game which involved baring those intriguing curves and feasting his mouth and his hands on them, until he had sated his inconvenient hunger.

He shook his head, trying to clear the powerful images from his mind. 'Do you want to try learning poker?' he asked.

'Is it easy?'

'Not really.'

'In that case, I'd love to.'

He raised his eyebrows. 'Don't say I didn't warn you.'

He shuffled the cards and dealt them and watched her brow pleating in concentration as he explained the rules to her. To his surprise he didn't have to repeat them and she seemed to grasp the concept of the game with remarkable speed.

He had expected—what? That he'd beat her without trying and soon become bored with effortless victory as had happened so often in the past? He was midway through the second game when he realised she was good. Actually, she was very good. And he was having to keep all his wits about him to compete against a mind which was more agile than he'd given her credit for.

She was bright, he thought in confusion. She was very bright.

'Are you sure you haven't played this before?' he questioned suspiciously.

'If I'd played before, then why would I have allowed you to explain all the rules to me?'

'Gamesmanship?'

'That's a very cynical viewpoint, Luis,' she said as she studied the fanned-out cards in her hand.

'Maybe life has made me cynical.'

She looked up and extended her bottom lip in an exaggerated pout. 'Oh, poor diddums!'

It wasn't an expression he knew but the meaning was clear and Luis found himself laughing in response. But that confused him even more, because women didn't usually amuse him, unless it was with the light, teasing comments they sometimes made when they were removing their clothes. Women had their place, but humour rarely featured in it. And suddenly he found himself intrigued by this badly dressed woman with her surprisingly street-sharp grasp of the complex card game. 'You do realise,' he said slowly, 'that I know practically nothing about you.'

She looked up and the light from the lamp shone directly into her face, turning her eyes the colour of clear, bright honey. And Luis suddenly found himself thinking: *They are beautiful eyes.*

'Why should you?' she questioned. 'It isn't relevant to my work. You don't need to know anything about me.'

'A woman who deflects questions about herself?' he drawled. 'Can this really be happening, or am I dreaming?'

'That's an outrageous generalisation to make about women.'

'And one which happens to be true. Generalisations usually are.' He leaned back against the chair and narrowed his eyes. 'So how long have you worked for me now? It must be a year?'

'It's two and a half, actually.'

'That long?'

'Time flies when you're having fun,' she said.

He heard the flippant note in her voice as he continued to study her. 'Being a housekeeper is an unusual job for a woman your age, isn't it?' he observed slowly.

'I suppose so.' She shrugged. 'But it's a good job if you don't have any qualifications. Or if you need somewhere to live,' she added, almost as an afterthought.

He put his cards face down on the table. 'You don't have any qualifications? That surprises me. You are clearly bright enough—judging by the way you've just picked up a relatively complicated card game.'

Carly didn't answer straight away and not just because his words sounded so patronising. She didn't want to tell him about her hopes and dreams—she didn't want to *expose* herself in any way to him because she sensed a certain *danger* in doing that. If it had been any other time, she might have distracted herself with a task which needed doing and hoped he'd forget about it. But it wasn't any other time—it was now—and she was out of her usual comfort zone. She couldn't pretend that she needed to go and see to something in the kitchen because she suspected he would overrule her. Luis wanted to talk and Luis was paying her wages. And what Luis wanted, he generally got.

'I've been trying to make up for lost time,' she said. 'Which is why I did those evening classes. And why I've taken a couple of the science exams I really ought to have taken at school.'

'You've been studying *science*?'

She heard the surprise in his voice. 'Yes. What's the

matter with that? Some people do actually *like* those subjects.'

'But they're not usually women.'

'Again, another outrageous generalisation.' She shook her head in mock despair. 'That's the second sexist thing you've said within the space of two minutes, Luis.'

'How can it be sexist if it's true? Look at the stats if you don't believe me. Men dominate the field of science. And maths,' he added.

'Which might have a lot more to do with teaching methods and expectations than because they have scientifically superior brains.'

His eyes glittered. 'I think we'll have to differ on that.'

Carly could feel herself getting hot as he ran a speculative gaze over her and once again she was aware of that whispering feeling of danger. 'As you wish,' she said, wanting to change the subject and talk about something else, but it seemed he was having none of it.

'Which science were you good at?' he persisted.

'All of them. Biology and chemistry. Maths, too. I loved them all.'

'So why—?'

'Did I flunk my exams?' She abandoned all pretence of playing the game and put her own cards down on the table. She didn't want to answer this, but she knew Luis well enough to recognise that he wouldn't let up. And pain grew less over time, didn't it? As the years went by you could talk about things which had happened and make them sound almost *conversational*. 'Because my father was…well, he was very ill when

I was younger and as a consequence I missed out on quite a bit of school work.'

'I'm sorry,' he said, and Carly almost wished he hadn't because it was harder to keep things in perspective when his voice had softened like that.

'Oh, these things happen,' she said.

'What exactly happened?' he probed, his dark eyes narrowed. 'What aren't you telling me, Carly? People have sick parents but still manage to pass exams.'

His persistence was as difficult to ignore as it was surprising, since he wasn't known for taking an interest in the personal life of his staff. And suddenly Carly found herself telling him. It was, she realised, a long time since she'd told anyone because people didn't want to hear hard-luck stories, did they? It was the modern trend to portray your life as if it were just one long, happy party; to act as if you were having fun all the time.

'It was one of those long-term chronic things,' she said, her voice growing quieter. 'He couldn't get out of the house much, so I used to come home from school, and sit and tell him about my day. Sometimes I'd read to him—he liked that. Then by the time I'd cooked supper and the nurse had come in to put him to bed, I'd be too tired to do my homework. Or maybe I was just too lazy,' she added, her attempt to lighten the mood failing spectacularly, for not a flicker of a smile had touched his suddenly sombre face.

'And did he recover?'

His voice was still doing that dangerous thing. That soft thing which was making her feel things she had no right to feel—certainly not about him. It was making her feel *vulnerable,* and she'd spent a lifetime trying not to feel like that. Carly pressed her lips together. She never cried about it these days, but the mind could still play funny tricks on you, couldn't it? Sometimes an innocent question could make your eyes well up without warning and she didn't want that happening now. Not in front of her boss. She shook her head. 'No. I'm afraid he didn't. He died when I was nineteen.'

His ebony gaze seemed to pierce right through her skin.

'And what about your mother?' he questioned. 'Wasn't she around to help?'

This bit was more difficult. It was hard to convey what had happened without making Mum sound like some kind of wicked witch, which she wasn't—she was just someone who could occasionally be a bit misguided.

'She wasn't very...*good* with illness. Some people aren't,' said Carly, injecting that breezy note into her voice which she'd mastered so well. The one which implied that she totally supported her mother's decision to live out her own failed dreams through her beautiful, younger daughter. She remembered the way her mum used to talk about Bella making it big through modelling, but saying that you needed to pump money in to get money out. And that had been what had driven her. What had made her bleed their dwindling bank account dry—a big gamble which had ultimately failed. And even if it had succeeded—so what? As if material success could ever cancel out all the sadness which had been playing out at home. 'My mother was busy helping my sister launch her career. She's a model,' she added.

'Oh?' Luis's eyebrows rose. 'That's a term which

usually covers a multitude of sins. Would I have heard of her?'

'You might have done,' said Carly. 'Though maybe not yet. She does lots of catalogue work. And last year she was hired for the opening of a new shopping complex in Dubai.'

'I see.'

Carly heard the trace of sarcasm in his voice and she bristled. Because that was the thing about families, wasn't it? You could criticise your own until the cows came home, but woe betide anyone else who attempted to do the same.

'She's doing a lot of swimwear shoots at the moment and lingerie modelling. She's *very* beautiful.'

'Is she?'

Carly could hear the doubt in his voice and all her own insecurities came rushing in to swamp her, like dark strands of seaweed pulling her down into the water so that she couldn't breathe. Did he think that someone like her was incapable of having a beautiful sister, with hair like white gold and naturally plump lips, which made you think she'd had Botox? A sister whose ankles and wrists were so delicate that sometimes you worried that they might snap, like spun sugar. Because Bella was all those things—and more.

And didn't she *have* to believe that her sister would one day achieve the success which she and her mother had yearned for? Otherwise it would make all those years of sacrifice and heartbreak count for nothing. It would make the memory of her father's reedy voice as he'd called in vain for his wife all the harder to bear. It would make the debts and the loss of their house seem a complete waste. And it would stop Carly from shrugging and accepting fate the way she'd learned to. Because the last thing she wanted was to feel bitter, when she remembered screwing up her application form for medical school into a tight little ball and hurling it onto the fire.

'Yes,' she said fiercely. 'She's the most exquisite woman you could ever wish to meet.'

For a moment, Luis didn't say anything. He thought her mother sounded shallow and uncaring, but he wasn't particularly shocked by that. She was a woman, wasn't she? And he had yet to meet a single one who could be trusted.

But it must have been hard on Miss Mouse. Even if she was trying to make it sound as if she was okay with it, he could see her struggling to contain her emotions. And for once he felt a certain empathy with her, even though dealing with a woman's emotions was something he tended to steer clear of. Because this was different. This wasn't someone who was breaking her heart just because she'd put on a couple of kilos, or because a man refused to buy her a diamond ring.

Instead, he saw a bright girl who was good at science, who had flunked her exams because she'd been busy caring for her father. But he wondered who had been looking out for her.

He remembered flitting in and out of consciousness after his recent operation, wondering who had been stroking his brow during the surreal night which had followed. The woman with the soft voice which had washed over him like a cool balm. Next day he'd asked the nurse if he had been hallucinating and she'd told him it had been the girl with the ponytail, in the old raincoat. He remembered frowning and wondering who she was talking about. A kind girl, the nurse had added, and that was when he'd realised that she'd meant Carly.

She had visited him a few times after that and in a strange way he had found himself looking forward to her visits—mainly because she always seemed able to plump up the pillows and make him feel even more comfortable than the nurses. She'd sat beside him rather primly and had suggested he breathe deeply and move his ankles around. Actually, in a quiet way she had been a bit of a *tyrant*, but he seemed to have responded well to her general bossiness. And then one day she'd just stopped coming, and that had been that.

He picked up his coffee and sipped it. Despite her occasional bursts of fierceness, her company had been surprisingly tolerable since they'd been alone in the house, even if she did insist on scurrying away to her room at every available opportunity. Even if she seemed to play down every womanly trait she possessed…

At least tonight she wasn't wearing that ugly uniform she always insisted on, though she had chosen a cotton shirt in yet another forgettable shade of beige. It was not a colour palette he would have ever chosen for her. With those eyes the colour of iced tea he might have dressed her in flame—or maybe scarlet. He gave the glimmer of a smile. Even if she was the antithesis of a scarlet woman.

His gaze flickered to her hands. Working hands, with short, unpainted nails which matched her scrubbed face and no-nonsense hairstyle. Briefly, he wondered why she was content to sublimate her femininity like this. Was it because she had stood for too long in the shadow of her beautiful sister? Or just that caring for her father during her formative years had blotted out her more frivolous side?

He thought that her childhood sounded pretty grim. Or maybe it was that all families were essentially dysfunctional. The wounds they inflicted never really healed, did they? He thought of his own family as the rain began to batter against the window again.

'This weather is crazy,' he said, his voice growing hard with frustration.

'Of course it is. We're in England.'

'But we don't have to be.' He put his cup down with a rattle and stared at her. 'Do you have a passport?'

'Of course I do.'

'Good.' He picked up his cards again. 'Then make sure you're ready to leave first thing tomorrow morning.'

'Leave?' Carly blinked. 'Leave for where?'

'St Jean Cap Ferrat. I have a house there.'

'You mean...' She looked at him in confusion. 'Cap Ferrat in the south of France?'

He raised his eyebrows. 'Is there any other?'

'But why do you want to go there, and why so suddenly?'

'Because I'm bored,' he said silkily.

Carly looked at him uneasily. She'd heard enough stories about his Mediterranean villa to know what it was like. It was where the beautiful people hung out. Where someone like her would never fit in. 'I...I think I'd prefer to stay here, if that's okay with you.'

'But it is not *okay* with me,' he returned, his voice edged with a steely arrogance which cut through her like a blade. 'You are being paid an enormous amount of money to make my life easier, Carly, which means doing as *I* wish. And number one on my wish list is to get out of this damned rain and feel a little warmth on my skin again. So why don't you wipe that dazed look off your face and start packing?'

CHAPTER FOUR

HATEFUL, ARROGANT MAN.

Even the beauty of her surroundings couldn't blot out Carly's indignation at the way Luis had spoken to her just before they'd left England.

You are being paid an enormous amount of money.

Yes, she knew that.

To make my life easier.

She knew that, too. So did that give him the right to treat her like a portable piece of property who could just be shifted around when it suited him? Her mouth tightened. But what Luis wanted, Luis got, didn't he? And if the South American billionaire decided to uproot to his villa in the south of France because he was *bored* and wanted to feel the heat of the sun on his body, then that was exactly what would happen.

But Carly forced herself to stay positive as she packed her suitcase, concentrating instead on the massive bonus he was paying her. It made her dream of getting to med school one step closer. It was so close now that she could almost *taste* it. All she had to do was tolerate the arrogant Argentinian playboy for a little while longer and then she would be free.

They had spent a surreal morning getting here,

boarding a private jet, which had flown them from London to Nice, where they'd been spotted by a lone paparazzi who apparently spent his days waiting for famous passengers to arrive on the incoming flights. Carly watched as he leapt in front of them, shooting off a role of film as Luis walked through the airport terminal.

He wasn't striding at his usual powerful pace, but his walking stick didn't seem to deter the attentions of a group of women who converged on him, looking like beautiful clones with their sun-kissed hair and frayed denim shorts. Instantly, they began to thrust pieces of paper in front of his face.

'Sign for me, Luis?'

'Want to come to a party later, Luis?' asked one, boldly trying to shove a card into the top pocket of his denim shirt.

But despite his waving them away with an impatient hand, the girls simply took out their camera phones and started clicking frantically instead.

'Does that happen very often?' asked Carly as they climbed into the powerful car which was waiting for them outside the terminal.

'Walking through an arrivals lounge when you get off a plane?'

'There's no need for sarcasm,' she said tightly. 'I meant, that kind of fan girl attention.'

He shrugged. 'Everywhere I go.'

'And does it get too much?'

He shot her a sardonic look. 'What do you think?'

She hesitated. 'I think that your life is…strange. That it manages to be both very public and very isolated at the same time.'

'Ten out of ten for perception,' he said mockingly.

She clipped her seat belt closed as the car began to pull away. 'Yet you didn't take any of those women up on their offers,' she observed, 'when many men in your position might have done.'

He gave a short laugh. 'You don't think that I've grown jaded with that kind of liaison? That those kinds of women are as interchangeable as the tyres I used to get through during a race?'

'That's a mean thing to say.'

'But it's true.'

The words came out more hotly than she had intended. 'Funny how it's never stopped you before.'

'Why would it stop me?' He raised his eyebrows. 'If a man is thirsty, he would be a fool not to drink. You think I should turn down some beautiful, beddable blonde because we have nothing in common other than the fact that our raging hormones seem hell-bent on collision?'

Carly shook her head. 'You are outrageous.'

His lips curved into a smile and his dark eyes gleamed. 'But you knew that already, Carly—I'm just answering your questions as honestly as I know how.'

Yes, he was, thought Carly. And didn't she *admire* his honesty, even if it made her feel uncomfortable at times? He wasn't pretending to be someone he wasn't, was he? Maybe the emptiness in his eyes was an inevitable consequence of having your appetite jaded by being offered too much, too young.

'So do you *like* being famous?' she asked suddenly.

'You make it sound as if I had choice in the matter, but I didn't.' He rested his palms on his denim-covered thighs and flexed his fingers. 'I didn't seek fame. All

I wanted was to race and to be the best in the world—the acclamation was just an inevitable spin-off of that.'

But as he met her amber eyes he remembered that there had been other spin-offs, too. Success on the scale he'd known meant that you could write your own rules as you went along and he'd done exactly that, hadn't he? Big time. He had turned his back on responsibility. He had taken from women but had never given anything back. He hadn't needed to. He had known unbelievable wealth and adulation but nothing had ever filled the dark space deep inside him. Maybe that was the price you paid for fame.

'Maybe I shouldn't have taken on as much advertising as I did,' he said slowly. 'But I was young and the success went to my head and it seemed crazy to turn down that kind of money. And my sponsors were keen for me to do it. Actually, that's an understatement. They wanted someone to sex up the sport as much as possible and I was considered perfect for the role.'

And motor-racing was as sexy as it got, Carly realised. Even she could see that. All that power and testosterone and money—and Luis had exemplified it all with those show-stopping good looks and hard, sexy body. No wonder beautiful strangers thrust their phone numbers at him at airports with innuendo in their voices and hunger in their eyes. No wonder that even women like her weren't immune to his charm.

'And once you're famous, you can't undo it,' she said slowly. 'You can't go back to the person you were before.'

'No. You can't. The world has an image of you and there isn't a thing you can do to change it.'

'Well, that's not quite true. You could…' The words were out before she had time to think about them.

He raised his eyebrows. 'Could what?'

'Nothing.'

'Tell me. I'm interested.'

She shrugged. 'You kind of *bring* publicity on yourself by dating the sort of women who give tell-all interviews to glossy magazines after you dump them.'

'You think I should have them sign a confidentiality clause before I take them to bed?'

'I don't know, Luis—I'm your housekeeper, not your counsellor.'

Turning her head, she peered out of the window as the car ascended a terrifyingly narrow road which spiralled its way up a dizzyingly high, green mountain. 'Gosh, it's so beautiful out there,' she said.

'Are you deliberately changing the subject, Carly?'

'I might be.'

He laughed. 'Ever been to Europe before?'

She watched as a bright scarlet sports car squeezed past them in the opposite direction, screwing up her eyes as she wondered if it would make it. 'Just a package holiday to Spain—two weeks in Benidorm in a hotel with my mother and my sister. It was fairly… basic.'

'Then you may be in for something of a treat,' he commented drily as his phone began to ring and, pulling it from his pocket, he answered in Spanish.

The rest of the journey passed quickly and Carly wondered what her sister would say if she could see her now, in a chauffeur driven car, travelling through some of the most expensive real estate in the world. She probably wouldn't have believed it. Come to think of it, she was having a bit of difficulty believing it herself.

The car rounded a bend and she caught her first glimpse of Luis's house—a *belle-époque* villa which he told her he'd bought from an Arabian prince, a friend of a friend, who just happened to be a sultan.

For Carly, it was yet another illustration of his rarefied life, a life which she'd seen only fragments of before. But suddenly it was being pieced together in front of her eyes, like some kind of rich and lavish jigsaw puzzle. He knew sultans and kings. Supermodels and politicians converged on his houses like flocks of glamorous butterflies. But he had no real base, she realised. He flitted from gorgeous house to gorgeous house, but there was no place to call home. Despite all his expensive real estate, Luis Martinez was nothing but a rich and pampered gypsy.

She looked up at the villa as their car drove through the gates, thinking it was like some kind of sumptuous fortress. Dazzling white and shielded by tall dark cypress trees, it sat high in the hills overlooking little azure coves and inlets.

'Are there many staff?' she asked, suddenly nervous.

'Just the usual. And your French counterpart is called Simone. You'll like her.'

Simone was waiting to greet them in a vast reception area with corridors leading off in different directions, like the spokes of a wheel. Tall vases filled with orange roses and spears of eucalyptus were reflected back in large ornate mirrors. A classical statue of a young woman tipping water over herself stood in one corner.

Carly looked around, thinking that it was a bit like

being in a museum and that his French housekeeper was scarily chic. Simone's grey dress skated over her slim figure, her hair was cleverly tinted, and, though she must have been pushing fifty, Carly suddenly felt shabby in comparison.

'I'm going straight to my study,' said Luis. 'To answer some of Diego's increasingly hysterical emails, before he blows a fuse. Simone, this is Carly's first time in France.' He ran his finger thoughtfully over his broken nose. 'I think we might put her in the blue room overlooking the bay.'

There was a split second of hesitation. 'But might Mademoiselle Conner not disturb you, if your rooms are so close?' Simone's smile was fixed. 'I have made up one of the guest houses in the grounds, which might be more…suitable.'

'Carly hasn't travelled in Europe very much before. We might as well give her a decent view.' His eyes were as flat as hammered black metal. 'That won't be a problem, will it?'

'Mais non!' Simone gave a little wiggle of her hands. *'Pas de problème.'*

Carly realised that Luis was watching her and found her cheeks growing warm beneath that hard-eyed scrutiny. And suddenly she was conscious of something more than *consideration* in his dark eyes. Was he looking *at* her, rather than through her, or was she starting to imagine things? She felt her breasts growing heavy and her cheeks flushing, and she thought she saw his eyes gleam in response. *As if he had guessed what she was thinking.*

'That's very kind of you,' she said awkwardly.

'It's nothing. Enjoy the view. I'll see you later. Massage after lunch?'

'As long as it's not a heavy lunch.'

'You see how *stern* she can be, Simone?' he questioned mockingly. 'Don't worry, Carly, I will allow you to police what I eat, if it makes you feel better.'

His words only increased Carly's confused feelings. Was she misreading the signs again, thinking that he was flirting with her? Thinking that a man like him would be looking at someone like *her* with hunger in his eyes? But no matter how much the logical side of her brain tried to tell her that she was mistaken, her instincts were telling her that she was right. His eyes *had* grown smoky with something like desire and she wondered if Simone had picked up on it, too.

She watched as he walked off down the corridor, thinking how much he had improved. She doubted he would need that stick for much longer…soon he would be back to his fighting fit and glorious best.

She swallowed. And when he was? What then? She supposed she would just go back to ironing his sheets and keeping the house in a constant state of readiness for his infrequent visits. It would be as if this whole bizarre interlude had never happened.

And it would be better that way, she told herself fiercely. She wouldn't have to run her hands over his oiled flesh any more, nor feel droplets of water splashing on her skin as he broke through the surface of the water to emerge beside her in the pool, like some dark sea lion. They could slip back into that other, infinitely less threatening relationship they'd had before. The one where she just faded into the background of his busy life and he barely noticed her. And this would all be like a distant dream....

'I shall give you a quick tour,' said Simone. 'Though I warn you that the house can be a little overwhelming on a first visit. Don't worry about your suitcase—someone will take it to your room.'

She followed the Frenchwoman along one of the long corridors, trying to remember what led where, but as Simone had said—the place was a little overwhelming. Doors led off into high rooms most of which overlooked the sea. Carly counted two dining rooms, one with a glass ceiling, which Simone told her could be retracted to open up to the sky. On the ground floor was a gym leading out onto a large pool area with terrace, and on the upper floor was another terrace offering a wrap-around view over the mountains which towered over the back of the house. She thought it was the most beautiful place she'd ever seen.

When at last she was shown to her room, Carly stood open-mouthed trying to take in the Mediterranean view, and a bed made up with linen so white that she felt she'd have to scrub her skin before she dared climb in between the sheets.

'And this,' said Simone, 'is where you'll be staying.'

Suddenly, she could understand the Frenchwoman's reservations about putting her here, because it was a room which was fit for a king. And Luis had given it to *her*. Carly could feel a stupid lump rising in her throat. 'Here?' she questioned, horrified to hear the crack in her voice. 'You mean, I'm staying in here?'

'Yes, here,' said Simone, her voice now sounding almost gentle. 'I will leave you to change. Lunch will be served on the smaller terrace, just after two. Can you remember how to find your way back there?'

'I...think so.'

But after the housekeeper had gone, Carly walked around like someone in a trance, running her fingertips over the billowing white drapes which framed the fabulous view. Out on the terrace, there was a table and chairs and even a lounger. She would be able to read her textbooks out here *and* get some sun.

In the bathroom toiletries were lined up, like in some upmarket department store. Lavender-infused bath salts stood next to a big old-fashioned tub. Thick, soft towels lay in neat piles, like drifts of clouds. There was even a little vase of white freesia perfuming the air. Carly buried her nose in the petals. Flowers in the bathroom—imagine that! Another wave of emotion hit her and, try as she might, she couldn't seem to put the brakes on it.

Because for the first time in her life she didn't feel like second best. Like the geeky child who always dressed in practical clothes while her sister floated around in pretty little dresses. That same geeky child was now staying in a billionaire's home, in a fancy suite of rooms which had clearly been designed to accommodate his upmarket friends. She wondered what Bella and her mother would say if they could see her now.

But as she began to unpack the contents of her suitcase, she realised that this temporary change of circumstances didn't really change anything. You couldn't make a silk purse out of a sow's ear. She remembered what her mother used to say: *Oh, Carly's got the brains, but Bella's got the beauty.* And to her mother, appearances had been everything.

Carly looked around. Everything here was top of the range—all sleek and clean and shining. Everything except her. The full-length mirror reflected back a woman with a hot face, crumpled clothes and untidy hair. Was she really insane enough to imagine that Luis had been looking at her with *desire*?

She glanced at her watch. Surely she could do *something* with her appearance. If she got a move on then at least she could wash her hair and change into something more presentable for lunch.

But she still felt like an alien as she stripped off and stood beneath the cool shower, self-consciously aware of her fleshy body as she applied creamy soap and shampoo. Afterwards, she blasted her hair dry and had just pulled on a clean set of bra and pants, when there was a knock on the door.

Perhaps it was Simone. Grabbing her discarded towel and holding it in front of her, she walked over to the door and pulled it open.

But it wasn't Simone who stood there.

Carly felt as if someone had just pulled the rug from beneath her feet because suddenly her knees felt shaky.

It was Luis.

Luis, whose black hair was ruffled and damp—presumably because he was fresh out of the shower, just like her. Luis, whose fine linen shirt was clinging to his torso, outlining every hard sinew. And suddenly her perception of him underwent a dramatic shift. This was the man whose half-naked body had become almost normal to her. So why did the fully dressed version suddenly seem way too intimate? She wondered what it was about those faded jeans and damp hair which made her bones feel as if they had turned to jelly. As if she were in danger of melting at his feet.

Because wasn't that what all women did around him? What she had sworn she would *never* do?

Her fingers dug into the soft towel held chastely against her breastbone. She should have felt embarrassed by her own near-naked state. She should tell him she wouldn't be long and close the door on him.

Or *he* should have felt embarrassed at seeing her that way. Shouldn't he apologise for disturbing her and tell her that he'd see her outside on the terrace?

But he didn't.

And neither did she.

They just stood there staring at each other like two people who had just been introduced and she could hear her heart pounding like a drum. Her breasts felt heavy and there was a soft, molten ache between her legs and in the middle of this confusing state came anger, and fear. Because she didn't *do* this kind of stuff. She didn't feel desire any more. She didn't want to. Because desire was unpredictable—and, more importantly, it was *dangerous*.

She shook her head slightly. 'I didn't hear the bell,' she said, licking her dry lips.

He frowned. 'What bell?'

Act normal, she told herself. Pretend that nothing's happening. Because nothing is. 'The lunch bell.'

His eyes narrowed. 'That's because nobody's rung it.'

'Oh. Right. Did you…' she shrugged her shoulders, telling herself this was crazy, but still she stayed rooted to the spot '…er…did you get all your emails answered?'

'No.'

'Diego won't be very pleased.'

'I imagine he won't,' he agreed drily. 'But right now I'm not really thinking about Diego.'

'Oh. R-right.'

Luis felt his throat grow as dry as sandpaper and even her stumbled response didn't dissolve his growing hunger. He knew he should leave *right now* but he couldn't seem to drag his eyes away from her. Not because she looked particularly sexy, because she didn't. Her pale legs and faded bra straps were unremarkable and, for him, it was no big deal to think that beneath that towel she was almost naked. He was used to naked women.

But this was Carly and, for once, her long hair was loose. Freed of the usual tight ponytail, it looked like silk and smelt of bay leaves and he found himself wanting to run his fingers through it. To twist one thick strand possessively around his wrist and to draw her head close enough to kiss her. He wondered what those unpainted lips would taste like. He wondered how the lush curves of her generous body would feel if they were moulded against him.

But it was more than that which drew him. More than the rampant and unexpected lust which was raging around inside him, and a sexual frustration which was making him ache.

She looked clean. That was it. Clean and pure. Her face was untouched by artifice and her iced-tea eyes were wide and dark. She looked like snow before it got trampled on. Before it became all grey and slushy.

And he was the kind of man who did the trampling, wasn't he? He stamped on women's hearts and hardly even noticed he was doing it. He was cruel and insensitive—that was what they said. And she was the last kind of woman he should be lusting after.

But none of that seemed to matter. All he could think about was the aching in his groin which felt as if he were about to *explode*. 'Carly,' he said unsteadily, even though he hadn't been planning to say her name like that.

Her eyes widened. She licked her lips again and made them gleam. 'What's…wrong?'

Her words whispered over his skin like silk and suddenly Luis found himself fighting temptation as he'd never had to fight it before. In the past, if he wanted a woman—he would simply take her, if she was willing. And they were always willing.

But even though her lips had parted with unconscious longing, she was staff, and everyone knew that sleeping with your staff was a recipe for disaster. Even if she weren't, she was all *wrong* for a man like him. She was caring and wholesome. She was the clean light to the darkness which filled the space where once he'd had a soul. What right did he have to mess with her? To take her just because he could and then to leave her broken-hearted afterwards?

'No, nothing's wrong,' he said abruptly. 'I thought I'd show you the way to lunch because I know how easy it is to get lost in this place, but, as usual, you're late. What is it with you?' He scowled at her. 'I'll meet you on the upper terrace in fifteen minutes—and for God's sake, get a move on.'

CHAPTER FIVE

THE INCIDENT AT her bedroom door unsettled her more
than it should have done. Carly told herself that Luis
had seen her in the swimming pool loads of times so
a glimpse of her unexciting bra strap was hardly likely
to send him into paroxysms of delight.

But while she might not be very experienced, neither
was she stupid. She could read people and their body
language—they were two of the traits which made her
believe that one day she might make a good doctor.
And she had *seen* the way he had looked at her when
she'd stood wrapped in her towel. That hadn't been
shock or revulsion she'd seen in the Argentinian playboy's eyes, it had been hunger—potent and powerful
and almost tangible.

And hadn't she felt it, too? Hadn't what had silently
passed between them made her feel as if she were being
swept away by something? As if some dark and invisible wave were dragging her towards something outside her control? She found herself thinking how cruel
nature could be, that her body should be so attracted
to someone who was out of bounds for about a million
different reasons.

She knew her cheeks were still flushed as she joined

Luis for lunch that day and she knew, too, that something between them had changed. That no matter how hard she focused her mind, she couldn't seem to make things the same as they'd been before.

Suddenly a new and achingly raw awareness had sprung up between them. She tried not to let it affect her work, but how could it not? The nervous trembling of her fingers when she massaged him reminded her of the first time she'd done it. She found herself missing the confidence which she'd acquired with practice. But what she mourned most was the loss of the ease between them. When for a while she'd felt as if they were almost equals. When she could say exactly what was on her mind and sometimes even make him laugh.

Now there was a terrible and fraught kind of *atmosphere* whenever they were alone. Their curious alliance must have been more fragile than she'd thought or maybe she really *was* naïve after all. Because now he seemed to go out of his way to avoid her unless absolutely necessary, closeting himself in his study and immersing himself in work and leaving Carly largely to her own devices.

Their days settled into an awkward kind of routine. Carly woke early and swam in the pool, long before any of the other staff were around, slightly worried that it might appear presumptuous of her to be enjoying the 'facilities'. She would swim furiously in an attempt to rid herself of the night-time demons which had been haunting her. And afterwards, she would lie floating on her back, looking up as the sun rose higher in the blue sky.

After that, she would take Luis through his exercises and give him a fairly rigorous massage before breakfast—a pattern she repeated three times throughout the day. And whenever she got the opportunity, she would scuttle away to some largely hidden corner of the vast complex to tackle some reading.

There had been a couple of visitors, each arriving unannounced on separate occasions—Carly had heard their giggles long before she'd seen them. A beautiful blonde and a foxy-looking redhead, who had sat wearing big sun hats and tiny bikinis, draping themselves around the pool without ever managing to get themselves wet.

And Carly had forced herself to stem the unreasonable jealousy which had risen up inside her. She told herself that, *of course*, Luis would have women round—he usually did—and she should be glad that he was showing very obvious signs of complete recovery. Though she noticed that neither woman stayed the night. Each was dispatched home in one of his luxury cars, usually a sign that he was bored.

He had been out a couple of times, too. His driver had taken him along the coast to Monaco, where, according to Simone, a Hollywood actress had taken over a famous restaurant to give a lunch in his honour.

That had been the day when Carly had uninterestedly pushed her *salade Niçoise* around her plate, telling herself not to behave like a possessive child. Of course he would leave her behind! Or had she really pictured herself bursting in on some glamour lunch wearing one of her pastel-coloured T-shirts with her knee-length denim skirt?

At least she'd managed to get through two books she'd been meaning to read for ages, and the fresh air, good food and regular exercise meant that, physically, she felt better than she'd done in a long time, despite her lack of sleep.

One afternoon, her thoughts were travelling along the fascinating labyrinth of quantum physics when a dark shadow fell over the page and she glanced up to see Luis blocking out the light. Behind him the turquoise waters of the infinity pool danced in the sunlight and beyond that was the infinitely darker blue of the sea. But the only things she noticed were his powerful body and that battered straw hat he always wore in the sunshine, and her mouth dried.

'What are you reading?'

She screwed up her eyes, wishing her heart would stop doing that noisy, drum-like thing. Wishing that by now she would have acquired some sort of immunity to him. 'I didn't know it was time for your massage,' she replied.

'That's an odd title for a book.'

'Very funny.' She held up the cover so he could see it.

'And why are you lying in the sunshine reading...' he narrowed his eyes, and read '..."*Quantum Theory Cannot Hurt You*"?'

'Stop laughing at me. You know why. I told you before that I like science.'

'I like cars, but I don't spend my time lolling round the pool reading maintenance manuals. There are plenty of novels in the library—just help yourself.'

'Thanks, but I don't particularly want to read a novel. This is...'

'What?' He lifted his walking stick and used it to point at the dog-eared dust jacket. 'Heavy? Indecipherable?'

'Completely fascinating,' she said quietly. 'In my opinion.'

He rested his stick against one of the sunbeds and gave short laugh. 'You know, you really are something of an enigma, Carly. What are you planning to do with all these qualifications you keep accumulating? Sooner or later, you're surely going to run out of exams to take.'

She hesitated. 'And is there something the matter with that?'

He gave a shrug. 'You'll just become one of those people with a stack of diplomas you never use.'

'Who says I'll never use them?'

He smiled. 'Science may make you *understand* why cornstarch is vital when making *alfajores,* but it isn't really necessary, is it?'

Carly felt a stir of resentment as she met the mocking question in his eyes, because wasn't that just *typical* of him? There was no praise or even a glimmer of surprise that his housekeeper should have been working hard at exams as she went about her lowly job. It hadn't even occurred to him that she might want more from life than this. The world revolved around Luis, didn't it? Stung by his attitude, she turned on him.

'Maybe I'm not just stockpiling certificates,' she retorted. 'Maybe I'm going to use the exams to make something of myself.'

'Like what?'

'Like, a doctor.'

'You? A doctor?'

Any momentary doubt that it might not be a good idea to tell your employer you were planning on leaving immediately dissolved. Was he arrogant enough to think that she'd be fulfilled for the rest of her life keeping house for him and making sure his favourite cakes were on the table whenever he was in town? Watching and waiting in the background while he lived his life, without having any real life of her own.

'Why not?' she flared. 'Do you think I'm incapable of being a medic?'

'I hadn't really given it a lot of thought.'

What he meant was that he hadn't given *her* a lot of thought. Oh, he might have felt the odd flickering of desire—because she was a woman of child-bearing age who was closeted up with him, and that was how nature had programmed him to react. But he didn't really think about her as a *person*.

Carly stared at him. 'If you must know, I've already applied for medical school and I have a deferred place waiting for me. I'm planning on going just as soon as I've saved up enough money to support myself during the course. I've dreamt about being a doctor for a long time and I don't intend to give up on my dreams any time soon.'

She sat up and pushed her sunglasses on top of her head, but the jiggling movement of her breasts seemed to have distracted him. Or maybe he'd just grown bored with hearing about her dreams. Whatever the reason, he was suddenly staring at her as if he couldn't drag his gaze away. He was staring at her and glaring as if he liked what he saw and yet resented feeling that way—all at the same time.

'You've got a tan,' he said.

Following the direction of his gaze, she glanced down to see the glimpse of white where her shoulder strap had shifted. 'A bit.' She smiled, trying for a little levity to lighten the heavy atmosphere which had suddenly descended on them. 'That is what tends to happen when you expose your skin to the sun, Luis.'

'And you've lost weight.'

'Have I?'

Their eyes met. 'You know you have.'

'If I have, it wasn't intentional.' She shrugged. 'This climate doesn't...well, it doesn't give me much of an appetite, and Simone's been serving those delicious salads. And I've been swimming every morning—in this weather it seems criminal not to. All that helps.'

There was another factor, of course. One which she wouldn't be confiding in him any time soon—and the main reason why her normally healthy appetite seemed to have deserted her.

She wondered what he would say if he knew. If he'd be shocked to learn that these days she had grown to dread and long for their massage sessions, in equal measure. That just the thought of going anywhere near his warm skin started a terrible aching deep inside her. And it was getting worse. She found her hands wanting to linger on his flesh. She wanted to bend her head to the base of his neck and kiss the dark tendrils which curled there. She wondered how her attitude towards men and sex could have changed so radically. Was it possible that all her hard-wired fears of intimacy had been melted by daily exposure to Luis Martinez and his magnificent body?

'Don't you own a bikini?'

His impatient question startled her and Carly looked at him. 'A bikini?'

'You know, the garment of choice for most women

your age rather than something your grandmother might be seen wearing.'

Her cheeks grew hot as she looked down to where her thighs were outlined against the cushions of the sunlounger. 'I'm the wrong sort of shape for a bikini.'

'And what sort of shape is that?'

She lifted her gaze to his. 'Too fat.'

'You are not too fat,' he said impatiently. 'You're curvy, yes—but in all the right places. And men like curves. Actually, they like to see them, instead of them being hidden away behind shapeless clothes which are deeply unflattering.' His mouth hardened. 'You ought to give it a try some time. Stop moaning about the way you look and try doing something to change it, if it makes you unhappy.'

'You do say the nicest things, Luis.'

'Maybe it was something you needed to hear,' he said, unrepentantly.

She snapped her book shut. 'What time is it?'

'Ten after four.'

'Then we'd better go for your massage.'

'If you say so, Carly.'

'I do say so.'

But Luis didn't move. He couldn't. Because massage was the last thing he was thinking about right then. From here all he could see were her legs. Legs which had turned a shade of the *dulce de leche* he used to eat as a child. A paler shade than the syrupy sweet which used to seep out from the *facturas* pastries his mother used to make—back in the days before betrayal had slipped its lethal knife into his world and changed it for ever.

He felt that familiar little stab of pain but it was

overridden by the infinitely sharper spiralling of lust. He dragged his gaze away from her legs but today she was like a beacon who seemed to glow golden just about everywhere. Even her hair had caught the sun and there were pale licks of colour nestling in amid the sedate brown, making it look as if she'd spent hours at an expensive hairdresser's. He shifted his position a little, but it had little effect on the heavy aching at his groin.

'Give me fifteen minutes,' he said tersely. 'I need to make a phone call first.'

'Fifteen minutes it is.' She scrambled up from the lounger as if she couldn't wait to get away from him. 'I'll see you in the massage room.'

He watched her go and the sway of her hips made him harder still. Her swimsuit was riding up and revealing more of her bottom than she probably would have liked, if only she'd been aware of it. He suspected she would be appalled if she knew just how much of her creamy buttocks he could see, because she was a prude, no question. She dressed like a prude and she acted like one, too.

Yet he knew enough about women to realise that she was as jumpy as a box of newly lit fireworks whenever he was around. And then some. Did she think he was blind to the way her cheeks went pink whenever he walked unexpectedly into the room? Her newly acquired tan wasn't deep enough to conceal *that*. Did she think he hadn't noticed that her breasts were diamond-nubbed and straining, whenever they were in the pool together? Or that during his massage sessions her hands had gone back to that same trembling she'd had at the beginning.

It was a powerful kind of chemistry, and if it had been anyone other than Carly she would have made a pass at him by now. And in truth, that probably would have been enough to deflate his interest—or certainly to cut it short. The easy lay had never been a problem; it was the potentially unobtainable which had always intrigued him. He realised that he'd never met anyone who had actively fought her attraction to him before. It was incredibly...arousing.

Propping his walking stick against the lounger, he pulled his cell phone from the pocket of his robe and called his office in Argentina. For a while he allowed his mind to be taken over with the practical considerations of his business empire, while his assistant read out the list of bullet points she had prepared for him. Most concerned his global building projects: the luxury apartments being constructed on Uruguay's most beautiful beach and the new hospital in Santiago del Estero. As he listened to her neat summary, he realised that everything was going according to plan. The conservation measures he was instigating in the south of his country had been so successful that he'd been asked to chair a Pan-European convention in the fall.

But as he mentally filed away the information he was given, different images started crowding into his mind. Images which were painful and unwelcome. He tried to block them out, just as he'd spent the last four months blocking them, but for once it wasn't working. He stared at his walking stick and suddenly found himself remembering the accident with a crystal clarity which made him flinch.

It was all too easy to recall that strange split second of calm, moments before impact. And then the deafening crumple of metal as his car had smashed into the side of the track. He closed his eyes as he remembered the stench of burning rubber and the first hot lick of flames as the car had ignited around him. The distant sirens and muffled shouts of his rescuers had grown louder with their sense of urgency and panic. He remembered being trapped in that metal coffin, thinking that he was about to die.

And if he had died? What would he have had to show for his life? A bloated bank account and a shelf full of trophies. His mouth hardened. It wasn't much of a legacy, was it?

The sound of a bird calling out from one of the trees brought him back to the present. He looked around at the luxury pool and the villa which rose like an elaborate white cake out of the tiered green gardens. Dusky-pink roses and starry-white jasmine scented the air and his senses suddenly felt saturated. How beautiful it was, he thought, and, ultimately, how fragile. It could all be over in a heartbeat.

Couldn't it?

He felt something flicker and power into life inside him as he began walking towards the massage room, like a man in a trance.

Quietly opening the door, he blinked against the subdued light to see Carly with her back to him, lining up bottles of aromatic oils in a neat row. He stared at the set of her shoulders and the ponytail which hung down her back and he knew the exact moment when she heard him enter, for her long fingers stilled on a small vial which looked like some alchemist's potion. She had changed into her uniform and the ice-blue dress stretched across the broad beam of her bottom, emphasising its generous curves.

He also knew the exact moment when his painful recall became transmuted into desire. Only this time it wasn't the low-grade variety which had been nagging away at him for weeks. Suddenly it was gathering all the force of a tidal wave—whipped up by soft *dulce de leche* flesh and eyes the colour of iced tea.

He could smell the subtle bayleaf scent of her hair as she turned round and flicked her ponytail back and the gesture made her breasts jiggle beneath the uniform dress. Automatically, his gaze lingered on them and it took all his concentration to lift his eyes to her face.

'You...startled me,' she said.

'That wasn't my intention.'

'Where's your stick?'

With a start he looked down at his empty hands, only just noticing that he'd left it behind. 'I didn't even realise,' he said. 'I must have left it by the pool.'

'I'll go and get it for you.'

'No,' he said suddenly. 'I don't need it any more.'

'I think that's something your doctor should decide.'

'My doctor's not here, Carly.' He began to walk across the room towards her. And suddenly he was walking completely unaided, consciously free of support for the first time in months and he gave a low shout of laughter at the sense of exhilaration he felt. 'But you are.'

'I'm not qualified to give medical advice.'

'I don't need any medical advice,' he said, his shadow falling over her face as he came to a halt right in front of her. 'At least, not for what I'm planning to do.'

'Oh? And what's that?' she questioned lightly, as if

there weren't a hundred dark undercurrents flowing between them. As if her darkened eyes weren't unconsciously begging for him to kiss her.

'You're an intelligent woman, Carly. Don't ask questions to which you already know the answer.'

Her eyes were huge as she looked at him, but they were wary, too. She shook her head and he could see the rippling movement of her throat before she spoke, as if she were trying to swallow something which was stuck there. 'I don't know what you're talking about.'

'Oh, please. Don't *pretend*, Carly. You're too clever for that. Unless you're trying to deny the chemistry which has been building for weeks, or that you want to kiss me as much as I want to kiss you. You're driving me out of my mind with frustration, and I have the feeling that if I don't do something about it soon, then one or both of us are going to go crazy.'

Carly was trembling as he reached out and coiled his fingers around the back of her head and the unthreatening nature of the gesture meant that she found herself sinking into it. And once she had let him touch her, she was lost. She tried to think logically. To be that person who was good at science. To concentrate on the million reasons why this shouldn't happen. But all she could think of was how mesmerising it felt to have the tips of his fingers rubbing at her scalp like that, as if he was giving her an impromptu head massage. As if the tables had turned and he was the one now in charge. Oh, yes. He was definitely the one in charge. She could feel her eyelashes fluttering and the lids suddenly felt unbearably heavy. 'We can't do this,' she said desperately.

'Why not?'

'You know why not. I work for you—'

'I'll give you dispensation, starting from now.'

'That's not funny.'

'It wasn't intended to be funny. I've never been more serious.'

He was still stroking her scalp and Carly knew she should pull away before it was too late. *So why didn't she?* Because she liked his fingers in her hair and his black eyes looking at her like that? Or because all those feelings she'd thought were dead were now flickering to life inside her, and she was afraid to move in case they disappeared again?

Their eyes met and held.

'We can't,' she said again, more desperately this time.

'Stop fighting it. We can do any damned thing we like,' he said harshly as he pulled her face towards his.

But unlike his words, his kiss was soft. Soft and insistent and innocent enough to make her relax, until she felt her lips parting through no conscious effort of her own. She felt the flicker of his tongue against the roof of her mouth and, automatically, she coiled her arms around him, clinging to him with an eagerness which surprised her. She had watched him and wanted him for weeks and at last she was touching him.

And suddenly she was consumed by her need for him. The past became nothing but a desolate place which was retreating by the second. The present was here. Now. And she wanted to live every single second of it.

Did she make some kind of sound? Was that why he lifted his head to stare down at her with a gleam of pleasure in his black eyes? His mouth gave a flicker of a smile before he lowered his head towards hers again.

She didn't know how long that second kiss lasted, only that it was underpinned with a new sense of purpose. He levered her up against the wall, pushing the flat of his hand above her head for support, while with the other he stroked her face. And not just her face. His fingers moved down over her neck, drawing tiny little lines along her collarbone, and she shivered in response. Next thing she knew, they were skating down over her breastbone and she moved her body restlessly. She heard him give a soft laugh as he pulled at the zip of her uniform dress. She felt that first little tug of resistance before he slid it down to her waist and the material parted easily, leaving her breasts to slide free.

She felt the rush of air which cooled her skin and heard his muffled murmur of appreciation as he drew away to look at her. He didn't seem to notice her functional bra—nor to care that it was chosen with support rather than frivolity in mind. There was nothing but dark intensity on his face and a look in his eyes she'd never seen there before.

'Perfecta,' he uttered, cupping one breast in the palm of his hand, as if he was weighing it. His thumb flickered across one nipple and, despite the barrier of the bra, her puckered flesh tightened in a rush of pure pleasure.

'Oh!' she gasped.

'Still think we "can't"?' he mocked.

She couldn't think of anything except the way he was making her feel. His hand had slithered down to her dress and he was rucking it up. Her body felt hot. Her skin was suddenly too tight for her body and her pounding heart too big for her chest. She closed her eyes, hardly daring to breathe for fear that he would come to his senses, and stop.

But he showed no signs of stopping. On the contrary, he was now pushing her towards the narrow massage bed, which lay like a sacrificial table at the centre of the room, and she felt her bottom collide with the soft, leather surface. Instinctively, she dug her fingers into his neck, terrified that she was going to slip to the floor and take him with her and shatter all the sensual magic. Momentarily, his mouth curved into a hard smile.

'Relax,' he murmured. 'I wouldn't be doing this if I didn't think I was capable of following through.'

The sexual boast broke into the sweet fug of desire which had descended on her and the magic began to dissolve in a way which was chillingly familiar. Her body went from heated need to icy revulsion in one sobering second. Only this time she wasn't with some sleaze of a guy at a party, who was still smarting with rage at another woman's rejection. This was Luis.

Luis her boss.

Luis who bedded actresses and supermodels.

What was she doing?

Panic swept into her mind like the dark beat of flapping wings. With all the detachment which her scientific brain was capable of, she pictured the scene as others might see it. As Simone might see if she walked into the massage room. Carly with her uniform open to the waist—her breasts hanging out and her legs parted. And her billionaire boss with his hand up her skirt, eager to slake his frustration on the most accommodating woman to hand. Despite her lacklustre looks and lowly job, he had decided that he wanted to have sex with someone as unlikely as *her*. Someone who just happened to be in the right place at the right time.

Or the wrong time.

Appalled at herself, she pushed at his chest with the flat of her hand. 'No!' she said.

Perhaps he thought she was playing a game. As if she had suddenly decided to adopt the role of tease, because he dipped his head to brush his lips over hers. 'Oh, Carly,' he said, very softly. 'Just shut up and kiss me again.'

But the kiss was no longer working. It no longer felt like magic. Her mind was playing tricks with her as she started to remember that other kiss. The forced entry of an alien tongue, and then…then… The blood in her veins was now so icy that it hurt.

'No,' she said again, splaying the flat of her hand over his chest.

And maybe this time he realised she meant it. That her words weren't just the flutter of someone saying something because they felt they should. She could see surprise flickering over his face, as if nobody had ever stopped him before, and she wondered how she could have been so stupid.

Of course nobody had ever stopped him before.

She slid down from the massage bed but her fingers were shaking as she yanked the zip of her dress back up and tugged her skirt into place.

'What are you doing?' he demanded.

'What does it l-look like? I'm calling a halt to this before it gets completely out of hand.'

'I don't understand. One minute you're up for it, and the next you're acting like I'm the big, bad wolf.' His face darkened. 'I'm not crazy about women who play games. What's the matter, Carly?'

'What's the *matter*?' Moving away, she gripped onto the aromatherapy table for support, her heart racing so hard that she felt dizzy. 'Where shall I begin? With the total lack of professionalism we've both just demonstrated?'

'I told you that I was prepared to overlook that.'

Carly shook her head. She never got it right where men were concerned, did she? Maybe she was just one of those women who had *victim* or *walkover* written all over them. She looked at Luis, at his magnificent body in the faded jeans and white shirt and the way his sensual mouth seemed to form a natural, wilful pout. The wild black hair hung in tendrils around his collar and he looked just as much a pin-up as he'd ever been.

As if someone like him would seriously be interested in someone like *her* in normal circumstances. 'Well, I'm not prepared to overlook it,' she said. 'Because no woman likes to think of herself as a substitute.'

His eyes were suddenly watchful. 'What the hell are you talking about?'

'Oh, come on. This is *me*, Luis, not someone you've just picked up at a party. I've been in your life long enough to know what you're like. You're renowned as being a ladies' man. As a man who loves women.'

'Your point being?' he questioned coldly.

'That you're known for your love of supermodels and actresses. In all the time I've worked for you, I've never seen you date someone who…' *Say it, Carly. Just come right out and say it.* 'Someone like me!' she finished. 'Someone ordinary, who you're only making a pass at because I just happen to be around.'

He rubbed his finger up and down the uneven surface of a nose which had once been broken by a jealous husband, but when he spoke, his voice was curiously calm. 'You don't think I could have one of these leggy *supermodels* or *actresses* in my bed within an hour or two, if I wanted? That it might be more straightforward if I did?'

'So why don't you?' she challenged.

'Because it's you I want,' he said savagely. 'It may be wrong and it may be inexplicable, but I. Want. You. And you want me, too.'

Carly stared at him. His voice had roughened and grown hard with desire, but only one word stood out. His feelings for her were *inexplicable,* were they? He couldn't understand why he wanted her. Yet wasn't he only telling her what she already knew? That this could only ever be a one-off, which was only ever going to end in tears.

And she couldn't let it happen, no matter how much she wanted him.

She wondered how to handle it. She could storm out without any kind of explanation, but that wouldn't solve anything. From what she knew about human psychology, she guessed that flight might only sharpen his decidedly alpha traits. He might be fired up enough to hunt her down and kiss away all her doubts and she might not be strong enough to resist him again.

But if she told him the bare facts, then wouldn't that act as a natural repellent? He was a playboy, yes, but she suspected he had the double standard so common to many of his type. Didn't men like Luis see women as either good girls, or whores? If he knew the truth about her, he might *respect* an innocence which would put her off-limits to him, and stop this from happening ever again.

She met the hungry glitter of his gaze.

'Well, it's not going to happen, because I'm...'

'You're what?'

She tried to swallow down the complex mix of feelings, but suddenly it was no good and the words came spilling out of her mouth. 'I'm a virgin!' she burst out, and saw the narrow-eyed look of comprehension on his face. 'Yes! Now do you understand, Luis? I'm a freak—a weirdo—a twenty-three-year-old woman who has never had sex!'

And with that, she turned and ran from the massage room as if some deadly snake had slithered down from the mountain and was intent on biting her.

CHAPTER SIX

HE DIDN'T COME after her.

He didn't follow her to her sumptuous room over-looking the bright blue bay. He didn't push his way in and try to kiss away every one of her objections, which seemed to be diminishing as the minutes ticked by. Carly stood staring out at the sleek white yachts she could see skimming across the distant water and felt the plummet of her heart. Had she really thought he might? Hadn't she *hoped* he might?

Well, yes. If honesty was the name of the game, she *had*.

She bit her lip as doubt washed over her. Even if Luis had decided that making love to her was a bad idea after what she'd just told him, at least he could have reassured her that she wasn't some sort of freak, even if she'd used that description herself. He could have laughed it all off as behaviour which had just got out of hand. He could tell her what she already knew, that there was definitely chemistry, but that it would be a very bad idea to act on it. Then they could forget what had happened and go back to how it had been before.

She turned away from the window. Could she do that? Pretend that he hadn't kissed her breasts, or rucked up her skirt like that? Or that she hadn't enjoyed every glorious and forbidden second of it, until his boast reminded her just what kind of man she was dealing with.

Walking over to the mirror, she saw herself as Luis must have seen her. Her skin was flushed, her hair wild and her eyes didn't look like her eyes any more. She swallowed. This was a Carly she didn't recognise.

A Carly she'd thought was lost for ever. A woman who could feel desire and act on it, just like any other woman.

Throwing her discarded uniform into the laundry basket, she washed her face and changed, but as she brushed her hair and tied it back into a ponytail she wondered how she was going to fill the hours until supper. And what on earth she was going to say to Luis when she saw him again. How *could* she have told him about her virginity like that?

Her muddled thoughts were disturbed by a knock on the door and her dread was complicated by the thunder of her heart when she opened it to find Luis standing there.

But on his face wasn't the anger she had been anticipating. Wasn't that a trace of *amusement* she could read in his dark eyes?

'You have to realise,' he said drily, 'that if you want a man to run after you, it's usually better to choose a man who can actually run.'

She swallowed. 'I didn't want you to run after me.'

'Oh, but I think you did,' he said, dark eyebrows rising. 'Aren't you going to invite me in?'

'I don't think that's a good idea.'

'You have a better one? Like pretending nothing happened?'

'Nothing *did* happen.'

'No?'

She shook her head. 'No!'

His eyes narrowed. 'Look, why don't you open the door properly and let me in, so that we can have this conversation in private?'

'Is that an order?'

'If that's what it takes—then yes, it's an order.'

Carly hesitated, but she could see from his expression that he wasn't going anywhere. He wanted to satisfy his curiosity. He wanted to know *why* and at the end of the day he was still her boss, wasn't he? If they *had* to have this conversation then surely it was better without the risk of Simone or one of the other staff coming past and overhearing them.

'Oh, very well. Come in, if you must,' she said ungraciously, opening the door wider.

Luis walked into the room, his heart beating out a primitive tattoo as she closed the door behind him. He had just spent the last hour telling himself that this was a bad idea and that he should forget what had almost happened.

But he couldn't forget it. Or maybe he didn't want to. He couldn't forget the look of shame on her face as she'd blurted out her innocence to him. And he couldn't forget the way she'd made him feel when he'd kissed her. It had felt sweet and soft and powerful. But most of all it had felt dangerous, and he had always been hooked on danger.

He heard her footsteps behind him and turned to look at her. Beneath the light tan her face was tight with tension and she was chewing the inside of her lip. He found himself wanting to take that look of anxiety away. He wanted to make her melt again, only this time, he wanted to do it slowly.

'So why are you here, Luis?'

'Not to apologise, if that's what you're thinking.'

She seemed to have difficulty meeting his gaze. 'Then, why?' she whispered.

'I want to know why you spoke about your virginity like that.'

She flinched, as if his bluntness had startled her, but she treated his question in the same way she might have treated a polite enquiry about the weather. 'And how was that?'

'As if you were ashamed of it.'

Now some of her poise seemed to desert her because she stared at the floor and started rubbing her toe against the Persian carpet. There was a long pause before she lifted her head to meet his gaze. 'Why should that surprise you?' she said. 'It's not exactly something to be proud of, is it? We live in an age where we're bombarded by sexual images, and people who don't conform to the norm of having amazing sex all the time are regarded as freaks. Most women of twenty-three aren't like me.'

'You make it sound like a burden,' he said.

'In many ways, it is.'

He narrowed his eyes. 'Yet when I gave you the opportunity to liberate yourself from this state of self-imposed purdah, you turned and ran away.'

Her knuckles clenched. 'It was very generous of you to offer to "liberate" me,' she hissed. 'But I'm not some *charity case,* eager for the big stud Martinez to show me where I've been going wrong all this time.'

He raised his eyebrows. 'And where have you been *going wrong*?'

'It doesn't matter.'

'Yes, it does.'

'Please don't push it, Luis.'

'Why not? I think you should talk about it.'

And suddenly all the fight seemed to leave her. Her shoulders slumped as she sat down heavily on the edge of the bed and looked up at him. 'What do you want to know?'

'Everything.'

'That's a big ask.'

'I know it is.'

For almost a minute Carly didn't speak, trying to convince herself that he had no right to demand to know these things. Until she reminded herself that she had started the ball rolling. She had told him or, at least, told him some of it. She must have realised that someone like Luis would demand to know the full story.

She hadn't talked about it for years. Not since it had happened. She had taken it and buried it in a dark place somewhere deep inside her. She hardly ever thought about it now, only when she awoke from those occasional nightmares, the ones where she was clutching her throat and unable to breathe. Did that mean that on some subconscious level it still troubled her? And mightn't it be good to get it off her chest to someone, even if that someone just happened to be her boss?

'So why, Carly?'

His soft question slid in through all her defences, and suddenly she was back there. Back with those lights flashing and music pounding and that horrible dizzy feeling, which had ended with her bent double at the bottom of a frosty garden, being sick into one of the flower beds. In the bright, sunlit bedroom of the luxury Mediterranean villa, it seemed as if it had all happened to someone else. But it had happened to her.

'I was at a party,' she said tonelessly.

'When?'

'I was sixteen, but I probably looked older. I hadn't been out of the house for weeks because of Dad, so I went with a schoolfriend to this big party on the edge of town. For once, I was wearing make-up and I'd borrowed some of my friend's clothes and I felt excited. And there was this…this guy…' She stumbled over her words, trying to present them in the fairest possible light. Because hadn't she asked herself again and again if she'd somehow *deserved* what had happened to her? Wasn't that what women always did in situations like this? 'I'd had a couple of drinks—and so had he. He'd probably had a bit more than a couple, come to think of it.'

'So he was drunk?'

'A bit,' she said. 'But mostly he was just in love with someone else. Someone who didn't want him.'

'You're not making any sense, Carly.'

'Aren't I?' she said and she gave a hollow kind of laugh. 'Okay, then, I'll spell it out for you. I was supposed to be his substitute lover for that evening, though I didn't know it at the time. I was the lucky person he'd picked to make him feel better about himself. To make him know that he was still desired. Surely you can guess what happened next?'

'Oh, I can guess, but I'd rather be told.' His mouth

had grown hard. 'You say you want to be a doctor. Well, you'll make a much better doctor if you don't cling onto the past and use it like some kind of security blanket.'

There was a pause which seemed to go on for an uncomfortably long time.

'He started to kiss me,' she said eventually, her voice a stilted whisper. 'And then to touch me. At first I liked it. I liked the way it made me feel. But then....'

'Then what, Carly?'

His words sounded distant. As if they were coming from somewhere far away.

'He...' She winced with pain and shame. She could almost feel those fingers probing her, digging into her dryness and telling her she should have been wet. Telling her that she was frigid and useless. The clamp of those teeth was sharp on her breasts and the sound of her knickers being ripped apart seemed deafening. She had attempted to scream, but he had blotted out the scream with the vodka-soaked slick of his mouth. 'He...' Her voice shuddered to a halt as, wordlessly, she shook her head.

'*Raped* you?'

His appalled question broke the spell and Carly opened eyes she didn't even realise had been closed. She shook her head again. 'No. Not that.'

'But he touched you...intimately?'

'Yes.'

'Aggressively?'

'Oh, yes.'

'That's a definition of rape in many of the statute books,' he gritted out and there was a dark anger on his face she'd never seen before. 'What stopped him?'

'Someone came into the room to collect their coat and disturbed us.'

'And then you called the police?'

She didn't answer, not straight away, and in a way wasn't this the bit she was most ashamed of? That she had succumbed to pressure and other people's expectations and allowed them to take control of the situation.

'No. I decided against it.'

'You decided against it?'

'That's what I said.'

There was a split second of a pause. 'Do you want to tell me why?'

Carly met his eyes and their dark light washed over her. Dark light was a contradiction in terms, wasn't it? But that was what she was getting from him. And it was disarming. It was like a deep bath at the end of a long day. Like holding out your cold hands in front of a blazing fire.

'What stopped you from reporting it?' he said.

'My mother did,' she said baldly.

'Your *mother*?'

'She said it would be impossible to prove, that it would be his word against mine, and she had a point. He was insanely rich and well-connected, and could have hired the best defence lawyers. I was just an ordinary girl with a sick father and no money. I wouldn't have stood a chance. My name would have been mud. It would have been just one more thing to add to the stack of dark things which were building up at home. And it wasn't as if he actually *raped* me.'

'But what about the person who came in to collect their coat? Couldn't they have been called as your defence if they witnessed the attack?'

She gave a bitter laugh. 'It was a friend of his,' she said, 'who described it as "horseplay".'

For a moment he winced, as if her pain were his pain. *'Cabrón,'* he bit out, his eyes darkening as he walked over to the bed and sat down beside her.

Carly tensed, but the arm he placed around her shoulder felt protective, not seductive. Although she guessed that in some way it *was* seductive. He seemed to represent safety and she'd never really had that before. She wanted to lean against him and drink it in, but she forced herself not to. She had learnt to stand on her own two feet and she didn't need to lean on anyone, but, even if she did, it certainly shouldn't be Luis, because he was the antithesis of safe. Luis was all about danger.

'So that's when you started sublimating your femininity,' he said slowly.

'I don't know what you're talking about.'

'Oh, I think you do.' He nodded, as if something was suddenly making sense to him. 'That must have been when you started scraping your hair back into that damned ponytail, which means nobody ever gets to see it. Probably around the time when you stopped wearing clothes which might flatter you, or the make-up which most women your age wear. You must have thought that if you didn't draw attention to yourself then you wouldn't attract the wrong kind of attention. That by being invisible, people would look through you rather than at you, and it wouldn't ever happen to you again.'

His perception was unsettling and Carly could feel the sting of tears at the backs of her eyes. But she blinked them away, because to break down and cry in front of him would be the final humiliation. 'You think that suddenly you're qualified to act as some kind of amateur shrink, just because I've told you my sob story?'

'It's not a sob story, Carly. It's the truth. And I want to help you.'

'Well, I don't want your help,' she said, pulling away from his grasp and staring out at the terrace, where a fat bee was disappearing into the scarlet trumpet of an hibiscus flower.

'You might not want my help.' His voice was quiet. 'But you want me.'

Forcing her attention away from the pollen-brushed bee, she jerked her head round to look at him. Suddenly she realised that she was sitting on a bed next to him and she shouldn't be. She shouldn't be within six feet of him. And she definitely shouldn't be staring into his eyes like that and losing herself in their dark luminosity. 'No, I don't,' she whispered.

'Then try saying it as if you mean it.' His mouth flickered into a hard smile. 'Except we both know you can't.'

'I can't believe you're saying this. Do you really think it's…*acceptable*…' her voice shook '…to start talking about desire, in the light of what I've just told you?'

'Yes,' he said fiercely. 'Absolutely I do. What happened to you was bad, and the guy who took advantage of you was a piece of scum, but it happened a long time ago and you can't let it write the script for the rest of your life. Sex isn't *wrong,* Carly. It's natural. It's one of the greatest pleasures in life and you're missing out on it. Don't you see that?'

His fierce words were impossible to brush aside and

suddenly Carly realised that she felt better for having told him. She felt lighter—*cleaner*. As if she'd scrubbed years of grime away from her skin and stepped out into the sunlight.

And Luis had been the catalyst for that.

She stared at him. 'I'm wondering where we go from here,' she said. 'Do you think we can we go back to how it's been before?'

'Possibly.' He took one of her hands in his and turned it over, studying her palm as if he was examining her lifeline, and when he looked up again there was a question in his eyes. 'But I don't want to. And neither do you. Not really.'

He had lifted his fingertips to her face and was tracing a feather-light path down over her cheek and Carly had to resist the urge to close her eyes, because it felt so *right* to have him touching her. She swallowed as his thumb moved across the cushion of her bottom lip and suddenly it began to tremble.

'Luis,' she said, but it came out in a way she didn't recognise. As if she was making a protest without really meaning it.

And he smiled, as if he had just won a battle she hadn't even realised they were having, before lowering his voice. 'Tell me something, Carly. Are you saving your virginity for the man you will one day marry?'

His blunt question shook her out of her dreamy state and she blinked at him in surprise. 'That's a strange question to ask at a time like this.'

He shook his head. 'It's exactly the right question to ask because I need to know what's important to you.'

She wanted to tell him that she wasn't sure she could answer coherently when his thumb was rubbing her lip like that, but she didn't want him to stop. 'Then no. The answer is no. I wasn't *saving* it for anyone. It's not like money you put in the bank. It's just that I'd never met anyone who—'

'Makes you feel the way I do?'

His murmured assertion should have sounded unbearably arrogant, but it didn't. Because that was the truth, too. She shook her head. 'No.'

He leaned forward and replaced his thumb with his lips, brushing them over hers in a way which made her tremble even more.

'I want to be your lover, Carly,' he breathed. 'I want to show you how to enjoy pleasure, for pleasure's sake. You have helped heal me—so let me now heal you.'

'S-sexual healing?' she questioned unsteadily.

'If you like.'

She drew her head away from his. 'It's…it's a crazy idea.'

'Why?'

Why?

A million reasons flooded into her head. Sex wasn't supposed to be something you just *did*, was it, like some cold-blooded experiment carried out in laboratory conditions? Sex was supposed to be about passion. A lot of people thought it was only about *love*.

She looked into the hard gleam of his eyes and suddenly she understood what that journalist had meant when she'd written that article. His face was rugged and beautiful, yes, but his eyes really did look *empty*. As if you could jump into their black depths and never reach the bottom. And surely only a fool would choose to be intimate with a known heartbreaker like Luis Martinez.

Yet the detached, scientific side of her personality was impressed by his honesty. He wasn't spinning her lies by making promises he couldn't fulfil. He was offering to teach her the art of sex.

She imagined turning him down. Of going back to being the woman she'd been before. Carly the invisible. Carly the scared. But she hadn't felt invisible when he'd kissed her. Or scared. She had felt three-dimensional and desired—properly desired—for the first time in her life. Hadn't it come as a huge relief to discover that the creep at the party hadn't destroyed those kind of feelings for ever? That deep down she was still a functioning woman, with a woman's needs.

And didn't she want that? Wasn't it time for her to truly leave the past behind?

'So how would it work?' she questioned casually, but maybe her nonchalant tone didn't fool him because she saw him smile in response. '*If* I were to agree.'

'I hadn't actually given much thought to that,' he said. 'I thought that might have been a little...*presumptuous.*'

'I suppose it might.' But Carly didn't care about *presumptuous*; she just wanted him to begin. She wanted him to kiss her again and make her feel the way she'd done before. She wanted his hands on her breasts and in her hair. She wanted to know what would happen if that low ache deep inside her was allowed to keep building and building...

Letting her eyelashes flicker to a close, she elevated her chin, silently inviting him to kiss her. But his soft laugh made her eyes snap open.

'Oh, no,' he said softly. 'This is not how I intend for your seduction to happen, *querida*. It will not be here, or now. It will not be fast and furious with us grappling on your bed like a couple of greedy teenagers. It will be a slow and considered feast. A banquet guaranteed to satisfy all the senses, rather than something devoured without tasting properly. I want you to be sure that this is what you really want.' His lips curved into a slow smile. 'And when you do, there will be no holds barred.'

She wanted to contradict him. To listen to the small part of her brain which was questioning her own sanity. But the heat in her blood had other ideas and so she shrugged, as if it were no big deal. 'So...'

'So.' He stood up very quickly, as if he didn't quite trust himself to sit chastely beside her on the bed any more. 'You will meet me on the upper terrace at eight o'clock. I will instruct the chef to prepare something cold and dismiss the staff for the rest of the night. We will not be disturbed.'

A shiver of anticipation whispered over her skin.

'I should like you to wear a skirt or a dress and to leave your legs bare,' he continued. 'Oh, and make sure your hair is down. I don't want to see you with that damned ponytail.'

'Anything else?' she questioned, her sarcasm hiding the sudden hurt she felt.

'Yes. And this is probably the most important provision of all.' He looked down at her, his shadow suddenly enveloping her like a dark cloak. 'I need you to promise that you won't fall in love with me. I can do sex—very good sex, as it happens—but I don't do love. Do you understand, Carly? Because I mean it. And if you think this is going to end in wedding bells and clouds of confetti, then you're mistaken.'

Carly was in no doubt that he meant it. She could tell from the implacable note in his voice and the steely glint of his eyes. And while his arrogance was shocking, once again she couldn't help admiring his honesty. Luis would never spin her any impossible dreams, would he?

'There's no need to worry about that,' she said. 'Believe me, I have no desire to waft up the aisle in a cloud of tulle and then listen to a load of boring speeches. I'm going to be a doctor, not a housewife, and I'm certainly not in any danger of falling in love with you, Luis. I know you too well.'

He smiled. 'That's what I like about you, Carly. I like your clear-headed way of thinking.'

But as Carly looked into the hard glitter of his eyes she suddenly found herself wondering if she had taken on more than she could handle.

CHAPTER SEVEN

CARLY BECAME PROGRESSIVELY more nervous as she got ready for dinner that night. Her mouth had grown dry and her hands were trembling and she thought seriously about abandoning the whole idea and telling Luis it had all been a horrible misunderstanding. Could she really go through with losing her virginity to a man like him, who had laid out his exacting guidelines from the start? She thought about what he'd said about her appearance, about what she should and shouldn't wear for her seduction. He had been positively *brutal* in his assessment of her physical appearance, hadn't he?

Yet he'd said nothing which wasn't true. Dull anonymity had been her aim and it seemed she had achieved exactly that. But while fading into the background had worked brilliantly when she'd been his housekeeper, he had told her quite emphatically that it was inappropriate for her new role...

As what?

His lover?

She licked her lips as she pulled the scrunchy from her hair.

Or just someone who was jumping in way out of her depth?

She soaked in a long bath, then hunted around for something suitable to wear but that made her feel even worse. She had convinced herself that she didn't *care* about pretty clothes, but as she surveyed her plain skirts and T-shirts she wished that someone would suddenly appear with a magic wand and transform her wardrobe into something frivolous and...*pretty*.

She did the best she could, but it wasn't easy for someone who had become a stranger to titillation. She had no idea how to primp herself to look good and gain a man's attention. She hadn't worn make-up in years, and her only jewellery was a tiny pearl on a gold chain, which her granny had given her. She fastened it around her neck with still-shaky fingers, but when she surveyed her completed image in the mirror she knew she couldn't go through with it.

Her mother had been right all along. You really couldn't make a silk purse out of a sow's ear. What would Luis say when he saw her with her scrubbed face and her cheap clothes and a pair of sandals which were currently showcasing her unmanicured toes? How could she possibly trot down to the terrace like some sort of prize pony and prepare to give him her virginity?

She began to pace the room, but that only increased her paranoia. What if she phoned him and told him she'd changed her mind? He might be irritated, yes, but he would understand. *Wouldn't he?* He might even be relieved.

But still she hesitated as she walked over to the bed, where her cell phone sat on the table beside it.

What would she say?

A soft knock on the door was followed by someone

opening it and suddenly Luis was walking into the room. His face was dark with question as his narrow-eyed gaze swept over her.

'Have you started walking in without being invited?' she said.

'I thought I'd better come and find you,' he answered. 'But judging from the expression on your face, your no-show on the terrace might indicate something more than your usual poor timekeeping.'

She shook her head and suddenly she didn't bother to hide her feelings behind a wall of pretending not to care. 'Luis, I *can't*.'

He was walking towards her and she could feel the loud bashing of her heart against her ribcage. Though he was dressed down in jeans and a linen shirt, nothing could disguise the glossy patina of power which moulded itself to him like a second skin. Suddenly, he looked like the towering superstar he really was and Carly felt herself begin to shrink in comparison. *How on earth had she put herself in this situation?* What had he said about those beautiful women at the airport? *As interchangeable as the tyres I used to get through.*

Was she out of her mind to contemplate having sex with him?

He was staring down at her. He was so close that she could almost feel the warmth of his body and smell the sandalwood of his soap. She was aware that the bed was within touching distance and she felt torn now—wanting him to reach out for her and terrified of making a fool of herself if he did.

His voice was soft. 'Can't what?'

She bit her lip. 'Can't go through with this.'

'Lesson number one: expressing doubt is not the

most flattering way to greet your prospective lover. And neither is standing there with a look of horror on your face.'

'Luis, I'm serious.'

'Relax,' he said. 'And let me look at you.'

She lifted a self-conscious hand towards her collar as his gaze roved over her. The pink T-shirt was new and the plain denim skirt made her hips look less curvy than usual, but even so... 'I've got nothing particularly fancy to wear. And anyway, I certainly wasn't anticipating *this*.'

'But that's what makes you completely lovely,' he said unexpectedly. 'Your lack of calculation and your absence of expectation. Your naturalness is refreshing.'

She stared at him suspiciously. 'I thought you didn't like what I wore?'

He shrugged. 'I don't, particularly. You certainly don't make the best of yourself, but your simplicity has an appeal all of its own. Even the most hardened cynic can have his head turned by a pair of shining eyes and the glow of healthy skin. And at last you are showcasing one of your most beautiful assets.' He lifted a handful of hair and let it fall down around her shoulders. 'Your hair is the stuff of male fantasy. And right now, you are the stuff of *my* fantasy.'

'Luis,' she said breathlessly, realising that some of the tension had left her, only to be replaced by a new and very different kind of tension, and she saw from the darkening of his eyes that he felt it, too.

He moved his hands to her waist and pulled her close and her heart began thumping dangerously as she felt the warmth of his body against hers.

'Carly,' he said softly. 'Sweet, unexpected Carly.'

She didn't say anything and part of him was glad, because for the first time Luis felt the whisper of doubt, and maybe her words might have compounded that doubt. He saw the way she looked at him—all darkened eyes and parted lips. All innocence and wonder. And as he moved closer he was overcome by a wave of lust far sweeter than he had anticipated, and hot on its heels came the dark stir of his conscience.

His mouth tightened.

He must not hurt her.

He would not hurt her.

'Come here,' he said. He cupped her face with both his hands and slowly brought his head down as he began to kiss her.

At first, he kept it light and teasing—a touch of the lips so fleeting that it barely made contact, though he could taste the subtle flavour of her toothpaste and, for some reason, that drove him crazy. And then he deepened the kiss, flickering his tongue inside her mouth as he began to explore her fully clothed body, and she came to life beneath his touch.

It was the most instant and mind-blowing transformation he had ever encountered. Suddenly, she was all fire. The hands which had been lying inert on his shoulders now moved to curl possessively around his neck as he pulled her even closer.

She kissed him with a passion which took him by surprise. He groaned as she tangled her fingers in his hair and melded her pelvis against his. Her lack of guile and experience was making him feel… Luis heard the roar of his own blood. He wasn't sure *how* it was making him feel. Only that, for all his words about wanting a seasoned seduction, he was suddenly peeling off her T-shirt with the same kind of hunger as a hormonally charged teenager. Maybe even more. Because at seventeen everything had been out there waiting for him. Back then he had been completely entranced by women and yet to discover just how devious they could be. He soon found out that what you saw was never the truth. That thick cascades of hair were usually as false as the stories they spun you. That breasts this large usually owed more to the skill of a plastic surgeon, than to nature.

But not with Carly. He swallowed. God, no. Carly seemed...*real*.

He unclipped her bra and drew back as her breasts tumbled out—the fleshy mounds pale and her nipples the colour of cappuccino. She went to cover them up with her hands but he halted her.

'What are you doing?'

'I know they're too big,' she said.

'Are you kidding?' He smiled. 'They are perfect. Your nipples are exactly the right size for a man's mouth. Shall I show you how well they would fit into mine?'

It pleased him that she blushed as she let him remove her hands, leaving those caramel-coloured circles bare to his gaze. He saw her eyelids flicker as if she was fighting something inside her and then they closed as he bent to lick his tongue over one.

'Luis,' she moaned.

But now he said nothing; his teasing dialogue forgotten. In truth, he was in no fit state to talk. He felt himself grow harder as he sucked at her nipples and teased them with his teeth until she was making wild gulping little sounds at the back of her throat. Her denim skirt was restricting and it was with unfamiliar difficulty that he tugged it down over her hips and thighs, before it pooled at her feet. And when at last he put his hand between her legs her panties were very wet.

Gently rubbing at the moist panel of fabric, he carefully pushed her down on the bed and then drew away from her.

'Stay right there,' he commanded unsteadily.

Her voice trembled. 'You think I'm in any fit state to go anywhere?'

'You are a woman who constantly surprises me,' he said drily. 'So I wouldn't care to make a wager on that.'

Carly watched as he tugged the clothes from his body with an impatience which seemed charged with extra urgency, though his hand was completely steady as he placed a condom on the locker beside her phone.

She had expected to be daunted by the sight of seeing Luis completely naked and aroused and ready to make love, but she wasn't. The truth of it was that her starved and eager body felt nothing but *relief* as he finally dropped his boxer shorts to the floor and joined her on the bed. She could feel the rough hair on his chest squishing against her bare breasts as he kissed her. His hand skated down to her hips, his fingers slipping beneath the elastic of her panties, before sliding them down over her knees.

He kissed her breasts and he kissed her belly. He touched her intimately until she was writhing with pleasure and a hunger which had become all-consuming. Suddenly, she didn't feel like Carly any more—she felt like… Her head tipped back. She felt like a woman. A *real* woman, and suddenly the inequality of their experience didn't matter. Greedily, her fingers explored his body in a way she'd wanted to do for so long. So very long. She touched the angled bones and honed muscle. She skated her fingers over the silken surface of his skin and then she dragged her lips from his, grazing them along his jaw, before finding the warmth of his ear.

'Please,' she whispered, barely conscious of what it was she was asking for.

'Please, what?' he murmured, his fingers moving down to part her moist labia so that she jerked with pleasure. 'This?'

She supposed she must have nodded or said something, or maybe it was obvious just from the eager way she clung to him how much she wanted him. She felt him reach out for the condom and the tearing open of the foiled package sounded unnaturally loud to her highly sensitised ears. She knew a moment of trepidation as she felt him prepare himself, but then he was moving over her and she could feel the engorged tip of him pressing against her.

She looked up into his face and the weirdest thing was that the look which passed between them seemed like the most intimate thing which had happened so far.

'Luis,' she whispered.

'It may…hurt a little,' he said, his voice doing that soft and unsteady thing all over again. 'I don't know. I'll do my best to make sure it doesn't.'

And then he was easing himself into her. Slowly. Deliciously. Filling her as if her body had been nothing but an empty space, just waiting for him to fill it. It didn't hurt like the books and the stories sometimes said it did. There was a moment of acute discomfort—

but then it was gone. And that was the moment when pleasure began to swamp out trepidation and doubt and every other negative feeling and replaced them all with satisfaction, and joy.

He moved inside her. He coaxed her and teased her. He made anything seem possible. At first she thought the shimmering of something hovering on the edge of her understanding was a flicker of something impossible. But when it happened again she began to stiffen with fear that she might somehow miss it. Like closing your eyes when you were looking at a rainbow and when you opened them again it was gone.

'Relax, *querida*,' he murmured as he made another deep thrust inside her.

Perhaps it was the '*querida*' which took the fantasy one stage further, which made her believe that anything *was* possible. She was poised on the brink of something magical, reaching out for something which kept slipping beyond her reach…and then suddenly it was happening. Her body was contracting and it was all about everlasting rainbows as Luis tipped his head back and gave a helpless kind of groan.

And Carly's body seemed to splinter into a million beautiful pieces.

CHAPTER EIGHT

CARLY COULDN'T SLEEP, and in the end she gave up trying.

Slowly, she got out of a bed which was still rumpled and scented with the unfamiliar smell of sex. Looking down, she saw the indentation of the second pillow; tangible evidence that for the first time in her life she had not slept alone, and she felt her skin shivering with pleasure as she remembered.

She had slept with Luis.

She had given her virginity to the Argentinian play-boy with an eagerness which was making her blush even now.

Scooping mussed hair back from her face, she laid her palms over her hot cheeks. Because not very much sleeping had taken place, had it? It had been one long night of discovery.

She swallowed, remembering how nervous she'd been. How she'd been fretting and pacing in her bed-room, too scared to go down to supper. But somehow he had made it all okay. He had come to her room and started kissing her and, instead of being some big deal, it had just seemed to *happen*. As if it was all perfectly natural and normal, just as he'd said it should be. She had made love with Luis Martinez and he seemed to have enjoyed it just as much as she had done.

Supper had been forgotten and it had been almost ten when he had pulled on his jeans and brought back some of the neglected food from the terrace. They had eaten grapes and slithers of mountain cheese in bed, and he had opened a bottle of wine called Petrus and given a small smile when she had pronounced it 'really nice'.

And he had gone to his own room just as dawn had begun to filter through the sky in streaks of red and gold. Bending his dark head, he had kissed her and told her it would probably be easier if he wasn't there in the morning.

He was right about that, too. She knew that. It was nothing but stupidity which made her wish that he'd stayed all night; a flicker of yearning which she knew was dangerous and pointless. So she forced herself to concentrate on the practical instead, which she was good at. She told herself that no way would he want his staff to know how he'd spent the previous evening and she couldn't think of anything worse than Simone discovering him leaving her bedroom, looking tousled and unshaven. Something like that would only make her own position more difficult…though she hadn't actually given a lot of thought as to what was going to happen now.

Now that Luis had taken her as his lover.

Padding barefooted into the bathroom, she pulled on the fluffy robe which was hanging on the back of the door and knotted it tightly at her waist. She certainly wasn't going to do the whole guilt trip—not with herself and not with him. Even if it never happened again, she would always be grateful for the way he'd made her feel. He had set her free from the past. He'd made her realise that she was capable of experiencing the same kind of pleasure as anyone else.

What had he said to her before it had all happened? The one phrase which had stuck out in her mind.

I like your clear-headed way of thinking.

She knew why he'd said that. Because she'd told him she wasn't hung up on love, or marriage. Because she'd convinced him that she was able to regard this sexual experience with complete objectivity.

So why did she suddenly want to hug her arms around herself and dance around the room, while music played loudly inside her head?

The sun was higher now, turning the sea a deep shade of rose, and when she walked out onto the terrace the air felt still and clear. The house was quiet but her head and body were buzzing and for once the thought of losing herself in a few pages of quantum physics didn't appeal. She would catch up on her emails, then see what the day would bring. And if Luis had decided that one night was enough—well, she would have to accept it like a grown-up.

She logged onto her email account and found three messages from her sister. The first was titled Where are u? The second consisted of nothing but a long row of question marks, and the third announced, rather more dramatically, WHAT THE HELL IS HAPPENING?

Carly clicked onto this one first, but unusually the email wasn't peppered with smiley faces or descriptions of her sister's latest modelling jobs. For once, the message was all about Carly.

Saw a photo of your boss at Nice airport and it looked like YOU in the background. I said to Mum that nobody else would wear a T-shirt like that in the Côte d'Azur!!! Are you really in the south of France with Luis Martinez—and if so what the hell is going on?????

Carly smiled. She wondered how Bella would react if she told her the unbelievable truth. *Yes, I am here with Luis. In fact, I told him about my past and he's decided to teach me everything he knows about sex, which is fairly comprehensive as I'm sure you can guess.* Imagine drafting *that* into an email!

She clicked to reply.

Yes, it's true. I've been helping Luis with his rehab after his accident, and he decided it would be preferable if he got better in the sunshine. It's absolutely gorgeous here. Aren't I lucky? Love, Carly xxx

She hit the send button just as someone tapped on the door, but before she had a chance to answer—it opened quietly and Luis walked into the room. He was freshly shaved and his black eyes were alive with vitality and a spark of something else which already she recognised as desire.

'Hello,' he said softly as he closed the door behind him.

Carly's hand crept up to her throat as she realised that the white bathrobe was deeply unflattering and probably added at least ten extra pounds to her frame. 'I thought you'd decided that it was better not to risk being seen here.'

'Maybe I've changed my mind.'

'I haven't even brushed my teeth.'

'Then go and brush them now,' he instructed silkily. 'Because I like the taste of your toothpaste.'

She escaped into the bathroom and when she returned, it was to discover that Luis had dropped his clothes on the floor and was in her bed—completely naked amid the still-rumpled sheets.

'What are you doing?'

'Isn't it obvious?'

'But…what about the staff?'

'What about them? The only member of my staff I'm interested in is standing right in front of me, wearing far too many clothes.' He patted the empty space beside him. 'So come over here, *querida*, before I grow too impatient.'

Carly swallowed down the sudden apprehension which had risen in her throat. It would probably be better to resist him, when even now the gardeners would be arriving and the chef sending his assistant down to the markets in Nice to buy fresh fish and vegetables for the day. To tell him that this was an extremely unwise move and surely they could arrange a rather more discreet meeting later.

It would be much better.

So why was she walking towards the bed and pulling back the sheets?

And why was Luis shaking his head like that?

'No. Not yet. Lose the robe,' he instructed silkily. 'And don't tell me you're shy, not now, when I happen to know more about your body than any man on the planet.'

It was difficult to act nonchalantly when the harsh light of day was showing no mercy to her too-generous curves, but Carly did her best. 'I'm glad to see that nothing ever manages to deflate your ego,' she said, unknotting the robe and letting it fall to the floor, before quickly sliding between the sheets and colliding with his warm, hard body.

'Not just my ego,' he said as he guided her hand to his groin and bent his head to kiss her. 'Mmm. Toothpaste.'

He kissed her until she relaxed. Until her body had begun to call out to her with a hunger which was already familiar and impossible to ignore. And again, Carly was lost as her whole world became centred on what he was doing to her.

She closed her eyes as he cupped her breasts, his palms rolling rhythmically over her peaking nipples. She squirmed with pleasure as he moved over her, parting her thighs and positioning himself there. She gasped as he entered her with one long, slow thrust, her head tipping back as he began to move inside her. Her fingertips roved over his skin, greedily exploring all the different textures, from the hard, hair-roughened thighs to the silken expanse of his broad back.

She wanted to revel in this feeling of intimacy and pleasure, but her orgasm rushed upon her with the speed and power of a freight train crashing over eggshells. She heard him cry out almost immediately, that strangely vulnerable moan he made as he shuddered into stillness inside her. She cradled her arms tightly around him and snuggled up close, her head resting comfortably on his shoulder.

And then she fell asleep.

When she awoke he had gone, just as he'd done last night, and when she appeared at the breakfast table, Simone informed her that Monsieur Martinez had gone into Nice on business and she didn't know when he'd be back.

The morning seemed to pass like an eternity and Carly found it impossible to concentrate on anything. He didn't return until late in the afternoon and by the time he came to her room to find her, she was convinced he was regretting what had happened.

'Where have you been?' she blurted out, before she could stop herself.

He raised his eyebrows.

'I'm sorry. It's none of my business.'

He gave a short laugh as he pulled her into his arms. 'I needed space, and I needed to do some business without any distractions. But now I find I'm in the mood for distraction.'

He pushed her down onto the bed, removing her clothes with almost clinical efficiency, and as Carly looked into the hungry gleam of his black eyes she guessed that this was a demonstration that sex could be fast and furious, too.

Afterwards, she lay there feeling slightly dazed, drawing little circles on his skin and realising that he knew far more about her than she did about him. And in her dreamy post-orgasmic state, she felt she could ask him anything.

'Luis?'

'Mmm?'

She turned onto her side, propping herself up on her elbow so that spills of hair fell down over her shoulders and covered her breasts. 'Have you never wanted children of your own?'

His mouth tightened as he brushed away the curtain of hair to expose her nipple. 'Another word of advice,' he drawled. 'As a post-coital topic, fatherhood isn't really a winner. Be warned, any dreamy little references to babies is likely to send any future lovers running off into the sunset. They might worry that you're starting to fall in love with them.'

She ignored the stab of disappointment that he seemed totally without sexual jealousy; she didn't think *she* could have been quite so casual about any future lovers he might have. But she stuck to her guns. To consider the question logically, as she had been taught. 'You think a question about children automatically means I'm falling in love with you?'

'I know the signs,' he drawled.

'Well, in my case you are misreading them,' she said coolly. 'I'm interested purely from a human interest point of view. Most men want to recreate—it's in their DNA. Continuation of the human race, that sort of thing. You've built up a massive empire, you're a millionaire many times over, surely you want your own flesh and blood to inherit all that?'

Luis rolled onto his back and stared up at the ceiling. It was a topic he usually snapped the lid on—fast. He didn't like women probing and it bored him when they searched for feelings which weren't there. He wondered why was she was spoiling things by asking him this kind of question.

Yet Carly wasn't looking for the kinds of things which most women wanted, was she? A question he'd normally consider loaded, and which he would deflect with ease, sounded different when it came from her. With Carly, he had laid out all his ground rules from the start. She knew what he would or wouldn't tolerate. She was ambitious for a career, not marriage, and perhaps that was why he felt relaxed enough to answer her question.

'I think the human race will survive very well without any miniature versions of Luis Martinez,' he said drily.

'Any particular reason?'

'I can see that you're going to make a very good doctor.' He turned his head to meet her eyes. 'Since you're very persistent with your questions.'

'You're stalling.'

'So I am.' His eyes gleamed. 'What do you want to know?'

'Oh, I don't know. About your life. Where you grew up. Why you're so adamant you don't want children.'

He linked his fingers together and put them behind his head, allowing a slow stream of memories to pass through his mind. 'I grew up on a big ranch outside Buenos Aires,' he said. 'Where we farmed cattle in great rolling sweeps of land with the biggest skies you ever saw.'

She wriggled a little closer. 'We?'

'Me, my mother and my father. We were quite unusual in that there weren't loads of children running around. But I guess that made us especially close as a family, and my parents...' He shrugged. 'Well, they adored me, I guess. The farm was hugely profitable, my father had business interests in the city which were equally successful...'

'So everything was lovely?' she prompted as his voice faded away.

'For a while.' He looked at her and when he spoke again his voice had grown hard. 'My mother had a friend called Amelita, and she and her husband had a son about my age. Vicente was like the brother I'd never had, and the two families used to do everything together. We skied in the winter and hit the beaches in the summer. We ate Christmas dinner around the same table. We were all like one great big unit.'

He paused, not sure why he was telling her all this. Not sure that he should. Was it because she had shared her secrets with him and something was telling him that he needed to redress the balance? Or because he suspected that she was insistent enough to keep probing if he didn't?

'Go on,' she said.

He stroked her hair. 'I developed a love of speed early on and my father built a small go-kart circuit on our property for me to practise on, which was pretty innovative at the time. Vicente and I spent hours bombing around that dusty trail. Then at sixteen, I moved away to the San Luis province so that I could use the famous Potrero de los Funes track. I didn't come home that often, but when I did, things seemed different. I thought that my father and Amelita had grown...close. Closer than was right. I used to see the way she looked at him. The way she dressed around him. For a while I managed to convince myself that I must be mistaken, because I *wanted* to be mistaken. And she was my mother's best friend.'

He swallowed. His own sexual experience had been at a fledgling stage—he was barely out of single figures himself at that time. But he had been hit on often enough to realise that his mother's best friend really was coming onto his father. He remembered trying to talk to him about it and being shocked by the old man's sudden spurt of rage; his gritted threat to punch his only son. He had allowed himself to be placated by the furious denials which had followed, because hadn't it been easier that way, even if deep down he had known the words to be lies?

'And then one afternoon I rose early from my siesta,' he said slowly. 'The day was so still and so hot that I felt I could hardly breathe. I walked outside, seeking the shade of the trees, but it was no better there. There was no relief to be found anywhere. And then I heard a sound, something which seemed out of place in my home. I found myself walking towards the summer house and that is where I found them. My father and Amelita…'

Carly's hand flew over her mouth so that her words came out muffled. 'And were they…?'

'Not quite,' he said, repressing a painful shudder of recall. 'Amelita was in the middle of some kind of tacky striptease at the time, while my father…' His voice shook with rage. 'And all this while my mother slept in the house nearby. It was the lack of respect as much as the betrayal which made me want to kill him.'

He stopped speaking and she didn't say anything. She moved her hand to his face to try to comfort him, but he shook it off as if a fly had landed there.

'It all came out, of course. These things always do,' he said. 'I suspect Amelita made sure that it did, since my father was one of the richest men in Argentina. And predictably, it blew everyone's world apart. My mother never really recovered. She felt the sting of the double betrayal, of being cheated on not just by her husband, but by her best friend, too. She moved out of the ranch and bought a place in the city, but she stopped eating.

Stopped caring, really. She used to stay in her rooms, afraid to leave, haunted by the fact that people would be looking at her and mocking her. Didn't matter what I did or what anyone said, she refused to listen, and she died just three years later.'

'Oh, Luis. I'm so sorry,' she whispered.

He shook his head as he tried to hold back the tide of dark emotion which he had battened down for so long. But for once in his life, it kept on coming and some instinct told him that maybe it was better this way. He had never told anyone, and if he told someone who ultimately didn't matter, then couldn't he loosen some of his own dark chains? Because one thing he knew was that Carly would never go anywhere with this. He could see the makings of the doctor in her already, not just in her firm but ultimately gentle care of him, but in a moral compass, which was rare. She would not need to swear the Hippocratic oath to have her discretion guaranteed.

'You want to hear the rest?' he questioned bitterly. 'Because it doesn't make for a particularly happy bedtime story.'

'I want to hear it,' she said.

'The husband of my father's mistress also felt humiliated by the public laughing stock he'd become, but he sought a different remedy than the self-imposed isolation of my mother. He took what he thought was the only honourable way out. He put a revolver to his head and blew his brains out. It was Vicente who found him.'

She drew in a deep, shuddering breath. 'Oh, Luis.'

He stared up at the ceiling again. 'So there you have

it. Now do you see why I don't believe in family life
and happy ever after, Carly?'

There was a pause. He could almost hear her thinking aloud as she sifted through all the possible words
and tried to find the right ones to say. Except that there
were no right words. He knew that.

'Not...really,' she said tentatively. 'I mean—those
were terrible things which happened, but they weren't
really anything to do with you, were they? None of
that was your fault. Just because of the way your father behaved, doesn't automatically follow that you
would do the same. Infidelity and betrayal aren't he-
reditary, you know.'

He turned to look at her again. He could see empathy clouding her eyes and he couldn't help admire
her kindness, as well as her perception. Because Carly
was clever, he realised. Clever enough to realise that
there was more.

'But I've lived a life on the racing circuit,' he said
simply. 'And I've seen what it does to men—especially
to champions.'

'What do you mean?'

He shrugged. 'There are characteristics which make
men like me succeed. We're driven—literally—by the
desire to win. We spend years in pursuit of the elusive
perfect lap and when we achieve it we want to repeat
it, over and over again. There aren't many of us at the
top, but when you get there you realise that it is both a
seductive and a dangerous place to be. People revere
you. They want a piece of you. Especially women.'

'Women who are *"as interchangeable as the tyres
I used to get through"*?' she quoted quietly.

'Exactamente.' His face tightened. 'I have seen the

strongest marriages break down under the strain of all the temptations the sport has to offer. When the adrenaline is flowing and some sexy little creature puts on a skirt the size of a handkerchief and presses her breasts against your windshield, most men can't say no. Most are arrogant enough to feel they *don't have to* say no.'

'So.' She sat up, folding her arms across her naked breasts. 'What you're really saying is that world champions get given so much forbidden fruit, that they find it impossible to exist on normal fare like most normal people?'

He shrugged. 'If you like.'

'But you no longer race for a living, Luis,' she said. 'So how does that even apply?'

'My father wasn't a racer,' he said stonily. 'He was a farmer who'd been married for twenty-one years. Who used to tell me that my mother was his soulmate.'

'So what you're really saying is that you think men generally are incapable of fidelity?'

'That's one way of looking at it,' he said slowly. 'Yes. I think that's right.'

'So men really are the weaker sex?'

'Or the more realistic?' he countered coolly. 'How can two people possibly make promises of fidelity to each other, when they have no guarantee of keeping them?'

Carly didn't respond. His words had made her heart sink, even though she knew she had no right to be hurt by them. He had never promised her anything other than what he'd just given her, had he? In fact, he had explicitly warned her off the very things he had just been talking about. She pushed back the sheet and got out of bed. 'I need to use the bathroom,' she said.

She walked across the bedroom and closed the bathroom door behind her, though maybe you were supposed to leave it open in circumstances like these? She realised what a novice she still was and how little she knew about how to interact with a man on such an intimate basis. She told herself that she couldn't complain about his honesty, just because he was telling her something she didn't want to hear. She had to accept this on the terms he had offered her, or she would end up getting her heart broken.

She flicked cold water over her face and practised a few convincing-looking smiles in the mirror so that when she walked back into the bedroom she felt almost calm. At least, until she saw him sitting propped up against the bank of snowy pillows, looking very dark and rugged.

His black eyes seemed to pierce through her still-tender skin. 'Would you like to go out for lunch tomorrow?' he questioned.

'Lunch?' She blinked, because she had assumed that they would assume their normal boss/employee relationship during daylight hours. She had thought that they would be together only in bed. 'You mean— not here?'

He gave the faint flicker of a smile, as if her lack of imagination had amused him. 'No, not here. There is a whole beautiful coastline out there, *querida*—with some of the most famous restaurants in the world just waiting to be eaten in. There are beaches and mountains and tiny villages which are like stepping back in time. And since this is your first visit to France, I think it's time I showed you some of them.'

'But…I thought you'd decided it was best if we weren't seen together?'

'And maybe I've changed my mind.' His mouth tightened. 'I don't live my life trying to please other people, and neither should you.'

CHAPTER NINE

HE TOOK HER to Juan-les-Pins, to a restaurant on a beach, where he was recognised immediately. But Carly was still too busy thinking about what he'd told her to take much notice of the heads turning to watch them as they walked over the sand-covered boards to a table which looked directly over the lapping blue waves. She thought about his sad upbringing and the conclusions he'd drawn. Conclusions which had only been compounded by his championship status in the glamorous sport of motor racing.

He didn't think that men were capable of fidelity.

It had been a bald statement to make to someone you'd only just seduced and the message had been plain, even for someone as naïve as her. He was warning her off. Telling her to keep this bizarre liaison in the right place and not start building any fantasies. Because he wasn't stupid. He must guess that being sexually awoken by a man like him would be powerful enough to turn the head of any woman, no matter how much she protested that she wasn't looking for love or marriage.

They ordered shellfish salads, and iced lime juice flavoured with coconut, and Luis devoured his food with a voracious appetite before noticing that she wasn't doing the same. He put his fork down and looked at her, dark eyebrows disappearing into the tangle of his dark hair.

'Lobster not to your satisfaction?'

She prodded at the pink flesh with her fork and forced a smile. 'The lobster's lovely.'

'Is that why you're not eating any of it? Or is it because you're upset about what I told you yesterday?'

'I'm not *upset*. I'm grateful you felt you could be so honest with me. I'm just feeling a bit...'

He put his glass down. 'A bit what?'

She shrugged. 'Nothing.'

'Tell me.'

'Oh, I don't know. Overwhelmed, I guess.' Her gaze shot around at the tables, which all seemed to contain at least one female who looked as if she'd be at home on a catwalk. 'All the women here look amazing. As if they've spent the entire morning getting ready to have lunch in a chic restaurant, while I—'

'Look like someone who has spent the morning being ravished by a man who can't seem to keep his hands off her? Who is growing hard just by looking at her.'

'Luis,' she said faintly, her breath catching in her throat, because when he looked at her that way she just wanted to lean across the table and kiss him.

'Don't you think that any of them would prefer to be in your shoes?' His gaze dropped to floor level and the hint of a smile curved his lips. 'Or flip-flops, in this case.'

'Which were never bought with the intention of being worn in some ultra-smart restaurant on the Côte d'Azur.'

He glanced up. 'But you don't dress to be seen, do you, Carly? Or to be looked at. You dress to be invisible and to blend into the background. I thought that was the whole point.'

She could hear the white umbrella above them flapping in the light breeze which was coming off the sea. 'And I told you why.'

'But the reason no longer applies, surely? If I've set you free from your hang-ups about sex, then doesn't it follow that you might be a little more experimental about what you wear?'

'You think I look awful,' she said, in a wooden voice.

'I think those pale shades you like don't do you any favours. Your colouring is so fair that you need something more dramatic to set that off. If you don't like your appearance, then change it, but don't keep doing nothing and then complaining about it, because it's boring.' He leaned back in his chair and subjected her to a cool look. 'And there's no need to look at me quite so reproachfully. You *did* ask.'

'And you certainly didn't p-pull any punches in telling me,' she said.

'What would be the point of that? We're back to the whole question of honesty again.' He shrugged. 'Maybe it's time you stopped hiding some of your more spectacular assets and tried something new. So grab your bag.' He lifted his hand and signalled to the waiter for the check. 'I'm taking you shopping.'

'I don't like shopping.'

'You will. Like eating avocado—it's a taste which can easily be acquired.' His black eyes gleamed. 'So come quietly, *querida*, because I am still not fit enough to put you over my shoulder and carry you.'

Carly bit back a smile. When he looked at her that way, she felt powerless to do anything but agree. She didn't feel like herself any more; she had become one of those women starring in a rom-com, their lives transformed by a gorgeous man with a big wallet and a lot of attitude.

Clamping her hands down over her hair, they sped along the Croisette in Cannes in his open-top car before coming to a halt outside a screamingly smart boutique, where a burly man in uniform took Luis's car keys and went off to park for him.

But Carly's mood evaporated when she peered through the plate-glass windows at the glamorous sales assistants who were grouped around inside.

'I can't,' she whispered. 'I can't go in there.'

'I thought we'd decided to dispense with the self-deprecation?' he drawled. 'You can do anything you want. Starting right now.' He laced his fingers in hers. 'Come.'

Carly felt faint. He was holding her hand in public! He was walking inside as if he owned the place and telling one of the sales assistant that he wanted to see her in 'hot' colours.

'Scarlet,' he said. 'And definitely flame. And I think we might try yellow, too.'

Slipping into seamless French, he spoke animatedly to the woman, using his hands to draw curving shapes of a voluptuous body in the air. They were taken to a private area at the back of the store, where he showed no embarrassment about running his fingertips along a line of frothy lace bras, or deliberating between the virtues of the thong versus the camiknicker.

Carly's throat had grown dry with nerves. She felt

big and ungainly, like a giant in a land of tiny people. She wanted to tell him she'd changed her mind, until she remembered that it hadn't actually been her who had made it up in the first place. It had been Luis who had taken command of the afternoon, overriding all her objections and deciding what needed to be done. And judging by his relaxed attitude as he sat on one of the velvet sofas, sipping a tiny cup of espresso, this wasn't the first time he'd adopted this particular role. Maybe it was just a rite of passage for all the women who shared his bed. Though surely the usual rangy supermodel would do more justice to one of the delicate pieces of underwear which had been brought to the cubicle for her to try?

But to Carly's surprise, the wispy bra was deceptively supportive and the camiknickers transformed her rounded hips into an area of her body which suddenly looked glossy, and...inviting.

When she pulled on a yellow and white polka-dot dress, with its full skirt and shiny patent belt, she barely recognised the reflection which gazed back from the mirror, but even the sales assistant gave her a wide beam of approval.

'Mais, elle est jolie,' she said, on a note of surprise.

Luis gave a slow smile as Carly stood in front of him. 'Very pretty,' he agreed, picking up a straw sun hat with a yellow ribbon on—his black eyes piercing into her as he placed it carefully on her head. 'Now are you going to start believing in yourself?'

She could feel the silk next to her skin and the crispness of the petticoat beneath the fifties-style dress and, almost shyly, she nodded.

He smiled, his gaze alighting on a stick-like mannequin clutching a plastic bucket and spade at the far end of the store. 'I think we'll take a look at some bikinis while we're here.'

Soon they were laden down with glossy carrier bags, tied with bright pink ribbons, and Carly was persuaded to keep on the yellow dress and the matching espadrilles.

'You've bought me far too much,' she whispered, her heart pounding as Luis cupped her face in his hands, causing the sun hat to wobble precariously.

'That's for me to do and for you to accept. And now I'm going to take you home and show you something which is vital to the repertoire of any lover,' he said, brushing his lips over hers in a grazing kiss.

Carly was back on that same dangerous high as they sped along the mountain road. She kept trying to tell herself that none of this had any real substance, no matter how wonderful it felt. But her heart was stubbornly refusing to listen to what her head was telling her. She had told him she wasn't looking for the things which most women wanted—that her desire for love and marriage had been eclipsed by her ambition to be a doctor. But suddenly she was discovering that falling in love with Luis would be as easy as falling off a chair.

He took her straight to his bedroom when they got back, but she barely had time to register that this was the first time she'd ever been in his room because he was closing the door and walking towards her, with a look of fierce intent on his face.

His eyes were glittering as he began to peel off her yellow dress before carefully draping it over the back of a chair. Beneath it she was wearing some of the new lingerie he'd chosen and she saw his eyes narrow as he ran his gaze over her.

'*Perfecta,*' he said softly.

'I'm not perfect,' she said, until she saw the expression on his face. 'Th-thank you.'

'That's better.' He gave a small nod of approval as he cupped the embroidered swell of her breast. 'Because right now, you are completely perfect to me.'

Carly would have defied a marble statue not to have responded to that statement. She tried to play down its significance as he pushed her onto the silken rug and took off her new camiknickers, before putting his head between her thighs. She stiffened at the shock of the sudden warm intimacy of his tongue licking against her moist flesh. Her fingers started tugging at the wayward waves of his hair so that he lifted his head, his dark eyes gleaming as they surveyed her.

'Luis?' she said uncertainly.

'You just have to relax,' he said. 'I'm not going to hurt you.'

Wasn't he? She closed her eyes. She suspected he was going to do exactly that. Because there were different kinds of hurt, weren't there? She'd learnt in biology that the human heart was vulnerable in so many ways.

But her mind emptied as his tongue began to explore her. She clung to him as he whispered soft incitements in Spanish. And after she had sobbed out a powerful orgasm which left her dazed and shaking, she wondered how she was going to live without this kind of pleasure.

Or live without him.

She could taste the unfamiliar flavour of sex on his mouth as he slid up to kiss her.

'Unzip me,' he said.

She swallowed. 'Are you going to corrupt me even more?'

'I'm going to try.'

He taught her how to suck him. He showed her how to pleasure herself, while he watched. He took her to Monaco and Antibes and Saint-Paul-de-Vence, where they ate lunch in a famous restaurant, where paintings by Picasso and Miro hung on the walls. They ate *plateau de fruits de mer* in Nice and drank champagne in a little place called Plan-du-Var, high up in the mountains. Back at his luxury villa he would strip off her clothes with hungry hands and their sex would have a hot, hard urgency. And when she had gasped out yet another orgasm, he would stroke her skin and murmur that her body was everything a woman's body should be. By the end of that week, Carly was reeling—her senses so exquisitely stimulated that she could barely eat or sleep.

And all she could think about was Luis.

It was as if he had entered her bloodstream like a powerful drug. Suddenly, she began to understand something about the nature of addiction. You tried something which you knew was bad for you, and suddenly you were hooked. Hooked on a feeling which even a novice could recognise as love.

But none of this was real. That was what she kept bringing it back to. It was a brief fairy tale which was bound to end. Her feelings weren't real and neither was this situation. Seduced by his skill as a lover, she had found it easy to forget she was also Luis's employee. But she was. Nothing had really changed and now she was wondering what was going to happen when they left here.

'You've been very quiet,' he observed late one afternoon as they lay beside the pool and she tried, unsuccessfully, to read.

'I'm just sleepy.'

'Don't be evasive, Carly,' he said softly. 'I thought we had agreed to be honest with each other.'

She laid the book down on her stomach, her heart clenching as she looked at him. The growing ache inside her was making her realise she couldn't carry on like this. She couldn't keep burying her head in the sand and pretending the future wasn't out there. She couldn't keep pretending that she didn't care for him, because she did. 'I've been thinking.'

'About what?'

'Well, a couple of things really.' For a moment the world seemed to hold its breath and everything around her seemed to be green and blue and beautiful. The flickering gleam of sunlight danced on the pool and the sky was as blue as those rain-smashed delphiniums she'd seen in the garden back in England. She didn't ever want to leave here, but some day soon she was going to have to. Because they were living in a protected bubble and sooner or later the bubble was going to burst. 'About what's going to happen when we go back to England.'

Luis tipped his sun hat forward, so that the shadow of the brim fell over his eyes, because somehow it was easier to know that his face was in darkness. He thought about her question and how he was going to answer it. She was only saying what had been on his mind for days, and he knew he couldn't keep ignoring his commitments elsewhere. He had a doctor's appointment in London next week and a growing stack of engagements, which he couldn't put off any longer. He had meetings in Dublin and Buenos Aires and was due to make a visit to Uruguay, to oversee the second stage of his beachside development.

But this wasn't just about the logistics of his life; it was about how he was going to deal with a situation he had created. How he was going to extricate himself from it, with as little angst as possible.

He sighed. He liked Carly. He liked her a lot, but the longer this went on, the greater the likelihood that she would get hurt, because that was what he did to women. That was his *process*. And he didn't want to hurt her. He didn't want tears or recriminations. He didn't want her to degrade herself by trying to hold onto what they could never have. He wanted her to go away and be the fantastic doctor he knew she could be.

'I don't think that's going to be a problem,' he said.

'Maybe not. But we still have to face facts, don't we, Luis? There's no point pretending that nothing's happened, is there?'

Beneath the shadowed brim of his hat, Luis frowned. What did she think had *happened*? They'd had sex. She had been unfulfilled and uptight and crying out for some kind of affection. And he had given it to her. He had set her free. His mouth hardened. *That had been the deal.*

He looked at her, at the zingy new orange and cerise bikini which moulded itself to her magnificent curves. She'd left her hair loose, the way he liked it, and her skin had now turned a deep, caramel colour.

He'd done her a favour. And he would do her an even bigger one by setting her free.

'I don't think it will be a problem,' he said coolly. 'In fact, I'm planning on leaving almost as soon as we get back to England. I have a number of global projects which will keep me occupied for most of the winter. We'll hardly see one another, probably not until the spring.'

'Oh. Oh, right.'

There was no disguising her shock or her disappointment. He could see she was doing her best to smile, but he knew enough about women to realise that behind her dark glasses those iced-tea eyes would be blinking away the first prick of tears. Because he made women cry, didn't he? That was something else he was good at. He made them long for something he was incapable of giving them. He felt a twist of something which felt like regret, but it was gone in an instant.

'And you'll soon be going off to med school, won't you? You're going to be a doctor. The best doctor in the world.'

Carly was about to tell him that it would be at least a year before she could afford to do that. Because even with the bonus he was paying her, she still needed to pay her rent and feed herself through six long years of study. For someone who hadn't done any formal education for such a long time, she wanted to give one hundred per cent of herself to her course and not distract herself with part-time jobs.

Until she realised the implications of what he was saying, and all the practical considerations about her future slipped from her mind. She realised what was happening and suddenly she felt sick. Luis was ending it. Now. As clinically as he was able to remove her clothes, he was now taking a scalpel to their relationship. He intended going off round the world and when he returned, they would act as if nothing had happened.

Because nothing had.

They'd had sex, that was all. All it was ever intended to be. Only a fool would imagine that the act of *making* love would make someone *fall* in love.

And she was that fool, wasn't she? That fool who had started looking at him with a warm glow in her heart and stupid little fantasies building in her mind.

She swallowed.

She was only that fool if she let herself be.

Quietly, she closed the pages of her book. 'That's right,' she said, hoping her face didn't betray the pain in her heart. 'I will. The best doctor in the world,' she repeated.

He glanced over at her. 'And what was the second thing?'

She stared at him. 'The second thing?'

'You said you had a couple of things you wanted to talk to me about.'

Had she? Carly blinked and then remembered. In the parallel universe of a few minutes ago when there had still been hope in her heart, she had been about to tackle a few home truths. She had wanted to tell him something she thought he needed to hear, but now she thanked heaven that his words had stopped her in time.

Dimly, she registered the sound of an approaching car in the distance, then the slamming of a door and the clatter of heels. But the momentary intrusion was dwarfed by the cold and tearing pain inside her. There was no going back—or going forward. She and Luis were finished. It was over.

She stared into his face. 'It doesn't matter now,' she said, just as Simone began to walk out from the back of the villa, closely followed by someone with long blonde hair and a tiny denim skirt. Someone who looked oddly familiar but who really shouldn't be here.

Carly blinked. It was weird. Like seeing a double-decker bus in the middle of the desert. They were both things you recognised, just that one of them was in the wrong place.

Simone's face was expressionless as she looked at Carly. 'Your sister has arrived.'

'My sister?' said Carly in confusion, as the blonde in the miniskirt came clattering towards them.

CHAPTER TEN

CARLY SAT BOLT UPRIGHT. 'Bella?' she said, her voice rising in surprise. 'What…what on earth are you doing here?' But deep down, she knew. The reason was fairly obvious and lying sprawled on a sunbed which her sister was now standing beside as she slanted him the widest smile in her repertoire.

'Well.' Bella pushed a spill of platinum hair away from her tanned face. 'You told me you were here in Cap Ferrat and I happened to be in the area—'

'What are you doing in the area?' asked Carly, but Bella was shooting her a furious *don't-ask-me-any-awkward-questions* type of look and years of deferring to her sister's wishes was a hard habit to break, especially when you were already feeling emotionally wobbly. She forced a smile. 'Luis, I'd like you to meet my sister, Bella. Bella, this is Luis Martinez, who is—'

'Ex-champion motor-racer of the world,' purred Bella. 'Yes, I know.'

'Oh, that was a long time ago,' said Luis smoothly. 'Nice to meet you, Bella.'

Bella was staring at him with open admiration as he sat up and pushed back his battered straw hat.

'I hope I'm not intruding,' she said.

'Not at all,' he answered. 'As you can see, your sister and I were just catching the last of the afternoon sun. Would you like some coffee? A drink, perhaps?'

'Ooh, a drink would be wonderful. I've been doing the most horrendous shoot all day and I'm knackered. The photographer has practically had his lens up my bum all day.' She licked her lips. 'I don't suppose you've got any champagne?'

'I think we might be able to find some.' He glanced up at his French housekeeper. 'Simone—I wonder if you'd mind…?'

'Oui, monsieur,' said Simone briskly. *'D'accord.'*

'Here, let me get you a chair,' said Luis, and he stood up, a movement which seemed to completely captivate Bella, before walking across to the far side of the terrace towards a small cluster of sunbeds and chairs which stood there.

He was barely out of earshot before Bella turned to Carly, her mouth hanging open in amazement. 'What have you been *doing* to yourself?' she demanded. 'I hardly recognised you! My God—that *bikini*!'

Carly automatically tugged at the frilly bikini bottoms. 'You don't like it?'

'I'm not sure. I don't know if it's really *you*. It certainly looks expensive. What the hell is going on, Carly? How come you're lying out here with Mr Hunky and looking like you were born to it?'

'I've been… I've been helping with Luis's rehabilitation.'

'Is that what you call it? Looked pretty cosy when I arrived, I must say.' Her eyes narrowed. 'You're not…'

On her face was an expression which Carly had never seen before. Yes, there was amazement and disbelief, but surely that wasn't *jealousy* she could read there?

Bella flicked a strand of platinum hair over her shoulder. 'You're not...*involved* with Luis Martinez, are you?'

Carly looked her straight in the eye. 'Oh, come on, Bella, can you really see someone like Luis bothering with someone like me?'

'No,' said Bella slowly. 'I suppose when you put it like *that*.'

Carly was relieved when Luis arrived back with a chair, though less pleased when Bella removed her high-heeled sandals and proceeded to glug down a glass of the pink champagne, which Simone had just delivered on a tray.

She had forgotten just how glamorous her sister was. How a similar composition of genes could have ended up making someone who looked so different from her. They both had the same amber-coloured eyes, but that was where all similarities ended. Bella's were fringed with heavy dark mascara, which made her look like some kind of startled young deer. And her figure was amazing—nobody could deny that. She had always exercised to within an inch of her life and never ate carbs after six and it showed. Oh, yes. It showed. She could see Luis looking at her, his black eyes narrowed with interest, and Carly felt her heart beginning to sink with the inevitability of it all. Of *course* he would find Bella attractive. Any man would.

She found herself accepting a glass of champagne, even though it was only five in the afternoon, and the bubbles shot straight to her head as she sipped it.

'Carly tells me you're a model, Bella,' said Luis.

'Yes, that's right. Though I still haven't made it *quite* as big as I'd like. At least, not *yet*.' Bella smiled at him from behind her curtain of white-blonde hair. 'I suppose you must know plenty of people in the industry?'

'Some.'

'Perhaps you could introduce me sometime?'

'Perhaps,' he said, non-committally.

Carly sat listening in horrified fascination as Bella ladled out abundant amounts of charm. Was Luis enjoying talking to her sister as much as he appeared to be? She watched him smile as Bella told him a story about the elastic snapping on a pair of bikini bottoms as the photographer homed in for a close-up.

'But about three men dashed over to the rescue with their beach towels!' she said.

'I'll bet they did,' observed Luis.

Carly tried to smile but her mouth seemed stuck in some kind of awful rictus. The alcohol was making her feel *disassociated*...as if she was a spectator in all this and not a participant. She saw Bella glance down surreptitiously at her watch.

'What are you guys doing tonight?' she asked casually. 'You're not free for dinner, by any chance?'

'Sorry.' Luis gave her a quick smile. 'But Carly and I have an engagement which we can't get out of,' he said, without missing a beat.

Carly blinked at him.

They did?

'But we must see you some other time,' he continued. 'Just give us a little more warning next time.' He reached down and picked up his cell phone. 'And in the meantime, I'll have my driver take you back to wherever it is you're going.'

Carly could see the flicker of annoyance on Bella's face, the sulky pout which had made her pretty face crumple. The look which always used to get their mother eating out of her hand, but which seemed to be having absolutely no effect on Luis.

She could feel cold dread building inside her as she wrapped her sarong around her to see Bella out, waiting for the outburst she knew was inevitable—and she wasn't disappointed.

'You do realise you're in danger of making a complete and utter fool of yourself?' hissed Bella as they reached the front door.

'I don't know what you're talking about.'

'Oh, please! It's written all over you, and I'm your sister—I know you better than anyone. It's obvious to me that you're sleeping with him and that you can't tear your eyes away from him. I don't blame you for that—he's pretty amazing—the only surprise is that he's chosen someone like you. I don't want to be cruel, Carly, but you need to hear the facts. And you're heading for a crash if you don't pull yourself together, because it's clear what he's doing.'

Carly felt as if she'd been carved from wood. 'And what's that?'

'He's just playing Pygmalion,' Bella continued, really getting into it now. 'Transforming his mousey little housekeeper into someone who's happy to lie by the swimming pool, bursting out of her bikini. But it's nothing but a *game* for him. Don't you see? He's been bored—and incapacitated—and it's just something to keep himself occupied. He'll drop you just as quickly as he picked you up, and then where will you be?'

There were a million things she could have said in

response, but Carly just said the words she knew were expected of her, like someone who was reading from an autocue. *And wasn't Bella only speaking the truth?* 'Thanks for the advice—I'll certainly bear it in mind,' she said. 'Maybe we can meet up when I get back to England?'

Bella stared at her as if waiting for more and when it didn't come, she spoke again. 'And hopefully you'll have seen sense by then.'

'Hopefully.'

Bella shook her head and her blonde hair swayed. 'You're a fool, Carly Conner.'

Carly watched as her sister strutted across the forecourt of the villa and climbed into the car which was waiting. She stood there for a long time after the electronic gates had closed, until there was nothing but a tiny black dot in the distance, spitting up clouds of dust as it drove down the hillside.

She walked slowly back into the house. Now what?

Back to the poolside to finish her glass of champagne and for a conversation she didn't really want to have? Yet deep down she knew she didn't have an alternative. She couldn't avoid the truth for ever.

Luis had obviously been swimming while she'd been saying goodbye to her sister. His dark hair was dripping and his olive skin was sleek with little droplets of water. He walked along the edge of the pool and stretched and suddenly it was as if her vision had cleared. As if she was able to step out of the fog of lust and love which had clouded her judgement up until now. She saw him as Bella must have seen him. Famous, gorgeous, rich. One of the great playboys who'd had dalliances with some of the most beautiful women in the world. Had she *really* thought she could stand in their shadow for long? Even if he had managed to make her feel better about herself, did she really think she was able to hang onto him? To make him *love* her?

He looked up and met her eyes.

'She's gone,' she said flatly.

'Yes.' There was a pause. 'She's nothing like you, is she?'

'Not really.' Carly forced a smile. 'Were you attracted to her?'

'Was I attracted to her?' he repeated slowly. 'Why do you ask a question like that?'

Carly reminded herself that he had taught her not to have hang-ups about sex, so didn't that mean that she should start thinking about it the way that the rest of the world did? Like some kind of casual exercise to be enjoyed. 'Most men are.'

'Are they?' he said, his tone now ominous. 'What, did you think I wanted to bed your sister, Carly? Or perhaps to live out the fantasy of taking the two of you at the same time?'

Her skin had turned to ice. 'D-did you?'

He gripped his hands into two tight fists, which hung down by the powerful shafts of his thighs, his face darkening like thunder. 'No, I did not,' he gritted out. 'Just what kind of man do you take me for?'

Carly had never seen him so angry. His black eyes were cold and his shadowed jaw looked as hard as granite. 'I know what kind of man you are,' she said. 'Remember?'

'I may have had a chequered past, but I have treated you with nothing but respect since we became lovers,' he ground out. 'I've been up front with you every step of the way and as considerate as I know how. But it seems you couldn't wait to throw it all back in my face by making veiled suggestions that I might enjoy some sordid little tryst with your sister.'

'I didn't—'

'Yes, you damned well did!' Ruthlessly, he cut across her words, advancing towards her as he had done so many times before, only this time his face was not softened by desire. This time it was hard and cold with fury. 'Maybe in the past, my behaviour might have justified you making such a negative judgement because, God knows, I've certainly been no angel. But there are *limits* to what I would consider acceptable behaviour.'

'Luis—'

'Do you really think I would be willing to replicate that kind of massive betrayal, after what I told you about my mother?'

'I'm sorry,' she said woodenly.

'Even if you could think so little of me, do you really think so little of yourself? Haven't you learned anything, Carly? That sex is not wrong and that you can be just as confident and as beautiful as you make up your mind to be.' He shook his head. 'But you're still allowing yourself to be that same scared woman underneath, aren't you? Still so eager to believe the worst about yourself. What's making you do that? Do you miss the cloak of invisibility you wore for so long? Do you find it so terrifying to be out in the real world that you're looking for some excuse to escape from it again?'

She shook her head as his accusations rained down on her like spiky little hailstones. And even though she wanted to blot out what he was saying to her, somehow she was finding it impossible. *Was* she an emotional coward, eager to think the worst about everyone because it was easier that way?

Or was he?

'Maybe you're right,' she said, pushing her hair out of her face. 'But if I'm having difficulty adapting to normality maybe that's because none of this *is* normal. I feel like someone who has jumped into the wrong end of the swimming pool. I'm out of my depth and I don't fit in. Not here. Not anywhere, really.'

'Then *find* your depth,' he said grimly. 'You're an intelligent woman. Don't tell me that you're planning to go to medical school at the age of twenty-three and then start playing the shrinking violet again. You are capable of so much, Carly. Of anything you want, if only you have the courage to reach out and grab it.'

Carly sucked in a deep breath, terrified that tears were going to arrive just when she least needed them. Because although his words were intended as an encouragement—and they were—they were also intended as a farewell. Her lips wobbled for a couple of seconds before she could trust herself to speak. 'You're very good at dishing out advice, aren't you, Luis? But I wonder how good you are at taking it.'

He gave a bitter laugh. 'Why, is this now going to become some kind of tit for tat?'

'It's more about redressing the balance than scoring points,' she said, hating the sarcasm she heard in his drawled response, hating this new distance between them which was growing bigger by the second. 'You wonder why I was so eager to jump to the wrong conclusion about you wanting my sister? Well, why shouldn't I think something like that, when you told me emphatically that you didn't think men were capable of fidelity?'

'Now you're twisting my words.'

'Am I? Or am I just putting my own interpretation on them?' She stared at him. 'Because I don't think that you do believe that, not really. I think that's just your excuse for staying away from commitment.'

'My *excuse*?' he demanded.

'Yes.' Her voice dropped to a whisper. 'I think you were hurt so badly by what happened with your parents. I think you felt completely betrayed by your mother's friend and your father and maybe even by your mother, too, for allowing herself to fade away and leave you. I think the pain was so bad that you vowed never to let anyone get that close to you again. So you didn't. You lived the life you could, the life which was expected of you, the playboy with all the different homes and all the different women. But no matter how many there were it was never enough, was it? They could never fill that hole deep inside you. At the end of the day, you were still all alone. And you always will be if you carry on like this.'

'That's enough!' he bit out and suddenly he wanted to lash out at something. Anything. He wanted to smash his fist into that marble statue on the opposite side of the terrace and see it lie in shattered pieces. He wanted stop the hurt which was enveloping him in something so dark and clammy that suddenly he couldn't breathe properly.

'You may be planning to major in psychology, but so far you're way off course!' he snapped. 'Is this supposed to make me *want* you, Carly? Am I supposed to be *grateful* for this brutal character assessment of yours? To be so in awe of your unique *insight* that I will somehow see the light? And what do you suppose will happen next, hmm? Play out the scene for me, *querida*, so that I can see it for myself. Do I now drop down onto one knee and ask you to become my wife?'

The breath dying in her throat, Carly stared at him. His caustic words were like having a blade rammed straight into her heart, but she told herself that maybe he'd done her a favour. Because hadn't this liberated her from any dormant hopes she might have nurtured, no matter how much she'd tried to deny them? Wouldn't she now be free of the fantasy that, deep down, Luis might actually *care* about her?

She shook her head. 'I may have been innocent,' she said slowly. 'But I'm not stupid. And if ever I was going to marry anyone it certainly wouldn't be a man who didn't even have the courage to look at himself properly.'

His eyes narrowed. 'You accuse me—*me*—of lacking in courage?'

She shook her head. 'Oh, I'm not talking about the kind of courage which made you put your foot down on the accelerator and take your car through a gap so tiny that most men wouldn't have seen it. I'm talking about the emotional courage to face your demons and put them to rest. Just as I've had to do. I'm sorry I said that about Bella—that was just a lingering hangup from my own past. I had no right to accuse you of that, and I should have been strong enough to stand up to her.'

But she knew why she hadn't answered Bella's question about her involvement with Luis and why she hadn't dared stand up for herself. Because she didn't believe in the strength of what she and Luis had together. She hadn't wanted to see the pity or the glee in her sister's face when it all ended. And it seemed that her instinct had been right.

'Anyway,' she continued. 'At least this has given us the ending we both knew was inevitable, even if it hasn't been quite as amicable as we might have wanted. We both know that I can't go back to being your housekeeper.'

There was a long pause before he spoke. 'No. I guess you can't.' He flicked her a glance from between narrowed black eyes. 'So what will you do?'

She took a moment to compose herself. To behave as if they'd been talking about nothing more controversial than the weather. And didn't some stupid part of her wish that he'd fought a bit harder to get her to stay? 'I'll find another job until next September. I should have all the funds I need by then to take up my place.'

He frowned. 'But you told me that there was a deferred space available now. So in theory, you could go this September—if you had the funds.'

'Which I don't.'

'You could if I gave them to you. And before you say anything—don't. I can afford it and I want to. Please, Carly. Don't let pride stop you from taking what I am able to give. At least that way, you'll get your happy ending.'

She looked at him and thought that she wasn't the only one who could be naïve. Did he really think that this was her happy ending? She thought about the father who had betrayed him and the mother who had slowly slipped away from the world. She thought about how alone he was, amid all his trophies and homes and enough money in the bank to secure the future of the children he would never have.

And something made her say it. Made her kick her pride into touch and have the courage to declare what she'd known for a long time now. Couldn't she give *him* something, too? Not money, but something much more precious.

Hope.

'Okay, I'll take it. And I want you to know that I am very grateful to you for your…generosity, in all its many forms.' She sucked in a lungful of air but her next words still came out in a breathless rush, full of nerves and apprehension.

'But you should know something else, too, and that is that I've grown to love you, Luis. And I'm sorry about that, because I know it's the last thing you ever wanted. I didn't want to fall in love with you, but, somewhere along the way, I did. And I'm not saying it because I want anything in return, because I don't. I don't expect anything. I'm saying it because, deep down, you *are* loveable. And you need to believe that. It's not because you're sexy, or rich and not because you have a whole roomful of silver trophies and can fly a plane. You are loveable because you can be a very kind and thoughtful man, when you let yourself be. And maybe one day you might start believing in that enough to open your heart and let someone in.'

Her words died out to the sound of silence. There wasn't a flicker of response from the rigid figure who stood in front of her, though she thought she saw something flare briefly in the depths of those empty black eyes. But then it was gone, and he smiled. That easy, charming smile he could turn on like a tap, a smile which was as cool and as transparent as water itself.

'Interesting hypothesis,' he said, in a voice which sounded faintly bored. 'But you know that I'm not really interested in the emotional stuff you women are so fond of spouting. All I will say, for what it's worth, is that I think you're going to be a brilliant doctor.'

Carly stared at him. *He had completely ignored what she'd just said.* Had treated her words with contempt. Of course he had. Why should she be surprised when he was just being true to himself? He didn't *do* that emotional stuff and he never would. He'd told her that all along.

And it was that which made her quickly turn and walk towards her room, before she added to her humiliation by letting him see her cry.

CHAPTER ELEVEN

LUIS STARED OUT of the window, without really seeing the sombre grey of the November day. Why was he feeling like this? As if there were some heavy weight on his shoulders which was perpetually weighing him down? As if there were something gnawing away inside him, which he couldn't work out how to fix. And that didn't make sense. Especially since he'd kept so busy after putting Carly on a plane back to London and saying goodbye to her.

He had left the Côte d'Azur and travelled to New York, where he'd hired a personal trainer before getting straight back behind the wheel and winning a charity race in Brazil. He remembered staring at the gleaming trophy and thinking it would have been around the same time that Carly was starting at med school in England. And he couldn't shake off his feeling of disappointment that she hadn't bothered to contact him to say well done.

He knew their relationship was over—he was the one who had ended it, wasn't he?—but the race had been big news internationally, and hadn't he expected some kind of acknowledgement? If not exactly praise, then surely *something*. Perhaps a faintly mocking communication noting that he still seemed hooked on danger, but congratulating him on winning the race, all the same.

But there was nothing.

Not a phone call. Not a postcard.

Nothing.

Never had a silence seemed quite so deafening.

He remembered feeling disbelief, closely followed by a slow and simmering anger. After all he'd done for her she didn't even have the generosity of spirit to say *well done*.

He had buried himself in his work, throwing himself into every new task with the enthusiasm of someone who was just starting out in the cut-throat world of business.

But something inside him had altered. Something he hadn't expected. He found himself looking at things differently. He started making changes he suspected had been a long time coming. He sold two of his houses and a whole heap of office space in Manhattan. He realised that he preferred life without all the hangers-on and so he reduced the size of his entourage, and told Diego so. A Diego who kept looking at him from between narrowed eyes and asking was he *sure* he was okay?

Was he okay? Luis had felt his mouth harden in response to the question. Of course he was. Physically, he'd never felt better. His brush with death had made him look at the world with a sharper focus. His senses felt raw and heightened. In many ways, he had never been so grateful just to be alive.

Yet all he could think about was Carly. Carly lying naked in his arms, with her hair spread over his chest, talking in that soft, sweet way she had. Carly running her finger along his jaw and teasing him. Carly sending him a silent glance, which would make him think about something in a way he hadn't thought about it before.

He tried going to parties to get her out of his head, and there were plenty of parties. Slick, pared-down affairs in minimalist New York loft spaces or wild, poolside extravaganzas held outside the city.

Trouble was that he couldn't look at a swimming pool without thinking about her.

He couldn't look at a damned bed without thinking about her.

He would find himself standing motionless while some impossibly glamorous woman came onto him in a way which made his stomach crawl. And that was when he started to get worried.

He tried looking at the situation logically. He was only fantasising about her because she'd been like no other lover he'd ever had. Because she had walked away without a backward glance and seemed happy to leave it that way.

Yet she'd been part of his life for a long time, way before they'd become lovers. He told himself he was interested to see how her ambition was playing out— hell, didn't he have some sort of *right* to know?

And now he was back in England on the second round of interviews for a new housekeeper to replace her and it was proving harder than he'd imagined. The first stream of women he'd seen had been hopeless, even though they'd all been eager for the job. But there was something wrong with each and every one of them. Too flirty, or too unimaginative. Several had been no good at cooking and one even had a criminal record she'd tried to conceal. He had rejected them all and demanded that Diego find him someone more suitable.

He looked down at the list of 'more suitable' candidates in front of him. On paper some looked promising, but his heart wasn't in it. He thought how long it had been since he'd eaten a decent *alfajor*. How long since he'd played poker. Or had sex. How long since he'd been made to laugh, or argue or defend himself in the presence of a sharp and amusing mind.

And that was when it hit him, harder than an opponent's wheel flying off during a practice lap.

He didn't want a housekeeper. He didn't want someone to replace Carly, because she was irreplaceable. He wanted… He closed his eyes. He knew what he wanted but it was a big ask. Too big an ask, surely, after what he had done. He flinched as he remembered the way she had looked at him, with that hesitant expression on her face. How she must have met nothing but coldness in his eyes in return. But that hadn't stopped her, had it? She had taken a deep breath and told him she loved him—even though it must have taken an almighty leap of courage and faith to do so. She had hung on in there and said what she needed to say. She had conquered her own insecurity and told him that he was a loveable man. She had done that *because she thought he needed to know*. And how had he reacted? He had treated her declaration with contempt and acted as if she'd said nothing at all.

He shook his head as the door opened and he saw Diego's swarthy features set in a questioning look.

'Shall I show in the first applicant, boss?'

But Luis was already rising to his feet and shaking his head.

'No,' he said fiercely as a powerful sense of resolve washed over him. 'Forget the interviews.'

'But—'

'I said, *forget* them. I have something I need to do.' His heart was pounding as he slid his phone into his pocket and reached for his jacket. 'Somewhere I need to go.'

He drove down to Southampton in his bright red car, only just staying inside the speed limit. The sky was low and the air filled with drizzle and, even though it was only late morning, all the cars on the motorway had their headlights turned on so that shafts of golden light cut through the sombre greyness.

The medical school was situated in a green swathe of land on the edge of the city and it was nearly lunchtime by the time Luis finally parked up. He turned up the collar of his leather coat as hordes of students streamed past him and as he looked into all the unknown faces he wondered why the hell he hadn't bothered to call her first.

You know why you haven't called her.

Because she might just have told you to go to hell, and you just might have deserved it.

He made his way to some reception office and saw the girl behind the desk turn very pink when he asked where he might find a first-year student called Carly Conner.

'We're…we're not really allowed to give out that sort of information,' she stumbled.

He leaned over the desk and used a smile which had

never failed him. 'Do you think your medical school would like a substantial donation?'

She nodded.

'Then why don't you tell me where I might find Carly Conner?'

He was informed that the first-year medical students were on their way to lunch and the girl hadn't finished giving him directions before he was weaving across some courtyard towards a cafeteria, which was packed with crowds of students.

And that was when he saw her.

At first he almost didn't recognise her, because she looked *different*. As if she belonged. She was laughing and talking to a small nucleus of people, a bag loaded with books slung over her shoulder.

He felt the clench of his heart as he stood stock-still and watched her and maybe somebody noticed him because suddenly heads were turning in his direction. Across the crowded courtyard he saw the colour drain from Carly's face as she looked up and met his gaze.

She didn't move and, at first, neither did he. He felt as if the blood had frozen in his veins and he would be stuck to that spot for ever. And then he began walking towards her, his legs feeling heavy and wooden and somehow disassociated from him.

The students with her had formed themselves into a protective semicircle and Luis automatically picked out some young Adonis with hair like buttered corn and eyes of startling blue, who seemed to be unconsciously squaring up his shoulders as Luis approached.

She tilted her chin as he got closer and now he could see why she looked so different. She had changed in ways which were both subtle yet startling. Her hair was still long, but now it was weaved into a complex plait which hung down over one shoulder. And she was wearing *make-up*. Luis swallowed. Not much, just a lick of mascara and a slick of something which was making her lips gleam. She looked…amazing.

In her jeans and short jacket she somehow managed to fade into the crowd and yet to stand out from it. And instantly, he understood why she had refused to take the expensive clothes he'd bought her, for she would have no use for them here, in her new life. His heart clenched as he thought of the yellow and white spotted dress still hanging in the wardrobe of his French home. Of the space beside him in a bed which had never seemed empty before she had gone and left it.

'Hello, Carly,' he said.

Her expression was wary as she looked at him. She didn't look exactly overjoyed. In fact, that was an understatement. Her face had grown pale and tight and her eyes were cool.

'I'm not going to ask why you're here,' she said in a low voice. 'Because obviously you've decided you wanted to see me, but you really might have given me some warning, Luis.'

He was not expecting a reprimand and for a moment he was…*shocked*. He thought how any other woman would have hurled herself into his arms and the slight deflation he felt was almost certainly something to do with his ego. *And mightn't that be a good thing?* he questioned with a self-awareness which suddenly made him feel uncomfortable.

'I thought that if I'd warned you, you might have

refused to see me,' he said, his gaze training hard on her face. 'Would you?'

She shrugged as if she didn't really care. 'I don't know.'

'You need any help, Carl?'

The Adonis had stepped forward and Luis held onto his temper with difficulty as Carly shook her head again.

'No, I'm fine,' she said.

'I need to speak to you, Carly,' said Luis softly, flicking a dismissive glance towards the youth. 'In private.'

For a moment she hesitated. He saw emotions he didn't recognise, and some he did, crossing those iced-tea eyes, before she looked down at her watch.

'I've got half an hour before my next lecture, so you'll have to be quick.'

'I thought you were never on time.'

'That was in the old days. I've changed.' Defiantly, she met his eyes. 'We can walk in the grounds. Come with me.'

He was barely aware of the total silence which suddenly descended on the courtyard, or the excited chatter which rose up before they were barely out of earshot. The grass was sodden beneath their feet as they left the courtyard and the bare branches of the trees were etched in forbidding lines against the low sky.

'What are you doing here, Luis?' Her breath was like a cloud of smoke as it billowed out into the cold air.

He swallowed. He hadn't really planned what he was going to say because hadn't some cynical side of his nature wondered whether this might just turn out to be a form of catharsis. That he would take one look at her and wonder what all the fuss had been about. Why he'd been unable to sleep or to think of anything much which didn't involve Carly Conner with her clever mind and soft body and that way of prising out secrets he'd locked away from everyone else.

But it wasn't turning out that way. It was as he had suspected all along. His heart was tight in his chest, as if an iron band were squeezing all the blood out of it, and his pulse was racing with a feeling which felt like excitement and exultation and apprehension all rolled into one. He'd experienced something like it when he'd been waiting on the starting line at the notoriously tough twenty-four-hour race at Le Mans, or any of the other myriad dangerous racetracks he'd tackled during his race career, but nothing like this. *Nothing like this.*

He stared into eyes as cold as chips of ice and suddenly it all came spilling out from a place deep inside him. 'I love you,' he said simply and waited for her reaction as he repeated the words in a voice he'd never heard himself use before. 'I love you, Carly Conner.'

Carly shook her head and her hands clenched into tight fists. She wished she hadn't forgotten her gloves because then she could have avoided her fingernails digging into her flesh like this. But the sharp pain helped her focus on her anger, and anger was the safest thing she had to hang onto right then. She glared at him. How dared he do this? How dared he come here and disrupt the life which she was building for herself—day by day? How dared he, by coming out with something he probably didn't mean, undo all her good work of trying to forget him? How dared he come here and try to *break her heart* all over again?

'You don't "do" love,' she snapped. 'Remember? It's top of your list of requirements for lovers—that they won't dare to expect anything like that from you. No wedding bells or clouds of confetti for you. *Your words,* Luis. And I don't have time for meaningless declarations. If you're missing sex then f-find someone else. That shouldn't be a problem for someone like you.'

She made to walk away but his hand reached out and caught her arm and she wanted to shake him off, but she couldn't, *How could he do that?* she wondered desperately. How would her physiology lecturer explain it? How could just one touch from a man make you defy all your instincts? Send your pulse rocketing and fill your mind with thoughts you were intent on not having…

'You're right. I didn't *do* love,' he agreed, still holding onto her arm. 'Because it has never happened to me before. I never thought it could. I'd only ever seen love as a negative. As dark and destructive. As full of pain and lies and betrayal. I didn't realise that it could make you feel a part of something bigger than yourself. Could make you feel as if you were really alive. And you showed me that, Carly. You showed me that like nobody else ever could.'

'Stop it,' she whispered. 'Please, Luis. Just go away.'

He shook his head. 'I'm not going anywhere until you've heard what I've got to say. I miss you more than any words can say. Nothing seems to make sense without you there, and I was a fool to let you go.'

'You didn't *let me go,*' she said. 'You pushed me away. You know you did.'

'Yes, I did,' he said heavily. 'I hold my hands up to

that. So maybe it follows that I don't deserve your love, Carly. That I shouldn't be given a second chance, because I threw it all back in your face.' He swallowed. 'So if you tell me that you no longer love me and that you don't want me in your life, then I'll turn around and walk away from here and I will never bother you again. I give you my word on that.'

She stared at him and sucked in a deep breath. 'I don't love you.'

His eyes narrowed. 'I don't believe you.'

'You arrogant bastard.'

'If you didn't love me, then you wouldn't be looking at me like that. Your eyes wouldn't be asking me to hold you properly, nor your lips parting because you want me to kiss them.'

'Luis—'

'And I want that too, *querida*. So much. I want to kiss you and never stop.'

She stared at him and her mouth was trembling but not nearly as much as his hands as he reached out to pull her into his arms. 'Answer me honestly, that's all I ask. Do you still love me, Carly Conner?' he growled. 'Will you marry me and have my babies?'

'Babies?'

She pulled away from him and he saw her frown, like someone who was preparing for a cloud to burst on top of their head. 'But I'm going to be a doctor, Luis. I've worked hard to get here and I'm not going to give it up. I've got six long years of training ahead of me. Six years of me being based in the south of England, while you continue with your jet-setting life elsewhere? Is that going to work out? I don't think so.'

'You don't think it's possible?' He gave a low laugh.

'Believe me, anything is possible if you want it enough. And I want you more than I have ever wanted anything. I respect your ambition and I am prepared to work around it, to support you in whatever you want to do. Because while I can see that there are practical difficulties to be overcome, they are completely irrelevant. There is only one thing which is important and that is my next question and I think you owe it to me to answer it truthfully.' His voice quietened. 'Do you still love me, Carly?'

Carly didn't speak, at least not straight away. It was as if she recognised that her world was going to change irrevocably, no matter what she answered. She became aware of the loudness of her heartbeat and, incongruously, the fact that her leather boots were sinking into the muddy grass. She could see the bare trees which surrounded them and in the sky a dark flock of birds who were heading somewhere. She wondered where. To their own warmer future? She saw Luis's expression: his eyes were narrowed and the lines etched along the sides of his unsmiling mouth were deeper than she remembered. The faint drizzle had settled on his black hair—so that it seemed to have covered the tangled tendrils like a fine mist of diamonds.

She thought about the tears she had shed since she'd left France. About the great, gaping hole where her heart used to be. She thought about how much she'd missed their sparring. His teasing. And a million things in between.

She thought about the practical difficulties which lay ahead if she told him what he really seemed to want to hear. Of how on earth they might be able to align two obviously incompatible lifestyles to any degree of satisfaction.

And then she remembered what he had just said.

Anything is possible. And with Luis, she honestly believed it was.

She nodded, her mouth working furiously as she tried to control the emotions which were building up inside her and threatening to spill out. *I am not going to cry,* she told herself fiercely. *Because I have an anatomy lecture to get to.*

'Yes, I love you, Luis Martinez,' she blurted out. 'I tried very hard not to, but in the end I couldn't help myself.'

'Couldn't you?' he questioned softly.

'No. You were like a fever to which there was no known antidote and once you'd got into my blood, I couldn't seem to get rid of you. I still can't.'

'That bad, huh?' Tenderly, he smiled. 'That's not the most romantic declaration I've ever heard, but it's certainly the most original. Just like you, my clever, sweet Carly.'

And that was when the tears came and there was nothing she could do to stop them. They spilled down her cheeks and dripped onto the collar of her jacket, like giant drops of rain.

But Luis was there to dry them and Luis was there to kiss her and once they started kissing, they couldn't seem to stop, and Carly's heart seemed to burst out of her chest as he gathered her in his arms and held her.

She touched his shoulders, his hair and his face, as if she couldn't quite believe he was there. But he was. Every vital, warm, living and breathing atom of him. *He was there. With her.* And if she was to believe what he was telling her, which against all the odds she did, he wasn't ever going to leave her again.

She made it to her anatomy class, with seconds to spare.

EPILOGUE

'ARE YOU AWAKE?'

Carly gave a slow and luxurious wriggle as her eyelashes fluttered open to meet the soft question in Luis's black gaze. 'I am now.'

Dark brows arched upwards. 'Did I wake you?'

'Wasn't that your intention when you started playing with my breasts like that?'

He smiled. 'Do you want me to stop?'

She sighed and closed her eyes. 'What do you think?'

'I think you're endlessly fascinating, Dr Martinez, and I love you very much. And I want you to know that these last six years have been the best of my life.'

Her eyes fluttered open and she bit her lip with expectation, never tiring of hearing him say these words. 'Really?'

'You know they have, *querida*.'

Yes, she knew. Just as they had been for her.

It hadn't been easy to rearrange Luis's life to accommodate her demanding role as a medical student, but then she'd discovered that the best things in life always had to be fought for. And Luis wanted her to achieve her dream as much as she did. He told her how proud he was of what she'd done and what she'd achieved, in spite of all the odds being stacked against her.

These days, he travelled as little as possible and had made his main base in England. From their sprawling Hampshire estate with its easy proximity to the sea, he now masterminded his latest business success—three ocean-going cruise ships as well as a flourishing yacht business. As for the rest of his global concerns, somewhere along the way he had become—as Carly told him with some pride—a consummate delegator. He employed the best people who gave of their best—and consequently the Martinez foundation had evolved, and was flourishing.

And even though he never really grew to *love* the English climate, he made sure he took them on plenty of sunny and luxurious vacations to compensate. Which was why Carly could often be found reading a haematology textbook on the beach, beside the clear aqua waters of the Caribbean.

She sighed, feeling Luis's thumb tracing enticing little circles over her nipple. From the window a clear river of light flooded in, illuminating the large bed in which they lay. She loved their home. They had bought a house overlooking the water not far from the medical school, from where she had graduated last week with honours.

But before the graduation ceremony had come their wedding, a wedding which Carly had resolutely refused to consider while she'd been in the middle of her studies. It had driven Luis crazy. For someone who had shied away from matrimony all his adult life, it had become one of his fiercest ambitions to wed her. The trouble was that he'd fallen in love with a woman who seemed resistant to wearing his ring.

'But you don't believe that men can do fidelity, remember?' she had flung at him, only half teasingly.

'Wrong tense,' he had growled back. 'I didn't—until I met you!'

The more he tried to persuade her to change her mind, the firmer she stood, but in a funny kind of way that had only made him love her more.

She had finally agreed to become his wife just before she graduated, telling him that she wanted to bear his name and to be Dr Martinez. And that simple declaration had thrilled him in a way which had left him shaken.

They had married in a small grey chapel overlooking one of Hampshire's green valleys and Carly had worn white roses in her hair and a simple dress, which had whispered over the flaggedstoned floor as she had walked to the altar to greet him.

Bella had been there, her initial poorly disguised jealousy at Carly's fate suddenly eclipsed by the presence of Luis's jet-setting friends at the ceremony. The Sultan of Qurhah was in attendance, with his beautiful wife and their gorgeous new baby. Niccolo Da Conti and Alekto Sarantos were easily considered to be the best-looking men there and the fact that they both happened to be billionaires only added to their appeal as far as Bella was concerned.

'Good luck with that,' Luis commented drily to his bride as he watched her sister slink across the room towards Niccolo, in a dress so tight that he privately wondered how she was managing to walk.

Carly turned in the direction of his gaze. 'But he's single, isn't he?'

'Yes, he's single.' Luis laughed. 'But if you think *I* was a commitment-phobe, let me tell you that Niccolo Da Conti takes the concept into a whole new stratosphere!'

'And you turned out to be the least commitment-phobic man on the planet!'

'Only because I met the only woman who could change my mind.'

'Oh, Luis.'

'Oh, Carly,' he murmured indulgently.

Her mother had been there, too; a mother amazed by Carly's 'luck' in finding herself such a rich husband. And if Carly was disappointed not to have been commended for working her way through med school—she kept it to herself. She'd learnt that there were some things you could never change and therefore it was a waste of time even trying.

She'd learnt so much, along with the demands of medical science.

That her love for Luis grew stronger with every day that passed and that she wanted to have his baby before too long.

That a man whose heart had been wounded only needed the constant love of a woman to repair it. And that love was boundless and limitless.

She'd learnt that sometimes things happened which you wouldn't have even dared to dream about. She was living that dream and so was Luis. He didn't want a life in the fast lane any more. His days as 'The Love Machine' were over. He told her that he'd never really believed that one woman could be everything for one man.

But now he did.

'Come here,' he growled softly. 'I have something I need you to hear.'

Carly smiled as she turned her face to his. 'What is it?'

'I love you,' he said, his arms tightening around her waist. And then he said it again in Spanish just before he kissed her.

* * * * *

'I have not chosen my bride yet,' Zahid said, and he took her champagne glass and placed it on a window ledge, then pulled her back to where she had been just a second or two ago. 'If I had I would not be about to kiss you.'

'Oh…'

Well, that settled that, then, Trinity thought. There was nothing to stop them other than her fear and the fact that she could not stand being held by a man. Except she was being held now and there was no urge to run—there was no urge to do anything other than receive the lips softly descending on hers.

Would he be able to tell her terror from her kiss? Trinity wondered.

No, she quickly realised, because there was no terror—just the melting of fear and the bliss of his lips and the stroke of his tongue.

She sank into his embrace without thought, and the press of his body against hers felt like a reward.

His mouth *did* make the pain disappear, his kiss *did* allow her to forget, and Trinity found out something new—it was very hard to kiss and smile at the same time, but she was trying.

Carol Marinelli recently filled in a form where she was asked for her job title and was thrilled, after all these years, to be able to put down her answer as 'writer'. Then it asked what Carol did for relaxation and, after chewing her pen for a moment, Carol put down the truth: 'writing'. The third question asked, 'What are your hobbies?' Well, not wanting to look obsessed or, worse still, boring, she crossed the fingers on her free hand and answered 'swimming and tennis'. But, given that the chlorine in the pool does terrible things to her highlights, and the closest she's got to a tennis racket in the last couple of years is watching the Australian Open, I'm sure you can guess the real answer!

Recent titles by the same author:

THE ONLY WOMAN TO DEFY HIM
THE PLAYBOY OF PUERTO BANÚS
PLAYING THE DUTIFUL WIFE
BEHOLDEN TO THE THRONE
  (Empire of the Sands)

**Carol also writes for
Mills & Boon® Medical Romance™!**

**Did you know these are also available as eBooks?
Visit www.millsandboon.co.uk**

MORE PRECIOUS THAN A CROWN

BY
CAROL MARINELLI

MILLS &
BOON

Published in Great Britain 2014
by Mills & Boon, an imprint of Harlequin (UK) Limited,
Eton House, 18-24 Paradise Road, Richmond, Surrey, TW9 1SR

© 2014 Carol Marinelli

ISBN: 978-0-263-24993-4

Harlequin (UK) Limited's policy is to use papers that are natural,
renewable and recyclable products and made from wood grown in
sustainable forests. The logging and manufacturing processes conform
to the legal environmental regulations of the country of origin.

Printed and bound in Spain
by Blackprint CPI, Barcelona

MORE PRECIOUS
THAN A CROWN

To my lovely Facebook friends,
who cheer me on when my heroes misbehave.

PROLOGUE

'Has anyone seen Trinity?'

Dianne's voice carried through the still night. It had become a familiar cry this past year or so, and one that Sheikh Prince Zahid of Ishla had grown more than a little used to whenever he spent time at the Fosters' residence.

Zahid had been a regular guest to the household since he had been sixteen but now, about to turn twenty-two, he had made the decision that this would be his last time he would stay here. The next time he was invited he would politely decline.

Zahid walked through the woods at the edge of the Foster property. He could hear the sounds of laughter carry across the lake on this clear summer night. Zahid was flying back to Ishla soon and he hoped that his driver would arrive early rather than promptly, for he really would rather not be here. The Fosters were throwing a party to celebrate their son Donald's graduation and, given that they had added the fact that Zahid too was graduating, it would have been rude to decline.

Next time he would.

Zahid did not enjoy their company, he never really had. Gus Foster was a politician and it seemed to Zahid that he never switched off. His wife Dianne's sole purpose in life seemed to be to stand by her man whatever Gus did. Since Zahid had known the family, there had been the humiliation of two very public affairs as well as the scandalous revelations of sleazier encounters and not once had Dianne's plastic smile wavered.

After tonight he would not have to see it again, Zahid thought. Neither would he have to make polite small talk with the obnoxious Gus. He only did it because he was a friend of their son Donald.

Well, as much as Zahid had friends.

Zahid was a lone wolf and very independent. He preferred the company of a beautiful woman on a Saturday night rather than this type of thing, but obligation had brought him here.

When he had been sixteen and a boarder at a top school there had been a random locker inspection and a wad of cash and drugs had been found in Zahid's locker. They had not been Zahid's. It hadn't been the mandatory suspension that had been the problem, though. It had been the deep shame that such a scandal would cause his family.

On hearing the news, Zahid's father, King Fahid, had immediately boarded his jet to fly from Ishla to speak with the headmaster, not to cover things up, for that was not how things worked in Ishla. Instead, Zahid had explained to Donald, the king was on his way to England to apologise and take his disgraced son home. Once in Ishla, Zahid would have to publicly apologise to the people of Ishla.

'Even if you didn't do it?' Donald had asked.

Zahid had nodded.

'It is up to the people if they forgive me.'

Zahid had stepped into the headmaster's office with his back straight and his head held high, ready to meet his fate, only to find out that there had been a misunderstanding.

Donald, the headmaster had informed the prince and king, on hearing about the locker inspection, had panicked and placed the money and drugs in Zahid's. It was Donald who would now be suspended and the school offered its sincere apologies for the disruption the incident had caused the king.

As the king and young prince had stepped out of the headmaster's office, there had stood Donald with his father, Gus.

'Thank you,' King Fahid had said to Donald, 'for being man enough to admit the error of your ways.'

'You miss the point,' Gus had said to the king. 'My son would never do drugs, he did this to help a friend.'

The Fosters had taken it on the chin.

Gus had even given a speech in Parliament, stating that even the most loving, functional families were not exempt from the perils of teenage years.

Functional?

Zahid had frowned at the choice of word then and was frowning now as he walked, recalling that time all those years ago.

The Fosters had appeared on the front pages on the Sunday newspapers. Dianne, smiling her plastic smile for the cameras, Gus with his arm around his suitably sheepish-looking son. The only one who had spoiled the picture-perfect image had been Trinity—she had been dressed in her Sunday best but, rather than smiling, she had scowled at the cameras.

Zahid actually smiled as he recalled the photo from

yesteryear but he wasn't smiling a few seconds later when a streak of blonde caught his eye.

There was Trinity.

She was hiding a bag of clothes beneath a tree and wiping lipstick off, and jumped when she heard Zahid call out and start walking towards her.

'Trinity!' Zahid said. 'Your mother has been calling for you. Where have you been?'

She swung around to face him. 'Please, Zahid, can I say that I've been with you?'

'You know I don't lie.'

'Please,' Trinity said, and then sighed. Zahid was so austere, so formal and so rigid that it was pointless even trying to get him on side. Yet, just as she went to walk off and face the music, he halted her.

'If I am going to cover for you, first I need to know what you have been up to.'

Trinity slowly turned. Even when she had asked Zahid to cover for her, she'd never really expected him to agree, yet it sounded now like he might. 'I was at my friend Suzanne's,' came her cautious reply.

'Doing what?'

'Just…' Trinity shrugged.

'Just what?'

'Dancing.'

'You have been to a party?'

'No! We were just listening to music in her room and dancing.' Trinity almost rolled her eyes as she attempted to explain to his nonplussed expression, because clearly that wasn't the type of behaviour Zahid would understand. 'We were trying on make-up, that sort of thing.'

'Why are you hiding clothes?' Zahid looked at what she was wearing—a long-sleeved top and a pair of jeans—and then he watched as Trinity screwed her blue eyes closed, no doubt to come up with a suitable lie.

Trinity was, Zahid knew, a skilled liar, only what he didn't know was that she wasn't trying to lie now. She simply didn't know, in this, how she could tell the truth, when it was just a feeling she had.

How could she explain that Suzanne had suggested she borrow some clothes because Trinity hadn't liked the way her aunt's new husband had been looking at her in the dress her mother had bought for her? Trinity didn't understand enough herself, let alone know how to explain it to Zahid, just how awkward Clive made her feel.

She refused to call him Uncle.

He was the reason that she'd run off.

It was the reason that Trinity was always running off at family things and, given that Zahid was only ever there on family occasions, he saw this behaviour all too often.

'Last time I was here, I caught you climbing out of your bedroom window,' Zahid said, and watched as Trinity did her very best to keep her face straight. 'It is not a laughing matter.'

No, it wasn't a laughing matter, Trinity thought, but the memory of it made her smile. Zahid had refused to believe she had simply been hungry and, rather than facing all the guests, had simply been trying to sneak into the kitchen. He'd brought her out a plate of food and then watched as she'd climbed back up to her room, using a tree and the trellis. Given her practised movements, it had been a presumably well-worn path for Trinity.

'I haven't done anything wrong,' Trinity said.

'Perhaps not, but on family occasions you should be here.' It was black and white to Zahid yet sometimes with Trinity it blurred to grey. She was so spirited and wilful and just so visibly unimpressed with her family that at times she made Zahid silently cheer, not that he would let her know that. 'You don't just disappear.'

'I know, I know,' Trinity started, but then a mischievous smile prettied her sulky face. 'So, what's your excuse, then?'

'Excuse?'

'What are you doing in the woods?' And then, as realisation hit, she started to laugh. 'Sorry, that was a stupid question.' Zahid's frown only deepened the more she tried to explain. 'Well, I guess you needed to...' Trinity stopped then. There was not a single vulgar thing about Zahid and, no, now that she came to think of it, Trinity could not imagine Zahid popping into the woods to answer the call of nature! 'My mistake.'

'I went for a walk so that I could think.' Zahid looked down at her. Of all the Fosters, Trinity was the only one he would miss. Yes, she made him smile at times, but he wasn't smiling as he saw that since her last escapade Trinity had changed. She had, in fact, grown into a very beautiful young woman. Her hair was blonde and had been cut in a jagged style, her eyes were huge in a too-thin face and they sparkled as she waited for him to speak. 'If you were in Ishla you would be expected to support your parents and mix with the guests...'

'I'm not in Ishla, though.'

As they started to walk back towards the party, Trinity tripped a little.

'Have you been drinking?'

'No.'

'Are you sure?'

'I think I'd remember if I had.'

He turned her to him and took her cheeks in his hands. He saw her dilated pupils and neither quite recognised the lust between them yet. 'Blow.'

'You're breath-testing me?'

'Blow,' Zahid said, and she did, but he could smell no alcohol.

'What are you up to, Trinity?' Zahid asked, except his hands did not leave her face and neither did Trinity want them to. Yes, he was boring, yes, he was yawn-yawn dignified, but sometimes when he smiled, sometimes when his subtle humour went completely over her parents' heads, he made her laugh. She had never understood what women saw in him. Donald was bitterly jealous and complained often to his family that women only went after Zahid for his title.

Tonight Trinity would beg to differ.

Now she understood his attraction, for those black eyes made the skin on her cheeks flare with heat and the height of him, instead of intimidating her, had her wanting to stand on tiptoe and lift her face to his like a flower to the sun.

Now they recognised the lust.

Zahid looked down at her. She was like a little wild kitten that any minute might scratch but right now was temporarily tame, and Zahid was knocked sideways by her appeal.

'Am I to breathe out again…?' Trinity said, and as he went to open his mouth to tell her they should get back, Trinity blew into his open mouth. He captured her breath and then swallowed, and for the first time Zahid wrestled with self-control.

'You need to be more careful,' Zahid warned. 'You should not be walking alone in the woods at night.'

'In case a handsome prince happens to be walking by?'

'I could be anyone,' Zahid pointed out, but his hands were still on her cheeks.

Their lips were almost touching.

'You're you,' Trinity said, 'and I want you to give me my first kiss.'

Her mouth was, to Zahid, perfect and he was, rarely for him, tentative as his lips grazed hers for he was wrestling for control, forcing himself to hold back not just want, for the pulse of her flesh on his lips gave him more than the usual want, it filled him with need, and a man of Zahid's standing must never feel need that wasn't met.

For Trinity to feel him kiss her so tenderly, to feel that sulky mouth now soft against hers, was sublime.

A late developer, for six months now, or perhaps a little more, Trinity had loathed her body. The feel of another's eyes on her had made her feel ill. Family functions had been spent fighting hands that wandered, yet she was not fighting hands now. She loved the feel of Zahid's hands moving from her cheeks and down to her waist, and when her lips parted the slip of tongues was so mutual, so natural that Trinity let out a moan.

Zahid would have loved to linger, she tasted of cinnamon and was so sweet and warm, but the purr of her too-thin body beneath his hands, the sudden tip into sexual hunger from Trinity, the raw need in himself were enough for Zahid to attempt to halt things.

'That was not your first kiss.' His voice was not accusing, he was merely stating a fact, for never had a mouth had such an effect on him before and surely it had been a practised kiss.

'Okay, it was my second,' Trinity admitted. 'Suzanne and I practised a while back so that we'd know what we were doing, but this doesn't feel like practice, though,' she breathed, her mouth searching for his again.

'You need to get back,' Zahid said. His voice was just a touch stern, for he was cross at his own lack of control. His life was ordered, the women he dated were generally a few years older than him, not the other way around, and with reason, for emotion he kept at a distance and love was something to actively avoid.

Sex was the name of the game but it felt like more than that now.

Trinity's hands met at the back of his neck and she looked up at him. His hands were just above her hips and she knew that at any moment they would disengage, that he would take her back, but Trinity didn't want that. She wanted her first proper kiss to go on for longer, she did not want to return to her family and the house, but more than that, she wanted more time with Zahid.

He was far too tall for her mouth to reach his without Zahid lowering his head, so when still he did not, her mouth moved to his neck, and worked upwards, inhaling his lovely scent and feeling his hands digging deeper into her hips.

There was a strange push-pull, for he should push her off, take her hand and walk back, yet Zahid was resisting the urge to pull her into his groin. Trinity's tongue licked up his neck and then one hand did move. Zahid took her chin in his fingers and Trinity blinked up at him. She thought for a moment that she was about to be told off, but instead his mouth came down on hers and she found out that the first kiss had been but a precursor to bliss.

Trinity's eyes snapped open at the passion behind his kiss. She was a little shocked, a little heady and then, when she saw the usually remote Zahid so consumed, Trinity's eyes closed again and just revelled in the bliss of being so thoroughly kissed. One of his hands was stroking her hip and his tongue was sliding around hers and there was nothing but pleasure to be had. His other hand was on her shoulder but almost pushing her back in an attempt to resist pulling her in, yet it was Trinity who ignored the pressure and moved a delicious bit closer and discovered her home.

In the circle of his arms, pressed against him, she found herself.

Trinity loved the feel of his sex against her stomach and finally the bliss of the pressure of his hand pulling her in as his tongue duelled with hers. Now she moved up on tiptoe, wanting to feel that delicious hard length lower yet. Still fighting himself, Zahid pushed her down. It was like a match to gasoline for Trinity and she rose to her toes again and then it was she who pushed down and Zahid wrenched his face back, ending the kiss but not the contact of their groins, his dark eyes assessing her but with a smile on that stern mouth, which was shiny from hers.

'Don't stop,' Trinity urged, pressing herself to him, She was building towards something that felt like a faint wail of sirens in the vague distance. Her body was on delicious alert, seeking their direction, as Zahid did his best to contain her.

'We shall stop,' Zahid said.

'Why?'

'Because…' Zahid did not want to stop, but neither did he want to continue things here. 'Because my driver shall be here soon to take me back to Ishla, and you are too good for the woods.'

'Take me back to your palace.' Trinity smiled but then it disappeared, a note of urgency creeping into her voice. 'I need to get away…'

Zahid frowned. 'When you say—' He never got to finish, Dianne's shrill voice terminating their conversation.

'There you are. What the hell…?'

Zahid dropped contact as soon as he realised that her mother was there but Trinity still hung like a cheeky monkey around his neck.

'Mrs Foster, I apologise. I was—'

'Oh, it's you! It's fine, Zahid.' Dianne was instantly mollified when she saw that it was Zahid who her daughter was with. 'Zahid, your driver is here and, Trinity, you need to come and say goodbye to our guests…' They walked back through the woods and towards the house, Zahid frowning at Dianne's rather inappropriate response—surely she should be furious but she was chatting away as if nothing had happened. 'Clive and Elaine are staying. Trinity, I want you to go and get the guest room ready.'

His driver was waiting and he pulled Zahid aside to tell him that if he wanted to fly tonight, they needed to leave now.

Zahid said swift goodbyes, but Trinity caught his hand and he could see the tears filling her eyes.

'Zahid, what I said about you taking me with you. Do you think maybe—?'

'Trinity.' He could have kicked himself. She was

reading far too much into one kiss and he had never meant to confuse her. He was just glad that Dianne had disturbed them when she had.

'I have to go.' Zahid's words were a touch abrupt but better that than she even glimpse the effect she had had on him.

Her hand gripped his fingers and he felt the brush of her fingertips as he pulled away from her and glanced at his watch.

It was ten minutes after eleven and as he climbed into his car, little did he know that it was a moment in time he would regret for ever.

He looked out of the window and cursed his brief lack of control as the car pulled off.

It was better that he return now to Ishla, Zahid decided, for he did not like her unsettling effect on him.

Yet it was one kiss that he would always remember.

As for Trinity…

She saw his car drive off and on her mother's orders headed back into the house to prepare the guest room.

Trinity too would never forget that night.

But for all the wrong reasons.

CHAPTER ONE

'DECLINE.'

Sheikh Prince Zahid's response was immediate.

The king, his son and Abdul, the king's chief aide, were walking through the second palace of Ishla, discussing the refurbishments that were necessary if it were to be inhabited again. As they walked Abdul discussed the diaries of the royal prince and king and raised the matter of Donald Foster's wedding.

The Fosters had always imbued a certain discomfort in Zahid—loud, brash, their egos and need to further themselves at all costs had not sat comfortably with Zahid. As he had matured he had done his best to politely sever contact but Donald had remained persistent and they still occasionally kept in touch.

'But Donald has asked you to be his best man.'

Zahid's jaw tightened a fraction as Abdul spoke on. Zahid had not told his father that just last week Donald had called, asking him if he would be his best man at his wedding to Yvette. Zahid had said to Donald that, while flattered, he had duties in his homeland at that time and would not be able to attend. He had rather hoped that that would be the end of it, but of course Donald had persisted and it would now appear that a formal invitation had been sent, along with a repeated request that Zahid be Donald's best man. 'I have already explained that I cannot attend his wedding,' Zahid said to Abdul. 'Offer my apologies and arrange a gift…'

'Donald Foster?' The King halted and turned round and Zahid silently cursed Abdul for insisting that they go through the diaries now. He had been hoping that his father would not find out. 'That is the man who saved our family from shame…'

'That was a very long time ago, Father.'

'Our country has a long memory,' the king responded. 'You owe that man…'

'I have more than repaid my debt to him.'

Over and over Zahid had repaid his debt to Donald— he had been his friend when, perhaps, Zahid would rather not have been, he had secured invitations to functions that Donald would never have got into had he not asked Zahid to intervene, and over the years Donald had also borrowed significant amounts of money and made no effort to pay him back.

'Were it not for Donald,' the king pointed out, 'you would have been brought into disrepute. More than that, you would have brought our country into disrepute. When is the wedding?'

'It is in two weeks,' Abdul said, then looked at Zahid. 'We could rearrange your schedule.'

'First a wedding and, given the speed it's been arranged, soon it will be a christening…' Zahid pointed out, and the King tutted.

'I would support a polite declining of your attendance at a christening for a child conceived out of wedlock, as would our people, but the wedding…'

To the king's surprise, Zahid took no more persuading, for he interrupted with a brief nod and then turned to Abdul. 'Very well, arrange my schedule but make it a brief visit, two nights at the most. I will fly out the day after the wedding.'

'If only it were that easy to get you to agree to more pressing matters,' Fahid commented, but Zahid did not respond, for he knew what was coming next—his father had brought him here for a reason, Zahid was sure. 'We need to speak about the renovations that are needed here.'

Memories stirred for both the king and Abdul as they walked through the second jewel of Ishla. The second palace was where Zahid and his sister Layla had been born and raised. Even on their mother's death, when Zahid had been seven, they had lived here. The king had been heartbroken at the death of his wife, Annan, but thanks to the privacy the second palace had afforded them, he had been able to grieve largely in private.

Zahid deliberately kept his face impassive as they discussed the work that needed doing, but he knew that just the fact his father had chosen to speak with him here meant that the reins were tightening.

His father had long since wanted him to choose a suitable bride. So far Zahid had resisted, he liked his freedom far too much, but this was a working royal family and Zahid's skills in engineering were being utilised, his vision for Ishla was taking shape, and more and more his time was spent here.

It was time for Zahid to raise a family.

'There is much work to be done,' Abdul said. 'The chief architect is concerned about some erosion on the cliff face and, as we thought, the great hall and the master suite are in need of structural repair.'

'How long will that take?'

'Six months to a year is his best estimate,' Abdul said, and went into further detail. It wasn't as simple as commencing work—the second palace contained many valuable pieces that would need to be catalogued and stored before work could even begin.

'You do realise, Zahid,' the king said to his eldest son, 'that once it gets out that activity has commenced at the second place, our people will assume that we are preparing the palace for the crown prince and his bride.'

'I do,' Zahid replied.

'And does six months to one year sound like a time-frame you could operate within?'

Black eyes met black eyes and there was a small stand-off. The king had raised a leader, which meant Zahid would not simply be told what he should do.

'I think that at this stage, it would be premature to go ahead with the renovations.' Zahid did not flinch as he defied his father's request that he marry soon.

'Your country wants to know that they have a prince who will—'

'They have a prince,' Zahid calmly interrupted, 'who shall one day rule fairly and wisely. I do not need a bride to assure them of that.'

'You need an heir,' the king said. 'If something should happen to you, they need to know that the line will continue.' He let out an irritated breath. Zahid refused to be pushed into anything, which the king grudgingly admired, but the people needed reassuring. Time was running out for the king and so he chose now to play the one card he had that just might persuade Zahid to submit to his will. 'Of course, should something happen to you, it would be Layla's son who would be next in line.'

Zahid's jaw gritted because Layla did not have a husband, let alone a son.

'Perhaps,' the king continued, 'if the crown prince chooses not to marry yet, another royal wedding might appease the people.'

'Father...' Zahid addressed him as a father and not a king, trying to reach for his softer side, for the king truly adored his daughter. 'Layla does not like any of her prospective husbands.'

'Layla needs to understand that with privilege comes responsibility. I am thinking of inviting the Fayeds to dine here at the palace next week.'

Zahid thought about Layla, who had kicked, screamed and bitten when her father had once attempted to drag her out to meet suitors.

She was a rebel, a challenge, and reminded him of...

Perhaps it was the wedding invitation but Zahid's mind drifted back in time and he recalled Trinity. Not the kiss but the fire in her eyes and a spirit that would not be crushed. Imagine Trinity being forced to marry. It would never happen.

'You wouldn't do that to Layla,' Zahid said, but the king nodded for Abdul to leave them for a moment and, once alone, he addressed his son.

'Today there are reports in the news that I have lost weight. Last week it was reported that during my last overseas trip I was hospitalised. Soon I will not be well enough to leave Ishla for my treatments and the people will know that I have little time left. They need to know the future is secure.' It was said without emotion and should be accepted the same way. Feelings were frowned upon, especially for a male royal, but Zahid could not allow Layla to be used as a pawn. If he married then he could change things for Layla, who, unlike him, believed in foolish things like a marriage based on love.

It was not just the king that Layla had wrapped around her little finger. History meant that Zahid too, was extremely protective towards his sister. Not that Layla knew why, for the time of the queen's death and its aftermath must never be discussed.

'I want to announce a royal wedding,' the king reiterated. 'I want to hear cheering in the street when you walk onto the balcony with your chosen bride.'

'Chosen?' Zahid's word was tart. For all the dining with families that would take place, for all the pomp and ceremony that went in to choosing a bride, both the king and Zahid knew it was a given. Zahid must choose Princess Sameena of Bishram and right his father's wrongs for Fahid had not chosen wisely.

Instead of choosing Princess Raina of Bishram, a younger Fahid had fallen in love.

Zahid though, would choose wisely. Sameena was his father's first choice, for the long-ago snub to the now Queen Raina still caused problems and both men hoped for friendlier relations between Ishla and Bishram.

Zahid, though, leaned towards Sheikha Kumu.

Her country, though small, was prosperous and had an extremely efficient army.

It was a business decision to Zahid and one he would not take lightly.

'You do not need to ask the Fayeds to dine just yet.' Finally Zahid relented. 'You are right: the people have already waited long enough for their prince to choose his bride. Six months to a year sounds a suitable time frame.'

'I am pleased to hear it,' the king said, and then called his aide to join them again. 'Abdul, do what is necessary for the renovations to commence.' He did little to contain the smile of victory that played on his lips as he continued speaking. 'And send out the invitations for potential brides and their families to dine.'

Zahid walked through to the master suite and on the king's instruction a servant opened the huge shutter and the sun streamed into the room and fell on a large carved wooden bed. Here, Zahid and his bride would first live till, on the king's death, they moved to the first palace to rule the land that he loved.

Zahid did not have six months left to enjoy being single for once his bride was officially chosen his playboy reputation must become a thing of the past.

It was a very sobering thought and one that did not go unnoticed by his sister.

As he prepared to fly to London for Donald's wedding, Layla came to his suite.

'Father says that the renovations are starting.'

'Correct.'

'Do you know who you will choose as your bride?'

Zahid did not answer, not that Layla let that stop the conversation.

'Perhaps Sheikha Kumu?' Layla fished. 'She is well connected and very pretty, or maybe Princess Sameena, she's so beautiful—'

'It is not about looks,' Zahid interrupted. 'I will choose the bride who will best serve our people. One who will understand that my heart belongs to them.'

Layla rolled her eyes. 'Ah, but I bet you take looks into consideration when you are choosing your lovers.'

'Layla!' Zahid warned, but she would not quiet.

'Why don't women get to go overseas? Why were you allowed to leave Ishla for your education?'

'You know why, Layla.'

'Well, it's not fair. At least you have had some fun before you choose your bride. Father is speaking about the Fayeds again. I don't want Hassain to be my first love.' She pulled a face and Zahid suppressed a smile. He wanted to tell his sister that when he was king he would change things, but that conversation was too dangerous to have just yet.

'I want to know what it is to fall in love.' Layla pouted.

Zahid could think of nothing worse than a mind dizzied by emotion. He truly could not stand the thought of a life lived in love.

Yes, there was a year of her life that Layla didn't know about.

The first year.

He looked at his sister who lived with her head in the clouds, yet he cared for her so. He could still remember her screaming in the crib, could still recall their father's repeated rejection of his second born, who he had blamed for his wife's death.

No, Layla must never know.

'Layla, the palace will be busy preparing for my wedding. You do not have to worry for a while.'

'But I do worry,' Layla said. 'Zahid, can I come to England with you? I would love to see the sights, and to go to a real English wedding...'

'Layla, you know that you cannot travel until you are married.'

'No,' Layla corrected him, 'the rule is that I cannot travel unless I am escorted by a family member. If you took me…'

'I am not taking you to England with me,' Zahid said. He would already have his work cut out with the Fosters and their debauched ways, let alone adding Layla to the mix. Zahid rolled his eyes. There was no doubt in his mind that his best-man duties would involve policing Trinity.

Once he had agreed to attend the wedding, Zahid had looked her up and his face had hardened as he had read on and flicked through images. Having completed school, or rather, as Zahid knew from Donald, a stint in rehab, Trinity had, it would seem, jumped straight off the wagon. There were several pieces about how she loved to party, combined with several images of her falling out of nightclubs. Things had gone quiet in recent years, though. She was now living in California and only came home on occasion, such as for the wedding of her brother.

His curiosity about Trinity surprised even Zahid. He could barely remember most of the women he had dated, yet the one kiss that he and Trinity had shared still remained clear in his mind, so much so that it took a moment to drag his mind back to the conversation.

'Can I come on your honeymoon, then?' Layla persisted.

'I will hopefully be busy on my honeymoon,' Zahid said.

'Not the desert part.' Layla laughed. 'After. When you travel overseas, can I at least come with you then?'

It was not such a strange request—sisters often travelled as companionship for the new bride.

'You might not like the bride I choose,' Zahid pointed out.

'*You* might not like the bride you choose.' Layla smiled. 'So I will entertain her so that you do not have to worry about such things as shopping and lunch.'

'We shall see.'

'Promise me that you will take me, Zahid,' Layla said. 'I need something to look forward to.'

'You are up to something?'

'No,' Layla said. 'I am just bored and I want something to dream about, something to look forward to.' She glanced at the clock. 'I need to go and meet my students.'

'Then go,' Zahid said, but Layla would not move till she got her way.

'How can I teach my students about the world when I have never even left Ishla?'

Zahid accepted that she made a good point. 'Very well, you can travel overseas with us when I take my bride on honeymoon.'

It was no big deal to Zahid.

Romance was not part of the equation in any marriage that he had in mind and that was the reason he said yes.

CHAPTER TWO

AN ASH CLOUD, perchance? Trinity's heart lurched in hope when she saw that her flight was delayed.

A really, really big ash cloud that would ground aviation for days.

Or maybe the baggage handlers could go on strike.

LAX had been busy, busy and JFK was much the same. Trinity knew she had been cutting it almost impossibly fine to get back in time for her brother's wedding and now that her flight had been delayed there was a very real prospect that the bridesmaid wouldn't make it to the church on time.

Had she been willing that ash cloud to appear perhaps?

Of course she had.

Just a nice natural disaster where no one got hurt and one where it could be explained in the speeches that, though Trinity had done everything she possibly could to get there...

Boarding.

Trinity watched as the sign flicked over and dragged herself to the back of the line. Even as she took her seat on the aircraft she was hoping for a black miracle.

A flock of seagulls perhaps?

Yes, an aborted take-off seemed preferable to facing her family, or rather her aunt and her husband.

When Donald had called Trinity to tell her that he was marrying Yvette, though she had given her congratulations and said that, of course, she'd be thrilled to be there, inside her stomach had churned.

On concluding the call, Trinity had actually dashed to the toilet to be sick.

She felt sick now.

A harried mother and baby took the seat next to her.

Why, oh, why, hadn't she used the money her father had given her to buy a business-class seat, Trinity thought as the baby told her with his big blue eyes that he was going to do everything in his power to scream all the way to Heathrow.

The take-off was impeccable, not a seagull to be found!

Then the captain came on and said that he would do his level best to make up lost time.

Trinity wished she could do the same—that she could push a few buttons and ride a tail wind if it meant that she could erase lost years. An ancient art history degree that she'd somehow obtained, as she'd struggled merely to operate, lay unused. Clubs, bars, dancing had been but a temporary escape from her pain and grief. California healing had beckoned, but neither reiki, nor chakra cleansing, nor the roar of the vast Pacific could replace what had been lost.

Her latest attempt to cure her repulsion to anything that hinted on sexual had been positive-reinforcement-based training.

Ha-ha.

Two thousand dollars later and several pounds

heavier, Trinity had decided that no amount of chocolate or affirmations were going to cure her particular problem.

She loved herself?

Most of the time, yes.

She'd just prefer not to be touched.

The meals were served and Trinity just picked at hers and refused wine. Despite what the newspapers said, she really only drank at family things.

Which it soon would be.

No.

As the cabin lights were dimmed Trinity tried to doze but Harry, as it turned out the baby was called, had decided now that he liked her. He kept patting her cheeks with his little fat hands.

'Sorry,' his mum kept saying.

'It's not a problem.'

Trinity tried to doze some more.

It didn't work.

The only consolation to attending the wedding was that she had just found out that, though at first he had declined, Zahid was going to be the best man.

She hadn't seen him since that night ten years ago and Trinity wondered what he would be like now, if he even remembered that kiss in the woods.

If he'd ever given her a thought since then.

Trinity closed her eyes and briefly returned to the rapture of being in his arms and the bliss of his kiss, but her eyes suddenly snapped open for she could not even escape to the sanctuary of them without recalling what had happened later that night and in the months that had followed.

There was so much adrenaline in her legs that Trinity

tried walking around the sleepy cabin, dreading what she must face later today. How she'd hoped her mother would tell her that Clive and Elaine hadn't been invited, how she wished her father, or even her brother, would step in.

No one ever had.

Skeletons belonged in the closet. Dirty laundry belonged in a basket.

Clive was more prominent than her father.

Nothing could be gained by speaking out. It was easier to simply smile for the cameras.

It wasn't, though.

All too soon the scent of breakfast came from the galley and, opening the shutter, she saw dawn.

The wedding day was here.

Trinity returned to her seat, where Harry was shrieking. 'Would you mind?' his mum asked. 'I have to go to the restroom.'

'Of course.'

Trinity held Harry, who stood on her thighs with his knees buckling as he screamed and screamed. 'Go, Harry!' Trinity smiled. Wouldn't it be lovely to be as uninhibited as Harry, to simply scream out your pain and not care a jot what others thought?

She didn't get to hold babies much. All her family was in the UK and none of her friends in LA had babies yet.

The sting of tears in her own eyes was terribly unwelcome and Trinity swallowed them back, telling herself she was being ridiculous. There was no comparison, Trinity told herself as she looked at Harry.

He was all big and chunky and wriggling.

Whereas *she* had been so tiny and so very still.

The sob that escaped Trinity's lips came from some-where so deep and buried that even Harry stopped his tirade.

'It's okay.' Trinity fought to quickly compose her-self and smiled into his curious eyes as he patted her cheek. 'I'm fine.'

Trinity had no choice but to be fine.

She just missed her baby so.

Ached for the time that her daughter had never had.

'Thanks so much.' Harry's mum was back and Trin-ity handed him to her but the bubble of panic was rising inside her and Trinity truly did not know if she could get through today.

She pressed her bell.

'Breakfast won't be a moment.' The steward smiled.

'I'd like a bourbon, please,' Trinity said. 'A large one.'

A few minutes later the steward returned with two tiny bottles of bourbon and a pussycat smile that told Trinity she was a lush.

Trinity didn't care.

At least it calmed her enough to get off the plane.

'Where the hell is Trinity?' Donald demanded, as he clicked off his phone. 'Yvette's in tears, there's not a sign of her at the hotel…'

Here we go again! Zahid thought as he felt the pull of the mad Fosters' vortex. A night out last night with Donald and co. and Zahid was remembering all too well why he chose only minimal contact. Gus had kept insisting that Zahid extend his visit, or come and stay later in the year, and Zahid had reluctantly explained

that he would be marrying soon and his time was now
to be spent in Ishla.

And now, it would seem, Trinity had gone missing
in action again.

Nothing changed.

'Why don't I call Dianne and see if there's an up-
date?' Zahid suggested, for it was the best man's duty
to keep the groom calm, but he had never seen Donald
so tense. He made the call and then gave Donald the
news. 'Your mother's at the airport and she says Trinity's plane just landed. As soon as she is through customs, she will take her straight to the hotel and help
her to get ready. Call Yvette and tell her that she can
stop worrying.'

'You can never stop worrying when Trinity's around!'
Donald challenged. 'I just hope she's sober.'

It wasn't Donald's comment that had a certain disquiet stir in Zahid. It was his reaction to the news
that Trinity had landed and that soon he would see
her again.

Over the years there had been a few near misses.
Zahid, when he had heard Trinity's plane was delayed,
had assumed that this would be another. But that she
was in the same country now brought a strange sense
of calm—the planets seemed more neatly aligned, the
stars just a little less random. They were in the same
country and finally, after all this time, they would see
each other again.

He wondered if she would be bringing someone and
briefly wrestled with the distaste of that thought but then
dismissed its significance. It had nothing to do with feelings, Zahid quickly told himself. After all, it was possibly his last weekend in England as a single man and

certainly there was unfinished business between them. It was natural to be hoping that she was attending the wedding alone.

Trinity didn't have to wait for baggage and she raced out of customs, her heart aflutter. Despite everything, she was looking forward to seeing her mum. Maybe things would be different now, Trinity hoped as her eyes scanned the crowd for Dianne. Maybe her mum would realise just how difficult today was. Maybe...

Her heart lurched in hope as she saw her mum, dressed for the wedding, just minus a hat. Trinity raced over and gave her a hug. 'I'm so sorry.'

'Have you been drinking?' was Dianne's only response to her daughter's kiss.

'I had one bourbon on the plane.'

'It's whisky,' Dianne hissed. 'You're in England now. Where the hell have you been?'

'The plane was delayed.'

'I don't want to hear your excuses.'

Trinity could feel her mother's fingers digging into her arms as they raced to get a taxi and Dianne didn't let up as they sped to the hotel. 'Yvette is in tears. She wanted her own sister to be bridesmaid and now you've made us look...' Dianne struggled to contain her temper. It had taken many, many dinners to convince Yvette's parents to choose Trinity for the role, but a generous helping hand towards the wedding bill had given them leverage and the Fosters had insisted that their voice be heard.

Oh, and so too would Trinity's voice be heard, Dianne remembered. She just had to tell Trinity that! 'I've told Yvette that you're going to sing near the end of the night.'

'Excuse me.' Trinity's mouth was agape. 'I can't sing.'

'You've got a beautiful voice.'

'Actually, I don't.' Trinity could not believe that they'd ask this of her. 'Mum, please, I don't want to sing, I just want to…'

Hide.

'When do you go back?' Dianne asked.

'Tomorrow afternoon.'

'So it really is a flying visit, then.'

'I've got an interview next week.'

'If you'd let your father help, you wouldn't be out of work.'

'I'm not out of work,' Trinity bristled, because she had a job at the beach bar and she certainly earned her money there, but Dianne pulled a face.

'If anyone asks, say…' Dianne thought for a moment. 'Say you're working in a museum.'

'You want me to lie?'

'Yes, please!' Dianne said. 'We didn't put you through an art history degree to have you working in a bar.'

'Ancient art,' Trinity corrected, and then smirked at her mum. 'What sort of museum exactly?' She watched as her mother's neck went red.

'Okay, a library, then. The reference section. At one of the big colleges.'

Nothing changed.

They got to the hotel and the shoebox of a room that had been booked for Trinity. After a lightning-quick shower she sat as her hair was brushed and coiled and pinned by her tense mother while Trinity quickly did her make-up. Moods weren't improved when her mother unzipped a bag and pulled out the most awful blue dress that Trinity had ever seen.

'You are joking?' Trinity said. 'It's so shiny I'm going to need sunglasses to wear it.'

'Had you bothered to come to any of the fittings then you might have had a say in what you were wearing. As it is…' She lifted up Trinity's arm and attempted to pull up the concealed zip that was located at the side. 'You've put on weight!' Dianne accused.

'No,' Trinity said. 'I gave you my measurements exactly.'

'Then why can't I do it up?'

Because you refused to believe I was ten pounds heavier than your goal weight for me, Trinity thought, but said nothing, just sucked in her stomach and chest as her mother tugged at the stupid zip until finally it was up.

'Is breathing an optional extra?' Trinity quipped.

'Yes,' Dianne snapped back. 'But smiling isn't. This is your brother's day.'

'Oh, funny, that, I thought it was Yvette's.'

'Trinity!' Dianne was struggling to hold onto her temper. 'Don't start.'

'I'm not starting anything, I was just saying…'

'Well, don't!' Dianne warned. 'You've already done your level best to ruin this day. All you have to do now is smile. Can you manage that?'

'Of course, but I'm not singing.'

'And lose the smart mouth.' Dianne secured her hat as she issued instructions. 'Go now and apologise to Yvette. I'm going to make my way to the church. I'll see you there and I'm warning you…'

'Noted.'

'I mean it, Trinity, I don't want a scene from you today.'

She should say nothing, Trinity knew that. She should just nod and reassure her mum that she'd behave, but, hell, she had a voice and as much as her parents loathed that fact, Trinity was determined to find it.

'Then just make sure I'm not put in any position where I might need to make a scene,' Trinity said, and her mother's silk-clad shoulders stiffened and Trinity watched as the feather sticking out of Dianne's hat shivered in anger as Trinity refused to comply with orders.

'Will you just…?' Dianne hissed, and turned around. 'Can you try and remember that this is your brother's wedding and not spoil a family gathering for once.' Her face was right up at Trinity's. 'For once can today not be about you?'

'Of course.' Trinity stared back coolly but her heart was hammering in her chest. 'Just make sure that you keep that sleaze well away from me.'

'Are you still going on about that? It was years ago…' Two champagnes on an empty stomach that was fluttering with mother-of-the-groom nerves and Dianne would not be argued with, and certainly she wanted nothing to spoil what *had* to be a perfect day. 'You will behave, Trinity, you will be polite and you will smile.'

It had been stupid to hope things might be different.

Nothing had changed, Trinity realised.

Nothing ever would.

'What are you doing?' Trinity asked, as she watched her mother's painfully slow attempt to write a text. 'I'll do it.'

'It's done,' Dianne said, as her phone made the small

whooshing sound that meant her text had been sent. 'I was just letting Zahid know that you're on your way to Yvette and that everything's back on schedule.'

As she took the elevator to Yvette's room for the first time that morning Trinity smiled.

As he pulled his phone from his pocket and read the text, so too did Zahid.

CHAPTER THREE

IT WAS NOT the bride who drew Zahid's eye as she entered the church; instead, it was the woman who walked behind her who held his attention.

There was a smile fixed on Trinity's face but her eyes were as wary and as truculent as the teenage Trinity's, but then they met his and Zahid watched as her pale cheeks infused with pink. For both of them there was a moment's return to a wood many years ago and a kiss that both wished had drawn to a more natural conclusion.

Zahid smiled, which he rarely did, and Trinity was so lost for a moment, so taken aback by Zahid's smile that as the bride halted, for a second Trinity didn't. She actually forgot her place, for it was as if she should simply walk on to Zahid—to go now and greet him as her body wanted to and wrap her arms around his neck, but instead, after a brief falter, Trinity halted and took the flowers from Yvette.

Zahid turned his back to her then and the service commenced.

The service was long, not by Zahid's standards, just terribly long to stand there and not turn around when he would have preferred to.

Though Zahid stared ahead, he was looking at her very closely in his mind and re-examining the Trinity he'd seen today.

Her dress was terrible. Like a synthetic sapphire, it lacked depth and mystery and it was far too tight. Her hair was worn up and dotted with violets that matched the dark smudges under her eyes, yet she looked, to Zahid, amazing. Sun-kissed, dirty blonde, fragile and sexy, she was everything he remembered her to be and more.

Trinity stared ahead, loathing that her shoulders were bare and wondering whose eyes were on them. She hated the loud sound of her aunt's husband singing a hymn, as if he meant the words, as if he were a decent man.

So, instead of dwelling on the man behind and to the right, she fixed her gaze ahead and stared at Zahid, a man who did not know the words but neither did Zahid pretend to sing. He stood firm and dignified and she willed him to turn around.

He didn't.

He could have no idea the torture today was for her, for she could tell no one about her past—that had been spelt out to her many years ago. His raven hair was glossy and immaculate, his shoulders wider than before and possibly he was taller. She saw the clenching of his fist in the small of his back and remembered that same hand on her waist when the world had seemed so straightforward. As he handed over the rings she was treated to a glimpse of his strong profile and her ears strained to capture whatever words he murmured to Donald.

Zahid was as conscious of Trinity as she was of him,

so much so that as they all squeezed into the vestry for the signing of the register, despite the chatter from others, he only heard her exhale in brief relief.

'Trinity…' her father warned as she leant against the wall to catch her breath, so relieved was she to be away from Clive.

Donald and Yvette signed the register and Gus added his signature with a flourish. Trinity watched as Zahid added his. *Sheik Prince Zahid Bin Ahmed of Ishla*.

'Leave some space for me.' Trinity smiled and then added her own signature.

Trinity Natalii Foster.

Her hand was shaking, Trinity realised as she put down the pen, only the nerves she had now felt very different to the ones that she'd had before.

As she stepped back from the register she caught the deliciously familiar scent of Zahid and as he lowered his head to her ear the tiny bones all shivered awake to the deep, long-buried thrill of his low, intimate voice.

'Natalii?'

'Born at Christmas,' Trinity said. 'Please never repeat it again, I hate it.'

Of course she had been born at Christmas, Zahid thought, for, unbeknown to Trinity he had returned to the Fosters' in the hope of seeing her in the new year after she would have turned eighteen.

Trinity hadn't been there.

She was here now, though, and Zahid spoke on.

'I thought that it was the bride's prerogative to be late.'

'You know how I loathe tradition.'

'Does that mean we shan't be dancing later?' Zahid

asked, and she turned to his slow smile. 'Given how you loathe tradition.'

Oh!

Trinity blinked for it was as if he didn't know she was dead inside, as if he didn't know that her frigid body no longer worked, yet it felt now as if it did, for a pulse was working high in her neck—Trinity could feel it, and her stomach was fluttering as it had years before on that night.

With Zahid beside her, she could remember the beauty, rather than dwell on the pain.

'I suppose we shall...' Trinity sighed, as if dancing with Zahid would be a huge concession. 'I'd hate to cause trouble.'

'Liar,' Zahid said, and his hand met the small of her back as he guided her out of the vestry.

With one brief exchange, with that small touch, she was back in the woods, innocent and unfurling to his hand, and it was actually dizzying to walk behind Yvette and Donald and through the congregation. More than that, it was exhilarating to step outside into the sun and, on the day Trinity had been dreading, she felt her heart soaring like the bells that rang out around them.

To be, for the first time, at such a function and be just a little bit taken care of, for Zahid's duty now was not just to the groom, was, to Trinity, amazing.

He stood for the wedding photos and even made the unbearable a touch less so as the family all gathered around.

'Smile, Trinity,' he said out of the corner of his mouth, and she forgot the shiver of dread that Clive was near.

'You don't,' she pointed out, and then frowned at her

own words because Zahid smiled so readily when their eyes met and held.

'It is not in my nature to smile.'

For some reason that made her giggle just enough for the photographer to get his shot and then they piled into cars and they met at the hotel.

As the bride and groom entered, one look at her very relaxed brother and Trinity knew that Donald must be on something.

Please, no, Trinity begged in her head.

He had promised her he was over that now.

She and Zahid sat at opposite ends of the top table and though she wished they were sitting next to each other, maybe it was for the best, Trinity thought, for just knowing he was here was distracting enough.

Anyway, they'd no doubt run out of conversation within two minutes, though she was dying to know what he was up to and desperate to know if he was seeing someone.

Surely not, Trinity consoled herself, because back in the vestry Zahid had definitely been flirting.

She struggled through the meal, her reward that awaited her dance with him, and soon enough it was time for the speeches.

To his credit, Zahid did unbend a fraction and asked for some sparkling water for the toasts!

God, he was so controlled, so well behaved, Trinity thought, stretching her legs under the table and slipping off her shoes as the speeches started and doing her best not to yawn, not because she was bored by the speeches but because jet-lag was starting to seriously hit.

Yvette's father went first, thanking everyone and saying how thrilled he was to welcome Donald into the family. Zahid's face was impassive but he privately thought that Yvette's father had the look of a man who had brought home a puppy for the children only to realise it was going to grow into the size of a small horse.

It was the small horse's turn next and Zahid watched as Yvette scratched anxiously at her neck as her very new husband took to his feet.

Donald thanked everyone too, especially his beautiful wife. 'I'd like to thank Zahid for all his help and for travelling so far to be here.' Donald smiled a loaded smile. 'You've been an excellent best man and I hope to return the favour when it is your turn to marry next year.'

Zahid's jaw clamped down as Donald rambled on and he glanced over at Trinity. Her cheeks were red, an angry red, and she was dribbling salt on her sorbet.

He hadn't wanted her to hear his news like that.

As Donald proposed a toast to the bridesmaids, Zahid watched as Trinity raised her glass...

But to a passing waiter.

Oh, Trinity.

He wanted to go over and halt her, to whisk her away, to explain that she had misunderstood.

It was the truth, though.

And this early in the evening the truth hurt them both.

Zahid duly stood and thanked the groom for his words on behalf of the bridesmaids, though privately he'd have liked to knock him out. Then he thanked everyone else that he had to and said all the things that a best man should, but then it came to the part where Donald should star, where this future king should demure and ensure that the groom shone.

'Donald and I…' Zahid glanced at his notes and then faltered, and Trinity looked up at the brief hesitation as Zahid silently recalled a teenage incident and saw it now through the eyes of a man.

They were your drugs.

He could see it so clearly now and yet here he stood, all these years later, paying the price for Donald's supposed valour.

Well, no more.

'Donald and I…' Zahid resumed his speech but he was not looking at his notes now '…attended the same school and later were students at the same university.' Trinity heard her father's cough in an attempt to prompt Zahid, and she looked at her brother's expectant face, but the glory never came. Zahid went on to recall a few antidotes and all in all it was a very nice speech—he just forgot to paint Donald as the hero in Zahid's life.

False duty had been more than repaid.

And so to the dancing.

Zahid stood over Trinity, waiting for her to join him on the floor, but it was a touch more complicated than standing for Trinity, because her already tight shoes refused to go back on, but finally she forced her feet into them. 'The things I do for my family,' Trinity said, as he led her to the floor. 'Not that they appreciate it.'

'I am appreciative…' Zahid said, as he loosely held her and they started to dance and she waited for him to finish his sentence.

He didn't.

'Of what?' Trinity prompted. 'You are appreciative of what?'

'That you are here,' Zahid said. 'That we see each other again after all this time.'

They both knew it was running out for them and there was no tail wind to help them catch up, no buttons to push that could change things.

Except he pushed the right ones.

Zahid was the only man who did.

'I loved your speech,' Trinity said, her words a little stilted, for she was cross with Zahid for flirting when he was about to be wed. Yet she was cross only from the neck up. Her body had seemed to overlook the fact he would soon be marrying the very second that she was in his arms.

'You're the only one who liked it. Your father looks as if he wants to kill me.'

'It's me he's shooting daggers at!' Trinity looked to the right and smiled sweetly at her father. 'I was late, you know?'

'You were.'

'And not looking out for my brother.'

Zahid looked down to those blue eyes again and wondered how much she knew, for he was sure that Donald was high. 'Is it nice to see your brother happy?'

'Donald wouldn't know what happy was if it was hand delivered and he had to sign for it.' She looked over at Donald, who was smiling and laughing to his bride. 'He's loaded,' Trinity said. 'Nothing changes.'

'You?' Zahid said.

'I don't go near anything like that.'

'I meant,' Zahid corrected himself, 'are you happy?'

'Not today,' Trinity said, then it was she who corrected herself. 'Actually, right now I am.'

'Because?'

'Because,' Trinity said, because in his arms she actually was and, no, she should not be flirting, she had been called a tease so very many times when she was unable to follow through, but she just needed one lovely thing to focus on, just the teeniest bit of help to get through the night and, for good or bad, Zahid was it.

'Because?' he said into her ear, and it was then that she succumbed.

'Because my brother has excellent taste in grooms-men.'

'His bride has terrible taste in dresses.'

'She does,' Trinity sighed. 'Though in fairness my mother would have lied about my measurements. She prefers me with an eating disorder, it makes her a more visible martyr...'

Trinity was, Zahid decided, rather wise.

'I'm supposed to be singing later,' Trinity said, and her hands moved up and linked behind his neck and, yes, they were back in the woods again. 'As I said to my mother, my name isn't Trinity Von Trapp.' She went to explain, because he probably had no idea what she was talking about, but then she remembered a long-ago Christmas and Dianne forcing them to watch the *Sound of Music* and Trinity giggling at Zahid's somewhat be-mused expression.

More than that, though, somehow he got her—she did not have to explain everything to Zahid.

'Rolfe might join you,' he said into her ear, and though Zahid would no more sing than fly to the moon a smile played on her lips as she pulled her head back, just enough that her back arched in just a little and Zahid's tongue rolled to his cheek as something else stirred to her words.

'I prefer the captain.'

It was a tiny dirty dance, but with words. The heat

from his palms was surely searing her dress and the way he simply let her be had her breathing freely for the first time since she could remember. With Zahid her body seemed to know how to work. He induced only pleasure and made it safe to be a touch wanton.

Then she remembered she was cross with him.

As the music ended, instead of sinking in for another dance, she pulled back.

'I'd better go and see how Yvette is.'

'I will check on the groom.' He gave a small nod. 'Perhaps later we dance...'

Trinity gave a tight smile as she walked off but she felt conflicted. No doubt Zahid thought her a party girl, no doubt he assumed where the night was leading.

He could never guess that she felt ill at the very thought of sex.

Only she didn't feel ill in his arms.

Trinity wanted to get back to him, only Yvette was teary and she either had raging cystitis or her bladder was the size of a thimble or more likely she really was pregnant, because she wanted to go to the loo on the hour every hour and Trinity had to help with the dress.

'Your brother...' Yvette was trying to tame her angry cheeks with Trinity's foundation. 'I just got a call from the hotel—he hasn't paid the reservation fee...'

'I'm sure it's just a mix-up,' Trinity suitably soothed.

She was quite sure to the contrary, though.

The night wore on and the only time they met was when Dianne introduced Trinity to a group that Zahid was in and, of course, one of them had to ask what she was doing with her degree.

'I'm thinking of moving to France.' Trinity beamed, deciding that it might not be such a bad idea actually and feeling her mother's tension beside her, 'but right now I work in a library at a large college—'

'The reference section,' Dianne interrupted, and Zahid watched the daggers that shot from Trinity's eyes.

Dianne was determined that Trinity would sing and trying to escape the inevitable, true to form, Trinity slipped outside for some air.

Zahid wasn't faring much better. All night Donald insisted on introducing him to everyone as his best friend from way back and slapping Zahid on the back as he did so.

It came as no surprise when Donald pulled Zahid aside near the end of the night and asked if he might have a word.

'I know that you're flying back after lunch tomorrow and that we might not get another chance to speak,' Donald said.

'You don't have to entertain me on your wedding night.' Zahid tried to smile, tried to keep things light, tried not to like this man any less than he now did.

'And I know that you've always been a great friend to me, as I hope I have to you.' *They were your drugs,* Zahid said again in his head, but he remained silent as Donald spoke on. 'The thing is, Zahid…' And Zahid listened as, again, Donald asked him to help—that if he could just take care of the honeymoon, then as soon as Donald was back he would repay him.

'I am not paying for your honeymoon.' Zahid interrupted the familiar tirade but with its latest twist. 'What I will pay for is three months of rehabilitation.'

'That's really generous but if I could just get these debts paid then I wouldn't need rehab. All I'm asking—'

'I have told you what I am prepared to do. I have

heard of a good clinic near Texas. A family friend had their son go there...'

'I've just got married I can hardly disappear on Yvette...'

'I would say that you have been absent from your relationship for quite some time,' Zahid said, refusing to be swayed. It was clear from looking at Yvette that Donald would soon be a father—it was time, then, that he grew up. 'If you go to rehab, I will take care of your debts.'

'Zahid, please, can you just—?'

'No.'

Zahid refused to negotiate.

'I will speak with the accounting firm that I use in the UK. The offer is there so long as you are prepared to meet my conditions.'

'You can afford to help me out without blinking.'

'That has nothing to do with it. Even if I had no money but you were determined to change, I would take a loan to pay for your treatment. I will not be used. You can work for a better life, or you can torch what you have. You choose.'

'Some friend!' Donald sneered.

Zahid stepped away from Donald and headed outside just as he heard Dianne start up with the familiar cry. 'Has anyone seen Trinity?'

Zahid was looking at her now.

She was a *bad* bridesmaid, if there was such a thing. The flowers were wilting in her hair as she drained her champagne glass and then muttered something very unladylike under her breath.

'Language, Trinity,' Zahid said, and she rolled her eyes.

'I hate weddings.'

'They are a part of life.'

'Well, if I ever get married it will be on a beach with no guests.' She glanced at him. 'What about you?'

'There will be many guests and it will go for two or three days. It will be a national holiday and the wedding date will be marked each year with the same...'

It sounded so horrific to Trinity that she actually laughed. 'I shouldn't complain really. So—' Trinity tried to keep her voice light '—when is your wedding day?'

'I will marry next year.'

It was ridiculous, Trinity thought, but as she stood there she was filled with a strange ache of sadness.

One kiss might not sound much, but that one kiss was her only pleasant memory even remotely attached to sex.

'You ought to go back inside,' Zahid said. 'Your mother is looking for you.'

'I loathe them,' Trinity said.

'It shows.'

'I love them, though.' He was surprised by her admission, not that she loved her family, more at the hopelessness in her voice. 'Do you get on with your family?'

'I do,' Zahid said. 'Most of the time.'

'Meaning?'

'Meaning most of the time I get on with them.'

'You're terribly straightforward.'

'Meaning?'

'Just that.'

'You should never assume,' Zahid said, for his thoughts were less than straightforward where Trinity was concerned.

'I don't want to go back in,' Trinity admitted. 'Do

you think anyone would really notice if I just disappeared?'

'You know that they would,' Zahid said. 'It will only go for another half-hour or so.'

She let out a breath. Half an hour felt like an eternity right now. 'I don't want to sing.'

'There are many things that I would prefer not to do.'

'But you do them.'

'Some of the time.'

'Would you sing?'

God, but she loved it when he smiled.

'No.'

His smile almost turned to a wince as Dianne's voice invaded them again. 'Trinity?'

He watched her jaw grit as the call continued and her mother's voice started to get near. Zahid took Trinity's arm and led her around the corner to where it was dark, and she could smell the pine from a tree and the thud of music and people in the distance and she wished they were back there in the woods.

'I wish you'd taken me with you that night.'

'I was tempted.'

'It didn't show,' Trinity said, and in sudden defence she mocked him a little. 'Have you been trained to hide your emotions?'

'Who said that I had any?'

She attempted a suitable reply but it dawned then that his hand was on her waist and the other was on her face when normally contact, any contact, was unbearable, just not tonight, and so she answered his question. 'Your kiss told me that you did.'

'Sex is not an emotion,' came his brusque response, but for the first time he lied and she knew it, for nei-

ther could deny what thrummed between them now. It
was more than lust yet it tasted almost the same, it was
more than want yet still he fought not to call it need as
he looked to her lips.

'Where were we?' Zahid asked, but the years could
not disappear. There was so much hurt there that for
Trinity it was not as simple as a kiss. So great was her
fear of contact she was petrified how she might react to
his touch. She knew about his reputation with women
and, of course, he assumed hers, but just as a kiss was
surely inevitable Trinity saw her way out and she leapt
on it and wriggled from his arms. 'I doubt your fiancée
would be very pleased...'

'I have not chosen my bride yet,' Zahid said, and he
took her champagne glass and placed it on a window
ledge then pulled her back to where she had been just
a second or two ago. 'If I had, I would not be about to
kiss you.'

'Oh.'

Well, that settled that, then, Trinity thought. There
was nothing to stop them other than her fear and that
she could not stand being held by a man, except she was
being held now and there was no urge to run, there was
no urge to do anything other than receive the lips softly
descending on hers.

Would he be able to tell from her kiss, her terror?
Trinity wondered.

No, she fast realised, because to his mouth there was
no terror, just the melting of fear and the bliss of his lips
and the stroke of his tongue.

Would he be able to tell from her rigid body that
she did not know how to respond, that her body refused to obey?

No, because she sank into his embrace without thought and the press of his erection against her felt like a reward.

His mouth *did* make the pain disappear; his kiss did, on a night she had been dreading, actually allow her to forget, and Trinity found out something new—it was very hard to kiss and smile at the same time but she was trying.

'What are you doing?' Zahid said, as she paused for a moment and allowed her mouth to stretch into the beam that this moment deserved.

'Smiling,' Trinity said. 'That's better.' For her lips could better relax against his now.

He kissed her deeper, and Trinity felt the weight of his mouth and the hastening of his tongue as he pulled her harder into him, she felt again the press of him on her stomach. The ugliest dress in the world fast became her favourite as his hands roamed the silk and located the not-so-stupid concealed zip and expertly slid it down just enough for his thumb to stroke her aching nipple.

The sirens were back, the sirens she'd heard but once, only they were louder now, closer now, with each and every stroke of his tongue.

Her hands were in his hair, she was back on tip-toe again but with the guide of his hand this time and the sirens neared dangerously close for both of them. She wanted him to lift her, she wanted her legs coiled around his hips. Visions of just that took over as Zahid struggled to halt her ascent, for he wanted to lift her, he wanted to be inside her but he would never compromise her.

'Not here...' Zahid pulled his mouth from her lips but they did not leave her face as she spoke. 'As I said, you deserve better than the woods. Do what you have to and then...'

She shivered at what Zahid left unsaid.

He kissed her ear and then peeled his face from hers and turned her a little. Lifting her arm, he dealt with the zip but did not leave things there. Instead, he kissed the sensitive flesh of her upper arm, and how he found her armpit sexy, she would never know, but clearly he did, because he was deep kissing her there now. Her panties were soaking. Trinity wanted to be back in his arms, but he turned her to face him and straightened her dress and then rearranged a few tendrils of her hair.

'I will be in in a moment,' Zahid said.

'Come in with me.'

'Trinity, go in.' Zahid's smile was wry for there was no way he could go back to the reception just yet. 'I'll be there soon.'

She almost floated in, just on a high from his kiss and the very real promise of tonight. Finally, finally, her body seemed to know how to respond, finally the curse was lifting.

It was possibly the very worst time to come face to face with her mother, closely followed by Clive.

'Everyone's waiting for you, Trinity,' Dianne said.

She just stood there, praying for Zahid to come up behind her, to take her hand, to just walk her away, but instead she faced this man with only the pathetic barrier of her mother between them.

'It's time to sing!' Dianne smiled.

'You want me to sing?' Trinity said, her voice a challenge.

'You know that I do.'

One moment she had been the happiest she'd ever

been, Trinity realised, but now she was suddenly the angriest.

Oh, she'd sing!

Trinity was ready to sing from the treetops now!

She marched into the hall, muttering, and strode up to the microphone.

Yes, she'd sing, Trinity decided, wrenching the microphone from its stand. She'd sing as loudly as she knew how if the microphone would just stop screeching feedback.

Her starting number would be, Trinity decided, 'I Was Seventeen Going on Eighteen', and she'd point to Clive as she sang, as she told the whole world about that night.

The skeletons were coming out to play, the linen basket was going to be emptied too!

Yay!

She felt as angry and as uninhibited as Harry had been on the plane, and there was no need to hide anything, none at all.

Zahid walked into the hall in time to see Trinity stalk to the microphone and start to tap at it, tossing her hair. Her eyes spelt danger and Zahid turned as Dianne came and stood beside him. For once she wasn't wearing that plastic smile and, as everyone had this wedding day, in crisis Dianne turned to Zahid.

'Stop her!' Dianne pleaded.

Zahid wasn't following Dianne's orders as he walked to the stage, it was to get to Trinity, because there was a recklessness to her that troubled him and Zahid would not let her look a fool.

'I'd like to dedicate this number to—' Trinity started,

but Zahid pulled the plug and her arm at the same time and hauled her from the stage.

'Put me down.'

'Not yet.'

'Put me down,' Trinity shouted, as he carried her over his shoulder behind the stage and out through the back exit to the elevators. It all became a little blurry then. She remembered him letting her down and Zahid demanding to know what was going on.

'Nothing!'

Jet-lag, champagne, nerves, fear, want all combined in desperate tears and then she lunged at him, desperate for escape, but Zahid denied her that. She tried to rain kisses on his face but Zahid held her at arm's length as she pecked away like an angry woodpecker who couldn't meet its mark. She wanted the sex he had promised, the bliss of escape with the one man who knew where it resided in her.

She wanted Zahid.

And so she told him.

'I don't reward bad behaviour.'

'You're not training a dolphin!' Trinity shouted, but then she started to laugh. 'I tried that, actually.' She put on an American accent. '"Positive reinforcement-based training"…and it didn't work!'

'If you want sex,' Zahid said, peeling off her dress and offloading her into the bed, 'then you can ask politely in the morning when you are sober.'

'Ask?' Trinity lay on the bed and laughed at his audacity. 'I have to ask?'

'Politely,' Zahid said. 'I want to hear the word "please" when you do,' but as he looked down at her, astonishingly, to Trinity, he smiled. 'You need to learn manners—your behaviour tonight has been shocking.'

'Really?' Trinity said. 'I thought that I'd behaved rather well.'

Zahid didn't have to come up with a suitable answer because less than ten seconds later she was sound asleep.

CHAPTER FOUR

ZAHID SAT WATCHING as Trinity started to stir.

Her bridesmaid's dress was over a chair, her shoes were on the floor, her hair was everywhere and her mascara had escaped her lashes and had moved to the pillow.

Zahid rang for breakfast and saw Trinity's eyes frown at the intrusion when a little while later the door-bell chimed.

'Just leave it there,' Zahid said, as the staff went to set up. 'Could someone draw a bath…?'

She sat up to ask everyone if they could please be quiet and get out of her room but Zahid shot her such a look that she ducked back under the covers and willed the sheikh in her bedroom to disappear.

Actually, Trinity realised, she was in his bedroom, she had to be because this room was massive and the bed seemed even bigger.

Oh, God.

As the maid came out and said that the bath had been run and Zahid said he would call soon to have the room tidied but that was all for now, Trinity had vague memories of kissing him.

Not outside, though. She remembered that that kiss

had been completely lovely. It was the inside attempt to kiss him that had her cringing in recall.

'Does that groaning mean you have a recollection of last night or should I call for a doctor?'

He didn't let her hide; instead, he whipped back the bedding.

'The first one.' Trinity stared up at a very, very beautiful man. His hair was tousled and he was no longer clean-shaven and stood over her in the morning-after version of yesterday's suit.

'How is your hangover?'

'It's not a hangover, it's exhaustion,' Trinity said. 'And forty-eight hours of no sleep, mixed with champagne and my toxic family...' She closed her eyes. 'Did I make a terrible scene?'

'I brought you up here before you could,' Zahid said, 'but, yes, you made quite a scene in the bedroom.' She could hardly breathe but then, when Zahid smiled down at her, so heart stopping was that face there was no 'hardly' about it—her breath was lodged in her lungs and it took a moment for her foggy brain to compute that Zahid wasn't cross. In fact, from the look he was giving her, any moment he'd be stripping the last of her clothing off.

Oh, God!

'Here!' He handed her a large glass of something cold and dark pink. She sat up a touch and when it met her lips, Trinity found out that it was watermelon infused with mint.

'I had no sleep on the flight. There was a baby next to me on the plane...' Trinity explained between draining her drink. 'We don't all have our own private jets to fly us to weddings...'

'You could have put on earphones.' Zahid remained unmoved by her explanations for last night's behaviour.

'You've never flown economy, have you?'

'Your father paid for business class,' Zahid said, because he had overheard Gus telling anyone who cared to listen how much his daughter still cost him, but more than that, Zahid simply would not let her lie.

'And I bought an economy ticket with it,' Trinity whispered conspiratorially. 'It's called ten hours of discomfort for three months' rent.'

'Then you should have taken an earlier flight if you knew that you would be unlikely to get any sleep.'

She lay back on the pillow and stared at him, sulking that he wouldn't give her an out.

Yes, she should have taken an earlier flight, but that would have meant a night in the family home and it had been the last place on earth she'd wanted to be. Economy and a screaming baby had been a far more palatable option.

'Here,' Zahid said. Taking the empty glass from Trinity, he hauled her back up to a sitting position as if she were a hospital patient, and then he sat on the edge of the bed with a plate loaded with tiny sausages and pancakes. He slathered them in maple syrup and, proceeded to cut it all up and then commenced feeding her.

'I was just tired.'

'Of course you were,' Zahid said. 'Eat.'

'You're not cross?'

'No.' He smiled at her but there was concern there. 'What was going on last night?' Zahid asked. 'You were very upset when I got you back to the room.'

Trinity shrugged. 'I'd just had too much to drink.'

'That's not what you said two minutes ago.'

'I just...' Trinity shrugged. She honestly didn't know what to say.

'You can tell me.'

Could she?

He was her brother's best man, a family friend... and, right now, the very best thing in her life, even if just for a little while.

She didn't want to spoil it.

'Things get a bit tense for me when I'm with my family.'

She waited for him to tell her how wonderful her family was and that she should behave better, but Zahid was actually trying to gauge how much he should say. After all, it was her family that he was about to criticise.

He popped a forkful of food into her mouth as he chose to let his ingrained diplomacy leave him a touch, for he wanted her to hear the truth.

'I find the Fosters hard work.' As she opened her mouth to say something he reminded her that it was rude to speak with her mouth full and so Trinity had no choice but to hear him out. 'After last night, I am severing ties with your family.' As she frantically chewed so she could get her words out, Zahid beat her to it. 'When I say the Fosters I don't mean you.' Trinity stopped chewing then as Zahid spoke on—she now wanted to hear what he had to say. 'When I think of you, I do not think of the Fosters, do you understand that?'

'I think so.'

'I need you to understand that when I sever ties with you, it shall be for different reasons entirely. Do you know what they are?'

Trinity gave a tiny shrug.

'If we were to meet in the future, my feelings and

thoughts about you would be very disrespectful to my future wife.' He tried to explain what Trinity could not possibly understand. 'My wife will be chosen with my country in mind.' He saw her frown break into a smile.

'I wasn't expecting her to be me.'

'I know,' Zahid said, smiling at the very thought of Trinity in Ishla. 'I'm sure you could think of nothing worse. I just want to make it very clear that when I sever ties with your family, it has nothing at all to do with how I feel about you.'

'Thank you.'

It was very nice to hear.

'And thanks for saving me from making a complete fool of myself last night,' Trinity said.

'It was no problem.'

'I was just having fun.'

His eyes said that he doubted, again, that he was hearing the truth but Trinity ploughed on regardless. In the sober light of day she certainly wasn't going to reveal the painful past and so she tried to turn the conversation to far lighter matters. 'So what does a sheikh prince do when he lets his hair down?' She stared at him for a long moment. 'I can't imagine you dancing.'

'We danced last night.'

'I mean…' She put her hands above her head and did a little dance in the bed and actually forgot she was only wearing a bra. He made her forget shame, Trinity realised as she put her arms down.

More than that, he erased it.

'I don't dance like that,' Zahid said.

'And we've established that you do sing. You don't drink?'

'No.'

'Because you're not allowed?'

'Because I don't want to.'

'Do you gamble?'

'Never.' He looked at her for a very long moment and then answered her question with one word. 'Sex.'

Trinity blinked.

'It is my vice,' Zahid said. 'We all have them.'

'Is sex a vice?'

'Apparently so.' Zahid gave a brief eye-roll. 'Though that defect will be removed soon.'

'Your wife might be a nymphomaniac,' Trinity said, and she got the lovely reward of his smile.

'We can always hope,' Zahid said, 'though it will not be something that is taken into consideration.'

'Well, it should be.' Trinity yawned.

'I shan't be raising the topic with my father.'

'We have to be down to join the family for breakfast at nine…' Trinity said, glancing at the clock and seeing that it was ten past eight as Zahid dipped the last of the pancake in syrup and offered it to her.

'You make a nice mummy bird,' Trinity said, and then duly opened her mouth, but the fork wavered there, just hovered where she couldn't reach it, and he pulled it back when she stretched her neck.

'Birds feed with their mouths,' Zahid said, and Trinity felt her insides fold in on themselves as he scalded her face with his eyes. Still she did not get that last piece of loaded, sugary pancake and her face turned to fire as he continued to speak. 'Okay,' Zahid said, 'you have two choices—breakfast with your family or we are otherwise engaged.'

'When you say otherwise engaged…'

Did he mean…?

Yes, Trinity realised as he took the last lovely bit of pancake and popped it in his own mouth, he did mean that, for his mouth was pushing her down to the pillow and he was feeding her terribly intimately now. Tongue, pancake and maple syrup were being pushed into her by his tongue and he didn't even let her close her mouth as she struggled to swallow.

It was moreish!

Filthy, messy, sticky and so very, very, nice, but as her mouth emptied and his kiss lingered on she moved her face back. 'I haven't brushed my teeth,' Trinity said, shy all of a sudden, but Zahid seemed more than happy to accept that she might need some space.

'I am going to have a quick shower,' Zahid said, licking the last remnants of maple syrup from her mouth and then releasing her, leaving her more than a bit breathless. 'Then, if you want, you can have your bath.'

It was up to Trinity. Whatever her choice, Zahid would not be joining the Fosters at breakfast.

Duty was done.

He just hoped now that it was time for pleasure.

Zahid stood and started to unbutton his shirt. 'When I come out I will ring for someone to come and sort out the room.'

Trinity nodded, surprised that he clearly expected her to be able to speak at her first sighting of his torso. His coffee-coloured skin gleamed and his dark nipples drew her eyes, but it was the very flat stomach and the snake of dark hair beckoning downwards that had Trinity suddenly look away and start pleating the sheet with her fingers.

'I won't be long,' Zahid said, and headed to the shower as she lay back on the pillows and blew out a breath, trying and failing not to think about him sliding off his trousers and naked on the other side as she heard the taps being turned on.

He was giving her the chance to leave, Trinity realised. The chance to gather her things and go to her own room. To have breakfast with her family safe in the knowledge that this would never be mentioned again.

If she left now, she would never see him again.

Trinity lay on the bed and listened as the taps were turned off and a few moments later he came out, carrying his trousers, which he put over the chair. One white towel was around his hips, the other around his neck.

'Still here?' Zahid smiled and took the towel from his shoulders and started to dry his chest and under his arms.

'Looks like it.'

'I'll get the place sorted.'

'I'll have my bath.'

She climbed out of bed and walked to the bathroom but turned at the last moment, in time to see Zahid take off the towel from his hips. And Trinity got more of a glimpse of what she was letting herself in for. It was darker than he, thick and tumescent, and so incredibly beautiful that rather than wanting to grab her dress and run or head for the other side of the bathroom door, she actually wanted to go back to bed.

'You should call your family,' Zahid said, as if it were completely normal to be chatting to her while naked, as if it was completely normal to want the plates cleared and the place tidied and all distractions put on hold before settling in for a lovely long session.

'Er, after my bath,' Trinity croaked, for she wanted nothing to burst the fragile bubble that she carried into the bathroom with her and only released once she had closed the door. The most fragile bubble she had ever carried, for she actually wanted sex, rather than wanted to want sex.

The lighting had been turned down and the huge sunken bath was filled with warm milky-looking water.

She felt all giddy and disorientated but in the nicest way. She looked in the mirror. Her hair was a disaster, her eyes on fire and her body felt as if it was filled with helium, so floaty and high was she from pancake-laden kisses and the promise of more to come.

There was a little card telling her the infusions that her bath contained—frankincense, neroli and argan oils—and that she was to add the bomb at her leisure.

It was the bomb of bath bombs, Trinity thought as she watched it spinning in the water, tossing out petals and the most heavenly fragrances that lured her to climb in.

She lay there in the just right temperature water, with her stomach pleasantly full and her thirst more than quenched, yet for the first time, the very first time since her very first kiss with Zahid, there was a stir of want for a very different pleasure.

Zahid thought her a party girl—that a morning sex marathon was surely commonplace for her.

He'd fall off his mummy-bird perch if he knew just how limited her experience was.

Yet as she lay there, recalling his kisses and her body's response to them, it dawned on Trinity that after all those years of therapy and Californian healing, which hadn't worked a jot, the answer could well be on the other side of the door.

If Zahid had so much as a clue how messed up she was

sexually then everything they had now would disappear. He'd either do the honourable thing and decline because nothing could ever come of them or, worse, she'd get pity sex, with Zahid being all careful and tender and asking if she was okay every five minutes.

Zahid wanted straightforward sex but there was nothing straightforward about sex for Trinity.

Yet she wanted Zahid to look at her the way he had this morning, she wanted the absence of fear that he brought, not just to her mind but her body too.

Still, if she was going to carry this off, then a confident, assured woman must walk out of this bathroom. Somehow she must present herself as the sexually experienced woman that he assumed she was.

'The maid has been.' Zahid knocked at the door. 'And your phone keeps buzzing. Do you want me to bring it in to you?'

'I'll be out in a minute, Zahid!' Trinity called to the closed bathroom door. 'About what you said last night... well, it would seem that I forgot to say please...' She could almost feel his smile behind the door as he answered her.

'Just remember to say thank you.'

Trinity ducked her head under the water but it didn't wipe the smile from her face. It should worry her really that the rather staid Zahid seemed to be the only person in the world who got her sense of humour. Most people frowned, or she had to explain and by then it wasn't so funny.

She didn't have to explain herself to Zahid.

Trinity looked down and saw her nipples peeking up out of the milky bathwater and she didn't understand why she was terrified but not scared.

This was all so…planned, so clinical.

No, not clinical…

Trinity blinked as she realised she had found the word she was searching for—Zahid put the sensual into consensual.

It was a very nice word to ponder as she climbed out of the bath. There were petals from the bath bomb in her hair and sticking to her skin but Trinity just wrapped herself in a robe and ran his comb through her hair.

What if she couldn't carry it off? Trinity thought. What if she started crying or broke down, or her complete inexperience told him that she hadn't a clue?

You'll *never* get a chance like this again, Trinity warned her reflection.

Kill or cure.

She opened the bathroom door, half expecting the slight chaos of this morning.

Instead, the room was in darkness, broken only by the candles dotted everywhere.

The breakfast things had been taken away, all clothes and things tidied, even the bed had that smooth freshly made look, except for the naked sheikh in it!

Trinity was terrified, of course, but nicely so, as she walked over to the bed.

'Nice bath?'

'Lovely.' She sat on the edge of the bed and wondered if the right thing to do would be to tell him but, no, as he welcomed her to his bed with a kiss, she wanted it just as it was.

His kiss made her shiver, the skill of his mouth told her to leave things to him but, just as she almost forgot to be frightened, the bleeping of her phone made her jump.

'Has anyone seen Trinity?' Zahid said, and actually

made her laugh as she rose from his bed and raked her hands in frustration through wet hair. 'I'll just let them know that I won't be joining them.'

She was *far* from grateful for the reprieve—now she and Zahid would have to start all over again, Trinity thought as she picked up the phone from the bedside and read her mother's text.

'They're about to start breakfast and she wants to know where I am.' Her voice gave a little squeak at the end, because he had rolled to the side of the bed and was fiddling with the belt of her robe,

'Text and say Zahid has taken you riding.'

'Horseriding?'

'Don't lie,' Zahid said, and pulled her hips so she was standing, trying to text, as he stayed very much on his side, leaning on one elbow, one hand on her bottom, guiding her hips to his face.

It was terribly hard to text with a mouth nuzzling your stomach. She could see his glossy black hair and feel his hot mouth and tongue as she tried to work out what to write.

Oh, my, Trinity thought as he continued to kiss her stomach, because she actually wanted to drop the phone and hold his head.

Dry from her bath, she was wet from his mouth.

She wanted him lower, yet she didn't.

She wanted fear, yet it steadfastly refused to arrive.

She wanted to run, yet she wanted to remain.

Somehow she hit 'Send' on her text.

'Now turn it off.' Zahid didn't lift his mouth from her skin as he delivered far from his final instruction. 'I want no distractions.'

CHAPTER FIVE

TRINITY TURNED OFF her phone but it did not make it to the bedside table because his mouth was really working her stomach now and instead she just dropped the phone to the floor.

All phones were off, there was a 'Do not disturb' sign on the door, day had become night and all Zahid wanted to do was enjoy.

The soft skin of her stomach tasted better than even he had imagined. Still warm from the bath, it responded so readily to him. Zahid felt the tension in her stomach shifting, he felt the taut muscles relax and then tighten again, but in pleasure as his mouth moved steadily down.

Zahid was working her quickly but for one reason only—he wanted her to come.

Zahid had considered taking care of things in the shower so that he might take more time, but he had chosen to wait.

He was ruing that decision now as he deep-kissed her stomach and his hands slid up her thighs, for he had wanted Trinity for a lot longer than perhaps he cared to admit.

What to do? Trinity pondered. What should she be doing about now? Her hands moved to his hair, more to steady herself, but Zahid moved his mouth lower, nibbling at golden curls then nudging her clitoris out with his tongue as his fingers slid inside a place that no fingers had ever touched.

It was just her mind that was scared, Trinity realised, not her body, for it responded so readily to him.

She could feel a tremble in her thighs as his fingers and tongue stroked her intimately, a tremble that had her wondering if she could remain standing, but his hands soon answered that though, for he released her sex for a moment and guided her to the bed.

She thought he would kiss her, but Zahid had kissed her mouth last night and again this morning, and the first more intimate taste of her had him yearning for more and so he slid down the bed.

'Zahid…' Trinity attempted to halt him, could barely cope with her inhibition, but then came his voice.

'Do you know how many times I have thought of this?' Zahid revealed.

Why was she smiling when she should be in tears?

She could only do this with him, Trinity thought. It could only be this way, Trinity realised, for if he had seen the look of brief horror on her face at such intimate exposure, Zahid would have surely stopped.

He could not see it, though, he was too focused on her sex and guided her hips so she was kneeling over his face.

As she hovered over him his mouth kissed up her inner thigh till it met its shy mark.

'Za—' His name did role from her tongue, it halted in Trinity's throat as his tongue rolled her somewhere deep. She had meant to tell him to stop, but by the time she got to '*hid*' the world as she knew it was different.

Trinity's expression had changed from horror to a

smile and then to a shocked state of bliss as all those years of frustration were swept aside by the masterful strokes of his tongue.

To him she unfolded and, though together, somehow the moment was private, the awakening exclusive to Trinity, which was how she wanted it to be, how it had to be if she wanted him to be this bold.

'I have a rose petal in my teeth,' Zahid said, though his mouth did not move away.

'They're everywhere,' Trinity breathed.

'Good,' Zahid said, returning to his heated mission. 'I find each one.'

She didn't actually have to *do* anything, Trinity realised, all she had to *do* was hold onto the bedhead and try not to moan as she followed instructions.

'Kneel lower...' Zahid breathed. 'Lower.' And she gasped as his face took more of her weight and, once it did, there was no chance of not moaning.

Unshaven, rough, wet and warm, he was everywhere that was needed, inside and out, as he devoured her with relish and his lack of inhibition gained hers.

Thank you, Trinity wanted to whimper, only not because of their earlier game—she had never been more grateful as he stirred her body beyond a simmer. She had to bite on her lip not to say it as he sucked and licked, and ran his stubbly jaw over her. His focus was so concentrated on her that Trinity didn't have to do anything other than rock to her body's tune and let out words that she would rather have kept in because they sounded so lame.

'That's lovely...' she managed. 'Lovely...' Because it was. It was as it should be and no less than that, just so nice to be lifted a little higher by his hands and his tongue kissed her more lightly, swirling her and then probing her, only pausing to tell her she was something, Trinity had no idea what, in Arabic.

'Fantastic,' Zahid translated between licks.

She felt it.

Those sirens were back and moving closer, but there was no sense of danger. She had never had an orgasm, but twice had glimpsed it with Zahid, yet she was on the very edge of one now.

'Zahid.' She said it in one word this time, for now she did want him to slow down.

'Why do you fight it?'

Because she didn't know what *it* was, till suddenly *it* was there and she rose to boiling. The zap of tension that raced up her spine, the shaking of her thighs almost shot Trinity from the bed. Zahid held her hips hard down and his mouth absorbed the energy that pulsed to his lips and tongue as Trinity sobbed out her pleasure. She released a few long-held fears as Zahid fought his— he wanted more, more of the same, more of everything with her. As he lifted her pink and warm from his lips, his mouth suddenly returned again, softly kissing, for he might never be there again.

Trinity wanted to collapse forward but she was already leaning on her arms as Zahid slid up the bed and let her down so she rested at the top of his thighs.

She looked down where he rose between her legs and just explored him a moment with her fingers. Zahid watched, incredibly turned on by her gentle ministrations, very close to coming for the feel of her on his lips had been incredible and the feel of her hands was sublime.

Trinity stroked what would soon be inside her; she felt the soft drizzle of him moisten her fingers and she was actually excited for the moment ahead. Still breathless from her first orgasm, she wanted to get back on the merry-go-round, loved it that the more she stroked, somehow he became even harder, and bigger too.

'You know…' Trinity said, and then stopped.

'Not unless you tell me.'

'I could get to liking this.' She smiled.

It was the most honest she had been.

'I could get to liking this too,' Zahid said, his face tense from withholding pleasure.

His words were more honest than he should dare to be, for a morning together was becoming far less than enough.

He could not think of that now. His mind was struggling just to remember what had once been routine—he reached to the bedside for a condom. Trinity halted him, for she wanted the softness of his skin to meet hers and she mumbled something about an IUD.

'A coil,' she explained, when he frowned.

She'd had one put in when she'd lost the baby, and had had it changed a couple of years ago, the fear of a random attack almost as petrifying as the fear of getting pregnant again.

'You're sure,' Zahid said, trying to cling onto the last shreds of common sense, for he never went without. 'Because if you get pregnant…' he made a slitting gesture to his throat '…it will be off with mine.' And Trinity actually laughed.

'Very sure.'

He held the base of his thick cock and Trinity lifted herself and lowered herself, loving the feeling of being on top, the control he gave an unwitting gift perhaps, but it set her free.

He filled her completely, she was sure, but then he pulled her hips right down and she shuddered a sob as she struggled to accommodate the full length of him and rose of her own accord to escape, but nature brought her down again. With Zahid her body did not need instruction, it just followed its own lead, until it was Zahid who slowed her down, but for reasons of his own.

He tried to keep things smooth, and although Trinity did her best to move slowly, all she wanted to do was grind against him. Zahid too gave up fighting it and simply let her be.

Was this what she'd been so scared of? Trinity thought as she looked down at Zahid, yet she knew there was no other she could be more herself with. Whatever colour she wore on the day, Zahid saw the person beneath, whatever lie her lips produced, Zahid seemed to extract her truth.

'I think I'm about to come...' Trinity said, and started to chase the feeling, but to no avail. Just as she thought she might not repeat the magic his mouth had given her, Zahid took over, bucking his hips into her, grinding her down to him, and there was nothing to chase, she was already here. The final swell of him inside and the lift of his hips tipped her over the edge and she came to the delicious sight of a very controlled Zahid momentarily out of it, pulling her down to her side and bucking into her for those last delicious strokes, where they met in a place where logic was left far behind.

It was sex, Zahid said to himself as he kissed her down from her climax. Good-morning sex that had been a long time coming.

It must remain as simple as that.

CHAPTER SIX

IT WAS FAR more complicated, though.

Zahid knew it.

It wasn't just that his people would never accept her as his bride. Or that she might not want to be one.

It went a lot deeper than that.

Zahid rolled away as he did after sex, but then thought twice and rolled back to face her again.

'Penny for them,' Trinity said, and it took a moment for him to register that she was asking his thoughts.

'Oh, it would cost a lot more than that,' Zahid said.

It might cost him his kingdom or, worse, he might lose his head, though not in the way he had joked about before. How could he run a country with Trinity waiting in his bed? How could he focus on his people when his mind would be so consumed by her?

It was no surprise when Trinity turned from his silence and picked up her phone.

Whatever he thought of them, they were her family.

'Eight missed calls,' Trinity said.

'You need to go down?'

'I don't want to,' Trinity admitted, 'but, given that I fly out this afternoon, it would be wrong not to put in an appearance.'

'I know.'

Zahid then made a huge concession. Yes, he had decided to sever ties but for her he would do the right thing. 'Do you want me to come down with you?'

Trinity shook her head and climbed out of bed and started to gather her things.

'What are you doing?' Zahid asked.

'I have to get ready. I need to go to my room.'

'You can get ready here.'

'It's going to be bad enough wearing last night's clothes in the elevator, I'm certainly not going down to face everyone in my bridesmaid's dress.'

'Go and have a shower,' Zahid said. 'I will have your things brought here.'

He took care of all the details so easily, Trinity thought as she quickly had a shower and this time she did make a bit of effort with her hair, blasting it with the hotel hairdryer and doing what she could with Zahid's comb.

Now came the hard bit and for once she didn't mean facing her family or facing her fears.

It was facing the man on the other side of the door and pretending what had just happened had been little more than a very pleasant interlude.

Now she had to give him up.

Maybe she could go to the pharmacist and ask for Zahid patches, like Donald had when he'd tried to give up smoking, Trinity thought, making a little joke to herself, trying to lighten the load on her mind. But no gradually reducing dose was going to wean her off Zahid. Trinity knew that already.

Cold turkey, here I come, she decided, opening the door and wearing a smile.

Zahid lay in bed, watching as she put on some make-up and then tied up her hair.

It was over.

He just didn't want it to be.

Or rather he did, for these feelings that he had for her did not sit right with him, these feelings spelt danger.

His mind flicked to his father, bereft on his mother's death, scarcely able to stand, let alone lead a country.

The same would not happen to him.

The dress she had bought for this morning was colourful and floaty and did not quite match her threatening tears as she took the case to the door.

'I'll drop it in my room on the way down.'

Zahid nodded.

So this was goodbye.

'You look beautiful,' he told her, for it was the truth.

'Thank you.'

She ached, not just from him but for him.

'What time is your flight?' Zahid asked.

Trinity told him.

'That is an hour before I am scheduled to fly,' Zahid said.

Their eyes met as they did the maths in their heads, as their brains raced to mental calculators to tap in more time.

One more kiss, one more taste, one more time.

'I could take you to the airport.'

'So I…'

'Leave your case here.'

She almost ran to him. Maybe she did, for suddenly she was back on the bed and in his arms and responding to the fierce promise of his kiss.

'Take as long as you need with your family,' Zahid

said as she wrenched herself off, 'but not five minutes more.'

They smiled because they both wanted that little sliver of time before they had to leave.

'Are you sure that you don't want me to join you?' Zahid offered again.

'I'd rather go down on my own.'

She looked at Zahid and there was a moment when she truly wanted to tell him the truth but the very fact that she hadn't meant that, no, he could not join her downstairs.

If he did then it would be a huge disservice to Zahid for, yes, he would do the right thing and make polite small talk with her family, even Clive.

She would not put him, even unwittingly, through that.

'Penny for them,' Zahid said, and Trinity just gave a pensive smile.

'They're not even worth that.'

They weren't, Trinity realised.

Not a pennyworth of thoughts did she want to give to a man who had no place in this room.

'Thank you,' Trinity said, and Zahid's eyes narrowed in a slight frown, for it had been a little joke that she might want to thank him but it sounded like she meant it.

'The pleasure was mine.'

One more kiss, and then just one more, before Trinity headed downstairs to where both Donald's and Yvette's families were gathered. Surprisingly it was a lot easier, knowing that if things got too difficult she could go back up to Zahid.

Even not by her side, he gave her a confidence that she had never had.

'I hear you're working in a library,' Yvette's mother said, and she almost went to correct her but for the sake of peace Trinity lied.

'In the reference section.'

She was the *perfect* daughter, circulating nicely, even pretending that she was listening as her mind roamed several floors upwards. Finally, when she glanced at the clock for the fiftieth time, it was time to say goodbye.

'I'm sorry I got so upset yesterday,' Yvette said as Trinity kissed her goodbye and wished her well for the honeymoon. 'I spoke to Donald last night and it was all just a miscommunication with the hotel.'

'That's good.'

They spoke for a suitable time and Trinity was just saying her goodbyes to everyone else, silently congratulating herself on a job well done and about to slip away to spend a final, magical hour with Zahid, when Donald pulled her to one side.

'Can I have a word, Trinity?'

She felt her heart sink and just closed her eyes as history repeated itself.

'You know how I hate to ask,' Donald said.

Except it didn't stop him from doing so!

'The hotel is insisting I pay for it all up front. How can I tell Yvette that I've messed up the honeymoon?'

'I haven't got it to give you.' That wasn't the issue, though and, not for the first time, she did her best to face it. 'Donald, you need help.'

'I need my honeymoon,' Donald said. 'It's just been an expensive few weeks. If I can just get away…'

Trinity was too worried to be cross.

So, instead of heading back to Zahid and the bliss of his arms, after a lengthy discussion she sat in the business centre of the hotel and pulled up her account as her time with Zahid slipped ever further away.

She didn't need to ask for Donald's bank details, she had already used them several times.

Thanks to flying economy and saving what she could, Trinity had just over eight thousand dollars in her account. 'How much do you need?'

'Well, there's the hotel, taxis, going out...'

'How much?' Trinity asked, and she couldn't even manage a shrill edge to her voice.

'Whatever you can manage.'

She left herself one hundred dollars and she was too tired from it all to be angry and too scared for her brother to be cross.

'Please, get help, Donald.' She gave him a hug when she stood.

Trinity truly did not know what to do.

She'd begged and pleaded with him over the years, she'd argued and threatened, had offered him the chance to come and stay at hers and just hang out by the beach, but all to no avail. 'I don't want anything to happen to you. I don't want to be at one of these bloody family things without you.'

'I'm fine,' said Donald, peeling her off, only she didn't want to let go.

'I'm scared I'm going to lose you.'

'Honestly, Trinity, there's nothing to worry about.'

'I love you,' Trinity said, 'and so I do worry.'

'Well, there's no need. Thanks for this.'

By the time she'd calmed down and sorted out her make-up to look as if she hadn't been in tears enough to go back to Zahid's room it was already time for she and Zahid to leave for the airport.

'I'm sorry, I got stuck...'

'It's fine.' Zahid pulled her into his arms as their baggage was placed onto a large gold trolley. It wasn't just sex he wanted from Trinity but this, that moment when he held her in his arms and she almost relaxed to him.

He could feel her heart hammering in her chest and, despite a brilliant make-up job, he knew there had been tears, and from the way she clung to him now he doubted that they had been happy ones. 'How was it?'

'Same old, same old,' Trinity attempted, forcing herself to pull back and smile, but she met very serious eyes. 'It was fine,' she said, adding another log to the fire of lies between them.

The traffic was light and in no time they were at Trinity's terminal. Zahid would go onto the VIP section and so they said their final goodbyes in the back of his car. Zahid raised his hand so that no one opened the door to let her out but her luggage was unloaded and it taunted Trinity from the corner of her eye.

'Take me with you.' Trinity smiled. She was joking, sort of, and then she wasn't. There was the threat of tears in her eyes again as she recalled the first time she'd asked him to take her with him. It was combined with this horrible feeling of impending doom.

Zahid had no idea what had happened that terrible night and rather than him see that, she moved in for a kiss, but Zahid halted her, his hand cupping her chin.

'I would love to take you with me,' Zahid said. 'You would be like a breath of fresh air in the palace...' And so very dangerous to his heart. 'You would be the biggest distraction, though.'

Normally, Zahid had no trouble ending things. It was just proving more than a touch difficult now. He actually wanted to take her hand and tell the pilot that there would be another passenger, to take her home to Ishla with him and to hell with consequences.

That was not him, though.

With Trinity he barely recognised himself.

Trinity too was having a lot of trouble remembering that she was supposed to be at ease with this, that it should be easy to simply kiss him goodbye, especially when Zahid started to make promises he surely would not keep.

'Give me your number and I will call...'

'Don't.' She pressed a finger to his lips. 'Don't say you'll call when you won't.'

He stared into very blue eyes and wished he was not going home to start the process of selecting a bride, wished for just a few more months of freedom...but wishes had to be denied when duty called.

'No doubt I'll see you in a few months at a christening.' Trinity attempted a brave smile but it wavered when Zahid shook his head.

Trinity was a luxury that even a married Zahid would find hard to deny.

'I think that this has to be it.'

'Such a terrible shame,' Trinity said, trying to keep things light, trying to pretend this wasn't breaking her heart. 'You could almost make family functions bearable.'

Zahid was struggling too as he tried to relegate it to a one-night stand, or one-morning stand, instead of lovers who were parting for good.

His goodbye was distant.

CHAPTER SEVEN

The cause of death has not been released and the
family have requested privacy at this difficult time.
*   A small, intimate funeral is being held today,*
followed by a private burial.

THEN THERE WAS the small spiel at the end of the report urging readers struggling with personal issues to 'ring this number'.

No doubt it would be engaged.

Trinity folded the newspaper and put it on the table in front of her as the steward came round.

'Can I get you anything before we start our descent?'

Trinity shook her head and got back to staring out of the window as morning continued to arrive.

She had always feared that this day would come but only in her worst nightmare had she thought that less than a month after the wedding she would be flying to the same church to say goodbye to her brother for the last time.

It had been a terrible month.

She had mourned Zahid, had ached to call him, to make contact somehow, though knowing that it was not what they had agreed.

No-strings sex, yet her emotions were more than frayed when she'd found out that ten days into their honeymoon Yvette had walked out on Donald and after that her brother had gone spectacularly off the rails.

It had from then on been a rapid descent into hell and Trinity actually couldn't remember when she'd last slept for more than a couple of hours.

Panic had descended when she had first taken the call and heard that Donald had died but it had been quickly replaced by numbness and she was grateful for that as she made her way through customs.

Her mum's family had naturally descended on the house. Her mother needed her sister but the thought of seeing Clive at this impossible time was more than Trinity could face.

Tonight she would stay at the hotel where the wake was being held before flying back tomorrow.

Yes, another flying visit.

She'd learnt her lesson and so, when her father had transferred money to bring her home for the funeral, she had flown business class this time, but she still hadn't been able to rest.

Heathrow airport saw its share of tears but it didn't glimpse Trinity's today for she held them back, petrified that if one escaped, the floodgates would open.

They nearly did.

As she turned, there was Zahid, the very last person she had been expecting to see, for the funeral was being kept low key. Her mother hadn't mentioned that Zahid would be there when she had spoken to her yesterday.

'You will be okay.'

It was a strange greeting. There was no embrace, just

the guidance of his hand on her arm as his driver took her baggage and they were led to his car.

'I wasn't expecting to see you.' Trinity didn't speak till they were in his car. 'Mum said nothing about you coming.'

'I only just found out. By the time I did you had already left for the airport…' Zahid did not elaborate. Now was not the time to tell her that he had finally caved and, unable to get through to Donald, he had rung Dianne to ask for Trinity's number, only to hear the news.

His plane had touched down twenty minutes before hers.

Trinity looked at Zahid. His lips were pale and his features taut. His thick hair was a touch too long and that tiny detail made her frown, for she had never seen him looking anything other than immaculately groomed.

'Let's first get you home.'

'I'm staying at a hotel,' Trinity said. 'You?'

'No hotel—I fly back this afternoon,' Zahid answered. 'When do you go back?'

'Tomorrow.' Her voice was dull and she went back to staring out of the window.

It was not his place to be angered by her lack of duty today. It was not his place to point out that surely she should be by her parents' side, not just for the funeral but in the days that followed.

It did anger him, though, for it just reinforced the fact that she bucked convention, that she refused to do the right thing, especially on a day like today.

They pulled up at the hotel and as the driver removed her luggage Zahid noted the time as they needed to leave soon for the funeral.

'You check in and change. I will wait in Reception.'

'Why?' Trinity said. 'Or are we pretending today that you've never seen me naked before?'

She was, Zahid decided as they headed to her room, the most volatile that he had ever known her and any doubt that he should be here today was erased from his mind.

She needed him today, Zahid told himself, still fighting that he might need to be with her today too.

'Your mother asked that I deliver the eulogy,' Zahid said, as Trinity tried to plug in her heated rollers then realised that she'd forgotten her adaptor.

'Great!' Trinity hissed, and then turned and gave him a bright smile. 'Great,' she said again.

'In what order?' Zahid asked. 'Is the hiss for the state your hair will be in, or that I have been asked to speak?'

'You choose.'

'Why are you…?' He halted. Now was perhaps not the time to ask why she was so angry at him, now not the time to tell her just the hell this month had been for him too.

'I'm going to have a shower,' Trinity said.

'A quick one,' Zahid warned. 'We have to—'

'I'm not going to be late for my own brother's funeral,' Trinity almost shouted. 'I do know how to tell the time.'

He arched his neck to the side as the bathroom door slammed. Zahid walked on eggshells for no one, yet he could almost feel them crunching beneath his feet as he paced the room.

Leave it for now, he told himself.

Trinity was not his and so he had no right to insist on better behaviour.

She was who she was and in truth he would not change her.

Zahid made a quick phone call and when the adaptor she needed was promptly delivered he sat as she came out from the shower wrapped in a towel and watched her eyes fall on the blinking light of her hair appliance.

Zahid did not expect her to thank him, so her silence came as no surprise.

She flipped open her case and like a depressed magician pulled out black, after black, after black.

Zahid turned his head as she dropped her towel and he heard her snap on her bra, then the sound of her pulling on her panties and then the tear of cellophane as she opened new stockings.

'I'm sorry for the imposition.' Trinity popped the tense silence with the tip of her anger. 'I know that you never wanted to see me again.'

'Of all your lies, and there are many, that is the biggest.' Zahid looked at her now, appalled at how much weight she had lost this past month, how her skin had paled. He silently berated himself about how much he still wanted her. 'How long did it take you to twist my words into my never wanting to see you again?'

'You said—'

'I said that this had to be it. I said my feelings for you would be inappropriate in the future.' He watched as she started to crumple and he knew enough about Trinity to know that any crumpling would be spectacular and so couldn't happen just yet.

To embrace at the airport would have opened the floodgates but his touch might just hold them closed for a little longer now. 'Come here,' Zahid said, and when she did, he pulled her to his lap.

Her skin did not arouse him this grey morning. Instead, he answered the tiny goose-bumps on her arms and her stomach in their plea for strength and warmth and held her tightly to him. 'I'm here to get you through today,' he said. 'Our stuff can wait. I will call you in a few days and then we can speak properly.' Zahid felt her nod on his chest. 'Today you have enough on your mind without being concerned about us.'

So much on her mind.

Not just that Clive would be there today.

It was the first funeral she had been to since her daughter's, which had been the loneliest day of her life.

'I'm here with you,' Zahid said, and he could never know just how much those words helped. 'Now, get ready.'

He did not avert his eyes as she dressed. There was no point—her scent was on him and his mind would caress her intimately later.

Right now, though, there was a funeral to attend.

As they took their places in the church Zahid recalled their last conversation. '*You could almost make family functions bearable.*'

Nothing could make this bearable, though.

As he stood to read the eulogy, she reminded him of a fragile flower blooming in winter surrounded by the ice of grief.

He looked at Donald's wife, Yvette, whose face was etched in bitterness, and wondered about her pain of the last weeks as her handsome groom had faded to the husband from hell.

Speaking at the funeral of a man you did not admire was a hard task but Zahid executed it well. He spoke of better times, of a younger Donald and family gatherings that...

Zahid glanced up from the notes he had written on the plane. Even as he had penned them he had known that the words were inaccurate, though the right ones to utter, yet Zahid never lied. His eyes turned to Trinity, who started down at black-stockinged knees, and there was the reason he had kept going back. Having admitted that to himself, he was able to speak the truth then. 'Family gatherings that I always looked forward to and will remember with deep affection...' He gave a pale smile as Trinity looked up. 'While we remember the good times,' Zahid said, and looked to Trinity, 'we should not ignore the pain left to us now.'

It was the only time Donald's life was painted as anything other than perfect, Zahid realised as the Fosters micro-managed their son's funeral.

The cemetery was awful. Zahid watched as Trinity held back despite her mother urging her to step forward.

Zahid moved and stood beside Trinity.

The light refreshments were downed with whisky back at the swanky hotel, yet when he wanted to be by her side, the Fosters still kept pulling him away, dragging him into other conversations when he so badly needed to be with her.

He saw her glance at the clock, knew that again they were running out of time and Zahid excused himself from second cousins and made his way over to the one who came first to him. 'How are you?'

'Fabulous!' Her smile was as dangerous as her eyes.

'How are you?' Zahid said again.

'I'm going to lose it in about thirty seconds from now.'

'You're not.'

'I might.'

'You won't,' Zahid said.

Zahid watched as she pushed on a smile as someone approached and offered their condolences but soon it was just them and she told him a little of what was on her mind.

'I don't understand how everyone keeps saying he was a wonderful man, how tragic it was and how sudden. I've been saying for months that this would happen.' She could not stand to be here even a moment longer.

'When do you fly?' Trinity asked.

'In a couple of hours.'

'We could go to my room.'

'I think that would be completely inappropriate,' Zahid said.

'Aww…' Trinity smiled that dangerous smile. 'A playboy with a conscience, how sweet!'

Crunch went the eggshells beneath his well-shod feet. 'You know, Trinity, if it wasn't your brother's funeral…' He halted, not just because Dianne had come over but because of the strength of the words he had been about to deliver, because privately he would like to take her aside and rattle her till she behaved, or tip her over his knee and spank her till she conformed.

He was angry, not just at Trinity but at himself for the foolish moment when he had even considered she might belong by his side, for she could barely behave at her own brother's funeral.

'We've decided to have people back to the house after all,' Dianne informed her daughter.

'I thought the whole point of having it at the hotel was that you wouldn't have to ask people to the house.'

'Well, your father thinks we should ask people back so I need you to go and open up and set up the drinks and glasses—'

'I'm not going back to the house.'

'Trinity…' Dianne had this black smile on in an attempt to disguise the venom in her voice. 'Go and open up and you are to greet—'

'I told you earlier,' Trinity said, 'I'd come to the hotel but I am not—'

'Grow up!' Dianne hissed. 'Grow up and show some respect for your brother's memory.' She walked off and left Trinity standing, her cheeks on fire with years of suppressed rage.

'I will take you back to the house,' Zahid said. He knew today must be agony for her, but there was a part of him that was very cross with Trinity. There were things you did, things that simply had to be done.

He took her rigid hand and led her out to his driver.

'In a couple of hours it will all be over.'

'It will never be over.'

He could not abide her melodrama. Zahid loathed raw emotion unless it came with an orgasm attached.

They pulled up at her house and he noticed her cheeks were no longer pink but instead as white as the lilies that had filled the church.

'Let's just set up then I'm going,' Trinity said. She let them in and started to pull out glasses from the dresser as Zahid sorted out the drinks.

Perhaps realising the reception she might get from Trinity, Dianne chose not to ring her daughter when plans changed yet again. Instead, she dialled Zahid. 'Could you ask Trinity to set up the guest room?'

Trinity said nothing at first when Zahid relayed the

message, she just marched angrily up the stairs and started pulling towels out of the airing cupboard. 'She's got a bloody nerve.'

Zahid was fast losing his patience. Yes, the Fosters were hard work but Trinity was behaving like a spoilt brat and, frankly, he expected more from her.

'Can you just, for five minutes in your life, do the right thing?' he said, as Trinity opened the guest-room door. 'Your mother has lost her son.'

She could hear the front door opening and cars pulling up and everyone starting to arrive, and she was past staying quiet, could not hold it in for even a second longer as she stood in the room where so much had been taken from her.

'She's lost more than her son,' Trinity said. 'How dare she pretend that it never happened? How dare she tell me to set up the guest room when she knows full well what went on in here that night?'

'What night?'

'The night *you left me* here!'

Oh, it had been but the tip of her anger back at the hotel, Zahid realised. He knew, with sick dread, the night she was referring to, he knew from the bleached whiteness of her lips and the anguish in her eyes what must have taken place.

He remembered Dianne telling her to set up the guest room for Elaine and Clive and her fingers grasping his as he'd climbed in the car.

Zahid even remembered the time.

Ten minutes after eleven was the moment that now he would regret for ever.

'My aunt's husband...' Trinity gagged. 'After you'd gone, he attacked me.'

CHAPTER EIGHT

ZAHID KNEW THAT how he reacted to this was important to Trinity so he fought for calm as he processed the news, but there was a dangerous instinct kicking in. One that might see him head downstairs this very moment, as the funeral party had now arrived, and for once it would not be their daughter who misbehaved.

'You need to let your parents know,' Zahid said, relieved when he heard his own voice, for it sounded calm, in control, when he felt anything but. 'They need to know what went on that night and why family functions are so hard for you.'

He had always been proud of his self-control but he was in awe of it when she responded to him.

'They know.'

Just two words but they were almost more than he could process. Zahid could hear long breaths coming out of his nostrils as Dianne called up the stairs for Trinity and he struggled to stay calm. 'Oh, Zahid, your driver said you need to leave.'

'You need to get your flight,' Trinity said, feeling guilty and panicked for telling him and seeing him fight for control. 'Please, Zahid, you can't say anything. It's my brother's funeral.'

He didn't care what day it was.

'Please, don't make this worse for me.'

He pulled her away from the room and wrapped his arms around her in the hall as Zahid for once struggled with what to do.

There were so many reasons not to do what he was about to, so very many, but he simply could not leave her here.

'Usually now you ask to come with me.'

'You always say no.'

'Not this time.' He neither knew nor cared what the reaction would be in Ishla, he just shoved away the thought that in a few days he was to dine with Princess Sameena and her family, then Sheikha Kumu three days after that.

He simply could not leave Trinity here and neither could he stay, because it would be impossible for him not to make a scene.

If his gaze fell on Clive, Zahid knew, there was no telling what he might do.

'You will leave with me.'

'I can't just walk out now.' Even if she had been threatening to just a few minutes ago, the reality was she could not simply walk out and leave, but Zahid had decided otherwise.

'Yes, you can,' Zahid said. 'I will sort it all out. You are not staying here to deal with this alone.' He took her hand and they walked down the stairs and headed to where her parents stood.

'I know it is not the best timing,' Zahid said, 'but I am taking Trinity back to Ishla with me.'

'Sorry?' Dianne blinked.

'I would like to have given you more notice but my return flight has already been arranged.'

So that his eyes would not drift around the room, Zahid stared down Trinity's father and almost dared him to protest, but no one would argue with Zahid in this mood. He was nothing but polite yet there was such a black energy inside him that in a matter of moments they were heading to the airport, only stopping at the hotel to collect her small suitcase.

'I only packed for today. All my things are back in America...'

'You don't need to bring anything,' Zahid said.

'What about work?'

'We'll sort that,' Zahid said, as they neared the airport. 'Tell me where you work and I will call someone.'

'The Beach Bar.' Trinity shook her head. 'It doesn't matter, I'm only casual.'

'I thought...' Zahid halted and let out a breath. He'd spent weeks making phone calls and trying to find out what library it was that she worked out.

Another lie.

What did he know about her?

Even as they boarded his jet, Zahid was quite sure that any minute she would change her mind.

'What will your father say?' Trinity asked.

'Don't worry about that now,' Zahid said. Usually he would let the palace know if he was bringing a guest but in this instance Zahid felt it would be better to speak face to face with his father.

As the plane took to the sky the practicalities of whisking her away were starting to make themselves known. Zahid did think of stopping somewhere en route but there was much for him to do back in Ishla.

He just wanted her away and safe.

She sat beside him and as the plane levelled out in the sky still she said nothing.

'Do you want something to eat or drink?' Zahid asked.

'No.'

'Do you want to rest?'

'No,' Trinity said, but she stood and Zahid watched as she walked towards the sleeping area. Her top was already off. 'I want you to make today bearable.'

'Trinity.' He walked in and watched as she stripped off her black clothes. 'What you need to understand is that once in Ishla we cannot—'

'What I *need* is one pleasant thing to focus on.'

'Sex won't make this better.'

'Oh, I think you could be wrong.'

'I'm not wrong,' Zahid said. 'When did you last sleep?'

Trinity couldn't answer that. Even thinking up an answer to the most simple question hurt too much right now.

Zahid pulled back the bedding. 'In.'

'I'm naked, Zahid.'

'If that's a problem for you I can see if the stewardess can find something for you to wear to bed.'

'It isn't a problem for me!' Trinity was so cross that he would not be goaded.

'Well, it's no problem for me either. Get some rest,' Zahid said, closing the door on her and taking a seat. But two minutes later she was out, thankfully wearing a robe and blinking at the bright lights.

'Can I have a drink?'

'Do I look like a flight stewardess?' Zahid said, deliberately turning away. 'Press the bell by the bed.'

'I don't want to press the bell.'

He did not turn round and finally she gave in and went back to bed. He watched as a few moments later the stewardess came and answered her call and returned a few moments later with a tray and a glass of sparkling water.

But trying to keep her in bed was like trying to squeeze a jack-in-the-box back into a box with a broken clasp.

'There's a noise.'

She was back again.

'A rattling noise.'

'Possibly because we are on a plane,' Zahid answered. 'Go to bed.'

'I can't sleep,' Trinity said, but she did as told.

For four minutes and forty-five seconds.

'Shouldn't there be a belt—?'

'I'll give you a belt,' Zahid said, standing, and he practically hauled her into the bedroom and threw her onto the bed.

'A leather one?' Trinity smiled.

'A human one.' He climbed onto the bed but not in it and lay beside her with his arm clamped over her. He turned her round so she was facing away from him but wedged against him.

'Go to sleep,' Zahid said.

'I can't,' Trinity said, 'because if I close my eyes…' So violent was the shudder that racked her, for a moment Zahid wondered if they had hit turbulence, and so loud were the sobs and tears that came then that the stewardess really had no choice but to knock and pop her head into the dark sanctuary in the sky to check if everything was okay.

'She's fine,' Zahid said as the door opened. And the stewardess nodded and closed it as Trinity wailed.

'I don't have tissue.'

'You have a giant one,' Zahid said, placing the sheet in her hand. And not once, as she sobbed, did he tell her to stop or that she should calm down. He just held her facing away from him, clamped down by him, so there was nowhere to hide.

'I gave him money,' Trinity sobbed. 'If I hadn't…'

'I gave him money too,' Zahid said. 'He called me from his honeymoon and said he could not pay the bill. If you want to blame someone, blame me.'

He could take it.

'I paid for his honeymoon,' Trinity said. 'I've lived on noodles for a month.'

'I paid for his honeymoon too, half the wedding party probably paid for his honeymoon,' Zahid said, and his words honed perspective.

He let her cry and then he let her sleep and he should have left then, Zahid knew. He should have climbed from the bed rather than hold her.

Zahid had not slept much in recent weeks either.

With Trinity resting beside him he finally did sleep but a few hours later the first stirring from her had him awake.

'I'm cold,' she moaned to a universe that did not answer.

He pulled the blanket higher on her shoulder then moved her tighter in to his embrace.

'Sleep,' Zahid said. They were five hours into their flight and it was already the most sleep that either had had in a while.

'I'm awake now,' Trinity said. 'Sort of,' she half explained, for she was in that lovely in-between place where things didn't hurt so much, or was it just that Zahid was beside her?

Zahid was beside her and they were on their way to Ishla!

She struggled to duck back into slumber, to not face the problems that surely awaited. He was still on top of the covers and, from the shirtsleeved arm that was over her, still dressed.

And again she was down to her bra and panties and had been put to bed by Zahid.

'Did I demand sex?'

'You did,' Zahid said, and smiled to the back of her hair. Then he remembered the reason she was there and the terrible thing that had happened to her. 'Trinity...'

'I don't want to talk about it.' She had heard the shift in his voice. 'Please.'

'Okay.' That she had told him was huge, Zahid knew.

'Is it going to cause trouble, you bringing me back to Ishla?' Trinity asked.

'Not for you,' Zahid said. 'But...' the ramifications of bringing her home at such a delicate time were starting to hit him. 'It is my birthday in a couple of days...'

'Will there be a party?' she nudged.

'No.' Zahid smiled. 'After that there are dinners to help make the wisest choice when I choose my bride.'

'Choose me,' Trinity said, and put her hand up in the air as if answering a question in class, and they both laughed. 'I've never heard you laugh,' Trinity said, as his hand came up to join hers.

'Neither have I,' Zahid said, capturing her raised hand and holding it there.

'Will you serve me without question?' Zahid said.

'I won't.'

He felt the resistance as she tried to pull her arm down and it was a game but a sad one for possibly the only way they could discuss it was to have a little play. 'Do you promise to remember to do your duty as I serve my country.'

'I don't.'

'And I don't need to ask if you will obey...' He released her hand and she moved it down and turned to face him and stared unblinkingly into his eyes.

'The closer you get,' Trinity said, 'the kinder you look.'

'The closer you get, the less I can see.'

'Can I be your mistress?'

'I would never take a mistress,' Zahid said. 'Which is why I would not have been at any christening.' She worried him so. 'Why would you want to be a mistress?'

'It was a joke, Zahid.' Trinity tried to turn it into that. In fact, she didn't want to be a mistress, just something of his.

'So how will you decide who will be your bride?'

'Alliances.'

She turned onto her back and chose to stare at the ceiling for she did not like his detached answer and it did not sound like him, or rather it did not sound like the Zahid that only she saw. 'So you'll marry for alliances with the hope love will grow?'

'Love is for fools and peasants, not for a future king.'

'Thanks,' Trinity said, and she turned and watched his haughty face twitch into a slight smile. 'Then I'm either a fool or a peasant.'

'I was not talking about you.'

'Of course you are. Just because you are going to be king one day, you think feelings are beneath you...'

'I am telling you how it is in my land,' Zahid said, refusing to be swayed. 'I am telling you my reasoning.' But not all of it. He chose not to tell her about his father's illness and when Layla had been born, for he could not share that with another and remain aloof, could not return to that memory and somehow stay detached, yet he knew to be fair to Trinity he must make things clear. 'I am telling you that in Ishla things will be very different between us.' He went to get up. 'I will have some refreshments brought in to you and then you should get dressed as we need to be out there when the plane starts its descent.'

'I know things will be different but we're not in Ishla yet,' Trinity said, as he rose from the bed and went to the door and she waited, breath held as Zahid halted and went against his own moral code, just for that one last time with her.

She watched as he turned and then undressed and it was Trinity who held the covers open this time. Naked beside him, it felt as if she had been cold for the entire month and had just remembered how it felt to be warm. 'Thank you,' Trinity said.

'I haven't done anything yet.'

'For making me happy. I shouldn't be happy today but I am.'

'You should be happy every day,' Zahid said, for even on the worst days they made the other smile.

His mouth was tender. It was a slow and long kiss for even if they did not have very long he still did not rush her.

Slow was the hand that explored her, that stroked

her breasts and then her hips, and Trinity could feel the building need in him. When she rolled to her back, when he moved deep into her, Zahid took his own weight on his elbows and their kissing stopped and he looked down at Trinity as she looked back at him.

She felt him build, yet she felt him hold back and it was his passion she wanted.

'You don't have to be careful around me.'

She saw the twist of pain on his lips, for the news had devastated him, she knew.

'You don't have to hold back,' Trinity said, because she wanted the Zahid who wanted her as she was, with no thought what had been. And right now she wanted his anger, for she was angry too and had every right to be—this was their last time. 'Please don't hold back on me, Zahid.'

He took her the way he wanted to and drove hard into her, but far from scaring her he drove her fear away, for her hands were pressing him in and her body was arching to his as they both refused to allow anything other than themselves in the bedroom.

It was Zahid who shouted and to feel him unleash just unravelled her more.

Deep, intense, blissful was the orgasm that met his and Trinity did her best not to cry out, but did and then frantically glanced at the door, but he brought her face back with his hand and his mouth took her moans and there was nothing she was scared of with Zahid.

'You were right,' Zahid said, looking down at the woman he would crave for ever. 'My feelings are beneath me.'

It took a moment for Trinity to understand his words.

Yes, his feelings lay beneath him right now, every one of them contained in her.

As a bell warned that they would soon be descending, Zahid knew he must leave feelings here.

He just wasn't sure how.

They quickly washed and dressed but instead of putting on his suit, for the first time she saw him in robes and wearing a *kafiya*.

He saw her startle.

'I...' She didn't know what to say. 'It all seems a bit more real now.'

'I don't know if I am making things worse for you,' Zahid admitted, for it had simply seemed right to bring her when he had found out what had happened. The reality, though, made little sense.

'I don't want to meet the women you'll...'

'I know.'

For the first time jealousy stirred in Trinity and despite herself she wanted to know more.

'Must she be a virgin?'

'Trinity, we need to get back to our seats,' Zahid said, for he did not want to discuss his future wife now.

'So you're not going to answer my question?'

'She must have kept herself only for me.'

He went to open the door but her words halted him. His kiss, his lovemaking, the way he had been with her had changed her world and Zahid deserved to know the gift he had given to her. 'I have.'

She saw the line between his eyes deepen as he tried to fathom her words.

'There's been no one but you, apart from...'

'Don't,' Zahid said. 'Don't put the two together, for what that bastard did does not count in any land that

I would rule.' He did not know what to believe. 'Trinity, the woman I took to bed that day was confident...'

'Not at first,' she admitted. 'Zahid, I've had issues since that night, I've tried so many things. I know I flirt, I know I seem bold but that's how I am with you...'

'I should have known!' Zahid said. 'I would have done things differently.'

'Exactly!' Trinity said, as the bell carried on pinging and then there was a knock on the door.

Zahid called out something in Arabic.

'Had I told you the truth, would it have happened?' When Zahid didn't answer, Trinity did for him. 'Of course not.'

'You *should* have told me.'

'No.' Trinity shook her head. 'Because then it would never have happened and I refuse to regret that it did. I know it can't happen again,' she said. 'I get it that it doesn't change things.'

But for Zahid it did.

CHAPTER NINE

TRINITY HAD NEVER really given his land much thought but as they neared she looked down at and knew it was not what she might have expected.

Old married new, for there were ancient villages, yet as they flew along the peninsula she saw too the high glitter of modern architecture, but most beautiful by far was the palace for it gleamed the brightest all.

'It's amazing.' When she got no response she glanced over at Zahid, whose face might have been carved from one of the stone palace walls.

'Zahid....'

There was no chance to talk. The plane was a second from landing and as it hit the palace runway, Zahid was actually grateful for the jolt of landing and the sound of wheels on the tarmac for it gave him two seconds away from his thoughts.

He had been her first.

He needed to process it, they needed to discuss it, but first somehow he had to clear his head.

A car drove them the short distance from the plane and though Zahid's driver did his best to keep his face impassive, Trinity could feel him repeatedly glancing in the rear-view mirror. It was the same when they arrived. The maids gaped in surprise as Prince Zahid arrived with a blonde foreigner dressed only in black and Trinity stood, her face burning, as Zahid spoke to a man in Arabic, who then walked off.

'That is Abdul, my father's chief aide, I have told him to let my father know that I wish to speak with him and to have a suite arranged for you.' He halted and turned as a very beautiful, raven-haired woman walked towards them with a curious expression on her face. 'This is my sister, Layla.'

'And this is?' Layla asked, when for once Zahid forgot his manners.

'Trinity,' Zahid responded, and Trinity watched as Layla raised an eyebrow and waited for her brother to elaborate. 'Trinity Foster.'

'It is lovely to meet you, Trinity,' Layla said.

'I am about to let Father know that I have a guest,' Zahid said. 'Layla, perhaps you could help Trinity to settle in and sort out some clothes and things for her. She came at short notice and so has nothing much with her.'

'Of course.' Layla smiled. 'This way.'

They were all so terribly polite, Trinity thought. Surely Layla must have a thousand questions but instead a maid was called and they drank mint tea as they waited for her room to be readied.

The king, though, did not hold back.

'Zahid,' the king said sharply. 'You said you wanted nothing more to do with that family...'

'I was not referring to Trinity when I said that.' He looked at his father.

'Perhaps,' the king said, 'but here the rules are different.'

'I am aware of that.'

'Here, you are not the man you are overseas.'

'I have brought Trinity here as a friend as, not for anything else.'

'It is not respectful to your future bride to be housing your mistress!'

'She is not my mistress,' Zahid said, for she no longer was. They had said their intimate goodbyes on the plane.

'Then why is she here?'

'For pause,' Zahid said. 'She has just lost her brother and there are family issues.'

'What does that have to do with you?'

When Zahid did not respond the king breathed out loudly. 'You are to say to Abdul that she is here to help Layla with her English.'

'Why lie?'

'It is not a lie,' Fahid said. 'Layla is, after all, helping to teach the girls of Ishla English and, given you have many functions and dinners to attend in the coming days, I assume it will be Layla who entertains her.'

'Yes.'

'And that will help Layla's English.'

'Fine,' Zahid said, and he looked at his father and saw he was visibly worried, for Zahid had never brought any friends from England, let alone a woman, back to the palace. 'It is just for a few days. You will hardly see her…'

'Why would I not greet your guest? Why, if you have nothing to hide, is she to be tucked away?' The king would prefer to confront the enemy, the woman who could seemingly so easily sway his son from the marriage that the king had in mind for Zahid. 'Tonight we will dine, and I would like to meet your guest'

'Trinity is tired from her travels.'

'Then we will dine early. Layla has to teach in the morning anyway.'

'It is nothing to be nervous about,' Layla said after Zahid had told Trinity a little later that she would be dining with the king tonight. 'You won't be expected to say much.'

Trinity smiled at Layla's rather wry comment.

'I talk too much,' Layla said, 'I question things and it itches my father.'

'Irritates,' Trinity corrected her, and Layla frowned. 'It irritates your father.' Trinity explained but she watched as Layla's cheeks turned pink. 'Zahid just said I was to help you with your English.'

'My English is perfect,' Layla said. 'Don't correct me again.'

Whoa!

They were all terribly polite, Trinity amended, *if* you remembered your place.

Yet Layla, in her own, very odd way, was lovely. 'Try this.' She held up a lilac tunic for Trinity but as soon as she tried it on, both women realised it was far too tight. It clung instead of hung and gave her more curves than were polite in Ishla.

'Oh, no.' Layla laughed, making the same cut throat gesture that Zahid once had. 'Try this one instead.' But as she handed her a pale mint one that would hopefully fit better, Trinity suddenly stopped smiling as she stared at her refelction.

Yes, she had lost a lot of weight this past month, just not from her breasts—for once she actually filled her bra.

Layla misread the sudden silence.

'I am sorry you lost your brother. I would die if something happened to Zahid.'

'We weren't very close in the last few years,' Trinity admitted.

'It must hurt.'

'It does,' Trinity said, 'but I am very angry with him at the moment.'

It felt strange to be able to speak with Layla, who she had only just met, more easily than she could with her parents.

'There are other hurts,' Trinity said, glad when Layla did not ask her to elaborate.

Only it wasn't the other hurts that were worrying Trinity now.

As she slipped the tunic over her head, that brief second of privacy had Trinity's face screw up in a frantic, silent panic as she willed her brain to remember her last period, but with all that had happened since that day, the last month was a painful blur.

'That's better.' Layla smiled and helped Trinity arrange the tunic. 'There are some lovely gold slippers that go nicely with it, or these jewelled ones, which I think would go really well.'

'The gold are beautiful...'

'But I prefer the jewelled ones,' Layla said.

She was in Ishla, Trinity reminded herself as she accepted Layla's suggestion, but even a detail like slippers served to remind Trinity that she knew nothing about this strange land.

* * *

Zahid was rather nervous both for Trinity and himself.

He watched as she walked in and after a flurry of introductions took a seat on a low cushion. He was grateful to Layla, who quickly moved Trinity's feet so her soles were facing away from the king.

'My son tells me you live in America?'

'I have for a few years.'

'You studied?'

'Ancient art history.'

'You must take Trinity to the second palace.' The king looked at his son. 'I am sure she would be interested. Perhaps Trinity would like to start the cataloguing.'

'Trinity is not here to work.'

'It wouldn't be work.' Trinity smiled. 'I didn't know there was a second palace. I don't remember seeing it as we came in to land.'

'It is hidden,' the king said. 'I am sure Zahid will be grateful for that in the coming year.'

'Coming year?'

'Once married, Zahid will live there with his bride until it is time for him to be king.'

Trinity reached for her water. Suddenly the thought of going there, seeing first hand where Zahid would live, held little appeal, but taking a cool drink she forced her smile brighter and Zahid could only admire her composure, for he knew his father was goading her for a reaction.

'And then Zahid will rule from here,' the king continued.

'Well, you'll need a lot of baby gates.' Trinity smiled sweetly, looking around at the many treasures.

'The future princes and princesses shall not live here till they come of age.' The king's explanation only added to her confusion. 'There are many treasures at the second palace too but, you are right, it is less formal. A lot of the artefacts at the second palace have significant, personal meaning.'

There were treasures everywhere. Even the plate she was picking up sticky rice from could have held her attention for an hour or more. Gold and blue, the more she ate, the more of the pattern it revealed, and Trinity would have loved to simply clear it and turn it around.

'You should take Trinity over there tomorrow,' the king said to Layla.

'I have a class to teach tomorrow,' Layla said.

'And I would be the worst person to attempt to catalogue a palace.' Trinity smiled. 'It would never get done.' She looked at the plate again and then at the king. 'Among so many beautiful things, do you have favourites?'

Zahid caught Layla's eye, both waiting for the king to silence her, yet the king actually forgot to be cross for a moment and smiled. 'I do, though I have not looked at them in a long time. My wife collected amulets, they are stored in a mandoos, or rather, a wooden chest.'

'In the second palace?'

'No,' the king said. 'I had it moved here, not that I have looked through it in a while.'

They spoke easily through dinner but then the king turned to Layla.

'Perhaps it is time for you to retire,' the king said to his daughter, 'if you want to be alert for your students tomorrow.'

Zahid caught Trinity's eye for a brief second and

again they were back in the woods, Zahid reminding her how much freedom she had, for he could not imagine Trinity at seventeen, let alone Layla's twenty-four, being told, however politely, to go to bed.

After dinner they drank coffee that would surely keep Trinity awake till the small hours but soon the king retired, leaving Zahid to walk Trinity back to her quarters.

'You did well,' Zahid said.

'I wasn't aware it was a test,' Trinity snapped.

'I was just commenting...' Zahid halted. 'You are tired, it has been a long day. Perhaps...'

'Please, don't try to tell me when I need to go to bed again.'

'I wasn't,' Zahid said. 'I was going to suggest we take a walk on the beach. I thought that might relax you.'

'Isn't it forbidden?'

Zahid said nothing and they walked through the moonlit night, past the palace, but as Trinity turned in the direction of what she assumed was the path to the beach, Zahid's hand gripped her arm and halted her.

'It is this way.'

'Oh,' Trinity said, 'so where does that lead?' She saw his face shutter, acknowledged his lack of response to her question and, realising it was the entrance to the second palace, she let out a mirthless laugh.

'Trinity, I am sorry if my father upset you tonight but I have never lied, I have never tried to hide my truth.' His eyes were accusing. 'Unlike you.'

'I've told you why I couldn't tell you.'

'Have you?' Zahid said. 'You tell me only the pieces you want me to know and at a time of your choosing.'

'That's not true.'

'Are you sure?' Zahid asked, for she had lied about her workplace, her sexual history and he knew she had been in rehab too. 'Are you sure you are as honest with me as I am with you?'

Trinity tugged her arm away. She wanted to talk to him, to speak with Zahid, to tell the only person on this earth she could, just how deep her pain went, but for what? At a time of Zahid or the king's choosing she'd be gone. She was scared too to tell him that she was starting to worry about her absent period. She doubted either of them would go unnoticed if they bought a pregnancy test!

'What am I doing here, Zahid?' It was like waking up from a dream. This morning she had been at her brother's funeral, this afternoon she had found herself safe in his arms, and now she was walking deep in the night on a beach in Ishla. Trinity honestly didn't know what part of the day had hurt the most—losing her brother, losing her heart or losing to this strange land. 'Why did you bring me here?'

'Because, given what you told me, I could not leave you with them.'

'I can't hide here for ever.'

'I'm not asking you to hide.'

The beach was as white as powder and the sea the colour of her bridesmaid's dress but with more depth, and Trinity battled the urge to run along the beach and leave footprints or write their names in the sand and watch the ocean take them away.

'It's like paradise,' Trinity sighed, 'but with separate bedrooms.'

They faced each other and it was simply wrong not to be in the other's arms.

'What do you want?' Zahid asked.

'To wake up and not fancy you any more,' Trinity said. 'For even the sound of your voice to annoy me.'

'I hope for the same,' Zahid said. They both smiled reluctantly. 'Nag me.' He smiled again.

'Take up fishing and talk to me endlessly about it.'

They both wanted a kiss, even a touch would do, but it could not happen here.

Ever.

CHAPTER TEN

TRINITY WAS THE perfect guest.

Well, not perfect, for the palace was a little less ordered when she was around.

Zahid woke on the morning of his birthday to a folded piece of paper under his door and he was at first cross when he opened the makeshift card from Trinity, for she should not be wandering at night near his room.

Her words wished him a happy birthday but there was the notable absence of kisses under her name, just a smiley face and two words.

Better not!

And there was a stick figure, Zahid with a fishing rod.

He was no longer cross.

Once he was dressed in full military regalia, Zahid glanced to his bedside where the paper card lay.

Zahid did not keep mementos and he did not know what to do with this, for if he left it in his room, the maids would no doubt think it rubbish. If he put it in his drawer, perhaps it became more than it was.

A memento.

He pulled on long leather boots with a head that was

pounding, for even dressed as heir to the throne, even about to greet his people, Zahid's mind was full of her.

He would decide what to do with the makeshift card later, Zahid decided, folding it and putting it in his pocket for now.

As he walked briskly to his father's study he met Trinity on the way.

'Happy birthday, Captain.' She smiled and though they stood a suitable distance apart as she teased him lightly about his uniform they were back on the dance floor and the dirty dance started again, when it must not.

'Thank you for the card,' Zahid said, 'but it was unwise to come up to my room.'

'Oh, well.' Trinity shrugged.

Zahid gave her a small nod and then walked off but his stride was temporarily broken when she wolf-whistled.

Possibly he blushed.

Possibly not, Zahid quickly decided. Most likely he was cross.

'Where is Layla?' Zahid asked, as he joined his father in his study.

'She is late again,' came the king's curt response.

They did not do 'happy birthdays'.

Layla was happily late. Besotted with Trinity and when she should be meeting with her father and brother, she smiled widely when Trinity knocked and Jamila, Layla's handmaiden let Trinity into her room.

'I got a message that you wanted to speak with me,' Trinity said.

'I want you to join me when I take one of my English classes.'

'I'd be happy to.' Trinity smiled.

'Tomorrow,' Layla said, Jamila finished doing her hair and make-up.

'That would be lovely,' Trinity said, for tomorrow Zahid dined with Princess Sameena and her family and it would be nice to have her mind on other things.

'Walk with me,' Layla said, and Trinity suppressed a smile, for she could not be offended by the way Layla ordered people around, she was completely used to getting anything she asked for. 'We can talk on the way.'

Layla told her about the students she taught and how much she enjoyed the contact, even if it was online. 'It is by video call,' she explained, 'which means I can get to most of the schools. We have a lot of fun and they will be so excited to meet a real English girl.'

'I'm excited to meet them too.'

'They ask so many questions,' Layla sighed. 'Difficult ones.'

'Such as?'

'You'll see,' Layla said. 'I had better hurry. I am already terribly late and my father will be cross that I am not already there.'

He was, especially when a maid informed him that Layla was chatting with Trinity.

'Just how long is your guest here for?' Abdul checked as they went through the briefing for in a few moments they would walk onto the balcony.

'I am not sure,' Zahid said, ignoring Abdul's slight eye rise, but the king spoke on.

'Today there is much celebration in Ishla. Not only does the future king celebrate his birthday but work is to commence on the second palace.' He looked at his son. 'Soon the people will find out who their prince is to marry.'

This time it was Zahid who asked Abdul if he could excuse them.

'I would like the dinners to be postponed,' Zahid said.

'It is far too late for that. Princess Sameena and her family are joining us tomorrow,' the king said. 'And why would you want them postponed?' He dared his son with his eyes to answer him.

Zahid accepted the dare.

'I would like to spend more time with Trinity.'

'Before you make a commitment to marry a suitable bride?' the king checked, and when Zahid did not answer he continued speaking. 'Because you know that Trinity Foster would be a most unsuitable bride and one that the people would never accept.'

'My answer to your question was the correct one. I would like to spend more time with Trinity.' That was all Zahid wanted. Time for Trinity to get used to Ishla and perhaps see its beauty. Time in England as a couple to see if they could work things out.

Time even to find out that they were not suited for each other, Zahid thought, recalling their conversation last night and the card in his pocket with the stick-figure picture on. He did his best not to smile.

Yes, all he wanted was time, and he looked at his father. 'You know I have never made a decision lightly.'

'You understand the offence that would be caused if these dinners were postponed.'

Zahid swallowed, for he did not want to make problems for his country. 'I do.'

'And you know that I want a wedding, so if I postpone these dinners then I shall invite the Fayeds for dinner next Sunday?'

'Father.' Zahid was not interrupting the king for his own benefit. Layla had just walked in unseen by the king and her eyes widened in horror as she heard what was being discussed. 'Hassain too,' the king continued. 'I would like to speak first hand with the man who will soon marry my daughter.'

'No!' Layla screamed, and the king turned as she ran from the room.

'Layla,' Zahid roared as he went to chase his sister, but she had flown straight into a shocked Trinity's arms.

'What's happening?'

'Layla is overreacting,' Zahid said. 'Layla, what you heard was the end of a very difficult conversation...' But Layla would not be consoled. 'You need to calm down so we can go out to the balcony, and then I will explain properly.'

'I'm not going out there,' Layla sobbed.

Abdul approached and told them that the king was making his way to the balcony and it was time for Zahid and Layla to join him.

'No!' Layla wept. 'You can't make me.'

'Layla.' Zahid was stern, for he was used to dealing with his sister's dramas and all too often it fell to him to calm her down, but the reproach in his voice made Trinity shiver. 'First you will do what is right *then* we will talk.'

He ignored Trinity's raised brows and the purse of her lips as Layla joined her brother, but he could not ignore the disquiet of standing, smiling at his people, as his sister stood, not scowling for the camera, as Trinity once had, but meek and fearful for her future, by his side.

'You said I did not have to worry for a while…' Layla said once they were back inside, but her voice trailed off as her father entered the room.

The world, Zahid thought wearily, was far less complicated when it was faced without emotion.

'I need an answer from you, Zahid,' the king warned.

'And I told you I do not make decisions lightly.'

It was an impossibly long day. A formal lunch and then he inspected the army and later a semi-formal dinner that Trinity did attend, but she sat next to a red-eyed Layla. For once it was easy for Trinity to sit quietly, for she had a horrible taste in her mouth. A *familiar,* horrible taste in her mouth, and she took a sip of the fragrant tea at the end of the meal. It tasted like neat perfume.

When would her period come?

After dinner, when Trinity had excused herself to go to her room, Zahid asked to speak with Layla. It was not an easy conversation to have.

'I asked Father if he could postpone the dinners so that I could spend more time with Trinity.'

'You love her?' Layla frowned, for she could not imagine her stern older brother falling in love, as his focus had always been his country.

'You too!' Zahid rolled his eyes. 'I am supposed to give an immediate answer when I am trying to make up my mind what is for the best, not just by my people but by Trinity, by you too…'

'Of course you love her,' Layla challenged, 'or you would not have brought her here and be asking to postpone dinners.'

'Away from here, people date, they get to know each

other, they see if their differences will work better together, or if they should be apart...'

'You think I feel sorry for you?' Layla sneered. 'Well, I don't. You are going to be king, of course you must marry a suitable bride, but at least you have known love in your lifetime, at least you got to be free for a while before you started your family.' Layla started to cry. 'So don't ask me to understand how difficult things are for you when the man I will marry and spend all my life with is Hassain.'

She ran crying to her room and Zahid walked in the grounds, but it did not relax him because the day replayed over in his head.

He turned and looked as a noise disturbed him. He saw shutters open but he looked away when he realised it was Trinity's suite.

Perhaps she couldn't sleep either, Zahid thought; perhaps the air in her room was as stifling as it was out here, for there was no escape from his thoughts.

His eyes moved back to her window and he could only sigh as he watched her peek out and then turn.

One foot, followed by the other.

Zahid walked over quietly as Trinity shimmied down the short drop from her window.

'Are you averse to using doors?'

When she heard Zahid, Trinity jumped.

'I wanted to go for a walk.'

'So why use the window?'

'I didn't know if I could.'

'It is not a prison.'

'You told me this morning that I should not be wandering the palace at night.'

'I meant you should not be near my room.'

'Oh, please…' Trinity started, then halted, for last night the temptation had been great to creep in. Not that she would tell him that. 'There are so many rules, I'm never sure if I'm breaking one or not.'

'Just be yourself.'

'You're not, though,' Trinity pointed out. 'I barely recognised you when you told Layla off this morning.'

'Layla was upset. It was the only way to calm her down.'

'Perhaps, but I don't really know you at all, Zahid.' He didn't respond. 'Does anyone?'

'What do you want to know?'

'You. What you think about things, how you feel, or are you going to tell me again that feelings are beneath you?'

'I have not been fair to you,' Zahid said, and stopped walking. 'Perhaps it was easier to blame your past and your ways on the fact that we cannot have a future but it is more complicated than that.'

'It is,' Trinity said, 'because even if I didn't have a past I'm not sure I'd want…' She gave a shrug and Zahid waited but Trinity didn't say any more. Instead, it was Zahid who spoke on and told her a little of his family's history.

'My father was to choose Raina as his bride, a princess from a neighbouring land who is now Queen. The marriage would have profited our people, ensured swift progress. Instead, progress has been painfully slow.'

'Why didn't he choose her?'

'My father walked into the room and saw my mother. She had been crying because she did not want a loveless marriage and to be chosen by the future king, but then their eyes met and she changed her mind. My father says she smiled at him and in that moment his choice was made.'

'Did it cause problems?'

'Many,' Zahid said. 'It caused division and even today relations are strained. That can be rectified now, though, if I choose Raina's daughter, Sameena.'

'Oh, so you do lie, Zahid!' Trinity said. 'You told me that you hadn't chosen.'

'I haven't,' Zahid said. 'I would prefer not to go with the elders' choice because one of the other potential brides comes from a country with a very organised army—'

'I don't want to hear,' Trinity said, for she did not want to hear about any future wife, but she did want to know about the marriage of his parents and all the trouble that it had caused. 'Were your parents happy?'

'Yes, they were happy, while their people bore the cost of a decision made in a rash moment.' Zahid shrugged. 'And then, when my mother died, their king fell apart. That is what love does to a man. When I saw how my father crumbled on my mother's death I decided I wanted no part in a marriage that made one so weak. My father could barely move from his bed. What if there had been trouble with neighbouring countries, what if there had been an emergency and decisions had been needed to be made? He was incapable.'

'I doubt that could ever happen to you.'

'I never thought it would happen to my father, yet it did,' Zahid said. 'I want no part in a love that renders you incapable.'

It was a very backhanded way of revealing his feelings but Trinity just shrugged and started walking, thinking over his words. They actually made a lot of sense to her.

'So you want your own Dianne?'

'Excuse me?'

'Your own Dianne, standing smiling and plastic by your side and agreeing, without question, to whatever you decide.'

'Do not compare me...' He caught her arm and swung her round. It was rather a difficult conversation because to reveal the absolute insult that was meant that he had to criticise Trinity's parents, but another Dianne was the very last thing he wanted from his wife. 'I do not want that from a wife.'

'You told me so yourself. You want a wife who will obey and serve without question,' Trinity challenged. 'That's what my mother does, she stands idly by.'

'Your father has made many mistakes.'

'Oh, and you're exempt from making them?' Trinity checked. 'I'm sure my father would insist he was only doing the best for his family and constituents, that my mother doesn't understand what it takes to do the job he does. I'm quite sure if he loved her he wouldn't have had those affairs and I'm quite sure he blames her for what happened to me. It was her side of the family after all.'

Zahid stood there a touch breathless, furious at her challenge, reluctantly acknowledging her words.

'I don't want my past pardoned in some grandiose gesture,' Trinity said, 'only to be thrown back at me, and, no, I would never stand with a plastic smile, meekly accepting that you know best.' She gave him a bright smile. 'See, we're completely incompatible, but it works both ways, Zahid. I don't want your idea of a marriage. I want a love that burns and sometimes hurts, one that challenges me at every turn. I want a father for my children who does not hold onto his emotions, whatever the cost.' The absence of her period had Trinity for once thinking ahead and what she saw was not pretty. 'I don't want a family tucked away in the second palace, with their father an occasional guest, till they come of age and can move to the main one...'

'You don't understand.'

'I don't, Zahid.' She smiled a plastic smile that infuriated him. 'But that's okay—clearly, I don't have to. I just have to agree to your ways.'

'I would always do the right thing by my family but there are rules in place and those rules mean I must do the right things by my people.'

'Yes, Zahid.'

'And I would never cheat on my wife.'

'Yes, Zahid.'

'Stop agreeing with me.'

'Oh, sorry, I thought that was what you wanted.' Then she smiled a very slow smile and his face was rigid as she made him examine a truth. 'Why did we have to sever contact?'

'You know why.'

'Are you worried that you couldn't keep your hands off me, even with a wife by your side?'

'No!'

'Oh, just those pesky inappropriate thoughts, then.' Trinity winked. 'Well, that's okay, then,' she said, and ran off towards the palace.

Never, not once, had anyone challenged him so; never once had he questioned his own integrity so much; never had he wanted to chase someone so much, to catch her and turn her round, to press her to the jewelled palace wall and demand she retract her words.

And Zahid did just that. In a moment he had caught up with her and, yes, he pushed her to the wall but in the way that lovers did and he demanded then that she take back what she'd said.

That she retract.

'Retract what?' Trinity asked.

The truth.

She looked deep into his eyes, could feel his erection pressed into her, and she just stared and challenged him to kiss her, to break the strange rules of this beautiful land. And then she did the unforgivable. She smiled, the plastic smile of her mother, and Zahid pulled back, staring into the tempting pool of her mouth and trying to shift decades of thinking as his mouth moved towards her, but Trinity turned her head.

'I'm going to bed, Zahid, presumably alone.'

'Stay.'

'No!' Trinity said. 'I'm too good for a shag against the palace wall.'

'I would not do that to you.'

'You want to, though.' Her hand reached down and what met her hand did not deny the truth.

But though she returned alone to her room, Trinity did not go to bed.

She couldn't be pregnant, Trinity thought as she lifted her leg on the bed and pushed her fingers inside, feeling for the strings that would tell her the IUD was in place, but was unable to find them. She felt behind her cervix hoping to find them nestling there but, no, they were nowhere to be found.

Trinity undressed and examined her body. Apart

from slightly bigger breasts, there were no changes she could see. She didn't feel sick, she felt exactly as she always had. In fact, better than she always had, for the most part. Here in Ishla she was relaxed.

Not now, though.

She remembered Zahid's slitting gesture to the throat and how she had laughed at the time.

She wasn't laughing now.

CHAPTER ELEVEN

LAYLA WAS NOT quite so gushing with Trinity the next morning.

'Is everything okay?' Trinity checked, as they walked to her study where Layla would take her class.

'If Zahid does not choose his bride, the next bride will be me.'

'That is not what you want?'

Layla's black eyes met Trinity's. 'It would seem that it has nothing to do with what I want.'

'Layla.' Trinity's hand went to her shoulder, but Layla shrugged it off.

'Please, don't,' Layla said. 'I am cross with you even though deep down I know it is not your fault. I will not stay cross for long.'

They were all so honest, Trinity thought, but in the nicest of ways, because where else could you deny a touch because of the mood you were in?

Here they did not pretend.

'Do you want to do the class tomorrow?' Trinity offered.

'No,' Layla said. 'I have promised the girls that you will meet them today, they would be so disappointed if that did not happen. I too have told them that you are here in the palace to help me with my English but you are not to correct me in front of them. It is easier to say that than explain you are here to sabotage my life.' She saw Trinity startle. 'Sorry, was "sabotage" the wrong word?'

'I'm not allowed to correct you,' Trinity pointed out, and Layla narrowed her eyes.

'You can with my permission.'

Trinity thought for a moment. 'Actually sabotage is the perfect word. I'm so sorry, Layla.'

'See! I was right,' Layla said, but then she smiled. 'I know it was unintentional, though,' she said, and gave Trinity a hug.

They were friends again.

English with Princess Layla was far more fun than Trinity remembered her English lessons to be!

Really, it was more an hour of conversation, for Layla did not know how to read or write in English.

Layla did not know how to drive either, Trinity found out as the questions poured in from Layla's students and one of them asked how you would get to school in England if you did not have a driver like Princess Layla.

'You would walk, or get a bus or train,' Trinity said.

'I would take my driver,' Layla said, and they all laughed at the thought of their princess walking, or getting a bus or train, and so too did Layla.

It was fun.

Till the topic turned to weddings.

'Does the bride wear gold in England?' a little girl asked.

'She wears white,' Trinity said, wondering if it might be a touch difficult to explain just how diverse weddings could be. 'Well, traditionally she wears white.'

'We are going to say goodbye to Trinity now,' Layla broke in swiftly, for she knew they would have many questions about weddings and it was something neither woman would, today, choose to discuss.

They all said goodbye and thanked her but still the questions came for Layla.

'My mother says that our prince is going to marry soon,' the same little girl said. 'Princess Layla, will they live at the second palace?'

'That is private,' Layla warned, which went against everything Layla's classes were about, it was why the students loved her so.

'You said, so long as we asked politely and in English, that you would answer our questions.'

Layla closed her eyes for a brief moment. 'Yes,' Layla said. 'Our tradition says that the future king will live at the second palace with his bride until it is time for him to rule.' She looked at Trinity, who had moved away from the camera and had tears streaming down her face.

It was cruel to hear about Zahid's future life and Layla nodded when Trinity stood. 'I'm going to go for a walk.'

'Of course.' Layla nodded. 'Wait one moment,' she said to her students, 'and I will be back.' She joined Trinity at the door. 'I am so sorry.'

'It's not your fault. Of course they have questions.'

'You did not need to hear them, though.'

Trinity walked through the palace grounds, overwhelmed with the impossibility of it all, because even a chance of future happiness for Zahid and herself would come at an appalling price.

As she wandered down towards the beach she saw

the entrance to the second palace that Zahid had steered her away from.

The garden was cool and shaded but as she walked further she saw it had its own private beach.

She thought there would be guards, or workers, but there seemed to be no one and when she turned a handle on a huge carved door, as easily as that she was in.

It was agony.

A huge wooden staircase led upwards but that was not what first caught her eye. Neither were the portraits on the wall, but a glass cabinet that contained framed photos.

This was a home.

Layla was the image of Annan, who'd had smiling black eyes and the same long hair. Even Fahid looked happy but what had Trinity's eyes fill with tears was a younger Zahid.

He had even been a serious baby.

Only then, as she looked through the years, did she realise just how lucky she was to receive that smile so easily, for it would seem he shared it with few.

To torture herself she took the stairs upwards and soon found the wing that contained the master suite.

It had to be it, Trinity decided looking at the opulent bed piled with cushions, the bed where Zahid would sleep with his bride. Yes, it had to be it, Trinity thought as she opened huge shutters and stared out at the ocean, for it was a view fit for a king.

'What are you doing here?' Trinity did not jump at the sound of his voice, she was trying too hard not to turn round and to wipe her eyes without him seeing.

'Layla's taking her class. I just wanted to take a walk.' Trinity chose not to tell Zahid that they had been discussing his wedding. 'I wanted to think. I'm sorry I wandered. I never thought it would be open.'

'You don't need keys here.'

He came over and stood by her side. 'You were crying?'

Trinity nodded.

'About your brother?'

Trinity gave a soft shrug then shook her head.

'No.' She looked out at the ocean again and thought of her brother, for without him she would not be standing here. 'You know, if it weren't for his death, we would never have spoken again.'

'That is not the case,' Zahid admitted. 'I had thought about you a lot in the last month. I told you Donald asked for a loan for his honeymoon. The first time was on the night of his wedding. I refused him and offered to pay for rehab instead. The second time...' Zahid hesitated and then continued. 'It was me who called him. I did not get around to asking for your number, though. He was in a bad way and he said again that he needed a loan. If anyone should have guilt for lending money...'

Trinity turned her head. 'No.'

'I had rung every library in Los Angeles,' Zahid said, and watched as her shoulders moved in a soft laugh. 'One by one I ticked them off and in the end I rang your mother. That is how I found out that he had died.'

'Why were you trying to call me?'

'I think we both know why,' Zahid said, 'even if it must remain unsaid.'

Must it?

'Trinity, since our first kiss you have not left my mind.'

'Oh, please.' There was still anger there. 'You never

gave me a thought. If Donald hadn't got married we'd never have seen each other again. You left me that night and you never looked back.' Tears were streaming down her cheeks but they were silent ones. 'You never came back.'

'I did come back,' Zahid said. 'In the new year, after your birthday. I returned, not because I wanted to spend time with your family but because I wanted to see you, but I was told that you had gone into rehab.'

'Oh, is that what they told you?' Trinity gave a mirthless laugh. 'I always wondered how they managed to explain away six months of my life.'

'Where were you?'

She couldn't discuss it, it hurt too much, but Zahid would not let it rest. 'Why would Donald and your family say you were in rehab…?' His voice trailed off as the truth started to dawn on him.

'Tell me.'

'I can't,' Trinity said.

'You can,' Zahid said. 'When will you learn that you can be honest with me?'

She had never been honest with anyone, though, for she had never been allowed to be.

'There is an Arabic proverb,' Zahid said, '*what is hidden is more than what has been revealed so far.*'

She pondered the words for a moment and they were true, so true.

The loss of her baby was, for Trinity *more* than the event that had led to her conception. She had not had to work to separate the two, for her love for her baby had brought out a fierce protectiveness in her.

'I got pregnant…' Trinity said, and then quickly added, 'Please, don't say sorry. I wanted her so much.'

Zahid said nothing, just let her continue.

'My parents wanted me to have an abortion, I just couldn't. I knew right from the start that it wasn't the baby's fault. I went away to have my baby but I lost her at six months…'

For the first time ever he felt the sting of tears in his eyes. Even on his mother's death he had been aware he must hold things together, that he must not, even once, cry, but hearing the love in her voice, despite the pain, had the emotions Zahid despised so much coursing through him.

'Does she have a name?'

Trinity nodded. 'Amara.'

Eternal.

He did what he must not do in Ishla, he sat on the bed and pulled her into him and held her as she wept and did his best to comfort her, but Trinity was still drowning in fear, not for the baby she had lost but the one she might hold inside her now.

'You can talk to me.'

'How?' Trinity asked. 'When tonight you are dining with your future wife?'

'I will sort something out. I will buy us some time.'

'How?'

'Do you even want to be here?'

She was scared to say yes, scared to admit her truth, scared too, given how terrible it had been for her, that if she did admit her truth, if somehow she could stay, then he would forbid her from seeing her family.

'Trinity?' Zahid demanded, for he would move a mountain if he had to, but he had to know first if she wanted it moved. 'Do you want to be here?'

She stared at a man she trusted more than she had

ever trusted another person, but she could not bring herself to tell him what terrified her now.

She looked into Zahid's eyes.

Her instinct was to tell him, but Trinity had been raised to deny her instincts and she did not know how to trust.

'I want to be *here*,' Trinity said, and her meaning was clear for a second later she met his mouth, her drug of choice, and it was Zahid's too and this time he could not deny her.

Their mouths were on each other's, he could taste her tears and her face was flushed from crying and her lips swollen, and it wasn't even a choice for Zahid as to whether or not he kiss her, he gave in to need.

Desperate urgent kisses that had them tearing at each other's clothes till they were naked and they melted into the other as their skins met again and he pressed her down onto the bed. It was dizzying, it had to be, for thought would have told them it was so very forbidden, a single thought would have warned that they could be caught at any moment, that this was wrong, very wrong. Zahid had always held onto emotion but not for a second did he hold on now.

'Tell me what you want.'

'You!' Trinity replied. It was the only answer she knew. 'This,' she said, half sitting against the cushions as he knelt between her legs. His head lowered and Zahid's mouth, hungry and rough, took her newly sensitive breasts deep, and she loved it that with Zahid pain was a new pleasure.

Then, when her breasts were not enough, when her mouth could not quench days of denial, of fighting not to react to her taunts, ended as he knelt back on his knees and pushed her legs further apart. She briefly looked down as he positioned her and then seared inside. Trinity's head went back and she was drunk on the power of him unleashed and raw as his hands moved her hips to his will.

This was Zahid's will, this was his want and even before Trinity came his decision was made and he started to spill into her.

Trinity could even feel the contractions in her womb as Zahid gave her the most intimate part of himself.

'There,' he said, and she understood his word.

'There,' he said again, as he pulsed in the final precious drops, and she forced herself forward and looked down again and watched the milky white on his length as he slowly pulled out and then drove in to her again.

It was done now.

After, they lay on the marital bed catching their breath, her hair in his mouth, her cheek hot and warm by his, and Zahid closed his eyes, but not in regret.

Tonight he dined with Princess Sameena and her family, next weekend it would be Sheikha Kumu, yet the woman he loved lay in the marital bed with him now.

It was too late to cancel the dinners, it would be considered the height of rudeness as the invitations had already been sent out.

He would get through tonight, Zahid decided but first he would speak with his father.

Foolish or not, sensible or otherwise, Zahid had chosen his bride.

His head had no say in the matter.

'I will sort this.'

Her body was so flushed she shivered as she was suddenly drenched in icy fear.

'Shouldn't I be away from here before you say any-thing?' Trinity was starting to panic.

'I don't want you away from me,' Zahid said. 'It's time to start trusting me, Trinity.'

'Zahid…'

'I will handle this,' Zahid said. 'I am going to make a formal request to speak with the king.'

CHAPTER TWELVE

THE KING LOOKED down from his window and saw Trinity walk out from the entrance to the second palace.

Of course she would be interested in the second palace and want to see it, the king consoled himself. After all, she had a degree in ancient art history and the second palace was rich with treasures.

There was little consolation to be had a few moments later when he watched as his rarely dishevelled son walked out.

She must leave, the king decided.

And she would be leaving tonight.

He wanted Zahid back, the man who thought only of his country, a man, the king privately admitted, who must be spared the pain that he himself had endured, for a heart was only so big.

'Is everything all right, Your Highness?' Abdul enquired an hour or so later, when he walked in on the king, who was still deep in thought.

'It will be,' the king answered. 'What are you here for?'

'Prince Zahid has tendered a formal request to meet with you.'

Fahid's stomach churned for the words they would exchange in a formal meeting must be documented.

'I do not have time. We are to greet guests soon.'

'It is a formal request.'

'Which means I must respond by noon the next day,' the king countered, for he, better than anyone, knew the laws of his land.

'You are to arrange for Ms Foster to come and speak with me now.'

'Of course,' Abdul said obligingly. 'Though, given we are soon to receive Princess Sameena and her family, would tomorrow perhaps be a more convenient time to speak with a guest?'

No, the king thought, for this must be dealt with now and once and for all.

And the king knew how.

Zahid needed to find out just how unsuitable Trinity would be as his wife, he needed to see for himself the trouble she would cause—and tonight he would.

He turned to Abdul. 'Summon her now.'

The giddy high from making love had faded the moment Zahid had told her he would be speaking with the king.

Trinity bathed and as she came out of the bathroom her phone buzzed and Trinity let out a tense breath before answering.

'Hi, Mum,' Trinity answered. 'How are you?'

There was a long stretch of silence and it took a while for it to dawn on Trinity that her mother was crying.

'Your father wants to spread the ashes tomorrow. He wants it done but I wanted you here.'

'Who's going to be there?'

'Just family.'

'I can't, then.'

'Trinity, please…' her mother said, but without anger this time. 'I don't want to lose you.'

She might, though.

Zahid would have no part in the strange charades her family played. Zahid had already told her his thoughts on her family and that he was severing ties with them.

She loved them, though.

'You're not going to lose me but I'm not going to attend any more family functions if Clive is there.'

'Trinity—'

'I mean it.'

Finally, she did.

It was a teary Trinity that answered when Layla knocked at her door.

'I did not know that the children would upset you.'

'It was just children asking questions.' Trinity attempted a smile as she let her in.

'I know, they ask so many. All the difficult ones, of course. I did promise them that so long as they asked in English and it was a polite question, they could ask me anything.'

'Polite?' Trinity checked.

'Well, you know girls can ask difficult things and so I tell them when their question is not polite…' Layla gave an uncomfortable shrug at Trinity's questioning frown and elaborated a touch further. 'Today they ask about marriage but some of the older students ask about wedding nights and I don't think they are suitable questions.' Layla went a little bit pink. 'Or rather I don't know how to answer them.'

'I guess it could be awkward.'

'It is.' Layla admitted.

'It's good they feel they can ask questions, though.' It was Trinity's cheeks who were a bit pink now as she probed Layla for information, not that Layla could know the reason for Trinity's interest. 'I mean, where would they go here to find out about birth control and the like?' She saw Layla frown.

'Birth control?'

'If you don't want to get pregnant.'

Layla blinked. 'I thought I was the only woman who felt like that. I don't want to have Hassain's baby.'

'I meant,' Trinity swallowed as she realised the can of worms she was opening but Trinity desperately needed to guage how these issues where handled in Ishla and so she was more specific. 'What would a young woman do if she wanted to have sex but wasn't married.'

'It would never happen out of wedlock.' Layla's cheeks were on fire.

'You mean there are no unplanned babies born in Ishla?'

'Of course not,' Layla said, and Trinity just stood there as Layla continued. 'It must not happen, it cannot happen.' To Layla it was as simple as that.

But despite Layla's absolute assurance that it could never happen, it very possibly had and to the future king's potential wife.

Of course there must be unplanned pregnancies in Ishla, she knew that Layla was being naïve.

So what happened when a pregnancy occurred that wasn't planned?

Trinity did feel sick then but it was in fear for her unborn child.

Perhaps they'd insist on an abortion, just as her

mother had. Only when Trinity had begged to keep her baby had she been sent away.

Zahid would do the right thing, of course, but would that be by his country or by her?

'Trinity?' Layla dragged her mind back to the conversation, her black eyes alight with curiosity. 'What is this birth control?'

Trinity was saved from answering when there was a knock at the door. It was Jamila who spoke for a moment to Layla.

'My father has requested to speak with you,' Layla told Trinity.

'It's okay,' Layla said, when Jamila had left and she saw Trinity's pale face. 'He is fierce, yes, but he is fair too, and you have done no wrong.'

But by Ishla's standards Trinity had.

CHAPTER THIRTEEN

TRINITY STEPPED INTO the study and looked to the side as she curtsied, hoping that Zahid would be here, for she did not know how to face the king alone.

'How are things?' the king asked. 'I trust you are being well looked after.'

'I've been looked after beautifully.'

'How are your family?'

'I've just spoken to my mother.'

'How is she?'

'She's a bit upset. My father wants to spread my brother's ashes.' They chatted a little about that and Trinity started to relax.

'It is a difficult time for them.'

'It is.'

'Did you enjoy your time at the second palace this afternoon?' The king saw that he had sideswiped Trinity but he would not hesitate to tackle difficult subjects when the future of his monarchy was at stake. 'Are you going to lie and say you enjoyed looking at the antiques and jewels?'

'No.'

'Is your intention to trap my son?'

Trinity had stood blushing and unable to look at the king but now her eyes did meet his. 'Trap him?'

'It is a commoners trick and you,' the king said, 'are a commoner with a past.'

'I'm not going to stand here and be insulted.'

'Where is the insult? You are a commoner, yes?'

'Yes.'

'And one with a past.'

'The insult was that I might trick your son.'

'I apologise, then,' the king answered. 'I forget that you have ways to defy nature. I would have hoped you would not bring them here but perhaps it is better that you did, for an unplanned pregnancy would bring more shame than I can even dare to imagine. More than a drug scandal.' The king gave a tight smile. 'I apologise, that was not you but your brother.'

'I would prefer, if we must discuss this, for Zahid to be here.'

'When I discuss this with my son, I will be far less polite than I am being now. I am furious with him and for the first time ever I am disappointed in him. A few weeks ago we were discussing bridges, and hospitals and the education of our people. Now he speaks only of wanting time to sort out your differences, time to see if you two might work. That is not how things work here in Ishla.' He looked at Trinity. 'We are a kind and fair country,' the king said. 'Until someone interferes in our ways.'

'You want me to leave?'

'You were always leaving, Trinity.' The king was scathing. 'Now though, it is not a question of if you leave, it is *how* you leave that matters…'

'I don't understand.'

'Then think about it,' the king said. 'I shall arrange for a plane to take you home—is that England or America?'

'I want to speak with Zahid.'

'Of course you can speak with him, you will be joining us tonight for dinner.'

'Please, no,' Trinity begged.

'Oh, yes,' the king said. 'You can meet Princess Sameena, you can face your shame and then perhaps you will understand my rage.'

'I'll go.'

'Yes, you will, straight after dinner. And, Trinity, remember what I said. If you do care for my son, please think about what I said. It is *how* you leave that matters.

'One moment.' He paused as there was an angry knock at the door and Zahid barged in uninvited.

'Why did you summon Trinity without me?' he demanded.

'I wanted to see that she was being properly taken care of,' the king answered calmly. 'And to find out her how family was.'

'Don't!' Zahid stood livid before his father, for he could see the paleness of Trinity's cheeks and knew she was upset. 'You do not have time to respond to a formal request for me to speak with you, yet you summon Trinity in here—'

'She was telling me that she must return to England.'

'No.' Zahid's fists were balled.

'After dinner tonight, she is leaving.'

'Oh, no.' Zahid would not put Trinity through that. He was already dreading facing Princess Sameena and he would not foist the same awkwardness on Trinity.

'If there is an issue, you discuss it with me. Trinity is not leaving tonight—'

'I am.' It was the first time she had spoken since Zahid had stormed in. The king had made it crystal clear the shame it would bring if she were to fall pregnant.

Trinity knew that she already was and she had to get away.

'I was just speaking with your father. My mother called and she's upset...' Trinity hesitated, for she knew Zahid would not let her leave if there was even a chance she might see Clive, so she chose not to tell him about the ashes. 'I think she needs me at home.'

'It isn't about what she needs.' Zahid shook his head. 'First we speak—'

'There is not time to discuss this further now.' The king stood. 'Our guests are due to arrive. I am sure Trinity will want to get ready.'

As she put on her make-up Trinity finally understood the king's wise words. Zahid loved her and he would not simply let her go, but if she stayed...

Her only thought now was for her baby. She had no idea of the rules of this land. Even Zahid had spoken of choosing a bride on the strength of an army.

The king was right. If she wanted to leave then tonight Zahid had to see for himself what an unsuitable bride she would be.

'Perhaps you wear too much...' Layla hesitated, reminding herself that Trinity was a guest but her lips worried her as Trinity put on some dark red lipstick and then added more mascara.

Trinity was wearing the lilac tunic that had been too

tight even on her first day in Ishla. Her breasts seemed bigger than they had then, though Layla assumed that must be from her bra, because she caught a glimpse of it when Trinity bent forward for all the buttons were not done up.

'You missed…' Layla pointed to her own buttons as they went to head down to dinner.

Trinity ignored her.

Zahid's jaw tightened a little when he saw Trinity, not because of the glimpse of cleavage and not even because of her dark red lips. It was the dangerous glint in her eyes that had him on high alert as Trinity took her seat next to Layla.

The king made the introductions. 'This is Miss Trinity Foster, she is here to help Layla with her English. I asked her to join us so that we can say farewell to her, as she is flying back to England late tonight.'

Sameena bowed her head in greeting and Trinity did the same, and the introductions continued.

Zahid sat silent.

Oh, there would be words at the formal meeting for putting Trinity through this.

Many, many words.

He looked at Sameena and saw her downcast eyes and Zahid's shame turned to slight curiosity, for having a sister like Layla and after the time he'd spent with Trinity, he recognised swollen eyelids when he saw them.

Perhaps Sameena did not want to be here either.

The conversation was as sticky as the dates for everyone, given that Queen Raina of Bishram was the 'suitable' bride that Fahid had rejected all those years ago.

Only Layla was oblivious to the tension.

'We were talking in my class about transport today,' Layla said, filling in a gaping hole in the conversation as dessert was served. 'Can I learn to drive, Father?'

'Why would you want to drive when you can be driven?'

'I would like to drive. Do you drive, Sameena?'

'I do.'

'Do you work?'

'Layla,' the king warned, 'it is Zahid and Sameena's time to speak with each other.'

'We must go soon,' Queen Raina said.

'Perhaps Sameena and I could walk in the gardens before you leave,' Zahid offered, and Trinity knocked over her drink.

Better that than throw it in his face, Trinity thought as a maid mopped it up.

'Layla might like to join you.' The king smiled.

'Of course,' Zahid responded, and the Queen and King of Bishram nodded their consent.

'It was a lovely dinner,' Sameena said, as Layla walked behind them.

'It was,' Zahid said. 'Were you looking forward to it?'

There was a slight hesitation before she said yes.

'Is there anything you would like to say?' Zahid carefully offered, and Sameena glanced over her shoulder at Layla.

'She is listening to her music,' Zahid said. 'She has her headphones in.'

Sameena laughed and then she stopped laughing, for it was almost an impossible conversation to have. 'My mother is talking of abdicating,' Sameena said. 'Of course, that is just between us.'

'Of course.'

'Soon I will be Queen of Bishram.'

'What is your hope for your country?'

'I have many,' Sameena said. 'Naturally, I hope that relationships between our countries will improve, whatever choice you make.' Zahid looked at her and saw tears in Sameena's eyes.

'Be honest,' Zahid said, 'because whatever you say, I look forward to better relations between our countries.'

'Even if there is anger between them for a while?' Sameena checked, for her parents would be furious with Ishla if she was not the prince's choice.

'We will work well together,' Zahid said, as they carefully forged an alliance but one that did not involve a marriage.

There was a small chink of hope in his heart as he headed back, and Trinity did not like the edge of a smile on his lips or the look that passed between Sameena and Zahid as the families said their goodbyes. It served only to confuse her.

'I need to get my things ready,' Trinity said. 'My flight is soon.'

'You are not boarding the plane tonight,' Zahid said. 'You are not leaving till I have spoken with my father.' He strode over to the king. 'I would like to speak with you now,' Zahid said to his father.

'Not yet,' Fahid said. 'I would like more coffee.'

They returned to the table and the king smiled like the cat that had got the cream. 'That went very well.'

'Really?' Zahid checked. 'I have never endured a more uncomfortable dinner.'

The king looked at Trinity. 'You have been a wonderful guest. Forgive me for not serving champagne tonight, it would have been offensive to our guests. Of course, we are more relaxed here, and it is right that we wish you farewell with a toast.'

He gestured the waiter and champagne was poured. Trinity took the smallest sip of bubbles, for she did not want them to guess the reason she could not join in with the toast properly.

Zahid didn't even raise his glass of sparkling water, for she was not leaving tonight.

Trinity caught the king's eye and as the bubbles went down she topped up her glass and it was time to ensure that she and her baby left safely tonight.

'Is Queen Raina the one you rejected in favour of your wife?'

'Trinity…' Layla breathed, for there were things that must not be openly discussed.

'I get a bit confused,' Trinity explained.

'You are correct.' The king nodded.

'You must miss your wife,' Trinity said.

'Very much.'

They chatted further and after the king said what a wonderful, dignified woman Annan had been, the tone of the conversation moved down.

'You must get lonely,' Trinity said, and she felt the squeeze of Zahid's angry fingers on her thigh as he attempted to warn her quietly just how inappropriate that line of conversation was.

He looked at his plate and did not see the king give Trinity a small smile and he did not see the tears that flashed in Trinity's eyes. 'You're a good-looking man, Fahid. Surely…' she gave a shrill laugh '…you think about dating.'

'Perhaps I have had my time.'

'Oh, come on,' Trinity said. 'You could have your pick, a handsome man like you…'

She was flirting with his father, she was being inappropriate, and Zahid's rage simmered as again she knocked over her glass and then refilled it.

'How would a king date?' Fahid enquired politely.

'I have no idea,' Trinity admitted. 'Where I work, at the beach bar, we have a night for the over-forties…'

'Trinity,' Zahid warned.

'What?' Trinity turned to Zahid. 'I'm just being friendly.'

'I want to speak to you alone.'

He took her wrist, pulled her away, marched her through the palace and to her room.

She could spill her drink, she could be wild, but he had never thought he'd have to tell Trinity that she could not flirt at the king's table.

He turned her to face him and his eyes were black, not with anger but with disappointment, with pain.

'What on earth was that?'

'I was just having fun.' She gave him a look. 'Oh, sorry, that's not allowed here, is it?'

'Of course it is, but tonight—'

'Oh, am I misbehaving?'

'You know that you are.'

'So I'm just supposed to sit quietly while you go for a walk with your future bride, while you make simpering eyes when you say goodbye to her—'

'Do not even suggest that I flirted with Princess Sameena,' Zahid said. 'Tonight I have done everything I know how to secure us some time together, I have spoken with Sameena, I have asked for a formal meeting with my father and then you sit there, pissed, and you flirt with my father, the king.'

'I had two glasses,' Trinity lied, for she'd had none.

'Is that all it takes for you to act like a tart?' Zahid demanded. 'I don't get you, Trinity.'

'I never asked you to,' Trinity said. 'Am I not being respectful enough for you?'

'No,' Zahid said. 'You are not being respectful to yourself.'

'Don't worry, in an hour or so I won't be your problem any more.'

'Go to bed,' Zahid said.

'What?'

'You heard. Go to bed and I will speak with you tomorrow.'

Even at her supposed worst, he would not let her leave, Trinity realised.

Zahid, her eyes begged, let me go, for she was terrified what would happen if the king found out she was with child, not just for herself but for the shame it would heap on Zahid.

'Bed,' Zahid said.

'My flight—'

'Will be cancelled.'

'I want to go home.'

'You are not leaving now. It will all be sorted tomorrow,' Zahid continued, 'once and for all.'

'What if I don't want it to be sorted?' The grip on her arm loosened. 'What if I don't want to be your chosen bride.'

'I understand that you—'

'You *don't* understand,' Trinity choked, because for

the first time in her life it was almost impossible to lie.
'Because you've never asked.'

'I thought we felt the same.'

'No,' Trinity said. 'We don't. I don't want to be your
bride.'

'You're sure?'

'Very sure.'

Zahid gave a curt nod and she watched as the beautiful man she knew literally disappeared before her
eyes, for he was back to yawn-yawn dignified in that
second.

'I will have a maid come and sort out your things.'

CHAPTER FOURTEEN

In a land where emotions were considered best contained, it was Layla who broke the rules, for she sobbed loudly as the driver arrived to take Trinity the short distance to the royal jet. 'I will come with you to the plane.'

'We'll say goodbye here,' Trinity said, and hugged her hard. She would miss Layla so much.

She gave a small curtsy to the king, who gave her a brief nod in return, and then she stood before Zahid and did not know how to say goodbye.

'I will see you to the plane.'

This time she did not refuse.

It was a very short drive to the runway, but if it had been a hundred miles it would have gone by too fast for she was saying goodbye not just to Zahid but her baby's father too.

'I am sorry for my behaviour tonight.'

'It was funny really.' Zahid gave a pale smile. 'I'm sure my father has not enjoyed himself so much in years.'

'You're not cross?'

'Temporarily,' Zahid said, 'then you make me laugh.' He was not laughing now and he only ever had with her. 'I apologise for assuming,' Zahid said, as the car pulled up at the plane. 'I assumed this madness was mutual.'

'Madness?'

'That's what it feels like,' Zahid said, and then he looked at her. 'I enjoyed being briefly insane.'

'You can go back to normal now.'

'I can.'

She went to embrace him but Zahid pulled back. He was gone from her now. 'You will have a safe flight.'

'Will?'

'You are on my plane. Do you need anything?'

'No.'

'You have not worked, you gave all your money to Donald.'

'I'll be fine.'

Sometimes the apple did fall far from the tree.

'I don't know what to say,' Zahid said. 'I never expected to be saying goodbye.'

Would she call him? Trinity wondered as she looked into his eyes. Would she tell him from the safety of England?

Would it be cruel to do so?

For now she just needed to leave.

'Look after yourself better,' Zahid said. 'You have every right to stay away from that man.'

Trinity blew out a breath.

If her mother had her way, she'd be seeing Clive tomorrow.

No.

'I'm going to go,' Trinity said.

If she didn't she might just tell Zahid how much she loved him.

* * *

The king watched as his son returned to the palace and he felt a rare prick of guilt when he saw the confusion in Zahid's eyes, for he had not seen that look since Zahid had been seven and the king had lain in a stupor.

'Happy now?' Zahid shot at his father, as he headed up the stairs.

'You will be,' Fahid said. 'It hurts to lose someone you care for.'

'Don't you ever try to give me advice on this.'

'Her behaviour tonight was shocking.'

'Not to me.' Zahid halted on his climb up the stairs and turned. 'She pushes boundaries, she tests you at every turn, she wants to prove she is right in that she cannot trust you. If you knew what she had been through…' Zahid shook his head. He had never wanted less to be a future king. 'I'm going to bed.'

'We will speak in the morning.'

'We will speak when I am ready to,' Zahid said, 'and that might take some time.'

'There are dinners…'

'Cancel them.'

'Zahid.' The king attempted reason. 'Trinity needs to be with her family. It is right she be with them now. Tomorrow they spread the ashes…'

The king was not scared of danger, he had an army of his own and he would happily lead them, but as Zahid descended the stairs he caught a glimpse of fear.

'What did you say?'

'Her mother called. She wants her to join her family to spread the ashes.'

No.

A thousand times no.

Whether she wanted his love or not, he wouldn't let that happen.

'Why wouldn't she tell me that?' Zahid asked himself out loud.

A lie by omission, but still a lie.

He could not believe a single word that came from her mouth, Zahid realised, which meant that saying she did not want to be his bride might also be a lie.

Oh, there was unfinished business between them again and he was not going to wait months or years to address it this time—another sun would not set without this being sorted.

'I am going to England.'

The King stared at him. 'I forbid you.'

'Then I defy you,' Zahid said.

'You cannot defy me.' The king stared at his son but could only admire him.

'You raised me to be strong.'

'You turn your back on our people, our traditions…'

'If I have to, yes.' Zahid nodded. 'Right now, there is someone that I need to be with and I refuse to have her face things alone.'

'You select a bride in a few days…'

'Perhaps I already have.'

'She is not suitable.'

'For who?' Zahid said. 'She is more than suitable for me.'

'You know the rules.'

'Change them,' Zahid challenged. 'Is that not the point of being a king?'

'It is not as simple as that…'

'It's very simple for me,' Zahid said.

'Our people would not welcome her.'

'They would if you did.'

'And if she won't live here?'

'That is something Trinity and I will discuss but without an ancient rule book over our heads. I am going to England now.'

'She has your plane.'

'Then I will take a commercial flight.'

'Your judgment is blinded by lust.'

'No,' Zahid said. 'My judgement is *clarified* by love.'

'A king must first love his country.'

'Don't worry, Father. I will not repeat your mistakes.' Zahid stared his father down, and brought up what must never be discussed. 'Love did not weaken you, Father, it was her death that you could not cope with.' Fahid had not struck his son in decades but his hand was raised now. 'You could not cope,' Zahid said, 'but I did.' He looked at his father who stood with his arm raised. 'I was seven and I coped with the death of my mother. I dealt with your daughter who you could not bear to look at, I fed you with a spoon when you had no will to live.' Zahid understood then his father's fear for his children but it made little sense. 'Would you rather not have chosen her?'

'Of course not.'

'Do you regret a single day spent with your wife?'

'Only her last day,' Fahid admitted. 'I did not understand her pain, I thought it was normal for women to scream when giving birth...'

'So did the doctor,' Zahid challenged his father's guilt. 'And the doula too. You lost the woman you loved through no fault of your own. Well, I refuse to play a part in losing the woman that I love.'

Zahid turned from his father and went to walk out

and to summon his driver, but the king called him back. 'You could have the plane turned around.'

'If Trinity returns to Ishla, it will be of her own ac-cord.'

Fahid gave in then and looked at his son with slightly shocked eyes, for the day had come where his son was stronger and more knowing than he, a day that for any parent was a challenge, especially when you were king.

'Zahid.' The king halted him again. 'There is some-thing that perhaps you should know. Tonight, when Trinity was being inappropriate—'

'I will discuss the behaviour with Trinity, I do not have to discuss it with you. She does not know how to behave on occasion but—'

'Trinity knew exactly what she was doing,' the king interrupted, 'because I asked her to misbehave.'

Zahid frowned.

'I encouraged her poor behaviour. I thought it would be easier on you in the end if you saw just how unsuit-able she was.'

'When you say you encouraged, did you and Trin-ity discuss this?'

'We did.'

'Could I remind you that though you are my father and king—'

'And sick,' the king added hastily, for he could see the muscle leaping in Zahid's cheek and that his fist was clenched.

'Lucky for you!' Zahid retorted, but it strangled near the end and the king did not now fear his son, instead he was devastated for him. For the first time there were tears in Zahid's eyes and that was something Fahid had thought he would never see.

'Take my plane,' the king said, and for the first time since before Annan had died he embraced his son. 'Go to her now.'

CHAPTER FIFTEEN

ZAHID HAD BEEN angry about many things involving Trinity, but he had never been truly angry with her.

That changed as his plane streaked through the sky, trying to make up the hours between them.

Over and over he replayed last night.

The snap of jealousy about his walk with Sameena did not equate with a woman who did not want him.

Little liar, Zahid said to himself.

He should have known when his father had produced champagne that something was going on. And, no, she had not had even two glasses, for he had never met any-one more clumsy than Trinity last night and she had knocked over her glass…

Every detail he replayed and, apart from once, that glass had not touched her lips.

He thought of her cleavage and it had either been one helluva push-up bra or Trinity was pregnant.

Was that why she had run?

Was he so formidable that she could not share the truth?

He was formidable now!

Trinity arrived at Heathrow still dressed in the lilac dress and wearing jewelled slippers, and she startled when she caught her reflection in the mirror as she stepped into the VIP lounge, because what had started to feel normal felt very different here.

Assuming she would be heading for a taxi rank, Trinity soon found out that luxury didn't end at the landing of a royal flight.

A driver was waiting and he asked her where she wanted to go. She asked that he take her the short distance to the airport hotel.

As she went to check in, instead of asking for a shoebox, Trinity splurged and asked for a nice suite as she pulled out her credit card.

Well, not splurged.

She was simply tired of scrimping and foreseeing disaster and crisis when, really, the disasters and crises had not been of her own making.

When she should possibly be feeling at her most vulnerable and weakest, Trinity felt the strongest she ever had.

Things changed today.

Trinity stepped into the shower and decided that if her family wanted her there at such things, there were conditions that needed to be met.

And if they weren't met then her family would not be seeing the child she was carrying.

It was suddenly as simple as that.

Her time with Zahid had made her stronger rather than weaker; his absolute honesty made it easier for Trinity to know her truth.

She was too numb to start mourning their relationship, too focused on getting through today to break down.

She put on the hotel robe and tied a towel round her

head and was just sorting out the black clothes to wear for the spreading of the ashes later in the day when there was a knock at the door.

Assuming it was breakfast or someone to come and check the mini-bar before she let loose on the chocolate, Trinity opened the door without thinking and came face to face with a Zahid she had never seen.

Oh, she'd seen him angry on occasion but not once, despite all her shenanigans, despite all she had done, never, Trinity realised, had his anger been aimed at her.

It was now.

'How did you know where I was?'

She stood back as he marched in and tossed down his case and there was the same start of surprise at the sight of him in robes that Trinity had felt when she'd seen her own reflection in the mirror at Heathrow.

In England she'd only ever seen him in a suit and being terribly polite.

'Did you collude with my father?' He towered over her and she tried to stand her ground.

'I think "collude" is a bit of a strong word...' Trinity attempted.

'Did the two of you decide that you thought you knew what was best for me?'

'No,' Trinity said. 'We thought, or rather I knew, you were struggling...'

'Struggling?' Zahid frowned. 'What do you mean, struggling?'

'With the decision—' his temper wasn't improving, she could hear his angry breathing '—as to my suitability, so I thought—'

'You thought you'd make it easier for me?'

'Yes.'

'You thought you'd flirt with my father and pretend to be drunk and that that would improve matters?' Zahid said, and Trinity swallowed. 'You thought you that if you misbehaved I'd decide you were too much trouble?'

'I guess.'

'Why don't we stop guessing?'

'Zahid, the sex is amazing and all that but it's not going to carry us—'

'You think you're so good in bed that you defy my logic?'

'No,' Trinity said. 'Maybe.'

'You think my judgement is skewed?'

'A bit!'

'What, because I don't just say to hell with it, just because I don't decide on a whim to discard everything I have ever believed in, without due thought, you assume I am struggling.'

No, but she could not tell him that without revealing her truth.

She just didn't know how to tell him.

'Is there anything else you haven't told me?'

'No.'

'Are you sure about that?'

'Completely.'

Zahid picked up her black clothes. 'Where are you off to today?'

'I haven't made up my mind.'

'Do you want to be my bride?'

'No.'

'I'll take that as a yes,' Zahid said, 'because not one honest word has come from your lips since last night. Do you love me?'

'Is it a yes-or-no answer only?'

'Trinity!'

'Yes.' Trinity smiled. 'Yes, Zahid, I love you, but given I'm clearly a compulsive liar...'

She did the wrong thing. Trinity started to laugh at her own joke. 'Zahid,' she yelped, 'what are you—?'

She never got to finish.

Trinity had been tipped over his shoulder once before but it was different this time, she was being tipped over his knee.

'What I should have done a long time ago,' Zahid said. 'Three times I have come back for you and still you doubt me. I tell you this much! I put up with your drama and your carry-on.' His hand came down on her bottom through the thick dressing gown and Trinity shrieked, her hands moving to cover her bottom, but he brushed them away and gave her another slap.

'You do not make decisions about us without speaking with me.' His hand came down again and the wad of material was a hindrance so he ruched it up and brought his hand down on her bare pink cheeks. It stung, it hurt, but the passion that came with the delivery felt delicious to Trinity as he slapped her again.

'You do not lie to me,' he said, as his hand went to come down again and then stilled. Zahid halted, barely able to breathe as he looked down at her red bottom and realised for the first time he was out of control. 'Trinity...' His hand was in mid-air and he waited for her to shout, to tell him what a sick bastard he was, and then he heard her voice.

'One more, Captain.'

He rarely laughed and he'd never thought he'd be

laughing this morning. He was angry, though, still angry as he tipped her off his knee and onto the bed.

'I nearly came,' Trinity said. She was lying there, smiling up at him, watching as he stripped, and nothing was going to tame her and nothing could in this moment tame him.

'You are impossible,' he said to a very over-excited Trinity.

'You chose impossible,' Trinity said. 'Can we talk about this later?'

It wouldn't be much later for he was over her, and he did not need to part her legs for they wrapped around his hips in glee as his mouth crushed hers.

'The last one was true,' Trinity said, as he bucked inside her.

'I know.'

'How?' she begged as he as he thrust deeper. 'How do you know I love you?'

'Because...' His words halted as the sob from Trinity and the throb of her around him told him she might not hear his words, but he said them anyway. 'Because of this.' His answer released into her and it really was a simple as that, for with no one, ever, could it be so lovely. Only Zahid could right a million wrongs.

'Never leave me,' Trinity said, as he collapsed onto her.

'I never will.'

'I'll get things wrong.'

'Oh, I am sure you will.'

'Your father...'

'I have dealt with him,' Zahid said. 'You did not have to run away. Whatever our problems, we can work them out.'

Her eyes filled with tears because the reason that she had run was coming back to Trinity now; the reason for her terror was a secret she could no longer keep.

'Is there anything you are keeping from me?' Zahid said, only very gently this time.

'Yes.'

Finally, Zahid thought, the truth.

'I know you said it must never happen, I know I promised it wouldn't...' She could barely get the words out. 'I'm pregnant.'

She waited for anger, a slap even, just as her mother had, but instead Zahid pulled her tighter in his arms.

'That is why you left?'

Trinity nodded.

'You felt you could not tell me?' Zahid looked at her and how he rued that stupid slit-throat gesture he had made that day, given all that she had been through, and he answered for her. 'Of course you thought you couldn't.'

'You're not cross.'

'I'm thrilled.'

Trinity wasn't particularly used to anyone she loved being thrilled by her *mistakes*.

'I am sad that you could not come and tell me but I understand why.'

'Your father asked if I was trying to trap you,' Trinity explained. 'He saw us leaving the second palace.'

'You got one of his pep talks!' Zahid rolled his eyes. 'Do I look trapped?'

Trinity shook her head. 'I asked Layla about unplanned pregnancies and she said it could never happen...'

'Layla has never been out of Ishla. Layla believes

everything that is told to her simply because she does not know any different. My father wraps her in cotton wool and terrifies her with tales in the hope she will be too scared to ever make a mistake.' Zahid looked at her. 'How many times do I have to tell you that you can come to me?'

'I know,' Trinity said. 'I was just too scared to in this.'

'Never be scared to come to me.'

She looked at Zahid and knew she would never be scared again.

'I want you as my wife,' Zahid said. 'The decision is actually a very easy one, yet I have forced myself to question it many times. I never wanted love, I thought it had destroyed my father, but I was wrong.' He tried to explain better. 'I love my country, I wanted a clear head to rule it, yet my head has never been clearer than it is now. You distract me in a way that is good. It makes me want change, to tackle issues that are difficult, to rule not just with my head but with my heart.'

'What will the people say about the baby?'

'Most will be thrilled, some will say we bring disgrace, others will know we are not so different from their own families...' He smiled at Trinity. 'Controversy is good,' Zahid said. 'It allows for discussion and I think you are going to be a very controversial queen but a very good one.'

'What will your father say?'

'I have been spending too much time with you because suddenly I have the strange compulsion to lie.' He looked at her. 'Shall we tell him after the wedding? Would that make things easier for you?'

'It would.'

'What else are you scared of? What else do you think you can't discuss with me?'

'Nothing.'

'You're sure?'

Honesty had never been on Trinity's agenda. The way she had been brought up had been about smoothing over the bumps with lies, ignoring problems in the hope they would disappear, not sharing the scary, shameful parts.

It was time to change.

'I love my family.' She didn't know how best to describe it. 'They've lost their son, I don't want them to feel that they've lost their daughter too. I can't turn my back on them and I will go to family events.'

'Of course,' Zahid said, 'so what is worrying you?'

'You,' Trinity admitted. 'That you'll cause a scene, say something…'

'It is beyond unfair of your parents to expect you to see this man.'

Trinity looked at him and, yes, at times she was grateful for his excellent self-control and knew he was exerting it now.

'I'd already decided that,' Trinity admitted. 'I was going to ring them and tell them that if they wanted me there today then he wasn't to be.'

'Was?'

'I think we should just get through today and then I'll…' she screwed her eyes closed. 'I don't know what I want.'

'Maybe you need to tell him face to face that you don't want him around,' Zahid said, for clearly she could not rely on her parents to defend her as parents should.

He looked at her as she spoke.

'I don't ever want to speak to him.'

'Are you sure?' Zahid said, 'because I will deal with it if that is what you want.'

'That's not what I want.' She looked back at a very pensive Zahid and, no, she could not put him through this for the rest of their lives, could not ask him to attend functions and stand idly by.

'You don't have to be drunk to take to the microphone,' Zahid said.

'I wasn't drunk that night.'

He smiled in dispute.

'A bit maybe,' Trinity admitted.

'Well, you don't have to be to say what is on your mind.'

'If I do say something…'

'I'll be there.'

'I'd prefer you wait here at the hotel.'

Zahid shook his head.

'In the car, then.'

'No,' Zahid said. 'You are not facing this without me.'

'So, on top of everything else, I have to worry about you losing your head…'

'I won't lose my head,' Zahid said. 'You have my word.'

If ever she was grateful for Zahid's self-control it was today. It made Trinity strong when she questioned her own, it kept her calm enough to face what she had been unable to before.

Zahid dressed in an immaculate suit and Trinity had on her funeral clothes, but they were facing a difficult day together this time.

Zahid waved away his driver, for he could see she

felt awkward enough, and he drove them himself. As he did, Trinity mind flitted to anything other than what lay ahead.

'Poor Sameena...' She turned in sudden anguish. 'What will happen to the two countries?'

'A war perhaps,' Zahid said, then he stopped teasing her. 'Had you not decided to escape you would have found out that Sameena and I had a very polite conversation.'

'In the garden?'

Zahid nodded. 'Soon Sameena will be Queen and she looks forward to happy relations between our countries, whatever my choice. It was a very discreet conversation but reading between the lines she was asking me not to choose her.'

'She rejected you!' Trinity beamed.

'You're going to get so much mileage out of that,' Zahid sighed.

'I am,' Trinity said, and then stopped smiling, for Zahid was pulling up at the river that had been chosen for the occasion. It was a place the family had gone for drives to at times and where Donald had proposed to Yvette.

'Ready?' Zahid checked, and Trinity nodded.

'You can do this.'

'I don't think Yvette knows...'

'Well, let her find out,' Zahid said. 'Maybe some honesty will allow her to speak more openly about what she has been through. Her baby and ours are going to be cousins. Don't you want them to be close?'

'I do.'

'Lies haven't worked for a long time,' Zahid said. 'Maybe you could try the truth.'

'You promise that you won't—'

'I will not lose my head.'

He took her hand and they walked over to the small gathering, but as he went to give her hand a squeeze to offer support her fingers slipped away from his grasp, just not in the way they had on that awful night all those years ago. Instead of reaching out in fear to Zahid, it was an assertive Trinity who walked towards the small crowd.

'What's he doing here?' Trinity asked, pointing her finger at Clive. 'Why on earth would you ask the man who attacked your seventeen-year-old daughter to be here on this day?'

'Trinity!' Dianne said. 'Not now.'

'When, then?'

'Trinity,' Dianne said in low tones as Gus tried to hush her, but finally Trinity refused to be hushed.

'Why are we whispering?' Trinity said. 'I mean it, I want to remember my brother today. I want to think about Donald instead of remembering what this sleaze did to me that night.' She looked at Clive and she saw not a strong, angry man but the pathetic, weak creep that he was. 'I don't ever want to see you again and if I do, I'll be going to the police. And I don't give a damn what it will do to my family, or to your reputation, because I know what you did to me and I'm more than prepared to say it in court.'

'Come on, Clive.' Elaine started to walk off. 'She was always trouble,' she shouted over her shoulder, 'always making stuff up.'

'For God's sake, Trinity,' Gus boomed, 'it's your brother's...'

'I just want to say one thing.' Zahid's deep voice

was out of place with the shouting but even Trinity shivered at the sinister calm of his voice. 'I promised Trinity that I would not lose my head today and I shall keep my word.' He might be in Western clothes but he was a dangerous desert warrior and had she been on the end of his look that was aimed at Clive, Trinity would have run for her life. 'If my gaze ever falls on you again then know I shall keep my word to Trinity and not lose my head, because I won't need to. I will kill you in cold blood.'

'He doesn't mean it…' Dianne's smile was frantic but Zahid's cool disdain met her now.

'You can test the theory if you choose but, I tell you once, my people would expect nothing less from their future king.'

He watched every step that Clive took as he walked off and it was at the right moment that Trinity took his hand because the master of self-control was waning as Clive took one final look around. Trinity felt the zip of tension in Zahid, knew that at any second he'd change his mind and bolt after him, and perhaps Clive sensed it too for he ran the last of the distance to the car and Zahid turned and looked at Dianne.

'I do mean it.' He put his arm around Trinity and they walked down to the river.

It was nice to be able to focus on her brother today, nice to recall the good times with Zahid by her side, and it was actually, for the first time, nice to step into her home.

'Why has Zahid asked to speak alone with your father?' Dianne asked.

'You'll find out soon.'

'Should I check if there's champagne in the fridge?'

'Zahid doesn't drink,' Trinity said, and then smiled at her mum. 'And there's always champagne in the fridge.'

'I'm sorry, Trinity.'

From out of the blue they came—the words she'd never thought she'd hear.

'Thank you.'

'Can we start again?' Dianne asked.

'I think we have to.'

They did start again, right from square one, because after a quiet celebration where they shared the news that they would be married soon, it was not long before Trinity yawned and said she wanted to go to bed.

'Perhaps set up...' Dianne's voice broke off.

'Zahid will sleep with me,' Trinity said, 'or we can go back to the hotel.'

Zahid did not correct Trinity, for to hell with politeness, he would never set foot in the guest room.

He wished them goodnight and they headed to her single bed.

'What did she say?' Zahid smiled as they huddled in the darkness. 'When you started laughing in the kitchen?'

'It was wrong,' Trinity blushed. 'I can't tell you.'

'You can.'

'Okay.' Trinity took a big breath. 'Mum said that when your father dies, will she have a title?'

'She wants a title?'

'She's wants to be the Queen Mother.'

He laughed.

It was rare, it was deep and it thrilled her right down to her bones, and there would be so much more of it, Trinity would make sure of that.

'How could I have ever thought you boring?' Trinity sighed.

'Another thing you haven't told me,' Zahid said. 'When did you think I was boring?'

'For years,' Trinity said. 'Till you took me in your arms.'

EPILOGUE

'WHERE'S TRINITY?'

Zahid heard the whisper from Dianne as he stood in the palace gardens, waiting for his bride to arrive, and, yes, she was more than fashionably late.

Zahid stared ahead. He was dressed in military ceremonials with a red and white *kafiya* tied with gold braid, which indicated he was the groom. His concern was not that Trinity might have changed her mind, his concern was for all she faced not just today but in the two days preceding the wedding.

He stood with his back rigid, feeling all the eyes of the guests on him. It was forbidden that they see each other in the lead-up to the wedding. Tradition did not take into account that the news of the future princess's pregnancy might have broken forty-eight hours before the wedding service.

Tonight they would be in the desert, Zahid thought.

Tonight, whatever the people's reaction to Trinity, he could put her mind at ease and then, in a week's time, they were heading overseas.

As the guests coughed anxiously Zahid actually managed a smile. He had asked Trinity where she would like to go for her honeymoon and, even though they were getting on much better, her answer had been as far away from her parents as possible, so they were heading for Australia. He simply couldn't wait to get away with his bride. The only teeny fly in the ointment was that he had promised that Layla could join them for a week.

Love had been the furthest thing from his mind when he had agreed to that.

It was the closest thing now.

He had watched his father's skin pale when the scandalous news had first hit and, no, when the king had called for him, Zahid had not denied it.

As strong as he was, guilt had washed over him as he'd seen his father, so old and so thin, struggle to take in the latest change.

'I am sorry if you feel I have let down you and my mother's memory.'

'Your mother was as vague as your sister now is,' the king sighed. 'I went through the mandoos last night and I thought how she would be with the news. I held her favourite amulet and I just knew that she would have been delighted.'

Fahid called in Abdul, who immediately said he would issue the strongest denial.

'You shall neither confirm or deny,' the king said, and Zahid watched as Abdul's face paled when he realised the rumour was true, and then the king said the strangest thing to Zahid.

Words he could not wait to share with Trinity.

Yet he had not been able to get to her yet.

'I am so excited.' Layla's endless chatter did nothing to ease Trinity's nerves. 'You don't mind me coming to Australia with you?'

'Of course not.'

'I'm only there for a week…'

'It will be wonderful,' Trinity said, but she could not focus on Layla's conversation or the maids who were doing her hair. Outside the crowd was building and they stood silent, awaiting the news of the formal union.

Layla's chatter was not selfish. She was trying to take Trinity's mind off her pregnancy being referred to as a scandal in some of the papers and that Ishla was alight not just with wedding preparations but with the news that Zahid's bride might already be with child.

At the time she needed to speak with Zahid most, to finally lean on someone she trusted, it was denied. 'Have you seen your father today?'

'No,' Layla said. 'The men's and women's celebrations are kept separate.'

'You must have heard something.'

Layla went a little bit pink. She still felt guilty and a little embarrassed by her naïve reaction when Trinity had clearly needed her advice. Obviously this birth control thing Trinity had spoke of did not work!

'Only what I told you. Zahid asked one of the maids to pass on that you were not to be concerned, to just enjoy the celebrations and that you would be together soon.'

Trinity knew that Zahid would be there for her and no doubt he would already have discussed the revelation with the king. Zahid's rapid departure from Ishla had been noted and there had been an image of them coming out a famous obstetrician's office. As well as that, despite a hastily arranged wedding, despite the gold gown she was wearing, given that it was her second pregnancy, Trinity was already starting to show.

Only it wasn't the king's reaction that worried her, or the damage to Zahid. It was the how the people would respond that gnawed at Trinity. Their reaction mattered, not because it changed the outcome but because it might change how Trinity felt towards them. She had already had one pregnancy steeped in shame, she refused to let this be another.

'You look beautiful,' Layla said, as Trinity stood to have her headwear arranged.

'Thank you.'

'We need to go,' Layla said. 'You are already late.'

'I'll just be a moment.'

Trinity had been raised to care only what others thought, and what others thought mattered terribly now.

No, it didn't.

Trinity knew that their baby had been conceived in love, knew that Zahid and she were meant to be together. Since that night in the woods their love had waited patiently till the time had been right, and she had to trust the timing of their baby had been chosen too.

Trinity peeked out at the silent crowd, who gave no indication as to their response to her.

She would find that out on the balcony.

Right now she had a wedding to attend and she wanted to be there.

Zahid turned as she arrived and it was not the Trinity he had been expecting. Instead of being wary and truculent, her eyes shone with confidence and as her eyes met his her cheeks infused with pink as they did whenever she saw him.

And, yes, the papers would confirm that the rumours were surely right, for the soft breeze pushed the fabric of her dress and there was the curve of her stomach.

Zahid smiled, and, just as she had been at Donald's wedding, so lost was she that she did as her body instructed and walked to be by his side.

'You look amazing.'

'Thank you.'

He had expected a hurried question, to ask if all was well.

It was.

Whatever the ramifications, they would face them together.

The service was quick, given that it was held in the fierce midday sun, but the part she would always remember best was after Zahid made his vows and then offered her a bracelet that had an Arabic saying engraved in English.

'I mean it,' he said as she read what was inscribed inside.

What is coming is better than what is gone.

With Zahid it was always better, Trinity knew.

There was no kissing his bride. Instead, he took her hand and led her back to the palace.

Trinity smiled at her parents and at Yvette, who was a few months ahead of Trinity in her pregnancy.

They were friends now and, as Zahid had pointed out, their children would be cousins.

She would be taken care of too.

There was Princess Sameena, who curtsied to the new princess as her parents stood severely at her side, and they shared a small smile, for the future of both their countries was so bright.

The rest of the guests followed them and still Trinity did not ask his father's reaction to the news.

'We meet the people now,' Zahid said, and squeezed

her hand. The memory of Trinity scowling at the camera did not make him smile now. He was, not that he could show it, worried by the reception from the people. He did not want their wedding day to be one where he asked her to force a smile. 'It won't take long.' Zahid cleared his throat. 'If they are a little hesitant, know that soon they will take to the news…' He frowned as she simply nodded and Zahid actually wondered if she had been shielded from the scandal that had hit Ishla. 'They may—'

'Zahid,' Trinity said, 'I'm not going to apologise or be ashamed.'

'Good.'

As the balcony doors opened and they went to step out, they were halted, as instead of the happy couple leading the way King Fahid did instead.

Zahid blinked.

His father had at that meeting reminded his son that he was still king and that he would sort it.

Zahid had wondered how.

Now he knew, for Fahid walked out onto the balcony to the surprise of the people and met them with a smile they had not seen on his face since before Princess Layla had been born.

He held out an arm and welcomed the couple.

'He welcomed the news,' Zahid said, and Trinity swallowed.

'Really?'

'It took only an hour for him to say that he could not be happier. He does not have much time and this way he gets to meet our child…'

With the king's clear blessing, as the happy couple stepped onto the balcony they were met with cheers and waves. The silence had been broken for things that had never been discussed in Ishla were being talked about now.

How, Trinity wondered, as Zahid now kissed his bride, could she rue the years that had been wasted?

Time knew best.

They were together now.

* * * * *

*If you loved this story,
don't miss Layla's,
available in November!*

MILLS & BOON®

Want to get more from Mills & Boon?

Here's what's available to you if you join the exclusive **Mills & Boon eBook Club** today:

✦ *Convenience – choose your books each month*
✦ *Exclusive – receive your books a month before anywhere else*
✦ *Flexibility – change your subscription at any time*
✦ *Variety – gain access to eBook-only series*
✦ *Value – subscriptions from just £1.99 a month*

So visit **www.millsandboon.co.uk/esubs** today to be a part of this exclusive eBook Club!